VENGEANCE

M.S.

Fran

and

novel

VENGEANCE

M.S. POWER

First published in Great Britain in 2002 by Canongate Crime,
an imprint of Canongate Books Ltd,
14 High Street, Edinburgh EH1 1TE

10 9 8 7 6 5 4 3 2 1

British Library Cataloguing-in-Publication Data
A catalogue record for this book is available on
request from the British Library

ISBN 1 84195 219 2

Typeset by Palimpsest Book Production Limited,
Polmont, Stirlingshire
Printed and bound by
Creative Print and Design, Ebbw Vale, Wales

www.canongate.net

For Bryden and Linda Goldie,
with thanks

Woe to the youth whom Fancy gains,
Winning from Reason's hand the reins.

Rokeby,
Sir Walter Scott

Book One

1

The flashing blue lights of the ambulance and police cars gave the scene an even more doleful aspect, making the water in the canal look fetid and menacing, the dampened stones of the disused railway bridge that spanned it taking on a grotesque gleam, the restraining tape, erected by the police, fluttering like morbid bunting in the cold January wind.

Chief Inspector Robert Harvey hunched his shoulders against the wind and gave a small involuntary shudder. A particularly grim Monday morning, he thought. He kept his hands in his overcoat pockets even as he crouched down over the young man's body, watching in silence as Miles McVinnie made his preliminary examination, curiously irked by the small whistling noise McVinnie made through his teeth.

'Well?' Harvey asked when the doctor finally stood up.

McVinnie grunted, and stretched his back, easing the stiffness from it. 'Male. Late teens. Throat cut. Abrasions on both arms,' he said in a dull, matter-of-fact tone. 'That's as much as I can say for the moment.'

'You know what I mean,' Harvey insisted gruffly.

McVinnie raised an eyebrow and pursed his lips before replying. 'It *could* be another one,' he admitted. '*Could* be, mind.'

Harvey eased himself erect and stared at the doctor. 'Possible or probable?' he asked quietly.

McVinnie gave a thin smile. 'Possible.' He paused. 'Leaning towards the probable,' he added.

'Shit,' Harvey muttered.

'I'll be able to tell you more – hopefully – when I've done a proper examination,' McVinnie assured him, packing his little case, putting everything in its proper slot like a zealous mother preparing a picnic hamper.

'When will that be, Miles?' Harvey asked but in a tone that suggested he already knew the answer.

McVinnie gave a little laugh. 'As soon as I've finished.'

'Thanks.'

'You want a thorough report, don't you?'

Harvey nodded.

'Well, that takes time.'

'That's the one thing I don't have . . . time,' Harvey responded despondently, looking over his shoulder. 'Alan,' he called, jerking his head to summon Detective Sergeant Alan Kelly towards him.

'Guv?'

'Who found him?'

'Dunno yet, guv. A –'

'What d'you mean – you don't know yet?' Harvey demanded.

'Some woman phoned the station, guv. Just said there was a body down by the canal, then hung up. The call was made from a phone box a few hundred yards up the road.'

'Can we . . . ?' Dr McVinnie interrupted, gazing at Harvey, two medics with a stretcher standing behind him.

Harvey nodded.

'That makes four,' Kelly said in a low tone.

'We don't *know* that,' Harvey snapped, watching as the body was lifted onto the stretcher and carried to the ambulance. Then he sighed. 'Sorry, Alan.'

DS Kelly shrugged in the manner of a man accustomed to being snapped at.

'He probably *is* the fourth,' Harvey conceded wearily.

'Well, maybe this time . . .' Kelly began, but fell silent under his superior's baleful gaze.

Maybe this time . . . ? Chief Inspector Harvey allowed the speculation to take root in his mind, and gave a long, low groan. Ever since October of the previous year, when the body of the first youth had been found in an abandoned warehouse in Camberwell, through November and December, when the murdered bodies of two more young men had been discovered, Harvey had been saying the very same thing to himself: maybe this time there would be some small clue that would lead them to the killer. But there never was. Once a month he killed, always at weekends, all of his victims young men in their teens, all of them rent boys, all of them homeless. And he had killed them all in the same manner, slitting their throats so deeply as to almost sever the head. He never killed them *in situ*, left no trace of himself in the area where the bodies were dumped. To make matters worse, the killer removed any documentation that might identify the victims, if, indeed, they had carried any in the first place.

Three hours after the discovery of the body by the canal, Gary Hubbard drove his van to the building site. He was a small man, but burly, clean shaven with close-cropped dark brown hair. The site boss regarded him as diligent and reliable; his workmates saw him as cheerful and always willing to help out even if he was a bit of a loner insofar as he wouldn't ever go to the pub with them at weekends. Indeed, they all had a sneaking admiration for him as they accepted his explanation of an ailing mother who lived alone on the south coast. She would, he said, be unduly upset if he didn't visit her every Sunday.

Gary Hubbard parked his van and clambered out, but not before checking he had his flask and lunchbox. There was a particular spring to his step that morning although no one would have noticed that: all his mates saw was the usual cheerful Gary ready to listen to what they had all been up to over the weekend, and laugh with them as they described the scrapes they had got into, and thank them politely when they enquired after his mother.

At the exact time Gary Hubbard arrived at the London building site, a few hundred miles north, just outside Dumfries, Mrs Alice

Johnson walked to the foot of the stairs and called, 'Will you two boys get a move on, for heaven's sake?' She waited for a reply. When none came, she called again. 'Jimmy? Gregory? Will you please come down or we'll be late?' She cocked her head and listened, giving a small, doting smile when she heard the boys respond, 'Just coming!'

Everyone who knew Alice Johnson had the same thing to say about her: she was a *good* woman, a woman without a wicked bone in her body. They also said it was most unfair, wasn't it, the way life had treated her, putting her husband in a wheelchair, leaving her child-less and she the very one who would have made the perfect mother for any child. And yet she remained so bright and happy and smiling.

And Alice Johnson *was* happy. She was a philosophical woman and had long since recognised that happiness was relative. True, her husband Donald was crippled, but his mind was alert enough, and in an odd way his incapacity allowed her to treat him as the child she had never had, and compensated for this sadness. Almost. Real happiness, she would readily have admitted, came with the visits from her nephews, the twins Jimmy and Gregory. For weeks before their impending arrival she started to bubble. She sang little nursery songs to herself as she baked their favourite foods, and planned activities that would keep them amused. Not that they needed much amusing. They were such nice boys, so intelligent, so thoughtful, so adorable. And Alice did, in fact, adore the twins. She had grieved when their mother, her sister Kate, had abruptly decided to leave Scotland to pursue her career in London, and, of course, take the twins with her. For all her qualities Alice took a somewhat prudish view about unmarried mothers even when it applied to her own sister. And there was something else: although she would have scoffed at the suggestion, Alice Johnson had secretly hoped that the twins might be left with her to rear, and for some time had unreasonably resented Kate's decision to bring up her own children. But she was over all that now, although she still did, occasionally, play a little game with herself, pretending the twins *were* hers when they came to stay.

*   *   *

Upstairs, in what had been their mother's room in the days before she took off for London, Jimmy and Gregory Renfrew sat huddled together peering at a letter. There was a shoebox filled with such letters on the bed beside them, bundles of them tied with ribbon. From time to time the twins giggled.

They were by no means identical twins. Quite the opposite. At seventeen Jimmy had developed into quite a charmer: dark-haired, huge brown eyes, a face that could manifest total innocence whenever he wanted it to. Gregory, on the other hand, had the air of a slightly manic professor: unruly blond hair, a long pinched face, a curiously angular nose on the tip of which he wore his rimless spectacles. Everyone said that while Jimmy had the looks, Gregory had the brains, and this was more or less true. Certainly Gregory took life seriously while Jimmy seemed content to waft his way through it as though he hadn't a care in the world.

'I can't believe Mum actually kept these,' Jimmy observed scornfully, folding the letter they had been reading and stowing it back in the shoebox.

'Women always keep love letters,' Gregory informed him seriously.

'They're crap.'

'Women don't think so,' Gregory insisted, taking yet another letter from the box.

'You won't catch me writing any of this rubbish to no woman,' Jimmy was saying. 'Come on. Let's put them back and get downstairs.'

But Gregory didn't move. His eyes had narrowed and he stared at another letter in his hand, mouthing the words as he read.

'Come *on*,' Jimmy said again, standing up and reaching for the box.

'Shush,' Gregory told him.

Perhaps there was something in Gregory's tone that his brother recognised. He sat down on the bed again, and asked, 'What is it, Gregory?'

Gregory gazed towards the window. 'The bastard only wanted to get rid of us.'

'*What?*'

'Wanted Mum to have an abortion. Listen.' Gregory stared at the letter again. His hands were shaking. '"The only way we can hope to continue our relationship is for you to have an abortion. At this stage of my career you cannot possibly expect me to take on the responsibility of –"'

Jimmy snatched the letter from his brother. 'Let me see that,' he demanded. '"Responsibility of children. It is a decision you will have to make, Kate. If you decide against a termination it will mean the end of everything between us. Ever yours. Bob."' Jimmy licked small flecks of spittle from the corners of his mouth. 'The bastard.'

'Actually, that makes us the bastards,' Gregory pointed out. Then he shrugged. 'Anyway, doesn't really matter, does it, now he's dead? And Mum chose us.'

'But he wanted to kill us,' Jimmy insisted.

Gregory shrugged again.

Almost as an aside Jimmy said, 'We don't even know if he *is* dead. Mum could be just saying that.'

Then there was silence. It was one of those strange silences that often fell between the twins, a silence during which each knew precisely what the other was thinking. Without a word Jimmy folded the letter and replaced it in its envelope. Then he handed it to Gregory. They nodded to each other as Gregory put the letter in his pocket. Then they smiled and stood up. They put the shoebox with the other letters back in the wardrobe, and gave each other another slow smile. And then, as though nothing untoward had happened, they left the bedroom and hurried downstairs.

'And about time too,' Aunt Alice said, but in a kindly way.

'Just making sure we had everything packed,' Jimmy told her.

'And have you?'

'Oh, yes,' Gregory said, and gave Jimmy a sly look.

'Everything,' Jimmy added.

'Then have your breakfast and we can make a start. It's a long drive ahead of us, you know.'

2

DCI Harvey sat alone in his office, the autopsy report on the body found by the canal on the desk in front of him. He had just finished reading it, reading it diligently, although he had already known its contents: unable to wait, he had gone down to the lab and listened as McVinnie explained his findings in detail. And when he had finished speaking, McVinnie had sighed and given Harvey a commiserating look. 'That's all I can tell you, Robert.'

Harvey nodded gloomily. 'Okay. So the MO is the same. The same sort of weapon was used. But you can't . . .'

'Like I said this morning, he *could* have been murdered by the same person or persons.' McVinnie gave a wry chuckle. 'If it makes you feel any better, I'd say it was probable now.'

And that was as much as McVinnie had been prepared to say. Robert Harvey stood up and walked to the window of his office. He stared down at the car park below. The Scene of Crime Officers had come up with nothing either – nothing usable, anyway. The canal bridge was a favourite place for young drug addicts to congregate and there were literally hundreds of shoe prints, most of them half obliterated by others on top of them. Of course, any clear prints would be checked, but Harvey wasn't optimistic. He sighed, and turned back to his desk. At least the latest victim had had the decency to have a record. Petty stuff. But his fingerprints had been on the computer, which was more than could be said of the others, and that meant the long, harrowing procedure of identifying him could be avoided. Paddy Salmon, known as Fish. Seventeen. Born in Liverpool. Abandoned at the age of three and taken into care. First arrested aged fifteen in Piccadilly for breach of the peace. Harvey heaved a snorting grin. Breach of the peace in Piccadilly! Some peace. He looked up sharply. 'Come,' he said clearly as someone knocked on the door. 'Yes, Alan?'

'The team's ready, guv.'

'I'll be right there.'

DS Kelly hesitated.

'Yes?'

'Just wondering, guv,' Kelly said with an inquisitive glance at the file on the desk.

'Oh.' Harvey leant back in his chair. 'McVinnie says . . . he'll go as far as to say it's probable.'

Kelly nodded, but a small gleam of excitement appeared in his eyes.

'But we're going to treat it as definite,' Harvey told him. And then, almost to himself, he said, 'It's *got* to be.'

And he said the same thing aloud when he faced the team of detectives in the incident room. 'It's *got* to be the same killer. Same MO. Same weapon. Same type of victim.' He swung towards the information board and stared at the photographs of the four victims pinned to it. 'Peter Dunn. James Meehan. Ross Douglas. And now Paddy Salmon.'

'All teenagers. All homeless,' Kelly said.

'All rent boys,' DI George Pope added.

'We don't know that for sure about Salmon,' Kelly corrected.

Pope twitched. 'It's likely.'

'Likely, yes. But not certain,' Kelly insisted.

Robert Harvey overlooked the bickering. Maybe he hadn't even noticed it. 'So, we've got someone who preys on homeless young male prostitutes. And kills them. Why?'

Nobody volunteered an answer.

'Why does he kill them?' Harvey asked again. 'He doesn't abuse them in any way as far as we can tell. Forensics can find no sign of abuse, sexual or otherwise.'

'Maybe *he* just gives *them* a blow job and then kills them,' DS Jim Callaghan suggested.

Harvey winced.

'Trust you to think of that,' Pope said, and laughed.

'Never known anyone to kill like this without getting something in the way of pleasure out of it,' Callaghan said defensively.

'Maybe he gets his pleasure from the killing,' Kelly said.

Harvey nodded. 'Maybe,' he agreed. 'Anyway, whatever his reason, unless we find him he's going to keep at it, you can bet your life on that. So . . .'

'Back to the Dilly, I suppose,' Pope interrupted.

Harvey nodded again, and allowed himself a tight little smile as the team groaned. 'You all have photos of Salmon? Good. Maybe this time some of the other lads will have seen him go off with someone.'

'Yeah. But will they tell us?' Callaghan wanted to know.

'Oh, I think they might help now. Just impress on them that one of them could be next.' Harvey nodded to himself this time. 'I think they'll help now.' He looked up at the clock. 'Anyway, I've got to get home,' he went on with something of a grimace. 'I'll see you all here first thing in the morning.' He made for the door, stopped and turned. 'And for Christ's sake have some good news for me.'

As Harvey drove home, Gary Hubbard stepped out of the shower and started to dry himself. Then, naked apart from his watch, he sauntered into the sitting-room of his small flat. He slumped down in an armchair and lifted one of the cans of lager from the floor beside it.

It was a curiously pretty room: not, certainly, the sort of room you would imagine a burly builder being at home in. There was a daintiness about everything which was unexpected: a lot of chintz, small delicate ornaments on the mantelpiece and on the shelves between the video tapes, even a vase of fresh flowers – a bunch of mixed blooms of the sort easily purchased from petrol station forecourts.

Gary drank some lager from the can, holding it in his mouth for a moment before swallowing. He leant his head back and closed his eyes. Then, abruptly, as if an alert had been triggered in his mind, he sat upright. He looked quickly at his watch. Immediately he switched on the television and settled back to wait for the news.

'My goodness, I thought you were never going to get here,' Kate Renfrew said jovially, kissing her sons lightly on the cheek, and giving her sister a hug.

'Aunt Alice drives very slowly,' Jimmy said.

'Very *carefully*,' Gregory corrected.

'Thank you, Gregory,' Alice said.

Jimmy screwed up his face as though in agony. 'Don't say it . . . please,' he implored.

'Say what, Jimmy?' Alice queried.

'More haste, less speed. You always say that.'

'No I don't,' Aunt Alice said.

'I'm afraid you do, Alice,' Kate said.

'Do I?' Alice frowned. Then she brightened. 'Well, if I do, that's only because it happens to be true.'

And later, after they had eaten, and when the boys had gone upstairs to play on their computer, Alice turned from the sink and asked, 'Do I really say that all the time?'

For a moment Kate looked puzzled. 'Say what, Alice?'

'You know – more haste, less speed?'

Kate laughed. 'Yes. Yes, you do.'

'Oh, dear.'

'It doesn't matter, you know.'

'No. No, I suppose not,' Alice replied vaguely in that faraway voice she always used when she had something very different on her mind.

Kate took a stance, her hands on her hips and her head cocked. 'All right, Alice, what is it?'

'What's what?'

'What is it that's bothering you?'

'Bothering me? Nothing. Why . . .' She stopped talking and went back to washing the plates.

'Alice, it's *me* you're talking to. I know you. Something is bothering you.'

Alice Johnson put the last plate in the drainer and pulled the plug from the sink, watching the water vanish down the hole. Then she turned. 'It's just . . . it's . . . just the boys,' she admitted finally.

Kate was instantly defensive. 'The boys? What about them?'

'They were asking questions on the way down.'

Kate stiffened. 'What sort of questions?' she asked, moving to the table and sitting down slowly.

'Just questions.'

'Alice – for heaven's sake. Questions about what?'

Alice joined her sister at the table. She folded her hands meekly in front of her. 'About you, mostly.'

'About *me*?'

'Oh, they were very light-hearted about it. Making a joke of it, really.'

'Making a joke of what?' Kate demanded, sounding frustrated.

'About – well, about . . . it's so silly . . . about boyfriends you and I had when we were young.'

'Is that all?' Kate tossed her head back and laughed.

Perhaps it was Kate's dismissiveness that irked Alice. When she replied she sounded cross and scolding. 'No, it's *not* all. It was as though they knew something.' She fiddled with her fingers. 'You really should tell them the truth, Kate. You shouldn't go on pretending to them that their father is dead.' She looked up. 'They're bound to find out, and they won't thank you for lying to them.' She made a steeple out of her forefingers. 'They might already have found out.'

A frightened look appeared in Kate's eyes. 'What makes you say that?'

'I don't know. The way they asked the questions. Sort of making suggestions that they wanted me to agree with rather than actually asking me anything.'

'Like what?'

Alice twisted her wedding ring round and round on her finger.

'Like what, Alice?' Kate asked again.

'Well, one thing they went on about was that maybe we – you and I – were terrible flirts when we were girls.'

Kate laughed with relief. 'Well, there's not much harm in suggesting that, is there? All boys wonder if their mothers were flighty. Come on, Alice, even we wondered about Mummy.'

'It was the *way* . . . and then . . . then, I think it was Jimmy . . . Jimmy wondered if maybe you and his father weren't even married.' Kate tensed.

'I laughed that off, of course.'

Her sister relaxed a little.

'But they kept on and on. In the end I had to get quite sharp with them. That was when Gregory said . . . oh, he laughed when he said it but it wasn't a nice laugh, not his usual laugh at all . . . when he said maybe his father wasn't dead at all, maybe he'd just . . . done a runner, he said . . . when he found out you were pregnant with twins.' Alice sounded as though she was about to cry.

Kate was shaking her head. 'It's just their way,' she said, but she, too, sounded dismal.

'I think, somehow, they've found out, Kate.'

'They can't have,' Kate insisted.

'It sounded very much like that to me.' Alice reached out and held her sister's hand. 'Why don't you just sit them down and tell them the truth? They're young men now. They'd understand.'

Kate pulled her hand away. 'I will. I will.'

'You've been saying that for years.'

'I've just said I will,' Kate snapped.

'Very well. They're your sons.'

'Yes, Alice. They're *my* sons,' Kate answered sharply. And then she reached for Alice's hand again. 'I'm sorry, Alice.'

Alice smiled thinly.

'You've been wonderful about everything. And the boys adore you, you know.' Kate sighed and leant back in her chair. 'And you're right as usual. I really do have to tell them the truth, don't I? And I will. I promise. The moment I get them in the right mood.'

Alice cocked her head and gave her sister a quizzical, good-humoured mocking look.

Kate held up her hands. 'I will. I promise,' she insisted.

DCI Harvey parked his car in the narrow driveway. He didn't get out immediately but stared at the house, at the lights in the upstairs window. Then, with a small shudder and a wry face, he stepped out of the car and made his way indoors. Without even waiting to remove his overcoat, he walked to the sitting-room door and said, 'Turn that down.'

His son, Justin, lounging in a chair, one leg thrown over the arm, looked up. 'Yeah. Hello to you too.'

'Turn that racket down,' Harvey repeated. 'Where's your mother?'

'Upstairs,' Justin said, waiting until his father had withdrawn before adding in a loud voice, 'Getting all tarted up to take you out.'

Robert Harvey shut his eyes and gave a silent groan. He took off his coat and hung it carefully on the mahogany hat-stand that Helen was so proud of: proud because she had bought it at auction for a ridiculously low price. Then he started to make his way upstairs, calling out, 'I said turn that racket down.' He waited on the stairs until his son obeyed, and only then went into the bedroom. 'I'm home,' he announced, kissing his wife on the neck.

Helen Harvey was a thin blond woman a couple of years younger than her husband. She gave the impression of being about to be beautiful, but she had given that impression since the age of twenty and never quite achieved it. But she was handsome, people said. Definitely a handsome woman. With *presence*. She was also a woman of ambition, albeit her ambitions were for her husband and her son rather than for herself. And Robert was doing nicely: one of the youngest chief inspectors ever, and on the point of climbing to the very top of the ladder. Justin, alas, was another kettle of fish. Helen Harvey worried a great deal about her son. He seemed, in her terms, to be drifting. Couldn't make up his mind what he wanted to do. Wasting his brains. Getting what he wanted from life by using his undoubted charm and good looks. But she consoled herself with the thought that he was, after all, only seventeen, and all seventeen-year-olds went through that indecisive period, didn't they? Of course they did.

'I hear we're going out,' Harvey was saying, taking off his clothes and heading for the shower.

'You *know* we are, Robert.'

'Where?'

'The Raeburns.'

'Oh, God.'

'They're very useful. They know everyone who's worth knowing.'

'I'm sure.'

'Besides, it's good for you to meet *normal* people once in a while.'

'The Raeburns are normal?'

'Yes, Robert. And they talk about things other than crime and criminals. I'm not going to let *you* become a bore like so many of your colleagues.'

'Thanks,' Harvey said. 'And another thing,' Helen continued. 'I want you to have a serious talk with Justin.'

Harvey ran a comb through his hair. 'About what?'

'About his attitude for one thing.'

'He doesn't listen to me,' her husband said, and then, as though it had just struck him, 'His attitude?'

16

'Yes. He's getting far too cheeky by half.'

'Huh.'

'And I'm not happy about that friendship he's formed with David Parsons. Not one bit happy.'

Harvey grinned happily. 'I'm sure I remember you saying that the Parsons were – acceptable.'

'I did, Robert. And they are. But that David . . . well, he's very strange.'

Harvey chuckled. 'And Justin isn't?'

'I meant strange strange. You know . . . odd.' She lowered her voice conspiratorially. 'I think he likes boys.'

'Oh. Well, even if he does, it doesn't seem to have rubbed off on Justin. Not if the string of girlfriends he produces is anything to go by.'

'No, but it might.'

'I think not, Helen.'

'But you'll talk to him – just in case?'

'I'll talk to him if it makes you happy.'

'Thank you, Robert. Now please hurry up with your shower or we'll be late.'

'You know something: I bet he's not dead at all,' Jimmy said. 'Did you see old Alice's face when you suggested it?'

'Yep.'

'I bet what you like Mum's just been saying he is so we wouldn't go looking for him.'

Gregory nodded. 'She wouldn't mean anything bad by it, though. She'd call it protecting us.'

'I know that.'

'We could easily get Alice to tell us, you know.'

Jimmy wrinkled his nose. 'Not the same. Have to get Mum to tell us.'

'How, though?'

'You're the brains of this outfit.'

Gregory giggled.

'You know you are,' Jimmy insisted.

'Well, let me think about it.'

'Think all you want, Einstein. What I'd like to know is: if the bastard is alive, how do we find him?'

'Find him?'

'Find him – and what do we do about him?'

They looked at each other in silence for several minutes.

'Got to do something about him,' Jimmy insisted. 'He was quite happy to see us killed off. We can't let him get away with that.'

Gregory took off his spectacles and polished them.

'Be like letting him get away with murder,' Jimmy said.

'He didn't actually –'

'He *would* have, though. That's the point.'

'Yeah. I suppose he would,' Gregory agreed.

'No supposing about it. And you know the penalty for murder.'

They eyed each other in silence, seriously. Then Jimmy said, '*Death!*' and began to laugh. Then Gregory laughed. The two of them roared with laughter until the tears rolled down their faces.

3

DCI Harvey strode into the incident room and snapped, 'Yes, yes, I've seen it,' as Alan Kelly held up one of that morning's tabloids. ANOTHER BOY MURDERED. POLICE STILL BAFFLED. Baffled was hardly the word, Harvey thought to himself. You had to have something, some small clue to be baffled about, and so far he had nothing. He suppressed a yawn, just as he had suppressed several yawns the evening before as he listened to Duncan Raeburn pontificate on subjects he clearly knew nothing about.

Harvey stretched. 'I've just seen the Super,' he told the team. 'I'm to hold a press conference this afternoon.' He threw his overcoat over the back of a chair and sat down. 'I need something to tell them,' he said, and looked from face to face hopefully. He waited. 'Nothing?' he asked finally.

'Maybe something,' George Pope told him.

'Maybe something,' Harvey repeated without much enthusiasm. 'What something?'

'Well, Alan and I spent the evening down Piccadilly and we now know that Paddy Salmon *was* one of the boys.'

'And that's it?'

'That's all we're certain of, but . . . well, he was pally with a lad from Glasgow . . . a Jamie Scubin. Worked together. If anyone knows who Salmon went off with, Scubin will.'

'And Scubin – you talked to him?'

'Not yet. Wasn't there last night. Doesn't have an address. But he hangs about that charity place in Trafalgar Square every lunch-time. Hope to catch him there today.'

Harvey nodded. 'I suppose that *is* something.'

'You can tell the press we're making progress, guv,' Alan Kelly said.

Harvey gave a little snort. 'I was going to tell them that anyway.'

'Boss?' Pope interrupted.

Harvey glanced towards him.

'Can I make a suggestion?'

Harvey waited without moving.

'Those lads down there, in the Dilly . . . well, Susan gets back from leave tomorrow. I'm sure she'd have more luck with them than we did. I'd say they'd talk to her a lot easier than they do to us.'

'Maybe you have a point,' Harvey agreed. And then, after a moment's silence, he asked, 'You think the boys know more than they're saying, do you?'

'I think it's likely.'

'They were very cagey with us,' Kelly admitted. 'Protecting their own backs.'

'And you think Susan could get them to open up?'

'I think maybe they have . . . I think a woman might get them to say things they wouldn't tell men.'

'Hardly surprising,' Harvey heard himself say. And then, 'You still didn't get anything on the others –' he glanced towards the photographs on the board '– Meehan, Dunn or Douglas?'

Pope shook his head. 'That's what I meant, boss. I'm pretty sure some of them *do* know something but they're not saying.'

'Afraid of upsetting the other punters,' Callaghan put in.

Harvey nodded again. 'Well, follow up that lead on Scubin and try and get me something concrete by three.'

'Morning, Mum,' Jimmy Renfrew said.

'Good morning, darling,' Kate replied, immediately getting up from the kitchen table and pouring cornflakes into a bowl for her son. 'Is Gregory coming down?'

'Yep. Just coming.'

'And your Aunt Alice?'

'Snoring her head off.'

Kate filled a second bowl with cornflakes and set it on the table, timing it well. 'Ah,' she said, and smiled, as Gregory came into the kitchen. He saw the cornflakes. 'Thanks, Mum.' Then he studied his mother carefully. 'You're looking very smart this morning.'

'Smart?'

'Beautiful,' Jimmy said with a grin.

'That's better,' Kate said with a laugh. She enjoyed these moments of banter with her sons. 'I've got a very important client to see today.'

Gregory eyed his mother up and down. Straight-faced, he said, 'Must be *very* important.'

'Yes. *Very* important.'

And it was as if the importance of the client meant a great deal to Kate Renfrew. Although she had kept it to herself, it had been quite a struggle to get her business into profit. She had worked hard since coming to London; she had scrimped and saved, and slowly established a name for herself as an interior designer. Two years ago she had moved her small showroom to Chelsea – not the King's Road itself, but one of the small, chic lanes leading off it – and now, although not rich, she had sufficient income to indulge herself a little, indulge her sons also, which was far more important to her.

'Anyone famous?' Jimmy asked.

'Not in the way you mean. Not a pop star or anything.'

'What then?'

'A politician, actually.'

'A politician, eh? Well, you make sure he pays you something up front, Mum. You know what that bunch are like.'

'Oh, I think I can handle him,' Kate said with a smile.

'I'm sure you can, Mum,' Gregory said.

'Actually, he's very charming.'

'Huh. They're the ones you have to watch,' Jimmy warned.

21

'Was Dad charming?' Gregory asked suddenly, out of the blue, but making it sound casual.

Instantly Kate got up from the table and set about pouring herself another cup of coffee. 'Yes. Very charming,' she told Gregory tightly.

'I bet he always got his own way with you, though, didn't he?' Jimmy asked.

The twins saw Kate stiffen briefly. Then they heard her give a clipped, bitter laugh. 'Not always. Not always, Jimmy,' she answered, and took her time about turning and coming back to the table. 'And what have you two got planned for today?'

The twins looked at each other. 'The usual,' Gregory said. 'Go out and try to find jobs.'

'Ah,' Kate said.

Kate Renfrew was curiously ambivalent about her children leaving school and working. Of course they had to work. They had to become independent. And she tried to be enthusiastic when they spoke to her about their efforts to find jobs. But Kate also dreaded the day her boys would start earning their own money, would cease to rely on her, would, possibly, probably, definitely abandon the home she had made for them, and leave her alone. And the twins knew this.

'Not that we're likely to find anything,' Gregory said gloomily.

'I'm sure something will turn up eventually,' Kate told him, patting his hand. 'There's no great rush,' she added, and accepted the smile both boys gave her as one of gratitude. 'Anyway,' she went on, looking at her watch. 'I have to go.' She swallowed the last of her coffee and pulled her coat on. 'See you both this evening.' She kissed them both on the tops of their heads, gathered up her handbag and briefcase and hurried out to her car.

The house rattled as the front door slammed. 'Got that, did you?' Jimmy asked.

'Oh, I got it,' Gregory answered.

'Didn't always get his own way. Ha!'

'*We* know he didn't, don't we?'

'Sure do.'

'Wouldn't be bloody here if he did always get his lousy way, the wanker.'

Despite the cold, and the fact that he was wearing only a T-shirt, Gary Hubbard was sweating.

'Catch pneumonia, you will, working with just that on,' one of his mates warned him.

Gary just grinned.

'I'm telling you.'

'Don't you worry about me.'

'Not fucking worried about you, pal. Just telling you.'

Gary heaved concrete slabs into place, feeling his muscles stretch and ripple under the strain. He liked that feeling. Liked the fact that there wasn't an ounce of fat on his body; enjoyed the envious glances other men gave him as they eyed his physique. It was all a far cry from the puny kid who had been jeered at and taunted, and called Matchstick. A far cry, too, from the defenceless, frightened child forced to submit himself to abuse in the children's home all those years ago, years that hung over him like a cloud, at times suffocating him, at other times filling him with such uncontrollable anger that he found himself hugging his pillow and crying.

'Well? How do I look?' Kate Renfrew asked.

'Divine,' Hector Lord told her. 'Don't I just adore those earrings, though?'

'Behave yourself, Hector.'

'I *always* behave myself – alas.'

Kate laughed. It was one of the best decisions she had ever made, she thought, giving Hector Lord the post as her assistant. Gay as a merry-go-round, his outrageous chatter never failed to cheer her up, and the fact that he had no physical interest in her was a definite bonus. Yet he was the best company possible for an evening out: impeccably mannered, attentive, witty and without a truly bad word to say about anyone. More, he had become something of a confidant, listening to Kate's troubles and offering his advice with the best will in the world. Indeed, that very morning, spotting a worried look in her eye, Hector had asked, 'What is it, Kate?'

'What's what?'

Hector arched his eyebrows. 'Come off it, Kate. From the moment you walked in this morning I could tell something was bothering you.'

Kate sighed. 'Alice is down,' she said. 'She brought the boys back.'

'Ah. The interfering Alice.'

'Yes. No. No, she doesn't really interfere. Well, maybe she does – a bit. But – oh, it's so complicated.'

'The same old story, is it – tell the boys about their father or rue the day?'

Kate smiled again. 'Something like that.'

'Well, tell them then, for heaven's sake.'

'You don't know them,' Kate said. 'They'd want to know all the gory details – everything.'

'Well, tell them the gory details.'

'Hector, don't be so ridiculous. "Your father dumped me because I wouldn't have you both aborted." Can you imagine what that would do to them?'

'The point is you didn't, Kate – have an abortion. Anyway, from what I've seen of those two, they're tough little nuts. They'd probably feel they'd put one over on their father.'

'I'll see,' Kate said vaguely, and then, 'God, is that the time? I'd better hurry. See you when I get back, Hector,' she added, making for the door.

'Good luck, ducky.'

'I'll need it.'

'I'll have the champers ready.'

'You should have woken me,' Alice complained.

'Mum said to let you sleep,' Jimmy lied.

24

'She didn't exactly tell us to let you sleep,' Gregory corrected.

'But she didn't say to wake you either. We thought the sleep would do you good.'

Alice smiled. 'It did, to tell the truth.'

'We knew it would,' Gregory told her. He glanced towards Jimmy. 'We discussed it and decided you deserved a lie-in after that long drive down,' he fibbed.

'And before facing that long drive back again tomorrow,' Jimmy added. 'Sit down and I'll make you a cup of tea.'

'Oh, no, dear. I'll –'

'You sit down,' Jimmy repeated. 'It's *our* turn to look after *you.*'

Alice smiled sweetly and settled herself at the table. She watched as Jimmy brewed her tea, and said, 'No thank you, dear.' when Gregory asked if she'd like some toast.

'I suppose you're going shopping?' Jimmy asked, placing the cup and saucer carefully on the table in front of her.

Alice gave him another smile. She nodded and stirred milk into her tea. 'Yes. Just bits and pieces. Nice little things I can't find in Dumfries.'

'That cheese shop in Jermyn Street, eh?' Gregory asked, and his aunt laughed. 'Yes,' she admitted. 'Donald does love his cheese.'

'And chocolates from Fortnum's,' Jimmy said.

Aunt Alice gave another cheerful laugh. 'They're for *me*,' she replied. 'Are you coming with me?'

''Fraid not, Aunt Alice. Got things to do,' Gregory told her.

'Oh.'

'Sorry,' Jimmy apologised. 'All right?' he asked as Aunt Alice tasted her tea.

'Perfect, dear.'

Jimmy collected the dishes he and his brother and Kate had used and started to wash them in the sink. And from the sink he gave Gregory a knowing look and an encouraging nod.

'Aunt Alice?' Gregory began seriously.

His aunt paused with the cup halfway to her mouth. 'Yes, dear?'

'We wanted to ask you something,' Jimmy said from behind her.

'We wanted to ask *you* because we don't want to upset Mum,' Gregory explained.

'Oh, dear,' Alice said, trying to make the exclamation sound light-hearted but failing.

'We don't want you to – well, we don't want you to break any confidences,' Gregory said considerately.

'We just want you to tell us if we're right,' Jimmy said, coming from the sink and sitting down opposite her.

'Yes,' Gregory agreed. 'That way you won't really be *telling* us anything, will you?'

'Just confirming what we already suspect,' Jimmy added.

'Our Dad's not dead, is he?' Gregory asked bluntly, taking advantage of the flustered state Alice had got herself into.

'Oh, I really don't think I –' Alice began.

'He's not, is he?' Jimmy insisted.

Alice took a deep breath. Her top lip quivered. 'No,' she said quietly. 'No, he's not.'

The twins gave her a smile of encouragement. 'We guessed that years ago,' Gregory told her.

'Why won't Mum tell us about him?' Jimmy asked.

Alice reddened. 'She . . . she simply wants to forget about him. She doesn't want to talk about him for her own sake.'

'Was he *that* awful?' Gregory asked.

'No! Oh, no. It's just . . . you really should ask your mother,' Alice answered, shifting uneasily on the chair.

The twins watched her in silence, watching her give another little squirm.

'So,' Gregory said after a minute. 'Tell us about Bob.'

Alice jumped as though someone had stuck a pin in her.

'Oh, we know his name is Bob,' Jimmy said in an offhand way, somehow implying that they knew a lot more about him as well.

'Why didn't they get married?' Gregory pressed.

26

'Why did he walk out on Mum?' Jimmy wanted to know.

Alice was almost in tears. 'Don't, don't,' she pleaded.

'We only want to know about our father,' Gregory said reasonably.

'Everyone wants to know about their parents,' Jimmy pointed out.

'They were both very young,' Alice said in a tiny voice.

'We guessed that,' Gregory said. 'It doesn't take a genius to work out that Mum must have had us when she was nineteen.'

'Twenty,' Alice corrected as if the year made a significant difference.

'He wasn't a one-night stand, was he?' Gregory demanded sharply.

His aunt looked genuinely shocked. She shook her head vehemently. 'Good gracious, no.'

'That's something,' Jimmy said with a sour grin.

'They were . . . together two, two and a half years, I think.'

'Were they engaged?' Gregory asked.

Alice nodded, and winced as though the very thought of the engagement pained her still.

'So why didn't they get married?' Jimmy demanded.

'They just –'

'Was it anything to do with us?' Gregory asked quickly.

'With *you*?' Alice asked, standing abruptly and taking her cup to the sink, keeping her back to the twins. 'Of course it had nothing to do with you,' she said, and turned on the tap.

'Aunt Alice . . . ?' Gregory said in a low voice, making the two words sound like an accusation.

Alice rounded on them. 'It had nothing whatsoever to do with –' she began, and then stopped. 'You'll have to ask your mother why she never married,' she said, for the first time sounding annoyed rather than confused. She turned off the tap and walked quickly towards the door.

'What was Bob's last name, Aunt Alice?' Gregory demanded so sharply it made her stop in her tracks.

27

'Harvey,' she blurted without turning, and hurried out the kitchen door.

'Thank you, Aunt Alice,' the twins chorused.

'Harvey,' Gregory repeated as they heard her walk heavily up the stairs.

Jimmy nodded. 'Harvey. A very funny bunny,' he said, and they both started to giggle.

Jamie Scubin chewed his nails, eyeing DCI Harvey and DS Kelly who sat opposite him. He was a scrawny young lad, dressed in clothes that were for the most part a size or two too large for him. Round his neck, on a thin strand of leather, he wore, incongruously, a large crucifix more suited to a prelate than a child of the streets. He was clearly frightened but was trying desperately not to show it, narrowing his eyes and adopting a sinister look, his attitude cocky.

'Right,' Robert Harvey began. 'Jamie, isn't it?'

Jamie Scubin continued to chew his nails, twisting his head sideways the better to gnaw on a tasty sliver.

'There's nothing for you to be afraid of,' Harvey said.

Jamie snorted. 'Not afraid.'

'Good. We just want to ask you a few questions about Paddy Salmon – Fish,' Harvey went on.

'Don't know nothing about him,' Jamie said, but took a break from chewing his nails. He folded his thin fingers and placed his hands on the table in front of him.

'We know you were friends,' Harvey pointed out.

Jamie shrugged.

'Knocked around together.'

Jamie shrugged again.

'You know Paddy was murdered, don't you, Jamie?'

The boy looked down at his hands.

'Don't you?' Harvey persisted.

Jamie nodded.

'All we want to do is catch the person who killed him.'

Jamie Scubin gave a high-pitched, mocking laugh, leaning back in his chair and staring at Harvey insolently. Harvey raised his eyebrows.

'Done the others, hasn't he, and you haven't caught him yet,' Jamie pointed out with a heavy sneer.

'We don't know it's the same person –' Harvey began.

'*We* know,' Jamie told him loftily.

Harvey leant forward. 'How do you know, Jamie?' he asked intently.

Jamie Scubin ignored the question.

'How do you know, Jamie?' Harvey's voice was cold.

'Got to be,' Jamie conceded.

Disappointed, Harvey nodded anyway. 'Doesn't *have* to be, Jamie, but, yes, it's likely. That's why we need your help.'

'Got a fag?' Jamie asked suddenly.

'No. I don't smoke,' Harvey answered. 'Alan?'

Alan Kelly took a pack of cigarettes from his pocket and tossed one across the table. Jamie grabbed it and held it aloft, waiting while Kelly flicked his lighter and held out the flame. Jamie sucked hard, inhaling the smoke deeply into his lungs, taking a second draw even before exhaling the first intake.

'Now, Jamie. Did you see Paddy go off with anyone the night he was killed?'

Jamie nodded. 'Yes.' Then immediately he shook his head, 'No.'

Harvey gave a considerate smile. 'Which is it? Yes or no?'

'Saw him chatting up a few punters but I don't know which he went off with.'

Harvey nodded understandingly. 'Now, think, Jamie – can you remember if any of the punters Paddy was talking to that night . . . can you remember if you saw any of them talking to Peter Dunn, James Meehan or Ross Douglas?'

Jamie gave a little snigger. Harvey waited patiently. Kelly moved his nose to ease an itch.

'Look,' Jamie said finally. 'I dunno. Like . . . well . . . it's mostly the same punters, isn't it? See the same ones all the time. Just dunno if –'

'That's okay. That's okay,' Harvey pacified him. 'I get the picture. There are regulars, right? So the three other lads *might* have been approached by the one Paddy went off with. That what you're saying?'

Jamie nodded.

'Fine,' Harvey said.

As though to clarify things, Jamie added, 'I'm just saying the same punters are always around. Mostly.'

'Good. You're doing well, Jamie.' Harvey allowed himself a benevolent smile. 'Now, any of these punters strike you as . . . well . . .'

'Kinky,' Alan Kelly suggested.

'Mean any of them look like they might kill us?' Jamie asked with a grin. 'Wouldn't fucking go with them if they looked like that, would we?'

'He mightn't *look* like a killer, Jamie,' Harvey explained. 'Could be the most ordinary-looking man in the world.'

'We'd know,' Jamie said adamantly.

'You would?'

'Yeah. Sure we would,' Jamie insisted, but now he clearly wasn't all that certain.

'All right,' Harvey allowed. 'Let me ask you this: do any of the punters stand out in your mind? I mean, is there one you can remember above all the others?'

Jamie took a last draw on his cigarette and then stubbed it out in the small metal ashtray, taking his time about it. Finally he nodded. 'There is one we saw a lot.'

Harvey leant forward again. 'Can you describe him for me?

'Big bloke. I mean, big build but smallish. Sort of funny shape. Looks a bit too well built for his size. Know what I mean?'

Harvey nodded.

'Dead smart dresser,' Jamie went on. 'But looks all wrong.'

Harvey found that puzzling. 'What do you mean – wrong?'

'Didn't look comfy in his clothes.'

'Comfy?'

'Yeah. You know. Some guys can wear smart gear and some can't. He's one that can't. Makes them walk all stiff like they're not used to dressing up.'

Harvey beamed. 'Well done, Jamie. How old is he?'

Jamie shrugged. 'Dunno.'

'About?'

'Dunno. Thirty maybe. Maybe a bit more. Never took much notice of that.'

'So why do you say he's maybe thirty?' Kelly asked.

'Way he walks. Way he bounces.'

'Bounces?'

'Yeah. On his feet when he walks. Old guys don't bounce.'

'What about his face?'

Jamie Scubin looked stumped. He gave a small chuckle. 'Never looked at that.'

'You never looked at his face?' Kelly demanded, clearly finding that hard to believe.

'Just a face,' Jamie said. 'Another face. Don't care what they look like so long as they pay.'

Robert Harvey suddenly looked sad. He sighed, and then, as though to waylay his sorrow, he asked quietly, 'Was it in Piccadilly you saw this man?'

'Yeah. And King's Cross. And Trafalgar Square. Moves about. They all move about.'

Harvey nodded. 'On foot? Ever see him in a car?'

'Huh? No. Don't use their cars, do they? If they have cars. Can't do business if you're sitting in your car, can you?'

'Right. Thank you, Jamie. Now, you used the word "we". You said *we* know, and *we* saw him. Who else, besides you, saw this man?'

'Mates.'

'Names, Jamie.'

Jamie looked away.

'I just want to talk to them. They're not in any trouble. I just want to find out if they can add anything to what you've said.'

'Not going to give them no hassle?'

'No. You have my word.'

Jamie Scubin gave a wry smile as though he'd heard that promise before. 'Brian. And Eddie. And Wrench.'

'Brian who?'

'Dunno his last name.'

'And the others?'

'Only know Wrench's. Tommy Spanner. Look, can I get out of here now?'

'Sure. Sure you can, Jamie. Just before you go, though – if you ever see this man again or hear anything about him, will you let me know?'

'Okay,' Jamie agreed, standing up. 'Could murder a few more fags.'

'Give him your cigarettes, Alan,' Harvey said.

Kelly tossed the packet of cigarettes across the table.

'Cheers,' Jamie said, and pocketed the pack.

Jimmy and Gregory Renfrew sat with their eyes glued to the computer screen. Already the words ROBERT (BOB) HARVEY had been typed in. 'Not much to go on,' Jimmy observed.

'It's a start. More than we had this morning,' Gregory told him.

'Must be a million Robert effing Harveys.'

'Have to narrow it down, then, won't we?'

'Take for ever.'

'We've got something else,' Gregory pointed out. 'Remember what he wrote to Mum in that letter? "At this stage of my career". Remember?'

'Yeah. Yeah, you're right.'

'Must have a career, then. Not just some working-class creep.'

32

'Must be an important career too,' Jimmy said. 'One with pro-motion.'

'Exactly.'

'Think we could pump old Alice some more?'

Gregory looked doubtful. 'I don't think so. She'll be on a right guilt trip as it is.'

'Mum?'

Gregory shook his head. 'Don't want her knowing anything just yet.'

Jimmy hooted. 'Alice will tell her what she told us. She tells Mum everything.'

'Somehow I don't think she'll mention this.'

'Bet you she does,' Jimmy insisted.

'Doesn't matter. Might just make Mum come clean.'

'Christ, Mum will *never* tell us where he is,' Jimmy said.

'We'll find him,' Gregory replied with determination.

'Could be anywhere.'

'We'll find him,' Gregory insisted coldly.

'And when we do?'

Gregory turned from the screen and peered at Jimmy over his spectacles. 'Just let's find the bastard first,' he replied.

Kate Renfrew returned to her showroom looking despondent. She stood just inside the door for a moment, leaning her back against it, and closed her eyes.

'Don't worry, precious,' Hector Lord comforted her. 'The champers will keep.'

Suddenly Kate gave a huge smile. 'Open it, Hector. Open the lot. You and I have some serious celebrating to do.'

'You mean –'

'Got it! The whole damn house from top to bottom.'

'You're brilliant, lovey,' Hector told her.

'I couldn't agree more.'

And then they were dancing about the showroom, waltzing, as

Hector hummed a fair approximation of the dance from *The King and I*. 'Let's go out for dinner,' he suggested when they finally came to a halt, puffing.

'Yes! Oh, damn, no. I can't tonight. Alice . . .'

'Bugger Alice.'

'I can't, Hector. Another night. Maybe tomorrow?'

Hector adopted a camp stance. 'Oh, well, see if *I* care being stood up for some ancient Scottish hag,' he said with an exaggerated simper.

'You're a fool, Hector.'

'Tell me about it.'

DCI Harvey came back into the incident room. His face was red and small beads of perspiration dotted his brow.

'How did it go, boss?' George Pope asked.

Harvey grunted.

'That bad?'

'The usual. I think I pacified them, although they'll probably twist everything I said.'

'The tabloids will, that's for sure. You tell them we were making progress?'

Harvey nodded. 'That's about *all* I told them. I didn't mention Jamie Scubin or anything he told us. I want that kept under wraps for a while. The less the killer knows about what we know the better. Anyway, the TV nosies were there so you can all watch me make a fool of myself this evening.'

'What about the three names Scubin gave us, guv?' Alan Kelly asked. 'Want us to see if we can pick them up tonight?'

Harvey thought for a moment. 'You say Susan's back tomorrow?'

'Yes, guv.'

'And you think she might –'

'Motherly touch, guv.'

'Right. Right,' Harvey said, as though resigning himself to some fate he had the power to avoid but lacked the energy to do anything much about.

Gary Hubbard enjoyed cooking for himself. His kitchen was well equipped, and the various utensils and electric gadgets were not just for show. Indeed, his small kitchen would have done credit to many a professional chef. And that was maybe why he liked the long winter evenings: it gave him the time and desire to indulge his hobby. Not that he was a great cook. He wasn't, and would have been the first to admit it, but he was certainly an excellent amateur, taking great care not only with the ingredients he used but with the way he presented the food, if only to himself. That particular evening he made Chicken Calvados, and dipped button mushrooms in what was left of the batter, deep-frying them also. He boiled one large carrot and a parsnip together and, when cooked, he mashed them, adding a pinch of nutmeg and a knob of butter. He placed his plate on a tray, together with a can of Budweiser.

At ten minutes to six he settled himself in his armchair opposite the television, the tray on his lap.

It was a ritual in the Renfrew household. When Kate came home from work she went straight upstairs and took a shower. Then, slipping into something more comfortable, as she said with a coquettish smile, she came down, had a gin and tonic which one of the twins prepared for her, and watched the news on the BBC, making appropriate small noises of disgust as the newsreader relayed the various horrors that had taken place that day. Yet the wars and famines seemed only to disturb her for the half-hour it took to announce them. As soon as the weatherman started his liturgy Kate left the sitting-room to prepare the evening meal, often singing gaily to herself as she cooked, glowing as her sons sat in the kitchen with her, telling her what they had done during the day, listening and giggling as she told them of some absurd comment Hector Lord had made. That evening was no exception.

So, at five minutes to six Kate, the twins and Aunt Alice sat together waiting for the news to begin.

'You're very bubbly this evening, Mum,' Gregory observed.

'I'll tell you all about it later,' Kate replied, sipping her drink, smiling. 'Is that all right for you, Alice?'

Alice looked up.

'Your sherry?'

'Oh, yes. Yes. It's lovely.'

'Good,' Kate said.

'Aunt Alice has been taking nips from the bottle all day,' Jimmy lied.

'Alice! I'm shocked,' Kate said, and chuckled.

'Really, Jimmy. You know that's not true,' Alice protested.

'Shush now,' Kate interrupted, and leant forward in her chair as the newsreader appeared after a fanfare, looking serious, and started with the headlines.

For ten minutes or so there was nothing untoward: the government was still bickering about the ecu, Saddam Hussein was having the time of his life jeering at and humiliating the Americans and tribes were slaughtering each other in Rwanda, all of which gave Kate the opportunity to tut and grimace appropriately. And then, with the international calamities disposed of, the newsreader said, almost casually, that the senior police officer hunting the killer of four young homeless men had given a press conference, and immediately the newsreader vanished from the screen and film of the press conference appeared, with a voice-over stating that: *Chief Inspector Robert Harvey, the detective leading the investigation, answered questions concerning –*' That was as far as it got. Before she could stop herself Kate Renfrew leapt from her chair and switched off the television, the ice in her drink clinking as her hand shook.

'Mum . . .' Gregory protested in a sing-song tone.

'Aw, Mum!' Jimmy said.

'I don't want to hear about those dreadful murders,' Kate said quickly. 'It's too dreadful.' She swung round. 'Alice, would you help me get supper?' she asked, and hurried from the room.

'Yes, of course,' Alice mumbled and went after her.

Instantly Jimmy was across the room to put the television on again, but the newsreader had moved on to talking about cold-weather payments for the elderly. Angrily Jimmy switched it off. 'Shit!'

Gregory was grinning. 'I take it you heard what I heard?'

'Course I did.'

'You think . . . ?'

'Got to be, hasn't it?'

His brother nodded and widened his grin. 'Can't be any other Robert Harvey.'

'Not the way Mum reacted.'

Gregory put his hands behind his head. 'So, Daddy's a chief inspector. That fits.'

'It's brilliant,' Jimmy said.

'Could hardly be better.'

'No. And looking for a killer,' Jimmy added as though this had special significance.

'Yeah,' Gregory agreed.

'Great possibilities.'

Gregory nodded.

Jimmy lowered his voice to a whisper. 'Jesus, Greg, this could be really something.'

'You can say that again.'

'We could –'

Gregory gave Jimmy a sharp look and held a finger to his lips. 'Later. Wait until after supper and we're upstairs.'

'Right,' Jimmy agreed.

'I thought you were splendid, Robert,' Helen Harvey said. 'Most authoritative.'

'Huh,' Harvey grunted.

'Wasn't he, Justin?' Helen asked.

'Oh, very,' Justin agreed. 'But the question is: *are* you making progress or was that claim just to keep the hounds at bay?'

Robert Harvey eyed his son. 'We're making progress,' he replied. 'Slowly,' he added.

'Ah, well,' Justin said, suppressing a yawn and standing up. 'Good job there's plenty more disposable little rent boys available while you make your slow progress.' He glided to the door. 'Be home late,' he announced, and was gone.

'You see what I mean?' Helen asked.

'About what?'

'About Justin, of course. You really *are* going to have to speak to him.'

'I will,' Harvey promised.

'When?'

'Soon.'

'The way he just breezes in and out, it's – he treats this house like a hotel.'

'I said I'll speak to him.'

'It's that David Parsons,' Helen insisted. 'Justin's even adopting his silly mannerisms.'

'Helen, *please.*'

Gary Hubbard finished his meal and wiped his lips with a sheet of kitchen towel. He crumpled the paper in his fist and let it drop on to the empty plate. 'Progress,' he said to himself, and liked the sound of the word. 'Pro-gress,' he said aloud, and switched off the television with the remote control.

Gary put the tray on the floor beside his chair and leant his head back on the old-fashioned antimacassar – just one of the many items in his flat that he maintained belonged to his mother. Indeed, he had stated this so many times he was starting to believe it himself. And even in those more lucid moments when he admitted his fantasies, he saw nothing wrong in creating the mother he had never known.

38

Indeed, it was, in many ways, better than having a real mother. She could be exactly as he desired: loving and tender, warm and beautiful, allowing him into her bed for cuddles and whispers, fluttering her eyelashes against his cheek and pretending they were fairy butterflies. More than that: he could create a brace of mothers if he so wished, each one demonstrating his filial devotion. The old, crippled mother on the south coast had her uses, but she never entered his flat although she always came foremost in his mind when he felt like crying. Only the beautiful mother dwelt in his home, the bright, intelligent one with whom he could discuss things, the one who understood him.

Gary Hubbard pursed his lips. At that moment his thoughts were untrammelled. He didn't for one second believe that the chief inspector was making progress. In truth, he cared not a whit if he was or not.

The twins stared at the computer screen intently. Gregory had recorded the late evening news on video and, using the frame grabber, had transferred the picture of Chief Inspector Robert Harvey on to the computer. He flicked the image from the screen, tapping in:

ROBERT (BOB) HARVEY
CHIEF INSPECTOR

It was almost one o'clock in the morning and the house was quiet, a tense silence following what had been a hectic evening.

Once they had eaten, the twins had volunteered to do the washing-up. 'You and Aunt Alice go and have a natter,' Gregory said to his mother.

'Bet you have lots to talk about,' Jimmy added innocently.

They took their time with the dishes: Gregory washed, Jimmy dried. 'Mum knows she made a mistake switching off the telly like that,' Jimmy observed.

'Bet Alice is having a go at her right now,' Gregory said.

'Might be a good time –'

'Might,' Gregory interrupted. 'Have to get Alice out of the way.'

'Tell her to piss off,' Jimmy said with a cackle.

'Oh, sure.'

'Well, give her a hint, then.'

Gregory nodded. 'Ready?'

Jimmy beamed. 'Ready.'

But Gregory wasn't a great one for hinting unless it really suited him. He stood just inside the sitting-room, aware that Kate and Alice had abruptly stopped talking as soon as he opened the door. 'Mum? Jimmy and I would like a quick word,' he announced.

Kate Renfrew tried hard not to look flustered, and almost succeeded. 'Of course, dear,' she said, giving Alice a quick look of panic before facing her sons.

'It's kind of private,' Jimmy said.

'Oh, I'll –' Alice began, half rising from her chair.

'Can't it wait, dear?' Kate asked hopefully.

'It's important,' Gregory told her.

'Well, I'm sure Alice won't –'

'We'd really like to talk to you alone,' Jimmy said, as Alice stood up.

'I'm sorry, Alice,' Kate apologised, and then gave a little frown as though unsure what, exactly, she was apologising for.

'Thanks, Aunt Alice,' Gregory put in before anyone could change their minds, and sat down opposite his mother.

Jimmy closed the door behind his aunt, and joined his brother on the settee. Immediately Kate tried to sound light-hearted. 'So, what is this pressing matter you want to talk to me about?' she asked.

Gregory came straight to the point. 'Mum, why have you always told us our father is dead?'

Kate felt the blood drain from her face. Her fingers started to twitch. 'He –' she started.

'Mum, we've known for ages that he's alive,' Jimmy lied pleasantly.

'You –'

'He is, isn't he?' Gregory prompted.

Kate opened her mouth and blinked as though she was about to cry. Then she nodded, letting her hair fall over her face. 'Yes,' she said quietly. 'I just didn't want you to get hurt.'

'How would knowing he was alive hurt us?' Gregory asked.

'I thought you might look for him.'

'And?' Jimmy asked.

'And find him.'

'And?' Gregory mimicked.

'And you'd . . . and he . . . and he wouldn't want to know you,' Kate blurted finally.

Jimmy gave a harsh little laugh. 'We know he doesn't want to know us,' he said.

Instantly Kate asked, 'How do you know?' looking genuinely fearful.

Gregory came to the rescue. 'Because he dumped us when he dumped you, didn't he?' he pointed out logically, giving Jimmy a warning glance.

'Oh. Yes. Yes. Of course,' Kate said. 'I also –' she began to say, folding her hands on her lap and staring at them. The twins waited. 'I was also afraid that I might lose you,' she confessed quietly.

'You mean you thought we'd dump you like he did?' Gregory asked.

'No, dear. Oh, no. I just thought –'

Gregory gave Jimmy a nudge and both of them went to their mother, kneeling on either side of her chair, each putting a comforting arm about her. 'Hey, Mum. Come on,' Gregory said.

'You're our Mum,' Jimmy added fatuously.

'We're never going to leave you for *him*,' Gregory assured her.

Kate Renfrew was now weeping quietly, and through her tears she gazed at her sons, then gave them a kiss each.

'He's that police detective on the telly, isn't he?' Gregory put in quickly.

Kate nodded.

'Robert Harvey?' Jimmy asked.

Kate nodded again.

'Why didn't he want us, Mum?' Jimmy now asked.

Kate's head shot upright. 'What do you –'

'That doesn't matter, Jimmy,' Gregory interrupted quickly. He looked furious. 'Mum and him just decided to break up. That's it, isn't it, Mum?'

'Yes, dear. It wasn't that he didn't want *you*. He didn't even know you. It was me . . . I mean, *we* decided we weren't meant for each other.'

'It happens,' Gregory said sympathetically.

Jimmy kept quiet, still smarting under his brother's furious glare.

'Much better you broke up when you did rather than lived together not wanting to live together,' Gregory said philosophically. Then, abruptly, he stood up. 'Well, that's it, Mum. That's all we wanted to know.'

Kate looked momentarily bewildered. Then she gave a nervous titter. 'I love you both *so* much,' she said.

'And we love you, Mum,' Jimmy told her.

'I know you do. I know,' Kate said.

Gregory gave an exaggerated sigh. 'Now we don't have to talk about him any more, do we?'

'No, we don't,' Kate agreed readily. And then, spotting the look that passed between the twins, she said, 'You're not –'

'Not what, Mum?' Gregory asked, widening his eyes in innocence.

'Not going to . . . I mean, you won't try and –'

'Try and see him? Talk to him?' Gregory asked, sounding astonished at the implication. 'Hell, no, Mum.'

Kate relaxed and smiled again.

'You know what we *are* going to do? We're going to forget all about him, aren't we, Jimmy?'

Jimmy nodded. 'Too right.'

'He doesn't want to know us so why should we want to know him?'

'Right,' said Jimmy, nodding vehemently.

And so they sat at their computer with their father's name and occupation on the screen.

'What next?' Jimmy asked.

'Find out where he lives,' Gregory told him.

'How do we do that?'

'Follow him.'

'Huh?'

'Follow him from work.'

'You mean camp outside the police station and follow him home?'

Gregory nodded.

Jimmy liked the idea. 'Yeah,' he said enthusiastically. 'Just like *we're* the detectives.'

'We *are* the detectives,' Gregory told him sternly.

'Yeah, I guess we are, aren't we?' Jimmy frowned. 'Hey – you sure you'll recognise him?'

Gregory gave his brother a disparaging look. 'Think I'd forget a face like that?' he guffawed.

'Ugly bastard, wasn't he?' Jimmy snorted.

'Actually, I thought you look a lot like him,' Gregory said.

'Piss off,' Jimmy answered, giving Gregory a playful thump. 'Okay, so we follow him and find out where he lives. What then?'

'Then we have a good long think about what we're going to do.'

Jimmy narrowed his eyes. 'You mean like getting revenge?'

'Compensation,' Gregory corrected.

'Same thing.'

'Not quite. Not quite.'

Jimmy wasn't about to argue. Gregory had a way of bamboozling him which he didn't enjoy. 'Have it your own way.' He thought for a moment. 'When do we start?'

'No point in wasting time. Tomorrow. Let fat Alice go home, and then we'll start.'

'Right.'

Gregory swivelled his chair round to face his brother. 'Jimmy, you've got to take this seriously, you know.'

Jimmy looked affronted. 'Of course I'll take it seriously.'

'It's not a game.'

'I *know* it's not a game.'

'Good,' Gregory told him. 'He tried to have us killed, don't forget, so we've got to do this properly.'

Jimmy gave a sneaky grin. 'Do *what* properly?'

'Whatever we decide to do.'

Jimmy's face was a mixture of suspicion and admiration. 'You've already decided, haven't you?'

Gregory shook his head.

'Yes, you have.'

'I haven't.'

'But there's something ticking in that head of yours.'

Gregory grinned. 'Tick,' he said, and tapped his temple.

'Tick bloody tock,' Jimmy said, grinning happily again.

'Got to find out everything about him before we can really plan anything.'

'Like what?'

'His family –'

'If he has one –'

'– if he has one. His hobbies. His weaknesses. Everything.'

'And *then* we'll show him,' Jimmy said almost to himself.

'Like you say, Jimmy boy – *then* we'll show him.'

4

She might well have had the motherly touch as DS Alan Kelly had intimated, but DC Susan Dill didn't manage to glean much information from either Brian Smollet or Eddie Binns. Maybe Kelly was biased, or maybe the boys didn't recognise motherliness when they saw it. 'I could have strangled them,' Susan Dill told Chief Inspector Harvey.

'I know the feeling.'

'It was as though . . . as though they just didn't care.'

'Hmm?'

'Even when I warned them that they could be next on the list, they just shrugged it off.'

'Huh,' Harvey grunted.

'Smollet's answer was: when your time's up, your time's up,' Susan Dill explained, sounding shocked.

'And they couldn't help with the description?'

'They *didn't* help,' Susan replied. 'Whether they *could* or not I don't know. It was like they'd rehearsed everything. Came up with identical answers to almost everything I asked.'

'You questioned them separately?'

Susan Dill looked slightly offended. 'Of course,' she answered. 'To tell you the truth, boss, I think the man Scubin told you about might be a bit of a red herring.'

Harvey wasn't thrilled to hear that. 'Indeed? And what makes you say that?' he asked coldly.

'Well, you asked Scubin if there was any one punter who stuck in his mind, right?'

Harvey nodded.

'And he came up with that thirty-year-old dumpy.'

'I remember what he said,' Harvey said.

'Well, I asked Binns and Smollet the same question and both of them came up with totally different punters. Binns spoke of a man in his early sixties who keeps squirting breath freshener into his mouth, and Smollet – well, Smollet had a whole list. A right fairy, he called one, and a foreign bloke with a beard, an old man on sticks . . . oh, and an American.'

Harvey sighed. 'I see.'

'It could be any one of them.'

'Or none of them,' Harvey admitted wearily.

'Or none of them,' Susan Dill repeated.

Harvey rose from behind his desk and walked to the window, staring out, looking down and around him. Without turning, he asked: 'You said they gave identical answers to *almost* everything?' And when Dill didn't answer immediately he swung round, watching her as she nodded slowly, thoughtfully, as though trying to recall some tiny detail that for the moment eluded her. Then she shook her head. Harvey paced back to his desk and sat down heavily. 'What about the third lad . . . Tommy Spanner – Wrench?' he asked.

'He wasn't about last night.'

Harvey gave a quiet groan.

'I was going to go looking for him this evening.'

Harvey nodded. 'Right. Oh, and Susan. I'd like *you* to have another word with Scubin.'

'Sure, boss.'

Harvey lurched out of his chair and started to put on his coat. 'By the way, you and Alan working all right together?'

For a moment Susan Dill bridled. Then she relaxed and gave a thin smile. 'Fine. Thank you, boss.'

Harvey bobbed his head. 'Good. Good. See you in the morning.'

'Night, boss.'

46

*   *   *

'I'm freezing,' Jimmy complained.

Gregory ignored him.

'We could be sitting here for hours,' Jimmy said.

Gregory nodded, but said nothing.

Huddled in the Mini that Kate had bought them, they waited for Chief Inspector Robert Harvey to leave the police station. Indeed, Kate had offered to buy each of them a small second-hand car, but the twins had declined. 'We don't *both* need one, Mum,' Jimmy had said.

'I just thought it might prevent you fighting over who –'

'We don't fight,' Gregory told her sharply.

And it was as if only at that precise moment had Kate realised that, true, her sons didn't fight. Occasionally they squabbled, but they never seemed to have major disagreements, nothing they couldn't solve quickly and amicably.

'Anyway, I can't drive,' Jimmy said.

'I thought you might like to learn,' Kate replied.

'No point. Gregory drives enough for both of us.'

And although she couldn't quite follow the logic of that, Kate nodded and acquiesced. 'Very well, I'll simply buy a better one for you to share.'

And, so far, it had all worked out very well. Gregory was always behind the wheel, Jimmy beside him enjoying being chauffeur-driven, as he put it. Now, with the Mini parked opposite the police station, they waited. From time to time Gregory switched on the wipers to clear the sleeting drizzle from the windscreen, giving Jimmy an irritated look as he blew into his hands. 'It's not *that* cold.'

'Colder,' Jimmy said. 'Can't even feel my feet.'

Gregory chuckled.

'Always said you were insensitive.'

Gregory snorted.

'Oh, you can laugh. Just you wait till I have my feet amputated because of frostbite and you have to *carry* me everywhere.'

'Da-dee-da-dee-da-dee-da,' Gregory sang mockingly. 'He my brother.'

A bus swooshed past, rocking the little car.

'You still think you'll recognise him again?' Jimmy asked suddenly.

'Of course. Never forget a face, me.'

'Last thing I want is to drive all over London following the wrong person.'

'We won't,' Gregory snapped. 'Just be quiet, Jimmy. And watch.'

'I *am* watching,' Jimmy answered, straining his neck to peer at a car leaving the station car park. 'That him?'

'No.'

'Shit.'

'Be quiet.'

'This is stupid.'

'Just shut up, Jimmy, will you?'

'It's stupid,' Jimmy insisted. 'Sitting here like a pair of morons. We don't even know if he's *in* there. Could have gone home hours ago.'

'Then we'll come back tomorrow.'

'And the next day, I suppose.'

'If that's what it takes.'

'Jesus, Greg.'

Gregory rounded on his brother. 'Either we do this right or we don't do it at all,' he hissed.

'We're doing it, aren't we?'

'I told you we had to treat this seriously.'

'Nothing exactly serious about sitting here in the freezing cold waiting for someone who might not even be in there.'

'You want to quit?' Gregory asked.

'No,' Jimmy admitted sulkily.

'Well, stop moaning then,' Gregory warned. 'That's him,' he said suddenly as a dark Audi braked at the exit of the car park before swinging out on to the road.

'Hey – that's Mum's car,' Jimmy exclaimed.

'The same as Mum's car, stupid,' Gregory corrected, starting the Mini, and easing out into the traffic, checking to make sure his lights were on.

'Don't lose him,' Jimmy warned.

'Shut up, Jimmy.'

'Just saying.'

'Well, don't.'

'Sorry for breathing.' But he had forgotten the cold, and his eyes glittered.

'Apology accepted.'

Gary Hubbard looked at himself in the mirror. He had taken care about dressing, making sure his expensive dark trousers were neatly pressed, his black top free of those little bits of fluff that seemed inevitably attracted to it. He leant forward and examined his face, running a hand over his jaw to make sure he had shaved closely, leaving no stubble under his nose as he sometimes did by mistake. He took a small jar of gel from the glass shelf over the basin, dipped a finger in and spread some on both palms. Then he moved both hands across his short hair, making it gleam. That done, he washed his hands again, making certain to remove any remnants of stickiness from between his fingers.

In his bedroom he took a black leather coat from the wardrobe. He held it for a moment, pressing it to him. Then he put it on, fixing the hood neatly behind his neck so that it nestled on his shoulders like a monk's cowl. Suddenly he scowled. He walked to the window and stared out, grimacing at the sleet that slid sideways from the sky. He folded his arms, squeezing the arms of his leather coat several times. Abruptly he turned from the window, taking off the coat as he made his way back to the wardrobe. He hung the coat carefully on a hanger, and took out a short, dark-green windcheater, zipping it to his chin, then shoving his hands in the pockets, turning sideways and viewing himself. Satisfied, he shut the wardrobe and walked quickly into the kitchen, humming as he went. He cocked his head and listened, tutting as he noticed a tap dripping. He tightened it. The dripping stopped. Gary nodded his approval and took to humming again, changing the hum to a low whistle as he took a large butcher's knife from the rack. He tore a plastic freezer bag from the roll under the rack and slid the knife into it. Then he unzipped his jacket. He put the bag into his inside pocket. He patted the pocket, and zipped up the jacket again as he walked back to the sitting-room.

Gary looked about the room carefully like a man trying to imprint everything on his mind in case he never saw it again. Then he left the flat, switching out the lights and locking the door behind him. He paused on the landing, listening. Then he made his way down the stairs. 'Good evening,' he said politely to old Mrs Mooney who laboured her way arthritically up the stairs.

'Good evening, Mr Hubbard,' Mrs Mooney replied, bestowing a kindly smile on him.

'Well, that must be a weight off your mind,' Hector Lord said, holding the wine bottle at an angle and raising his eyebrows.

'Please,' Kate Renfrew said, giving her glass a push across the table. 'Yes. Yes, it certainly is.'

Hector gave her a quizzical look. 'You don't sound too convinced,' he told her, nodding to the waiter who suddenly appeared at his shoulder, enquiring if sir would care for more wine.

'No, I *am* glad it's all out in the open.'

'How did they take it?'

'Very well. Surprisingly well, in fact. Of course, they said they already knew, but I don't believe that for one moment. They couldn't possibly have known.'

Hector tasted the prawn and pasta confection, making a face that suggested he could have done better himself. 'So why are you still worried?'

'I'm not *worried*,' Kate said.

'So what then?'

'I wish I knew,' Kate answered, frowning, toying with her glass before finally raising it to her lips. 'I think I just expected them to react differently.'

'Throw a tantrum?' Hector suggested.

Kate smiled. 'No. They *never* throw tantrums. They were just too . . . *too* cool about it all.'

'You sound as though you wanted a row,' Hector said, leaning back to allow the waiter to put the fresh bottle of wine on the table. 'You women,' he went on. 'If things go badly you complain. If things go well you complain. No satisfying you.'

'I'm not complaining. It's just – well, you don't know the twins like I do,' Kate told him. 'There was something – oh, I don't know. I get this feeling when I'm around them sometimes. Vibes, I suppose. They give off vibes when they're up to something.'

'Everyone does.'

Kate shook her head. 'It's something special. Really, Hector. It's like electricity or something.'

'Oh, God,' Hector groaned, but smiled sympathetically too.

Kate smiled wistfully back. 'I'm sorry, Hector. I'm probably being silly.'

'Can we forget the beautiful twins for a moment, then? We're supposed to be celebrating.'

'Yes. We are, aren't we?'

Hector nodded.

'You're right – as always,' Kate admitted, and raised her glass. 'Cheers, Hector. And thanks.'

'Don't thank me, sweetheart. You got the commission.'

'That's not what I was thanking you for.'

*   *   *

51

'Where the hell does he live?' Jimmy demanded irritably. They had been following the Audi for almost half an hour, heading out of the centre of London, south towards Balham. Gregory didn't answer.

'Maybe he's not going home at all,' Jimmy suggested. Again Gregory said nothing. 'Maybe he knows we're following him and he's leading us a dance,' Jimmy said.

'Any more maybes?' Gregory finally spoke.

'Just saying.'

'He's turning,' Gregory said tightly. He took his time before following the Audi up Rigden Road, allowing two cars to pass before swinging the Mini left. Ahead of them they saw the Audi brake and indicate. Then the reverse lights gleamed. Gregory pulled the Mini into the side of the road, immediately switching off his lights, and together they watched as the Audi was reversed into the narrow, short driveway of number eleven.

'Bit posh for a pig,' Jimmy observed.

'Posh pig.'

'What's he doing?'

'*I* don't know, do I?'

'Can you see him?'

'He's just sitting in the car.'

'Why?' Jimmy asked, and instantly regretted it when his brother gave him a withering look.

It was another five minutes before Gregory tensed and gave a tiny gasp. 'Here he goes,' he whispered. Together they watched as Chief Inspector Harvey got out of his car and walked up to the house, letting himself in. 'Come on,' Gregory whispered urgently, opening the Mini door. They crossed the road and trotted towards number eleven, and noticed, just as they arrived, the light go on in the front downstairs room. They saw Harvey standing with his back to the window, talking to someone, gesticulating. Then another man walked across the room. Harvey followed him.

'Who was that?' Jimmy asked.

'God, Jimmy, if you ask me any more stupid questions —'

'I wasn't asking you,' Jimmy defended himself. 'I was just wondering.' Then he started to giggle nervously. 'Maybe he's bent. Could be his boyfriend.'

For some reason Gregory appeared to consider this a real possibility. Then he shook his head. 'Never make chief inspector if he was queer.'

'Suppose not,' Jimmy thought it wise to agree.

'Come on. We've seen enough for now.'

Gary Hubbard parked his van in one of the small streets behind Marble Arch. He locked it, keeping the keys in his hand, swinging them as he set off at a saunter down Oxford Street.

The January sales were in full swing, the street crowded with bargain-hunters. From time to time Gary paused to peer into shop windows. Once he was tempted to go into a shop and buy a pullover which took his fancy, but he decided against it even though it was allegedly reduced to half the original price.

At Oxford Circus he turned right and made his way down Regent Street. Although he did not increase his speed, he walked with a new crispness in his stride, and the change was a conscious decision. He was, he thought to himself, a man with a mission. As he passed the Café Royal he raised the collar of his jacket, averting his head from the doorman.

'That's Scubin,' DS Kelly said, nodding towards a group of young men loitering outside Boots on Piccadilly Circus.

'Which one?' Susan Dill asked.

'With the Nike top.'

'Smoking?'

'Yes.'

'Right. I'll see if I can get him to come for a coffee. If he does, give me half an hour, Alan.'

'Whatever you say.'

Susan Dill looked momentarily vexed. 'I'm not –'

'I know you're not.'

DC Dill started to walk towards Scubin. Then she stopped and came back, smiling in an embarrassed way. 'What's his first name, Alan?'

'It's Jamie.'

'Thanks.'

Susan Dill was in her late twenties, attractive in a quiet, unremarkable way. Unless you knew, you would never have taken her for a policewoman. 'Jamie?' she asked, coming up unnoticed behind the boy.

Jamie Scubin spun round. At first he looked frightened, but then, seeing a woman, he relaxed a little, even smiled tentatively. 'Who wants to know?' he asked, using the phrase he had heard on television a few times, and liked.

Susan Dill returned his smile. 'I do. Fancy a coffee?'

Instantly Scubin was suspicious again. He glanced past Susan, tossing the butt of his cigarette away. 'You the Bill, eh?' he demanded.

'Yes. But I just want a quick chat.'

'About what?'

'Look, I'm dying for a coffee. Why don't we –'

'Got nothing to say,' Jamie stated.

'Okay. Just a coffee, then?' Susan pressed.

'In here?' Jamie asked, jerking his head backwards towards the entrance of McDonald's.

'Fine.'

Scubin gave her another long hard stare. 'Okay,' he agreed finally. 'Thanks,' he said politely as Susan placed a coffee in front of him. And, in case she thought he was soft, 'You're not bad-looking for a copper. Could shag you myself,' he concluded with some bravado.

Small lines of laughter played about Susan Dill's eyes although, oddly, there was sadness in them also. 'That's some cross,' she said, looking pointedly at the huge crucifix hanging around Jamie's neck.

'Had it for years.'

'Oh?'

Jamie grinned. 'Nicked it,' he said as though about to goad her again. 'Nicked it from a punter.'

'Must have been a bishop,' Susan said with a twinkle.

'Naw. Just some nut. Into Jesus in a big way, he was. Jesus and Hitler.'

Susan Dill couldn't prevent herself laughing.

'Daft, isn't it?' Jamie asked, and then, after a moment's thought, added, 'Paid good money for it, though. Fifty quid for nothing.'

'For nothing?' Susan sounded sceptical.

'Well . . . nothing much.'

'I suppose you meet a lot of nuts?'

Jamie shrugged.

'Don't you worry?'

''Bout what?'

'About yourself. About getting beaten up, or worse.'

Jamie Scubin hooted. 'Punters aren't into that,' he said. 'Old gits, mostly. Spend all their time trying to get a fucking hard-on.'

'Tell that to Paddy Salmon and the others,' Susan said.

'If you'd caught him after Pete got done . . .' Jamie began, and then waved to a small man with a hunched back who walked into McDonald's and wandered about, sizing up what was available. 'That's Seymour,' Jamie explained, leaning forward confidentially. 'Know what Seymour likes?'

'I don't think I want to.'

Jamie giggled. 'It's nothing bad. Just likes us to strip off so he can look at us. Then gives our bums a few slaps. Sad old sod, eh?'

Susan Dill nodded.

'Easy-peasy money,' Jamie told her.

'Jamie, you remember the man you told my boss about?'

Jamie nodded.

'Seen him since?'

'Nah. Weekend punter, he is.'

'Have you thought any more about him?'

'For what?'

'To help us.'

'Help you with your enquiries, eh?'

Susan Dill smiled tolerantly. 'Something like that.'

'Nothing more to think about. Said everything,' Jamie told her. And then, as if the remark applied to that moment also, he stood up. 'Thanks for the coffee. Got to make a move.'

'Jamie –'

'Sitting here talking to you won't pay the rent,' Jamie told her with a grin.

'Before you go – is Tommy Spanner around?'

'Wrench? Yeah, he's somewhere. Seen him half an hour ago.' Jamie turned and looked towards the entrance. 'That's him,' he said. 'The one with that daft Pizza Express cap on. What you want him for?'

'Same as I wanted you for. A chat.'

'Want me to tell him?'

Susan Dill nodded. 'Thanks.'

'Right,' Jamie said abruptly, adopting the busy air of someone about to start work. Then he gave Susan Dill a slow stare. 'You take care, now,' he added.

'And you, Jamie.'

Susan Dill watched as Jamie Scubin scuttled to the entrance of McDonald's, and started to whisper urgently to Tommy Spanner. She couldn't, of course, hear what was being said, but it was all pretty amusing by the look of things. Both lads were grinning broadly. Then Tommy Spanner slapped Jamie on the shoulder, and made his way into McDonald's, walking deliberately towards her.

If the twins had waited another fifteen minutes outside Robert Harvey's home they would have seen Justin come out of the house, get into his father's car and drive away.

Justin Harvey had an arrogant air about him. An only child and intelligent, he had soon learned the art of manipulating his parents, playing one off against the other to get his own way. And get his own way he certainly did, most of the time at least. His mother, perhaps because she could not have any more children, worshipped him, always reluctant to scold him or attempt to control him directly, leaving that to his father. But at an early age Justin had realised that his father's attitude towards him was special. It was as though he, Justin, represented something Chief Inspector Harvey had always longed for. Yet it was more than that. It sometimes struck Justin that he was, in an odd way, a valued replacement for something his father had irretrievably lost.

And if, that evening, the twins had followed Justin, they would have seen him stop outside a house a few streets from his home – a street of expensive detached houses, houses with small front gardens managed by contracted landscape gardeners, each individually designed – and toot the horn of the Audi, seen David Parsons come wandering out of the house with that languid stride of his, and get into the car.

'Thought you were never going to get here,' David said, sounding petulant. Older than Justin by a couple of years, he was an extraordinarily pretty young man; not handsome, *pretty*: the sort of lithe and fragile creature Zeffirelli liked to cast in his films, the sort who appears vulnerable and pliable but who, in reality, is as hard as steel and dangerously persuasive.

'I had to wait for Dad to get home,' Justin explained.

David didn't answer.

'At least he lets me have his car,' Justin tried.

'Big deal,' David snorted, making it clear that he didn't think much of Chief Inspector Robert Harvey.

'He's all right,' Justin said. 'Anyway, it's my mother you have to worry about, not Dad.'

'Dear Mama,' David scoffed.

Justin grinned. 'I'm sure she knows you're bent.'

David bridled. 'Just a little crooked, Justin, if you don't mind. Not bent.'

And there was some truth in that. David Parsons, his parents divorced, was, as they say, privileged. Wealthy and idle, he was an advocate of the philosophy of not knocking it until you'd tried it, and David Parsons tried just about everything.

'I heard her tell Dad you were a bad influence on me.'

'Oh, dear. Corrupting her precious little darling, am I?'

'That's what she thinks.'

Gary Hubbard stood on the island under the statue of Eros, gazing across the road towards McDonald's, his eyes blank and emotionless like a buyer at a bloodstock sale reluctant to allow the opposition to know which lots he was interested in. Not that Gary was interested in anything that evening. He was on what he liked to think of as his weekly reconnoitre, just seeing what was about, what was available, which young man he could save. And that was the terrible thing about Gary Hubbard: his belief that by killing he was offering redemption.

'Jamie says you want to talk,' Tommy Spanner said, sitting down opposite Susan Dill.

'Yes.'

'I get a coffee too?'

Susan smiled. 'You get a coffee too,' she agreed.

'Maybe a burger?'

'And a burger.'

Susan Dill watched as Wrench attacked his Big Mac with a vengeance, pulling a face as relish trickled like contaminated blood down his chin. Instinctively she pushed a paper napkin towards him. Wrench finished his burger and wiped his mouth. He gave a low belch, and grinned. 'Enjoyed that,' he said by way of thanks. 'Okay, I'm listening,' he added, cocking his head to indicate he was paying full attention.

'Did Jamie just tell you –' Susan Dill started to ask.

'Said you wanted to know about punters,' Tommy interrupted.

Susan nodded. 'Did he tell you why?'

'Didn't have to.'

'No. No, I suppose he didn't.'

Tommy shrugged. 'Can't help you, though.'

'Maybe you can but just don't know it,' Susan pointed out.

Tommy shrugged again.

Tommy Spanner's off-hand manner suddenly irritated Susan Dill. 'For God's sake, Tommy,' she said in a loud whisper. 'Don't any of you *care?*'

Tommy was taken aback. 'Course we care. Care a lot. But it could be anyone. He's not going to wear some kind of fucking sign that says COME WITH ME AND GET KILLED, is he?'

Susan looked away in frustration.

Tommy tried to be reasonable. 'What we're trying to tell you is that the most normal-looking punters are often the most weird ones. Tell you a regular I've got. He's a big shot, a judge or something. Something big in the courts, anyway. *Real* normal, he looks. Got this flat out St John's Wood way. Never think there was anything funny about him. Married, too. Can just see him bouncing his grandkids on his knee and cuddling them. Know what he likes? I'll tell you. Likes me to pretend I'm going to kill him. Likes to have the shit beaten out of him, and all the time I have to keep saying *I'm going to kill you, you pervy bastard.*' Tommy started to giggle hysterically. Then, abruptly, he was serious again. 'Just can't tell who's the nutter and who isn't. Not till they get your knickers down anyway.'

'Tommy, I'm sorry,' Susan Dill heard herslf say.

Tommy gave her a forgiving smile. 'Nothing to be sorry about.'

The pub was quite full. A couple of minutes' walk from the London School of Economics, it was a favourite student haunt, and it was mostly students who drank there now. David Parsons seemed to know most of them. 'Oh, God,' he said.

'What?'

'She's only here. All alone and forlorn in the corner. Little Miss Huffy.'

'Shut it, David.'

'You're *not* going to have another scene, I hope.'

'Just shut up,' Justin said gruffly.

They pushed their way across the pub and, as they did so, Miranda Jay looked up and gave a wan smile. 'Hello, Justin,' she said quietly, and gave David a nod.

'Hiya,' Justin answered. 'You mind?' he asked, pulling out a chair to sit down.

Miranda gave another small smile.

'Get me a pint, will you, David?'

'Yes, *sir*,' David replied. 'Want anything, Miranda?'

Miranda Jay shook her head, keeping her green eyes fixed on Justin. She was a pretty girl with long blond hair, the colour of sand. She tossed her head frequently to keep the hair out of her eyes and, although she was unaware of it, she did it sexily.

'Yeah, look, I'm sorry about –' Justin began when they were alone.

'So am I,' Miranda said, but wearily, as though apologies were something that passed frequently between them.

'Forgiven?' Justin asked.

'Of course.'

Justin Harvey leant across the table and planted a kiss on Miranda's lips, closing his eyes as he did so. He snapped them open when he heard David Parsons say, 'Break!' and place a pint of lager on the table. 'Oh, thanks, David,' Justin said, then gave his friend a glance. 'You couldn't give us –'

'The lovebirds want to be alone to coo?' David asked lightly, but there was an edge to his voice.

'If you wouldn't mind.'

'Why should I mind?' David asked. 'Who am I to stand in the

path of true love?' he added with a tiny sneer, walking away, waving
to some other friends as he went to join them.

Miranda gave a small shiver. 'Ugh, he's so –'

Justin laughed. 'He's okay . . . when you get to know him.'

'I don't *want* to know him,' Miranda stated flatly.

Justin eyed Miranda intently. The truth was that she didn't want
to know anyone except Justin, and that irked him. Certainly he
liked her. Certainly he enjoyed the sex they had together. Certainly
he could do a lot worse. But certainly also Justin Harvey had no
intention of getting tied down. And, almost without meaning to, he
blurted, 'Look, Miranda, you know I like you. Like you a lot . . . I
mean *really* a lot. But like I told you at the start, I don't want to get
serious about *anyone* yet.'

Miranda stared at him.

'Couldn't we just lighten up a bit?'

Miranda still stared.

'Just enjoy ourselves without –'

'I'm pregnant,' Miranda announced dully.

Justin gave a high-pitched nervous titter. 'You're *what?*'

'Pregnant.'

And suddenly Justin was furious. 'Oh, come off it, Miranda. Don't
fucking try that old trick.'

'I'm pregnant,' Miranda said for the third time.

'And you're going to tell me it's mine, I suppose?'

'Of course it's yours. I haven't been with anyone else.'

Justin Harvey started to shake his head, his mouth slightly open,
his eyes disbelieving. 'That's what they all say,' he said, and drank
deeply from his glass.

Miranda started to cry, bowing her head and sobbing, her
hunched shoulders heaving.

'Oh, shit!' Justin exclaimed, and looked about as though for an
escape route.

It was then Miranda lashed out. On her feet in a flash, she smacked
Justin across the face as hard as she could with the palm of her hand.

'You selfish bastard!' she screamed at the top of her voice, and before Justin could recover she left the table, toppling his lager, and stormed out of the pub.

'Charming,' was how David Parsons described the scene.

Justin glowered at him.

'I'll get you another pint.'

'Let's get out of here.'

'We only just got here.'

'Let's go.'

'Your wish is my command.'

'Thank you for a lovely meal, Hector,' Kate Renfrew said, kissing her friend lightly on one cheek.

'Always a pleasure,' Hector told her, letting the engine of his smart little sports car idle.

Kate opened the door but didn't immediately get out. She stared at her house, wondering, 'What on earth do I have to face?' aloud.

'My guess is they won't even mention their father again,' Hector told her. 'Unless you do,' he added.

The lights in the sitting-room were on, and Kate peeked round the door, tutting as she noticed the television had been left on also. She switched it off, switched off the lights too, before making her way to the foot of the stairs and calling, 'Hello? I'm home!'

'Upstairs, Mum,' she heard Jimmy answer – cheerfully, she was pleased to note.

The twins both looked up and smiled pleasantly as Kate came into their room. It was one of their idiosyncrasies that they both slept in the room originally allotted to Gregory, keeping Jimmy's room for their clothes and storage: CDs of bands no longer in fashion, toys from their childhood, magazines and books, and the rest of the paraphernalia usually collected by teenagers.

'Did Hector behave himself?' Gregory asked with a smirk.

'Of course.'

'Where did he take you?' Jimmy wanted to know.

'Carlo's.'

'Cheapskate.'

'It was very nice,' Kate protested.

'Not good enough for you, Mum,' Gregory observed.

'Well, when you can afford it you can both take me somewhere you approve of. Did you go to the cinema?'

'Nah, we got a video,' Jimmy lied.

'Was it good?'

'Boring,' Gregory answered immediately.

'Oh, dear. What was it?'

'*Mission Impossible*,' Jimmy said, giving Gregory a surreptitious nudge, and a smile.

'I thought that was supposed to be –' Kate began.

'It was utter crap,' Jimmy said.

Kate held a hand over her mouth as she yawned delicately. 'I'm sorry you didn't enjoy it.'

'Our own fault,' Gregory admitted. 'Should have known better.' He leant back in his chair and stretched.

'You won't stay up too late, will you?' Kate asked.

'Be in bed before you are,' Jimmy said with a grin, and Kate suddenly gave a huge smile as she recalled the game she used to play with them when they were tiny, pretending she was going to bed early in the evening also in an effort to get them settled down for the night. 'Fancy you remembering that,' she said.

'Some things you never forget,' Gregory told her, and the way he said it made Kate look at him sharply. But Gregory's face was bland and serene.

'Well, I'll say goodnight,' Kate said.

''Night, Mum.'

''Night, Mum.'

'Love you both.'

'Yeah,' the twins chorused. 'Love you too.'

As soon as Kate had left the room Gregory recalled the information to the screen:

ROBERT (BOB) HARVEY
CHIEF INSPECTOR
11 RIGDEN ROAD
BALHAM

Then he flicked the picture of Harvey back on to the screen and studied it. He gave an amused little snort, and tapped in a new heading: MISSION IMPOSSIBLE.

Jimmy leant forward and read it. 'Brilliant,' he said, forgetting the idea had been his.

'Yeah, not bad. Not bad at all,' Gregory gloated.

'Thing is, though, we haven't decided what our mission is,' Jimmy pointed out.

'Can't decide that till we have all the information,' Gregory told him. 'And I mean *all* the information. Every last bloody detail.'

'That'll take some time,' Jimmy moaned. 'Take ages.'

'So?'

'Just saying.'

'Got all the time in the world, we have,' Gregory said with satisfaction. 'Don't care *how* long it takes. We need to know every single detail about him before we can plan things properly. Once we have everything we need, then . . .' He stopped significantly, and watched as Jimmy's eyes gleamed, just like his own.

Robert Harvey looked up from his newspaper. 'You're home early.'

Justin pulled a face. 'No pleasing some people. You usually give out to me for being home late.'

'I wasn't giving out to you. Just making a comment.'

'Oh, that's what it was. I see. Where's Ma?'

'Huh?'

'Ma. My mother. Where is she?'

'In the bath.'

'Oh . . . All right if David stays the night?'

For a moment his father looked puzzled. 'Where is he?' he asked vaguely.

'In the hall. Can he stay the night?'

'I suppose. Better ask your mother, though.'

'He's going to help me with –'

'Have a word with your mother,' Robert Harvey insisted, passing the buck before returning to his paper.

And Helen Harvey agreed, albeit reluctantly, and not before raising the usual objections. 'He only lives three minutes' walk away,' she said, brushing her hair vigorously, watching Justin in the mirror.

'He's going to help me with some job applications,' Justin lied glibly.

'He could go home when that's finished.'

'We don't know what time we'll get finished.'

'Oh, all right, then.'

'You really don't have to make your dislike *quite* so obvious, Ma.'

And, as she so often did, Helen countered with, 'How is Miranda?'

'Fine. Why?'

'You're still seeing her?'

'Of course. Saw her this evening, in fact.'

His mother beamed. 'She's *such* a nice girl.'

'That's why I go out with her.'

Helen swivelled on her stool. 'Justin . . . David, he's . . .'

Justin gave a harsh, brusque laugh. 'Ma, he's just a friend.'

'I'm sure, dear. But he's –'

'He's just a friend,' Justin repeated.

Gary Hubbard frowned. For some reason he couldn't quite identify, he felt uneasy. Staring across the road at McDonald's he watched the small band of rent boys being approached or accosting, making deals and walking off, sometimes beside the person they had spoken to, sometimes a few paces behind. Although he didn't know their names, Gary saw Jamie Scubin come out of McDonald's and speak urgently to Tommy Spanner: he had seen them both before although he had approached neither. He saw Tommy Spanner go into McDonald's and, some twenty minutes later, saw him come out again, this time accompanied by a young woman. Perhaps it was this that made him uneasy. Gary paid particular attention to the woman: she was the misfit. He studied her carefully, noting her carriage, her straight shoulders, her confidence, her stride: these were the things that worried him. Although she looked nothing like a policewoman there was, in the way she held herself, that aura of authority Gary had come to recognise and be wary of.

He moved his position. He saw the woman shake hands with the youth, walk briskly to the bottom of Shaftesbury Avenue, cross over and stop to talk to a man standing alone outside The Body Shop. They spoke only briefly. Then, together, they walked down the steps to the underground.

Gary pondered for a while, nodding to himself. He was smiling too as he crossed the Circus and headed back up Regent Street in the direction of his van. He wasn't upset. He hadn't planned to do anything despite taking the knife with him. He always carried the knife in his pocket on his evening excursions. It was like a comforter. And what he had witnessed had been a lesson. Something he would have to remember when the end of the month came round. He quickened his step. An addition to the excitement, he thought. And he needed that addition. After four killings Gary found something close to monotony creeping into his actions. He had read somewhere that killers very often *wanted* to get caught. He regarded that as nonsense. *He* certainly didn't want to get caught. Quite the contrary. He wanted to go on and on killing, executing his mission, finding peace as well as excitement in his deeds.

5

On the Friday morning of that week Chief Inspector Harvey sprang something of a surprise. He had decided to call in outside help, something he had been loath to do in previous cases; indeed, scoffing, as many of his colleagues still did, at what he termed the 'mumbo-jumbo brigade'. 'This,' he announced to the assembled team, 'is Anne Evans.' He waved a hand at the dumpy, dishevelled woman who had preceded him into the incident room. 'Dr Evans is a criminal psychologist,' he explained, and gave a small apologetic cough lest anyone think he had summoned her willingly. 'She will, we hope, be able to build up a profile of the man we're looking for.' And then, as though to waylay any questions that might accompany the quizzical looks that greeted his announcement, he continued, 'I propose to give Dr Evans all the information we have and see what she can come up with.'

Dr Evans smiled nicely.

'How long will that take?' George Pope wanted to know.

Dr Evans continued to smile. She was accustomed to scepticism and was unfazed by it. If anything, she quite enjoyed being regarded as a crank by the old school of ranked officers: it gave her infinitely more pleasure when they were forced, eventually, to acknowledge her expertise. 'Not long,' she answered curtly. 'If I get all the information today I should be able to give you an adequate profile before the weekend,' she added calmly, but with authority and confidence.

'Yes,' Harvey said, for no other reason than to break the silence that followed.

'Dr Evans, how accurate are these profiles?' Susan Dill asked.

Anne Evans allowed herself a small chuckle. 'That,' she said, 'depends greatly on what information you already have. By and large, though, what I *do* tell you will be accurate. But it's not like an identikit. I can't tell you exactly what this man will look like, though I *will* be able to give you some indication as to his age, and possibly his build. But my real function is to help you understand what *sort* of person he is, and even *why* he might be committing these murders.'

Harvey looked from face to face, his glance mutely enquiring if there were any further questions. When there weren't, he said, 'Right. Once we have Dr Evans' report I'll want Smollet, Spanner, Scubin and Binns brought in. I'll want them all to help build up an identikit of any punter they've been with who fits in with the doctor's findings.

'Christ, boss, that'll take for ever,' Jim Callaghan protested.

Harvey glared at him.

'You any idea how many punters these guys go with?' Callaghan asked.

'That's why I've asked the doctor to help – to see if we can narrow it down,' Harvey replied.

'Even so –'

'Just let me see what I can come up with,' Anne Evans interposed quietly. 'I might surprise you.'

'This is really *boring*,' Jimmy Renfrew complained. They were in the Mini, parked across the road from the Harvey house. They had been there for the best part of an hour now, watching. 'Can't we *do* something?'

'We will,' Gregory said.

'You keep saying that. When?'

'When we have all the information we need.'

'We know enough already.'

Gregory snorted. 'We know *nothing* yet.' He reached on to the back seat and pulled a flask of coffee towards him. 'Want some?'

Jimmy shook his head.

'Just be patient, Jimmy,' Gregory suggested. 'Trust me.'

'You don't tell me anything,' Jimmy protested.

'There's nothing to tell yet.'

'I know you,' Jimmy said. 'Bet you've got it all worked out and you're just not telling me.'

Gregory smiled quietly to himself. 'I've nothing worked out, Jimmy. Honest. Wouldn't work anything out without consulting you first, would I? I mean, we're in this together, aren't we?'

'I suppose.'

'No supposing. We are. You just keep the camera at the ready.'

'It's ready,' Jimmy assured him, peering through the viewfinder for good measure.

Then, as Gregory poured coffee from the flask into its plastic mug and drank, Jimmy said: 'Look!'

A taxi had come to a halt outside the house. The front door opened and Helen Harvey emerged. Immediately Jimmy lowered his window and started to photograph her.

'Get plenty,' Gregory warned.

'I am,' Jimmy said crossly. 'Who is she?' he asked. 'Must be his wife,' he answered himself.

Gregory nodded, but didn't speak.

Helen Harvey raised a hand to the taxi driver, and then turned. For some minutes she stood on the doorstep, talking to someone inside the house, giving the impression she was impatiently waiting for them to join her. Then, with a frustrated little shrug, she shut the door and walked briskly to the taxi.

'We going to follow her?' Jimmy asked, excited again now.

'Wait,' Gregory answered. He had barely got the word out when the door opened again, and Justin Harvey hurried down the path towards the taxi, pulling his coat on as he did so. 'Get him,' Gregory snapped.

Jimmy started photographing urgently.

'Get close on his face,' Gregory urged.

Jimmy adjusted the lens. 'Got it,' he said. They watched the taxi drive off down the road. 'Come on, then,' he goaded. 'Follow them.'

But Gregory shook his head. 'Not today,' he answered in a tone that made Jimmy look at him suspiciously.

'What is it?'

Very slowly Gregory turned his head and stared deep into his brother's eyes. Then he let a wide smile spread slowly across his face. 'You didn't notice?'

'Notice what?'

Gregory smiled wider.

'Notice what?' Jimmy asked again, sounding peeved.

'Let's get the film developed and I'll show you,' Gregory told him, deliberately mysterious.

'Show me what?'

'You'll see. You'll see.' Gregory started the car. 'We've cracked it, Jimmy.' He swung the car away from the pavement and drove in the direction of Chelsea Bridge.

'For Christ's sake, Greg —'

'Shh,' Gregory said, still maintaining his smile.

'No. Tell me. You said we were in this together.'

'Oh, we are, Jimmy.'

'Well, tell me.'

'All in good time. Let's get the prints and then you'll see.'

'See *what?*'

But it was as though Gregory didn't hear the question. He started to hum to himself. *Glow, little glow-worm, glow*, he hummed, and smiled and smiled.

It was curious how certain small things upset Gary Hubbard, causing him genuine distress. And it was strange also how, when distressed, he sought consolation by reminding himself of the second most stressful period of his life. He would sit crosslegged on the floor and surround himself with photographs of his time in the Falklands. His arms folded across his chest, he would rock back and forth, his breath coming out in short, noisy bursts like sobs. But he wasn't crying. Far from it. Indeed, such was the glint in his eyes, anyone witnessing his demeanour would be forgiven for thinking he was enjoying the images of horror littered about him. From time to time he would select one picture, pick it up and stare at it, turning it this way and that to view the corpse it depicted from every angle, then nodding as if the study had revealed something he had missed before, some detail that was only now significant.

At six o'clock that Friday evening, Gary gathered up the photographs and stowed them away safely in their folders. He had studied them for over an hour and was noticeably calmer now. He placed the folders in the drawer of the small desk he kept locked at all times. He strained his shoulders backwards so that the blades almost met, his hands linked behind his back. He stared upwards at the ceiling for a moment, and then shut his eyes, taking long, deep breaths. Then he shook himself, starting with his neck and working downwards, like a horse.

Gary didn't eat that evening. He had read somewhere that fasting heightened the senses, and he had come to believe it. He always fasted on those evenings when he heard what he had begun to think of as *the call*. And, in a sense, this call was very real. He *did* hear it: it screamed silently in his brain, just like other screams that tormented him occasionally, screams that had been stifled through fear, screams still suffocated as if to release them would again damage the small boy who had suppressed them in the first place.

Arms folded! Mother Margaret ordered, standing by the dormitory door and watching as each child crossed his arms over his chest to remind him that someone called Jesus had died on the crucifix to save him from eternal damnation, a Jesus he had already begun to hate. And as night edged its way towards day, and the children slept, Mother Margaret would make the rounds. Any child whose arms were unfolded would have the blankets stripped from him and a leather strap brought down hard on his skinny buttocks, and as each lash landed, through her breath, Mother Margaret would be saying, 'God needs soldiers. Obedient soldiers,' and all he could answer through his pain and tears was, *Yes, Mother. Yes, Mother* . . .

Gary stared out of the window. Under its coating of frost the ground reflected the streetlights and glistened. It still confused him how the boy and the soldier intermingled in his mind, blending into each other, small as toys, retreating, then marching boldly forward again, before falling back once more.

Small things worried Kate Renfrew also, although maybe *irked* would be a better diagnosis. And she was irked, probably unreasonably, when she arrived home and found the twins not in the sitting-room to greet her even though they certainly were at home. She regarded their absence as a slight, and there was an edge to her voice when she announced from the foot of the stairs: 'I'm home.' She relaxed when the twins responded immediately, coming hurtling down the stairs, both of them beaming.

'Hiya, Mum,' Jimmy was the first to say, giving Kate a peck on the cheek.

'Mum,' Gregory said, and kissed her too.

'That's better,' Kate told them, and then noticed Gregory had his jacket on. She frowned.

Gregory spotted the frown. 'Just got to nip out for a sec,' he explained. 'Be right back.'

'Where on earth is he off to?' Kate asked Jimmy.

'Got to pick something up.'

'What?'

Jimmy shrugged. 'Something we ordered.'

Kate wasn't about to let up. 'What did you order, Jimmy?'

Her son grinned and tapped the side of his nose.

'Ah,' Kate sighed, feeling a little thrill run through her. 'A surprise?'

Jimmy nodded.

'For me?'

'Sort of.'

'Sort of . . . ?

'You'll see, Mum. Won't be a surprise if I tell you, will it?'

Kate laughed gaily. It was one of the games she and her sons played: surprises. Not for any particular reason or occasion. Just something they delighted in.

'Right. Well, I'll go and have my shower,' Kate announced, running her fingers through Jimmy's hair.

'I'll have your fix ready for you when you come down,' Jimmy told her. 'You look as though you could murder a good *stiff* gin tonight.'

'Whatever do you mean?'

'You look knackered.'

'Well, thank you *very* much. That's just what a woman needs to hear, James Renfrew,' Kate said, flouncing up the stairs, feigning severe damage to her ego.

'Beautiful but knackered,' Jimmy called after her.

'Too late to redeem yourself now, young man,' Kate countered.

He was busy in the kitchen, mixing his mother's drink when Gregory came back. 'Got it?' Jimmy asked.

Gregory held up a large envelope. 'Got it.'

'Better hide it upstairs before Mum comes back down.'

Gregory nodded and headed for the door.

'Any good?' Jimmy asked.

'Brilliant.'

'That's my boy,' Jimmy said with a wink. 'Want a lager?'

'Lager? Champagne, mate.'

'Sorry. All out of champagne, sir.'

'Lager, then. Be down in a mo.'

'Miranda called,' Helen Harvey told Justin.

'Here?'

'Phoned,' Helen corrected herself.

'Oh. What did she want?'

'To speak to you. Justin . . . she sounded upset. You two haven't had a falling out or anything, have you?' Justin shook his head. 'No. Better give her a call back, I suppose.'

'You don't have to make it *quite* so obvious, Helen,' Robert Harvey observed quietly when Justin left the room.

Although she seldom bothered to do any, Helen was an excellent needlewoman, her embroidery delicate and highly praised. She didn't have to concentrate on it too deeply either, but could use the time to think about all the little things she felt were important. And she liked to believe that, in winter, seated in front of the log fire with her husband reading the paper opposite her, it gave a cosy touch to her marriage – that cosy family touch she was convinced marriage was all about. Now, she gave her husband a frown, pausing in her work, the needle held aloft, the collar of the blouse she was decorating stretched flat across her knee. 'I'm sorry?'

'Justin and Miranda,' Harvey told her.

'What about them?'

'Helen . . .' Harvey said simply, letting his voice rise on the word.

'I haven't the remotest idea what you mean,' Helen protested.

'Of course not.'

'I just happen to think she's a very nice girl.'

'I'm sure she is.'

'And it would do Justin no harm at all to start settling down a little.'

Harvey snorted. 'He's only seventeen, for heaven's sake.'

Helen gave him an accusatory glare.

'Yes, well, things were different then,' he countered.

'How convenient,' Helen said tightly.

'And *my* mother didn't push me –'

'I'm not pushing anybody,' Helen protested immediately.

'No?'

'No.'

'That takes care of that, then.'

74

Justin also, it seemed, had taken care of things. He came back into the sitting-room and dropped lazily into an armchair. His father looked at him briefly, and then went back to his newspaper. Helen gave him a tender, approving smile, completing a small, intricate portion of her design before asking, 'Everything all right, dear?'

Justin grunted.

'Is that a yes or a no?' Helen asked.

'A yes.'

'Oh, good.'

Justin yawned, making a noise about it.

'Tired?' Helen asked.

Justin nodded vaguely; his father made a little derogatory noise in the back of his throat.

'Why don't you have an early night?' Helen suggested.

'Might just do that,' Justin told her.

'That'll be a first,' Harvey said.

'There's a first time for everything, Dad.'

'True, true,' his father agreed.

'Or I might not,' Justin added, getting up and stretching. 'Might just nip round and see David,' he said, using the rather sneering tone he knew would provoke his mother.

But, for once, Helen Harvey didn't rise to the bait. Indeed, she acted as though she had not even heard the remark: she added two more stitches and then cut the thread with a tiny pair of scissors. 'There,' she said proudly, holding up her handiwork. 'What do you think of that, Robert?'

Her husband peered over his paper, and nodded his approval. 'Very nice,' he said.

'Justin?'

'Yeah,' Justin said, and then, as though somehow her action had made up his mind for him, he added, 'Won't be late,' and strolled out.

Helen Harvey put the blouse down on her knee and waited until she heard the front door close before saying, 'You should have said something.'

'Like what?'

'You know I can't stand that David Parsons.'

'Well, then, *you* should have said something.'

'You're his father,' Helen pointed out fatuously. 'He listens to you.'

'I hadn't noticed.'

Suddenly Helen was angry. 'That's just the trouble with you, Robert. You don't notice anything that's not connected with your work. Your own son is –'

Robert Harvey dropped the newspaper onto his lap. 'Helen,' he said. 'Helen.' He folded the paper in a resigned way and dropped it to the floor beside his chair. 'The boy is entitled to choose his own friends.'

'Not if –'

'The more you make it clear to him that you dislike David the more he's going to see him. It's called rebellion, or something.' He stood up. 'Anyway, you're only assuming David is gay.'

Helen gave a snort.

'And even if he is . . .'

'I don't want my son associating with –'

'Anyone who isn't white, middle class and heterosexual? Isn't that it, Helen?'

'That's quite unfair.'

Her husband shrugged.

'Things happen,' Helen went on, and then grimaced as though she wasn't quite sure what she had meant by the remark. She redeemed herself quickly. 'Just think what a scandal could do to your career, Robert.'

Robert Harvey gave a huge guffaw.

'Oh, you can laugh,' Helen told him, nodding her head.

'Well, Helen, I'm certainly not going to cry.'

His wife packed up her little bag of embroidery materials and stood up. 'You might one day,' she told him ominously. 'And then it will be too late.'

Gary Hubbard was convinced that something out of the ordinary was going to happen that evening, but his conviction was quite unlike that which riddled him when he had sought out and killed the four young men. It was as though, he thought, as he parked his van in Covent Garden and set off down the Strand, as though whatever mischievous being guided or, at least, took a hand in his actions had subtly communicated the feeling of impending extraordinariness.

And perhaps he was trying to dupe that mischievous being, to hex the bugaboo, so to speak, when, suddenly, he changed direction and started to stride across the bridge towards the National Theatre. He kept to the inside of the pavement to avoid being sprayed by the slush passing cars spewed at him. For a while it seemed as though he was the only one on foot: he had the bridge and, he fancied, the world to himself. But not quite. Without warning he heard someone call his name. 'Gary!' He looked quickly behind him. Nothing. And then, when there was a break in the traffic, he spotted a figure across the bridge waving at him. Gary screwed up his eyes and stared. He didn't wave back but stood quite still, staring. And, as he stared, he saw the person start to run across the bridge towards him, beginning to chatter even as he made his way. 'Knew it was you. What you up to, mate?'

Gary felt the tension ease from his bones. A flicker of a smile crossed his lips. 'Jesus, Jason, didn't expect to bump into you,' he said.

Jason Weaver grinned happily as though surprising people gave him particular pleasure. He was a wiry twenty-one-year-old, good-looking, even though a cast in his left eye sometimes gave him an evil, growling expression. Gary didn't know him very well although they worked alongside each other on the building site. Indeed, he had tended to avoid him, irked by Jason's tendency to boast about his sexual prowess, his conquests, his irresistible appeal to women.

Gary didn't trust people who boasted. He had long since learned that those who did were usually the ones who had nothing to brag about, the very ones who did nothing, using their boastfulness to cover their inadequacies. Now he studied Jason as though seeing him for the first time.

'What you up to?' Jason asked.

'Just . . . just going for a drink,' Gary Hubbard answered.

Jason Weaver looked puzzled. 'Didn't think you –' he began and then stopped.

'Didn't think I what?'

'Didn't think you lived up this way.'

Gary forced a laugh. 'I don't. Just felt like coming –'

'Me too,' Jason interrupted.

'Great minds think alike,' Gary said quietly.

'Oh. Yeah. Yeah, that's right,' Jason agreed tentatively. Then he brightened. 'Fancy going –'

'Sure,' Gary agreed.

'Great,' Jason said. 'Don't much like drinking by myself.'

'No, me neither,' Gary told him.

Jason Weaver, hands in pockets, swung his body from left to right. 'This way or that?' he asked, now rocking on the balls of his feet.

'Closer this way,' Gary said.

'Right.'

Together they continued along the bridge, both hunching their shoulders against the wind that had suddenly started to blow up in spurts.

'You still don't see it, do you?' Gregory asked, looking very smug. On the desk in front of them was a blow-up of Justin Harvey's face.

'Sure I see him,' Jimmy said.

'Ah, but that's all you see. *Him*. Look closely, Jimmy.'

Jimmy peered then grimaced. 'What am I supposed to be looking for?' he demanded, sounding fed up.

'You just keep looking,' Gregory told him. 'I'm going for a pee.'

Jimmy was still poring over the photograph when his brother returned. 'Can't see anything special,' he said without turning round.

'No?'

'No.'

'Oh, Jimmy,' Gregory said in a strange sing-song voice.

Jimmy Renfrew turned his head slowly and looked up at his brother. Then he gave a small, high-pitched gasp. '*Jes-us!*' he exclaimed.

'Good, eh?' Gregory asked.

'Good? Christ Almighty, you're fantastic.'

'Thought you'd be impressed.'

'Oh, I'm impressed. *Very* impressed.'

'Think I'd get away with it?'

'Hell, yes.'

'Gives us a load of possibilities,' Gregory said.

'You can say that again.'

'Gives us a load –'

'Yeah, yeah,' Jimmy said, and they both laughed.

And, certainly, Gregory's transfomation did appear more than promising. He had taken off his spectacles and dampened his hair and flattened it, making it look as though it had been cut. And he stood there in a pose that made him somehow look a little taller, more arrogant. He looked for all the world like the twin of Justin Harvey rather than of Jimmy.

Gregory gave a little twirl, and, as he did so, he said, 'Got to get talking to him, so we can hear what his voice sounds like.'

Jimmy nodded seriously.

'If I could get that perfected then we're really in business.'

Jimmy nodded again.

'Just *think* what we could do!'

'Shit. Anything. Anything we like.'

'Precisely.'

'Do a bank job,' Jimmy suggested.

Gregory grimaced.

'Well . . .'

'Do a lot more than that,' Gregory pointed out.

'And have it blamed on . . .'

'You've got it,' Gregory said quickly, excitedly. 'So, like I said, we've got to get close to him. Hear him. Pick up on his traits. See what he wears. How he acts. Everything.'

'Right.'

'And then . . .' Gregory said ominously.

'And then?'

Gregory sat down at the desk beside Jimmy and put an arm about his shoulders, and with his free hand he brought the picture of Chief Inspector Robert Harvey up on to the computer screen. 'Well,' he said. '*He* wanted to kill *us*, didn't he?'

Jimmy bit his lip and, in an awed voice, asked, 'You mean we kill him?'

He was surprised when Gregory shook his head, and replied, 'Oh, no.'

'What then?'

Gregory pondered. 'I haven't quite worked it out yet. But –' He stopped and grinned wickedly at his brother.

'But what, Greg?' Jimmy demanded.

'Well,' Gregory began slowly, drawling the word. 'Well, I thought we might kill *someone* all right,' he admitted. Then he raised the picture of Justin and studied it. 'Thought we might kill someone and have this bastard blamed for it.'

Jimmy stared at his brother in silence.

'You know,' Gregory went on very quietly as though he was in the process of planning something in his mind. 'Kill someone he knows. Leave a few clues leading to him. Have him arrested. Have him charged.' Then he giggled. 'Have him fucking convicted,' he concluded.

Jimmy found Gregory's giggle infectious. He started to giggle too, rubbing his hands together in delight. 'That's only bloody brilliant.'

Gregory struck a haughty pose. 'I thought so,' he said, and then burst out into uncontrollable laughter.

'Be even better if Daddy had to investigate and find out that –'

'Yeah. That's just what I was thinking,' Gregory agreed. He stretched and yawned as though suddenly exhausted. 'Anyway, that's the plan. What d'you think?'

'Sounds good to me.'

Gregory nodded. 'Okay. From now on we concentrate on pretty boy here,' he said, flicking a dismissive finger towards Justin's picture.

'Anything you say, Greg.'

Suddenly Gregory became menacingly solemn. 'Jimmy, this is serious stuff we're talking about, you know.'

'I know.'

'One mistake and it'd be us for the high jump.'

'I know.'

'And then Daddy dear will really have beaten us.'

Jimmy nodded. 'I know,' he said again.

'So . . . it's got to be slowly, slowly. Everything planned down to the last detail.'

'Right.'

Gregory laughed. 'Be like killing two birds with the one stone,' he announced.

'Only fair,' Jimmy said. 'There's two of us.'

'Exactly.' Suddenly Gregory's good humour vanished.

'What is it?' Jimmy asked anxiously.

'Just thought of something else,' Gregory replied.

'What?'

'What age would you say he is?'

'Dunno. Late forties?'

'Not him, stupid.'

'Oh, *him*.' Jimmy gazed at Justin's picture for a minute. Then he shrugged. 'Dunno. Same age as us, I suppose.'

Gregory nodded. 'Yeah.'

'So?'

'So that means the bastard was shagging her at the same time he was shagging Mum.'

'Shit! Yes.'

There was silence for a while, broken only by Gregory drumming his fingers on the desk. 'But he kept *him*,' he said finally but quietly as though meaning only to think it. 'He kept *him* and wanted *us* killed.' His brother looked too appalled to speak, and was relieved when Gregory gave him a smile. It wasn't a pleasant smile, however. 'And that, sunshine, was the biggest mistake he ever made.'

Gary Hubbard sat at the bar staring into his pint. Beside him, Jason Weaver was prattling on, enjoying himself hugely. Gary heard him talk but wasn't listening to him. Gary was worried. He knew he was about to be drawn away from his pattern, knew that Jason was going to be a victim, and he was trying to find a justification for this. He wasn't, he'd told himself repeatedly in those dark, despairing days and nights, just some ruthless, mindless killer. There was a purpose to it all. Yet he was sane enough to realise that killing was becoming a pleasurable thing, and this shocked him. He sat up with a jolt as he felt Jason's hand on his shoulder. 'What?'

'Just saying,' Jason answered, his words slurred.

'Saying what?' Gary asked, perhaps hoping that whatever Jason had been saying would justify what he knew would happen.

'Just saying that . . .' Jason started to laugh stupidly. 'Can't think what I was saying.'

'Must have been a lie. They say that, don't they? If you can't remember what you were saying, it was a lie?'

No doubt it was the combination of Guinness and tequila that made Jason react the way he did. All of a sudden he had swung off his stool and was standing, weaving, to one side of Gary, looking ready for a fight, his fists clenched. 'You fucking calling me a liar?' he demanded.

Gary didn't even look at Jason. He had been accosted by so many drunks while in the army that this was nothing new to him. He knew he could cripple the other man with a single blow. He raised his eyes and smiled apologetically at the barman.

'Hey, you –' the barman said warningly to Jason.

'You fuck off,' Jason roared.

'Right,' the barman said, and made to lift the telephone by the till.

'Come on, Jason,' Gary intervened quickly, giving the barman a wink. 'Come on. Nobody's calling you a liar. Don't go spoiling a good evening, eh, mate?'

There was a wonderful calm in Gary's voice, and something oddly hypnotic about it too. It was the sort of voice he had used to lull uncomprehending Argentinian prisoners into a sense of security before he and his colleagues had shot them rather than face the trek back with them across frozen wasteland. There was compassion and understanding in the voice, and Jason Weaver was seduced by it. As if by magic all his belligerence disappeared, and he was smiling as he threw both arms around Gary. 'Let's piss off out of here if we're not wanted,' he said into Gary's ear.

Gary smiled back but only with his lips. His eyes had a faraway look to them as he nodded and finished his pint in a single gulp. He stood up, put an arm about Jason's waist and manoeuvred him out of the bar and on to the street, nodding to the barman as he did so, watching as the phone was replaced without a call being made.

The two men paused on the pavement, their breath streaming from their mouths. Small flakes of snow had started to fall, not enough to settle, but enough to make all the passers-by duck their heads and watch their step.

Then, without a word, Gary Hubbard guided Jason Weaver towards the underpass.

'Where we going now?' Jason slurred.

'I know a place,' Gary told him.

'All right, mate?'

'I'm fine.'

'Yeah, me too,' Jason said, and then added. 'You're sound, pal.'

The underpass, once a small, daemonic, underworld city, was virtually abandoned now, now that the council had decided to sweep away those unsightly residents along with the rest of the city's garbage, leaving it inhabited only by the ghosts of the homeless, the drunk, the mad. Yet a few, too desperate, too numbed to think of finding some other warren, returned each night and erected crazy cardboard structures. And when they felt the coast was clear they lit small fires, giving the area an even more ghastly air. They gathered round the flames, taking on the aspect of phantoms, motionless figures with hands outstretched towards the meagre warmth.

On the right as Gary steered Jason deeper into the underpass was a small area that remained uninhabited even by the desperate. Water covered the concrete ground, rippling in the fiery light as it seeped from the road above and trickled down the walls, distorting the graffiti, making the words illegible, the figures even more demented paranoiac visions.

Jason had taken to humming to himself contentedly as he permitted himself to be guided, and Gary willingly allowed the tune to drip into his brain; it helped to quell the argument that was raging there. It had been his intention to get Jason back to the van. To drive somewhere safe. To kill him unobserved, without hurry. But for some reason his intentions were being thwarted. He still had his left hand about Jason's waist, his right hand inside his jacket, clasping the hilt of the knife. And suddenly the ridiculous tune Jason persisted in humming became a taunt, a dare. Gary Hubbard felt himself start to shake.

'She says she's pregnant,' Justin Harvey said.

David Parsons guffawed. 'They all say that,' he answered. 'Claiming to be with child is the oldest snare in the world. More fool you if you fall for it.'

Justin shook his head. 'Miranda's not like that.'

'Of *course* not,' David countered sarcastically.

'No. Seriously. She'd never –'

'Look, Justin, take it from me, she –'

'What if she is, though?'

'No big deal,' David announced and tipped more vodka into Justin's glass.

'Steady,' Justin said.

'You're not driving. And . . . you could stay the night.'

Justin ignored the invitation. 'What d'you mean – no big deal? Not for you, maybe, but . . .'

'Just tell her to get rid of it.'

'What if she won't?'

'Marry her and settle down to married bliss,' David said glibly.

'For Christ's sake. This is serious.'

'If she loves you she'll do what you want. Anyway, I'm quite sure you can persuade her to do what's best.' David Parsons half filled his own glass with vodka and added a splash of Coke.

Justin gave a low, forlorn groan. 'I can't just –'

'You'll have to. If you don't . . . well, you don't want the silly cow trotting round and telling your dad about it, do you? The shit would really hit the –'

'She wouldn't.'

'Oh, she might.'

Justin placed his glass on the table and put his head in his hands. 'Oh, Christ, he'd kill me.'

'Well, solve everything, that would, wouldn't it?' David asked with a titter.

'Mum would go spare.'

'Well, then, you'll just have to face Miranda and talk her into doing what you want . . . unless, of course, you fancy making your beloved parents into grandparents.'

Justin snorted.

'Look,' David went on. 'Just go round and see her and talk to her. She might not be as unreasonable as you think.'

Justin nodded gloomily. 'I'll do it tomorrow.'

'Want me to come with you?' David asked with a leer.

'That's all I need.'

'Just trying to help. Never could understand why she doesn't like me.'

'Not everyone likes you, David.'

'No? You do surprise me.'

Justin finished his drink. 'I'd better go,' he said, and stood up.

'What time are you going to see her?'

'Oh. Tomorrow evening. That's what I told her on the phone.'

'Well, good luck.'

'Yeah. Thanks.'

'Let me know what happens.'

'Yeah.'

The twins lay in their beds, both of them with their arms folded behind their heads.

'What're you thinking?' Jimmy asked.

'What we were talking about,' Gregory answered.

'Me too.'

'We're agreed, aren't we?'

'Yep.'

'And you're not all of a sudden going to start saying how boring it all is?'

'Nope.'

'Good.'

'I'll do exactly what you say.'

'Good.'

'Start in the morning?'

'First thing.'

Jimmy laughed gleefully.

'What's so funny?' Gregory asked.

'It's just so perfect.'

'Yeah. It is, isn't it?'

'I hate to admit it, but you're quite a genius, Greg.'

'We both are,' Gregory corrected with munificence.

'So we'll start first thing in the morning, then?' Jimmy asked.

'Crack of dawn.'

'Stick to him all day.'

'Like leeches.'

Jimmy sniggered. 'Suck him dry.'

Gregory gave a huge, noisy yawn. 'In a manner of speaking. 'Night, Jimmy.'

''Night.'

Justin Harvey was not an impulsive person – not when it came to confiding in his parents, anyway. So it was a sign of the genuine pressure he was feeling when he got home from David's and asked, 'You alone, Dad?'

Robert Harvey, dozing by the fire, looked pointedly about the room, and said, 'It would appear so. Why?'

'I mean – where's Mum?'

Harvey straightened himself in his chair. 'Gone to bed,' he answered. He looked at his watch. 'Just where I should be,' and made to rise.

'Dad, can I talk to you?'

Harvey blinked. If not exactly astonished, he was certainly very surprised by Justin's request. He could not recall his son ever wanting to speak to him before, not with the secrecy and urgency his tone suggested. He watched Justin fidget for a moment and then, clearing his throat, he said, 'Of course. Of course. Sit down, why don't you?'

Justin sat down opposite his father, and twisted his fingers, making a steeple of them and then destroying it. 'Dad, I might have a problem.'

Harvey folded his arms, and gave his son a wide-eyed stare. 'Just might?'

Justin nodded.

'Better tell me about it, then.'

'It's Miranda.'

'Ah.'

'She says she's pregnant,' Justin said bluntly, eyeing his father from under frowning eyebrows.

'Ah,' Robert Harvey said again.

It was not the reaction Justin had expected. The small noise, half sigh, half an expression of understanding, was a far cry from the explosion he had anticipated. 'And it's yours, I take it?' he heard his father ask,

Justin shrugged. 'That's what she says.'

'What do you say? Is it or isn't it yours?'

Justin didn't answer.

'There's a good possibility it's yours?' his father probed.

Justin nodded.

'How good a possibility?'

'Almost certain.'

Harvey nodded slowly, pensively. 'Let's suppose it is. What is it you want me to say?'

Justin gave a tiny smile. 'Tell me what to do.'

'What do you *want* to do?'

'I don't know,' Justin said. 'David says I should try and make her get rid of it,' he added, looking away and missing the wince that passed across his father's face.

'How involved *are* you with Miranda . . . I mean, I mean is this a serious relationship or just –'

'Just,' Justin interrupted. 'I think, though, that maybe *she* thinks it's serious.'

'Have you asked Miranda what –'

'She only told me yesterday. I haven't had the chance to.'

'Well, that's one thing you'll have to do, Justin. Go and see her.'

'I'm seeing her tomorrow evening.'

'Well, when you see her, sound the girl out. Don't go in there bull-headed. Try and be a bit diplomatic. But the first thing you have to do – before you see her – is decide what *you* want,' Harvey advised, continuing immediately when he spotted Justin about to speak, 'and once you've decided *that*, you'll have to persuade Miranda to fall in with it.'

'And if she won't?'

'We'll deal with that when the time comes.' He stood up with his back to the fire and rocked on his feet. 'Just don't make a mistake, Justin. Don't do anything you might regret for the rest of your life,' he said. 'And for God's sake don't say anything about this to your mother yet,' he warned, allowing himself a small conspiratorial smile. 'Now, I'm off to bed, and I suggest you do the same.' He took a couple of strides towards his son and placed a hand on his shoulder. 'We'll work something out,' he said reassuringly. He withdrew his hand abruptly as though he suspected the tender gesture might, in the future, be held against him.

Justin gazed up at him. 'Thanks, Dad.'

Gary Hubbard had broken all his own rules, and, staring down at the dead body of Jason Weaver, he felt afraid for the first time. Despite the cold night air he was sweating, though not from any exertion. The killing had been ridiculously simple. Drunk and maudlin, Jason had accepted Gary's arms about him as a gesture of friendship, of love between mates even, and had smiled in a befuddled way as Gary slit his throat. Even now he was smiling as though death was quite a joke. No, Gary was sweating with fear. Fear of what, he wasn't certain, which made it all the worse. He wiped the knife on Jason's jacket and stood up. He felt dizzy suddenly and started to sway. He heard the sound of footsteps approaching, the light click of high-heeled shoes, walking slowly. He heard voices. Women's voices. He knew he should run from the scene but he couldn't move. And then, 'Hey,' he heard, and looked up.

A few yards away two prostitutes, arm in arm, stared at him, stared at the knife he held in his hand, stared at the body on the concrete, their mouths falling open little by little as the horror of what they saw finally penetrated their consciousness. Then one of them gave a tiny, strangled scream and her companion joined in with a long, low, baying sound like a hound in full cry. Then they were both screaming their heads off, cowering together, backing away but too terrified to take their eyes off Gary Hubbard.

Suddenly Gary was running. He was racing from the underpass and up on to the bridge. He was careering along the bridge, gulping in freezing air, feeling it sear into his lungs.

When he reached the Strand he stopped and leant one hand against a closed kiosk, panting. Then he started walking as quickly as he could without drawing attention to himself. He was slowly regaining control, issuing orders to himself, trying to erase the kaleidoscope of images that flaunted themselves in his mind. He passed the Strand Palace Hotel and turned right towards Covent Garden, heading for his van. As soon as he saw it parked there he felt an enormous weight lifting from him. But not for long. When he reached the van he stopped dead. It wasn't just that it dawned on him that he had lost his keys: he could *see* them lying on the ground beside Jason Weaver's body, glinting. He put his arms on the roof of the van and sank his head on to them, giving a low groan. A drunk staggered towards him. A dog, sitting beside a young beggar, barked. Gary stood upright. The drunk changed course, tacking away, muttering. The dog whined and settled down.

He used his knife to force the lock on the driver's side of the van. Inside, the door shut, he felt better, safer. He took a deep breath to steady himself, then he fumbled underneath the dashboard, loosening the wires. He selected the two he wanted and, with a sharp jerk, wrenched them free. Like someone who had done all this before, he touched the wires together and gunned the engine into life. He sat back, revving the engine gently. He set the windscreen wipers in motion, watching as they cleared away the thin layer of snow, leaving glistening designs. *Glow, little snowflake, glow*, loomed into his thoughts, bringing to mind, also, another time he had sung the ditty, using 'snowflake' instead of 'glow-worm': yomping through the blizzard in the Falklands, allowing the silly song to register in his brain in case his very consciousness froze.

He reversed the van carefully and drove back across the bridge to the underpass at a sedate pace. Perhaps the two slags had just run off, glad to be left unmolested. Perhaps his keys might be retrievable. Perhaps . . . but already he could make out the flashing blue lights of police cars and, in the distance, following him, the melancholy wail of a speeding ambulance. But by now Gary Hubbard was calm again, in control, thinking logically. True, he felt his spine tingle as the traffic police waved him and the cars preceding him through, telling him gruffly to 'keep moving, keep moving'. Gary nodded at them, and kept moving. All he could think about now was how he was going to get into his flat without his keys – without waking up the neighbours, that is. But he would find some way. He always did. He was a survivor.

Kate Renfrew was in that hazy state, not yet asleep, not fully awake, a time when things that worried her came to mind. And Kate was worried. She was well aware that the twins had their secrets, things they would not allow her or anyone else to share. But recently, ever since she had reluctantly admitted to them who their father was, they had become . . . well, *estranged* was how she thought of it. Not all the time. They would be their normal, happy, cheerful selves, chatting to her, laughing, and then, in the twinkling of an eye, they would shut her out almost, answering her questions curtly, being vague about what they had been doing, frowning as though warning her she was overstepping some mark they had drawn. She had spoken to her sister about it on the phone, but Alice had been her usual useless self, telling Kate not to keep imagining things.

'I'm not imagining anything,' Kate protested. 'I'm sure they're doing –'

'Kate,' Alice interrupted sharply. 'You're *not* sure. You can't be. You only *think* they might . . .'

'I know my sons,' Kate snapped.

'Well, ask them, then. Just ask them what they're up to.'

'Thank you, Alice,' Kate said in that withering tone she reserved for her sister. 'That's most helpful.'

'I can't think of anything else you can do.'

And neither could Kate. So, she left things as they were. Not enquiring. Just happy that her sons appeared not to have changed in their affection for her. Indeed, in those times when she wasn't excluded, the twins were more than attentive. Even Gregory, which was curious since he had always tended to be reserved, cautious with demonstrations of tenderness, while Jimmy was the opposite: effusive, tactile, always the one to land the first kiss, the first to compliment her on a new dress, a change of hairstyle.

And it was with Jimmy's tenderness in mind that Kate finally fell asleep, a smile on her lips. Everything would be all right. Be fine, as the twins always said.

6

'McVinnie wants to see you, boss,' Susan Dill announced the moment Chief Inspector Harvey came into the incident room.

'What about?'

'He didn't say, boss.'

'Is it urgent?'

Susan Dill gave a small shrug of ignorance.

'I'd better call –' Harvey began but stopped as the door opened and Anne Evans came bouncing into the room.

Waylaid, Harvey nodded to her. Then he gave her a thin smile. 'I'm glad someone's feeling good,' he said. He looked about the room. 'Where's Pope? Go find him.'

'Me?' Alan Kelly asked.

'Yes, you.'

DS Kelly stood and made for the door. Before he reached it, however, DI Pope walked in carrying a plastic mug of coffee.

Harvey glared at him and waited pointedly until he and Kelly had taken their seats. 'Right,' he said, glancing at Anne Evans, walking across the room and sitting down himself, leaving her centre stage. But just as she was about to speak Pope said, 'Boss, Doc McVinnie was looking for you.'

'I know,' Harvey snapped.

'Sorry. Just –'

'I know,' Harvey said again. 'Dr Evans?'

Anne Evans stood in front of the information board, facing the team. She looked at each of them in turn and, as she did so, a slow transformation seemed to take place. The bounciness left her. The fuzzy impression she first gave vanished. And when she finally spoke there was a hardness to her voice that was surprising.

'The first thing I have to say is this: what I tell you is merely a guide. It is by no means a description. I have read all the reports and what I tell you is my deduction of the *type* of person you're dealing with.' She paused to let that sink in. 'These deductions are based on what we have learned from other psychological profiles, patterns already set. Certain things, of course, can be learned from the method he uses, but these are physical and not as accurate as the psychological. Understood?'

She waited again, watching as everyone nodded.

'Good. To begin with you are probably looking for a younger rather than an older man. Someone between the ages of twenty-five and thirty-five. He is undoubtedly very strong. Although all the victims have been young, and not particularly muscular, it is surprising what strength people can muster when they are about to be killed. To overpower them and restrain them while he kills them takes a great deal of stength. This does not necessarily mean he is tall. All I'm saying is that he is definitely well built and muscular.'

She paused again, this time to dab the side of her nose with a hankie.

'It is almost certain he is a loner. By that I do *not* mean a recluse. He probably has a job. At a guess I'd say it was a job that requires strength. Labouring. Lifting. Using heavy machinery. His colleagues, if he has any, probably won't find him strange, although I doubt he mixes with them much, either at work or socially. He is unlikely to be married. He probably lives alone or with an ageing parent. More likely alone. What is unusual about him is that he appears not to be driven by any sexual motive. None of his victims has been sexually abused by him. So the question is: why does he kill them? And why does he only choose rent boys? It could quite simply be that he regards rent boys as an obscenity, and has taken it upon himself to rid the world of them. That, however, is unlikely, I think. In my

94

experience, all serial killers who choose a specific category of victim have a far more *personal* reason for their actions. And these personal reasons can be extremely complex and appear quite illogical to us. It could be, for example, that he was at some time a rent boy himself, and hates himself so much for having been one that he is on a sort of saving mission: saving other men from experiencing this self-hate.'

DS Jim Callaghan sniggered.

'I know,' Anne Evans permitted herself a small understanding smile. 'I know it sounds ridiculous but that is the way the minds of these people work. Or it could be that he believes by killing them he is offering them a better, safer alternative to the –' Dr Evans again smiled, this time sadly, '– to the life they are leading. Interestingly, he appears to get no *pleasure* from the killings. If pleasure is involved, almost inevitably there is some mutilation other than the actual cause of death – in this case the cutting of the throat. There is also the fact that he removes all identification. This could mean he wants to spare the victims the humiliation of being identified – identified as prostitutes, that is. So, we know he feels sorry for his victims. However, the longer he goes unapprehended, the less these emotions will count. He will find himself driven, and will become less selective.'

Harvey, like a schoolboy, held up his hand. 'You mean he'll keep on killing?'

'No question of it. He's not a clever man. Not even a very cunning man. I'm sure he believes he is doing good, and it is this which makes him particularly dangerous.'

'What about the weapon he uses – does that tell you anything?' Susan Dill asked.

Anne Evans nodded. 'Yes, it does. He is clearly very deft with it.'

'A butcher?' suggested George Pope.

'Possibly,' Anne Evans said, but clearly she wasn't enthused by the suggestion. 'However, I think you might be looking for someone with military experience. An ex-Para. The technique he uses – the clean severing of the recurrent laryngeal nerve to stop the victim screaming – is part of the Para training, not something you pick up or chance upon out of the blue, not when it's used consistently as in this case. So, to sum up, a youngish, fit, strong man, a loner, possibly with a military background, who appears quite normal to those who know him. Is that any help?'

Harvey gave a low chuckle. 'It's more than we had to begin with.'

'Good.'

'You can't tell us how to catch him, I suppose?' asked Alan Kelly not altogether jocosely.

'That's not *my* job,' Anne Evans answered pleasantly enough.

'Pity.'

'One final thing,' she said. 'When –' her eyes twinkled '– *if* you catch him, he will probably offer very little resistance. And that's not because he *wants* to be caught. Some killers do, but not this one, I think. It's because he doesn't believe he's doing wrong. Anyway, good luck.'

As Anne Evans was outlining her deductions in the incident room, Gregory and Jimmy Renfrew were making a few deductions of their own.

Earlier they had parked the Mini down the road from the Harvey house, and waited patiently for Justin to appear. When he did, setting off on foot up the road towards the Tube, they left the car and followed him, keeping their distance. And now, outside the London School of Economics, they stood a little way off watching as Justin spoke to a pretty girl, talking intently while the girl gazed at him.

'Must be his girlfriend,' Jimmy decided.

'Maybe,' Gregory agreed.

'Got to be. Look how she's looking at him.'

'Hmm,' Gregory said. 'Maybe she *wants* to be his girlfriend.'

'Wish we could hear what they're saying,' Jimmy said.

'What *he's* saying,' Gregory corrected. 'He's doing all the talking.'

'Looks like he's giving out to her.'

Gregory nodded.

Jimmy giggled. 'Maybe she wouldn't give it to him last night.'

Gregory ignored that remark. He was much more interested in what was going on opposite, his eyes narrowing as he watched a willowy guy join Justin, only nodding briefly to the girl, and then put an arm about Justin's shoulder and lead him away. Gregory saw Justin turn his head and say something to the girl: a question obviously, since she nodded, and then moved away from the entrance to the college.

'What now?' Jimmy asked.

'We follow *her*,' Gregory answered firmly and with no hesitation.

'Shouldn't we split up? One of us follow her and the other –?' Jimmy was suggesting, trying to be helpful, and looking crestfallen when his brother shook his head.

'We can always pick up on him again later,' Gregory answered.

'Oh, right.'

'But I do see your point, Jimmy,' Gregory added expansively, nodding sagely. 'We will have to split up from time to time, I'm sure.'

Jimmy brightened and there was an added spring to his step as they followed Miranda Jay away from the college. And he was happy to agree with Gregory when he explained, 'Thing is, Jimmy, we'll learn a lot more about *him*, I think, when we know more about the company he keeps. Like her,' he said, quickening his stride as Miranda hurried to make it across a pedestrian crossing while the traffic was halted by someone else. 'And that other guy who took him away while he was talking. Seemed pretty close, those two, if you ask me.'

'Yeah, they did, didn't they?' Jimmy agreed.

They hurried after Miranda, darting across the road and down into the Underground, catching up with her and standing directly behind her as she purchased her ticket. Earls Court.

Outside Earls Court station Miranda turned left. She walked with her head down, looking disconsolate. When she turned left again into Dower Street, Gregory warned, 'Better hang back a bit.' They waited on the corner, letting Miranda get ahead of them. She crossed the street and walked slowly up the steps of number eighteen. She fumbled in her pocket for the keys to the door. Only when she had gone in and closed the door behind her did the twins trot up the street to the house. Immediately Gregory ran his eye down the long list of occupants lined up beside their individual bells. He pushed one at random. A man's voice, sounding only half awake, answered the intercom. Gregory muttered something incomprehensible. 'What?' the voice demanded. Again Gregory muttered. The buzzer unlocking the door sounded. Gregory grinned. 'Works every time,' he said to his brother, and pushed the door open. 'You wait here,' he ordered, and walked into the house.

DCI Harvey returned to the incident room after walking Anne Evans to her car. He had clearly made up his mind about something. 'Right,' he said even before the door was shut behind him. 'I want all of you out on the streets tonight. I want Scubin, Smollet, Binns and Spanner picked up and brought in. I want them kept apart and I want each of them to try and give us an identikit of any punters who fit in with what Evans just told us.'

'Jesus, guv. You know how many that could be?' Jim Callaghan protested.

'I don't care if it runs into thousands,' Harvey snapped.

'It bloody well could.'

'Maybe not,' Susan Dill put in pensively. The rest of the team looked at her.

'Susan?' Harvey asked.

'Well, boss, when I was talking to Scubin and Spanner in McDonald's they pointed out some of the regulars. They all seemed to be older men. I got the impression younger men don't usually go for rent boys.'

'It'll still be a hell of a lot,' Callaghan said.

Harvey glared at him as if he was about to make some caustic reply but was beaten by the phone. Alan Kelly grabbed it, listened and offered it to Harvey. 'It's Doc McVinnie, guv.'

Harvey took the phone. 'Miles?' he said, and then listened. And as he listened he scowled. 'But you're not sure?' he asked eventually, and listened again. 'Right. Right. Thanks, Miles. I'll be right over.' He held the phone in his hand for several seconds before replacing it in its cradle. 'Shit,' he said quietly, apparently intending only to think it. He looked surprised when George Pope coughed and asked, 'Bad news, boss?'

'I don't know,' Harvey replied. He stared down at the phone. 'I don't know,' he said again, and then swung on his heels and left the room.

'What about this one?' Kate Renfrew asked, holding up a swatch of curtain fabric.

Hector Lord studied it, tapping a pencil against his lips. 'Hmm,' he said, not sounding too enthusiastic. 'I prefer the blue.'

Kate smiled. 'Good. So do I.'

It had been a busy time, but Kate thrived on pressure even though it meant working late into the evening and hence seeing less of the twins than she would like. Typically, she had taken the trouble to sit them down and explain that she had a really important commission, a dream job, she called it. And the twins had been wonderful about it, encouraging her, praising her, telling her it was no more than she deserved. They had also lied.

'Did I tell you the twins have got a job?' Kate now asked Hector Lord.

'*Your* twins? *Working*? Good grief. Miracles never cease.'

'Don't be so catty, Hector.'

'Doing what, am I allowed to know?'

'They're very enterprising.'

'I'm sure.'

'They –' Kate began and then stopped with a chuckle. 'I'm not quite sure.'

'Must be *very* enterprising indeed, then.'

'They did tell me. It's . . . well, it's something to do with delivering things. They use the Mini. Speciality things,' she explained, as much to herself as to Hector. 'You know, out-of-hours deliveries.'

'Not pizzas, by any chance?'

'Don't be silly, Hector. Nothing like that. Flowers, I think. Surprises. Yes. That's it. You know, unexpected birthday presents and the like.'

Hector gave her a baleful look.

'Some company – I think it might be connected with Harrods – caters for the unusual.'

'Oh. That would suit the twins, all right.'

'Well, I think it's very clever of them.'

'Oh, very.'

'And they're working very hard at it. They leave the house even before I do most mornings.'

'Most industrious.'

'*I* think so.'

'You would.'

'And they're not home until all hours.'

'Slavery.'

'I'll slap you,' Kate Renfrew said.

'Yes, please,' Hector replied.

Gary Hubbard spent several hours replacing the lock on his front door. He had been forced to kick it in the night before, wrenching it from the frame. But one kick and the lock had yielded, disturbing no one.

The new lock fitted. He tested it repeatedly, twisting the shiny new key several times in the lock. Satisfied, he went inside his flat and closed the door firmly behind him. He stood with his back leaning against the door and breathed a huge sigh. He felt safe again.

*   *   *

DCI Harvey stared down at the body of Jason Weaver.

'I thought you'd better have a look,' McVinnie said.

Harvey nodded. 'Who's heading the —'

'Donnelly.'

'Ah.'

Miles McVinnie coughed. 'The MO is the same, but . . .' He hesitated. 'Look, perhaps you should talk to Donnelly.'

'I will. Just tell me what —'

'Same MO,' McVinnie interrupted quickly, repeating himself in the process. 'I'd go so far as to say the same weapon was used. But there's a difference: any amount of ID left on the body. And this lad appears to have had a job.'

Harvey looked at him sharply. McVinnie shrugged.

'You're positive about the weapon and the method?' Harvey asked.

McVinnie nodded.

'When was he brought in?'

The doctor checked the notes on a clipboard by the slab. 'Twelve forty-eight last night.'

'Name?'

'Jason Weaver. Age twenty. Home address, flat 6, Merryhill, Camberwell.'

Harvey gave a wry smile. 'But nothing, I suppose, to identify —'

'There's these,' McVinnie interrupted, sounding very pleased with himself as he held up a small plastic bag containing three keys on a plain ring. 'Found beside the body.'

'Could be *his*,' Harvey said pessimistically, indicating Weaver.

'Could be. We won't know until later. And even then . . .' McVinnie shrugged again.

Harvey nodded. 'You'll let me know?'

'If Superintendent Donnelly allows me to,' McVinnie answered with an impish grin.

'Donnelly's an asshole.'

'Nevertheless . . .'

'Nevertheless nothing. You'll let me know, Miles?'

'Unofficially.'

'Any damn way you like.'

'It would make it a lot easier if you cleared it with Donnelly,' McVinnie pointed out. 'He certainly won't take kindly to you stepping on his toes – again.'

'I'll clear it with him.'

'Yes, I bet you will.'

'I will, I will.'

And so it was that Harvey went immediately, if reluctantly, to see Superintendent Peter Donnelly. Not that there was any real antagonism between the two men or, indeed, any justification of Harvey's assessment of the superintendent. Harvey's dislike was based on simple jealousy and a resentment that Donnelly had been selected ahead of him for promotion. And that certainly rankled. The two men had worked together on several occasions and there could be no doubt that Harvey had proved himself the more capable and successful. But Donnelly understood the politics and ingratiated himself with all the right people, kow-towing with magnificent delicacy.

It came as rather a surprise that Peter Donnelly welcomed Robert Harvey into his office with something close to affability. 'Robert. Long time and all that. Sit, sit.'

Harvey sat down, forcing what he hoped was a friendly smile.

'Coffee?'

Harvey declined.

'So, to what do I owe –'

'I need your help, Peter,' Harvey said with consummate humility.

Donnelly glowed. 'Of course. Anything I can do, just ask.'

'I was about to,' Harvey said, irked at Donnelly's habit of interrupting.

Donnelly gave a tight little grin. 'And I'm listening.'

'You know I'm investigating the killings of –'

'Indeed. How's it going?' Donnelly asked but in a way that suggested he knew it wasn't going all that well.

'Slowly.'

'But surely?'

Harvey inclined his head.

'Good. Good.'

'I've been told that the body of a young man was brought in,' Harvey continued, getting some small satisfaction as Donnelly narrowed his eyes suspiciously. 'Last night.'

Donnelly nodded. 'That's right.'

'I wondered if there might be a connection between his death and the ones I'm investigating.'

'What makes you ask that?'

'I'm just wondering. Not asking.'

'Oh.'

'Would you have any objection if I took a look at the body and had a word with the pathologist? Who's doing the autopsy, anyway?'

'McVinnie,' Donnelly said.

'Oh, I know Miles. Would you object if I had a word with him? I mean . . . there's probably no connection, but you never know.'

'No, you never know,' he agreed although he seemed to be talking about something else. 'Fine. Talk to McVinnie.' He beamed. 'Anything to help a colleague.'

'Thank you.'

'Anything else?'

'Well, yes, as a matter of fact,' Harvey said, trying desperately to play at being subservient. 'I was hoping you might be able to tell me a bit about –' He stopped as Donnelly sucked in his breath noisily. 'Don't worry, I'm not going to interfere,' he added quickly.

'What do you want to know?'

'Anything you care to tell me.'

Suddenly, surprisingly, Donnelly laughed, and it was a pleasant laugh, the laugh of a man who felt secure in his position.

'Here's what I'll do, Bob. I'll have a full report sent over to you. How's that?'

Harvey was stunned. 'I'd certainly appreciate it.'

'Consider it done.' Donnelly stood up. 'You'll have it this after-noon.'

Harvey stood up too. 'Thanks.'

'Who knows? I might have to call on you for help one day,' Donnelly said although the small smile on his lips indicated he thought this was unlikely.

'If ever I can —'

'We really should meet more often, don't you think? A drink from time to time?'

Harvey nodded. 'Why not?'

'Why not indeed. Nice seeing you.' Donnelly held out his hand.

'And you,' Harvey agreed, taking the hand and shaking it, wondering what was making Donnelly so affable.

The Superintendent walked Harvey to the door. 'If there *is* a tie-in, we might work on it together, eh?'

'Of course we'll co-operate.'

'Hmm. I meant we might work closely together on it.'

Harvey nodded. 'Yes.'

'Good. Two heads and all that,' Donnelly said with a laugh.

'Yes,' Harvey said again.

'Just let me know what you think when you've read my report, will you, Robert?'

'Of course.'

'Good.'

'There weren't, I suppose, any witnesses?'

Donnelly beamed. 'As a matter of fact, there were.'

'Oh?'

'It will *all* be in the report. Witnesses. Evidence. Everything.'

'Fine.'

'*Full* co-operation.' Donnelly said pointedly.

'Thank you.'

'Which will, I trust, be reciprocal?'

'Of course. Of course.'

To Jimmy it seemed like an eternity before Gregory came out of the house, grinning from ear to ear. 'Round one to us,' he said.

'Tell me.'

'They're all bedsits. Nice enough, but just bedsits.'

That wasn't what Jimmy wanted to hear: he had already guessed that much for himself. 'So?'

'Expensive ones,' Gregory added, teasing.

'Greg, for shit's sake.'

'Her name's Miranda Jay. Age nineteen. She's in number two.'

Jimmy was impressed. 'How'd you find that out?'

'Easy when you know how.'

Jimmy pouted. 'I thought we were in this together.'

'Just joking. Met this guy on the stairs.'

'And he just gave you all the information?'

'Well, yes. He was stoned out of his mind,' Gregory said with a grin.

'Gave him a load of crap about meeting this girl and forgetting which room she was in. Then, when I described her, he said, "Oh, that'll be the lovely Miranda Jay – you Justin?"'

'You think Justin's –'

'Got to be.'

'Poncy name.'

'It is a bit.'

'More than a bit. What now?'

'Oh, I think a cup of coffee, and then we can wander back and pick up the trail of *Justin.*'

Jimmy laughed. 'Jus-tin,' he sang in a mocking tone.

'Or maybe his pal.'

They started to walk back towards the Underground. 'Something about him, the pal,' Gregory said thoughtfully.

'What d'you mean?'

Gregory shook his head. 'Dunno. Just a feeling.'

'You and your feelings.'

'Intuitions, please.'

Superintendent Peter Donnelly kept his word. At one o'clock the report on the death of Jason Weaver was delivered to Robert Harvey. Alone in his office Harvey read it carefully. Then he phoned McVinnie. 'Miles? I've seen Donnelly.'

'Oh. And?'

'And we're co-operating.'

McVinnie gave a low snigger. 'You mean *he's* co-operating.'

'Something like that. Anyway, he's got no objection to my talking to you.'

'I see.'

'And he's sent me over a full report on the incident.'

'I see,' McVinnie said again. 'That *is* being co-operative. I wonder what he wants in return.'

'He wants in on our investigation.'

'Ah. You watch yourself.'

Harvey gave a raw laugh. 'Don't worry about me, Miles. I know how to handle dodgy Donnelly. Now, about those keys. Three, am I right?'

'Yes. Two Yales and one for a Ford of some sort.'

'Any number on it?'

'Just a minute.'

As McVinnie went off to check, Harvey whistled quietly to himself, Donnelly's words 'full co-operation' rattling in his brain. He knew what that meant: he would do all the work and Donnelly would make damn sure he took the credit. Well, he wasn't going to get away with it this time. Harvey scribbled down the number on the Ford key as McVinnie gave it to him. 'Thanks, Miles. Nothing else?'

'Not for the moment. If there is —'

'You'll let *me* know?'

'Of course.'

'Cheers.'

Harvey put the phone back in its cradle and sat thinking for a moment. Then, in one economical gesture, he stood up, gathered up the report on Jason Weaver and strode out of his office.

And minutes later it was with the same determined stride that he entered the incident room. 'Okay, listen up,' he said, glancing about to make sure all the team were present. 'We *might* have another one.'

'Oh, Jesus,' George Pope swore.

'It's just a might. But let's hope we do because this time we have something to go on.' He opened the folder. 'Young man found murdered in the underpass by the National Theatre. Jason Weaver.' He paused before announcing, 'Donnelly's heading that investigation.' Although his face remained impassive, he smiled inwardly at the reaction: at least he knew he had the full loyalty of his team. 'I've had a word with him and we're going to co-operate on this one – if it turns out that Weaver *is* another one.'

'What makes –' Susan Dill started to ask.

'Miles McVinnie says the MO is the same. Says he's pretty certain the same weapon was used – and used by the same killer.' He looked up to see if there were any more questions. 'Now,' he turned back to the report, 'the body of Weaver was brought in in the early hours of last night. The alarm was raised by a couple of tarts, Emma Simpson and Katherine Beldon. They share a flat. They've been interviewed and have given a vague description of a man they saw with the body. But I want you, Susan, and you, Alan, to talk to them again. See if you can't get something more substantial.' He waited until Dill and Kelly had nodded their agreement. 'The victim lived at home with his parents. He was working as a builder. Not a rent boy as far as we can tell. George, I want you to go over to the parents. Find out everything you can about the lad. Whoever interviewed them for this –' he tapped the report '– did a crap job. I'm certain there's more we can learn. Jim, we have the building site he was working on. I want you to come with me and talk to his workmates. Nobody's bothered to talk to them yet.'

'Right, guv.'

'Finally, there were three keys on a ring found near the body. They *might* be Weaver's. On the other hand . . . George, before you go to see the parents, drop in on McVinnie and get those keys. One I'm told fits a Ford . . . Shit, I have the number but I've left it upstairs. Get the number and find out what make of Ford it belongs to. Then contact all Ford dealers and tell them to let us know immediately if anyone comes in looking for a replacement. It's a long shot, but you never know.'

'Right, guv.'

'Well, let's get a move on.'

The team stood up.

'Oh, one other thing,' Harvey said. 'Any information we pick up stays in this room, understood?'

The officers smiled.

'As far as anyone outside this team is concerned we aren't making much progress.'

They all nodded.

Harvey shrugged. 'Anyway, McVinnie could be wrong. Weaver might have no connection whatsoever with the others.'

'You think he does though, don't you, boss?' Susan Dill asked.

'I hope he does,' Harvey answered. He sighed. Then coughed. 'We'll meet back here at –' He looked at his watch. 'At four.' He gave a little smile. 'That'll give us time to go through what we've uncovered and have a cup of tea before you all go out for a night in Piccadilly.'

'Gee, thanks, guv,' Alan Kelly said.

'Welcome.'

The twins were in the sitting-room when Kate got home. They had her drink ready. They had the casserole that she had prepared the night before in the oven. They were very relaxed and attentive.

'Good day, Mum?' Jimmy asked.

'Exhausting but, yes, very good. And you?'

'Busy.'

'And what did you have to deliver today?'

'The usual. Flowers, mostly.'

'And that hamper,' Gregory put in, before giving Jimmy a knowing look, and adding, 'not finished yet, either. Got two more deliveries to make later.'

'Oh, dear,' Kate said. 'I was so looking forward to an evening together.'

'Got to earn the shekels, Mum,' Jimmy said.

'*Earn the shekels*,' Gregory mimicked when Kate had gone upstairs for her shower. 'Where did you get that from?'

'The inner recesses of my brain,' Jimmy answered, beaming.

Gregory looked as if he was about to smile also, but changed his mind. 'You sure you're clear about tonight?'

'Course I am.'

'You won't mess up?'

'No.'

And then, perhaps feeling he was being condescending to his brother, Gregory added, 'We did really well today, didn't we?'

'Sure did.'

And they had done well. After leaving Miranda Jay's flat and having a coffee, they had returned to the LSE and waited for David Parsons to come out. At lunchtime he did, and the twins were delighted to see that Justin was also waiting for him.

'Very chummy,' Jimmy observed.

Gregory nodded.

'If they split, who do we follow?' Jimmy wanted to know.

'The friend,' Gregory told him without hesitation.

'Right.'

Justin and David parted at the Underground, but not immediately. They stood outside the tube talking for quite a while, and it seemed Parsons was advising Justin about something, stabbing his finger at his friend's chest from time to time and looking serious. Then, as they finally parted, he tapped Justin on the cheek.

'Sweet,' Jimmy observed.

Justin watched David go down the stairs, and then set off up the road on foot. Instantly, the twins raced after Parsons, pushing through the turnstile after him. Once on the train they were careful to make themselves as inconspicuous as possible, staying at the far end of the carriage, just occasionally glancing in David's direction. When he got out at Green Park, they followed. Clearly he had a specific destination in mind. He didn't hang about or saunter, but headed down past the Ritz and turned right. A few hundred yards down that street he went into a bar.

'Do we go in?' Jimmy asked.

Gregory thought for a moment. 'You do,' he said finally. 'I'll wait out here.'

'Oh.'

'What's the matter?'

'Nothing.'

'You don't have to do anything. Just have a drink. Keep out of his way. Watch him until he comes out.'

Jimmy nodded. 'Okay.'

'Off you go then,' Gregory said.

Alone, Gregory started to pace up and down the pavement, playing a sort of slow-motion hopscotch on the paving slabs, avoiding the joins. It was an odd place and time to admit, if only to himself, that since the discovery that the man who had fathered him had wanted both himself and his brother aborted, Gregory had been possessed of the idea that the only thing that mattered was some terrible revenge, a revenge that would certainly involve killing. And now, turning and making his way back towards the entrance to the bar, he remembered reading somewhere, in a novel probably, that murder could be a most pleasurable pastime. And that was exactly how Gregory was beginning to feel about it. He was a few yards from the bar when Jimmy came hurtling out, grinning from ear to ear. 'You bastard!' he told Gregory. 'You knew, didn't you?'

'Knew what?' said his brother, wide-eyed.

'It's a queer bar,' Jimmy announced. 'Fucking fairyland in there.'

'You serious?'

'Too damn right I am.'

'I honestly didn't know,' Gregory said, almost to himself.

'Well, it is. And our friend is as camp as washing-up liquid. And a regular. Knew the barman well. Knew a few of the other queens too.'

'I see,' Gregory said.

'Took a shine to me, the poof,' Jimmy announced, not sounding too displeased.

'He *what*?' Gregory asked, jerking his head up.

'Took a fancy to *moi*.'

'How do you mean?'

'Kept looking at me. Fluttering his stupid eyelashes. Kind of smiling.'

'Did he say anything?'

'Didn't give him the chance. Let's get out of here.'

They started to walk back towards the tube station, Gregory with his head down pensively, Jimmy skipping along.

'You think he'd recognise you again, Jimmy?' Gregory asked suddenly, stopping and facing his brother.

Jimmy shrugged. 'Dunno. Maybe. Had a good look at me, anyway.'

They walked a little further. 'You're sure he fancied you? You're not just saying that?'

'I told you. He fancied me.'

The next question Gregory asked had a curious tone to it, light-hearted and jocose, but with an underlying intensity to it. 'You think you could pick him up?'

Jimmy stopped dead in his tracks. 'Piss off, Greg,' he snorted.

'No, I mean ... I don't mean you'd *do* anything, for Christ's sake. But could you pick him up? Get him to go somewhere with you?'

Jimmy cocked his head. 'Probably. Yeah. Sure I could. Why? What are you up to now, Greg?'

Gregory grinned. 'Just thinking.'

And later, when they had eaten the casserole and kissed Kate goodbye, promising they wouldn't be too late yet at the same time advising her not to wait up for them, and were sitting in the Mini outside the Harvey house, Jimmy asked, 'What *are* you plotting, Greg?'

'Just let me get it all worked out first, eh?'

'All *what* worked out?'

'Everything . . . Here he comes,' he added, nodding towards the house as Justin came out of the front door and hurried towards his father's car.

Harvey was in the incident room well before four o'clock. His visit to the building site where Jason Weaver worked had been a failure. Only the security guard was on duty. The weather, he said, was too wet for building. And, no, he hadn't a clue about the names of the men working there. Have to see the site boss for that. And, shit, no, he didn't know who the site boss was. Have to ask *them* about that, he said, nodding towards a billboard that gave the name of the building firm in charge of construction: Ballard and Hobson.

Harvey had better luck at Ballard and Hobson, but not much better. Certainly they could give him the name and address of the site manager, but as to the labourers, no chance: casual workers most of them. What were all the questions for, anyway?

Harvey sent Jim Callaghan to check on the site manager, and returned to the station to wait for the rest of the team.

Callaghan was, in fact, the first back. He looked none too happy.

'Well?' Harvey demanded.

Callaghan struggled out of his coat, and hung it on the peg behind the door. He took a notebook from his inside pocket and started to leaf through the pages.

'Just tell me, Jim,' Harvey said wearily.

'Huh? Oh, right, guv. Saw the site manager. Stuart Hale. Got a list of everyone working on the site for the past six months. Weaver's one of them.' He tore a page from his notebook and passed it to Harvey.

'That the lot?' Harvey asked, running his eye down the eleven names.

'So he says.'

Harvey looked up.

'No. I believe him. He wasn't trying to –'

'No addresses?'

Callaghan shook his head. 'But there's supposed to be a break in the weather tonight. He's hoping they can get back to work tomorrow.'

Harvey nodded.

'I warned him to say nothing to anyone until we had a chance to get over to the site and question them.'

Harvey nodded again. 'Good.'

'And I didn't say *why* we –'

'Good,' Harvey interrupted. Then he noticed Callaghan hovering. 'What is it?'

'Guv, could I slip home for an hour?'

Harvey looked annoyed.

'It's just . . . well, Beth's –'

'Oh, yes. Sorry. I forgot. When is it –'

'Four weeks.'

'Yes. Yes, of course. Go on home.'

'I'll be back at –'

'Seven will be time enough.'

'I'll be back at seven.'

As Callghan got back into his coat and opened the door, Susan Dill and Alan Kelly came in. Harvey looked across at them expectantly. 'Anything?'

'A lot more than is in that report, boss,' Dill said.

'Tell me.'

'One thing that's not in the report is that the man the girls saw by the body had a knife in his hand and menaced them with it. Actually moved towards them.'

'So they saw him? Clearly?'

Dill winced. 'They saw him all right. But not that clearly. They can't seem to give us a *clear* description of him.'

'They're downstairs now, guv,' Kelly said. 'Putting together an identikit. Trying to, anyway.'

'All they can remember is – it fits what Dr Evans told us – smallish and stocky. About thirty. Close-cropped dark brown or black hair,' Dill told him. 'Emma Simpson's our best bet. Been on the game longer and tough as they come, but pretty shaken just the same. Still, she seems to remember more.'

'And it was definitely a knife?'

'Oh, yes. They're both positive about that.'

'And when he ran off, did they see –'

Dill was already shaking her head. 'All they can tell us is that he ran through the underpass. Where he went after that, they've no idea.'

'And his clothes?'

'There's no light down there, guv,' Kelly said. 'In the underpass. Best they could say was dark trousers, maybe jeans, and a zip-up jacket.'

Harvey reached out and took Donnelly's report from the desk. He flicked through the pages. 'It says here that the man seemed to be holding Weaver when –'

'That's not what they're saying now, boss,' Dill said.

'What *are* they saying now?' Harvey asked irritably.

'They both say they didn't even notice the body until after he had . . . what they say is they saw *something* on the ground but didn't know it was a body until after the man had run off. When they came into the underpass and walked towards the scene the man was already moving towards them.'

'With a knife still in his hand?'

'That's what they both say.'

Harvey shook his head. 'That doesn't sound like our man. That and the keys. He's been so careful.'

'Up till now,' Dill said.

'Maybe he panicked?' Kelly suggested.

Harvey shook his head again. 'He's not the sort to panic. And Weaver wasn't his usual kind of victim.' He continued to shake his head. 'There's something –' he began, but stopped and looked towards the door.

George Pope came in, saying, 'Sorry I'm late, boss,' and there was something about his apology that made Harvey infer he was apologising for more than his tardiness.

'Nothing, I suppose?' Harvey asked.

''Fraid not. The parents are shattered. He was one of five children. Just an ordinary working lad. Nothing unusual. Except –'

Harvey looked up hopefully.

'Except they can't understand what he was doing up the West End. Spent all his time in and around Camberwell. He never said anything to them about going up West that evening.'

'Would he have?'

'They think so. They're a very close family. The only explanation they can offer is that Weaver recently broke up with his girl – he might have gone up West just to avoid her.'

Harvey grunted. 'Friends?'

Pope shook his head. 'No close ones. Just boozing pals. All local. Apparently none of them knew he was going up West either.'

'What about his workmates? Ever go out with them?'

'Now and then. Usually Friday nights they went for a drink after work. Just a couple of pints, then home.'

Harvey gave an enormous, despondent sigh. He glanced at the report again. 'You get the impression he was a heavy drinker?'

Pope shook his head. 'No. He drank but . . .'

'It says here he was well pissed.'

115

'Maybe drowning his sorrows,' Dill suggested. 'Losing his girl.'

'Maybe,' Harvey agreed. 'Maybe,' he repeated as if to find some comfort in his mild agreement. He tossed the report back on to the desk. 'Anyway, perhaps we'll get something from the workmates tomorrow.'

'Or the girlfriend,' Pope suggested. He looked at his notes. 'Lisa Doherty. Seeing her tomorrow,' he told Harvey, and then, noticing the tetchy look that swam over his boss's face, he added quickly, 'She's away today. Gone to see her gran in Northallerton. That's –'

'I know where it is,' Harvey said grumpily. He sighed again and got up. 'Well, you'd better all take a break before you hit Piccadilly,' he said. 'It could be a long night.'

Jimmy tried to suppress a yawn, but failed. 'Don't tell me you're tired,' Gregory mocked.

'Nah, just yawning.'

'Good. It could be a long night.'

Book Two

7

To say that Justin Harvey was tense would be putting it mildly. Sitting opposite Miranda in the café, his untouched cappuccino in front of him, small nerves in his temple twitching, he kept glancing at his watch and fingering the winder as though to speed up time. 'And that's your final word?' he asked.

Miranda nodded. 'Yes,' she answered quietly.

'Not much more to say then, is there?'

'No.'

But maybe there was a little more to say. 'Look, Miranda . . . I mean . . . Okay, I believe you. It's mine, but I can't . . .'

Miranda interrupted him with a doleful gaze. 'You don't have to do anything, Justin,' she said emotionlessly.

'You mean –' Justin started hopefully.

'I mean I just want you to go away and leave me alone.'

'I –'

'Just go away, Justin. Out of my sight.'

'Oh, sure, and let you –'

'Get out of my life, Justin,' Miranda said, her voice rising threateningly.

Justin looked about him nervously in case anyone had heard. He uncrossed his legs and made as if to rise. Then he leant forward. 'I'm not going to let you ruin *my* life, Miranda,' he said in a low whisper.

She raised her hand as if to strike him, but Justin caught her wrist. Only when she lowered her head and started to sob did he release it. Then he stood up and stared down at her. After a moment he put both hands on the table and bent down again, putting his mouth close to her ear. 'Just get rid of it,' he said, and then stalked from the café, staring straight ahead, not noticing the two teenagers sitting quietly in the corner, their eyes following him intently. As the door hissed to a close behind him, their gaze shifted to Miranda, sitting alone, her head still bowed.

'Now,' Gregory said, making the word a command.

'Right,' Jimmy answered, clearly aware of what his brother intended.

'Just be cool,' Gregory warned. 'Don't spook her.'

'I won't.'

'Just remember what we rehearsed.'

'I will.'

'Good luck.'

Jimmy Renfrew got up and walked over slowly but positively, stopping by the chair Justin had vacated. 'He's a bastard,' he said and, as Miranda looked up at him in surprise, he added, 'All right if I sit down?' He didn't wait for an answer, settling himself into the chair and leaning his elbows on the table. 'Been watching,' he said.

'Oh,' Miranda said, looking embarrassed.

'Hey,' Jimmy told her, 'no need to be upset . . . I mean, not about . . . you know. Pity you didn't swipe him one,' he concluded with a grin.

Miranda Jay gave a tiny smile. 'You know Justin?'

'Oh, I know him. *Not* one of my favourite people, I have to say. Yours neither by the look of it.'

'We —'

'It's okay. You don't have to tell me,' Jimmy reassured her in a kind voice. He pointed to her coffee. 'That's cold. Let me get you another.'

'Oh, no. No. No thanks. I just want to —'

'Go home?' Jimmy asked.

Miranda nodded.

'You live near here?'

Miranda nodded again.

'Well, in that case I'll walk you home. My name's Jimmy, by the way.'

'I'm Miranda,' she told him, studying his face for the first time.

'Nice name. I like it.'

'You don't have to walk —'

'I know I don't *have* to. I'd like to. Just to make sure you get home safely.'

Suddenly Miranda relaxed. 'You're sweet,' she said, with a smile.

'That's better.' Then Jimmy frowned. 'Bet that clown never even paid for your coffee.'

'No, he didn't.'

'Typical.'

'You know Justin well?'

'As well as I want to,' Jimmy told her, standing and holding the back of her chair as she rose.

He paid for the coffee and held the door open for Miranda. Just before he followed her out he gave Gregory a wink. His brother nodded without smiling. He waited a minute and then got up to follow.

Gary Hubbard had been busy. The killing of Jason Weaver had had a curious effect on him. It was as though for the first time he recognised the seriousness of what he had done; or rather, he realised that he was in danger of being caught, which was not quite the same thing. His carelessness in losing his keys had been a blow, but he had not panicked. He had thought about it carefully. The keys were the only evidence that linked him to Jason. The police undoubtedly had them. It was up to him to make sure they were not traced back to him. And suddenly Gary realised he was enjoying himself. It was the first time he had truly to pit his wits against the police; the first time he was in real danger of being identified. Yet, oddly, this also pleased him. In a sense it gave him status.

After he had changed the lock on his front door, choosing a Chubb to replace the old Yale lock, he walked down to the street and slipped the spare Yale key down the grating of the drain. Then he turned his attention to the van. He removed all his belongings from the back, storing them in the hallway of his flat. Then he checked the glove compartment, taking everything out of that too. When he was satisfied there was nothing left in the van except an old newspaper on the passenger seat, a copy of *The Sun*, he brushed it out thoroughly. Then he put a screwdriver in his pocket and drove to Dagenham. He headed to the scrapyard, setting his mileage gauge to zero as he passed the main entrance. He drove a further half-mile, stopped and turned the van, pulling to the side of the road and parking. He got out, waited for an articulated lorry to pass, and opened the bonnet. Then he removed the oil filter, and tossed it over a low hedge surrounding a piece of wasteland that hoardings promised would be transformed into a supermarket later that year. He wiped his hands on a few pages from *The Sun*, and chucked them over the hedge too. Then he drove back towards the scrapyard.

He had just turned into the gates when the engine seized, making him smile contentedly. He jumped out and removed the front and back number plates, wrapping them in what was left of the newspaper. Then, on foot, he made his way to the Portakabin that served as an office.

In the incident room Kelly and Callaghan had shoved two desks together. Spread along the length of them were the identikit pictures the four rent boys had helped to compile. George Pope and Susan Dill stood just behind Kelly and Callaghan, none of them looking particularly pleased.

'What d'you think?' Pope asked.

Nobody answered.

'The boss is going to love this,' Pope said.

Again, nobody answered.

Finally, 'It's not our fault if the little shits can't agree—' Callaghan began.

'It's not their fault either,' Susan Dill snapped, coming instantly to the defence. 'Everyone sees people differently.'

'Not *that* differently,' Callaghan insisted, pointing to the likenesses strewn across the desks. 'There's no two of them that look any way alike.'

'Yes there is,' Dill said. 'If you bother to take a close look, that is.' She pushed her way to the desks and started sorting out several identikits into a small pile. Then she swept the others aside and lined up her selections in a row. She pointed to them one by one. 'That's Scubin's. That's Smollet's. That's Binns'. And that one's Spanner's. Granted, the shape of the face is different, but take a good look at the features. Look at the eyes. All of them are close set, very close to the nose. And look at the nose: it's almost identical, stubby and turned up.' She glanced at the rest of the team, and by their silence concluded she was getting somewhere. 'Then there's the mouth. You could almost lay one on top of the other and they'd come out the same.'

'She's right, you know,' Alan Kelly conceded.

George Pope took to nodding. 'Could be,' he allowed.

'You're never going to get two descriptions *exactly* the same,' Dill insisted. 'I think the boys did a really good job.'

'Jim?' Pope asked Callaghan.

'Maybe.'

Susan Dill gave him a smile.

'Yeah, I can see what Susan means,' Callaghan now said.

'Let's hope the boss can too,' Pope added.

'It's all we've got,' Kelly put in.

'Tell me about it,' Pope answered.

'Right,' Gregory said. 'Tell me about it.'

In their bedroom, Gregory sat at the desk, turned towards Jimmy who lay sprawled on the bed, looking very pleased with himself. He held out one hand, palm upwards. 'See that? That's where I've got her eating from.'

Gregory wasn't impressed. 'Just tell me what happened,' he demanded. 'You took long enough about it.' He had got home several hours before Jimmy returned, and had had time to think the worst.

'You told me not to spook her.'

'Just tell me, Jimmy.'

Jimmy sat up. 'Well, I walked her home.'

'I know that. What did you find out?'

'I'm coming to that,' Jimmy said, clearly enjoying his moment of control. 'She comes from Oxford. Just outside. Islip, actually. Old man's got a bob or two, it seems. She's an only child, poor little love.'

'Jimmy . . .' Gregory said, making the word a warning.

'Been going out with Justin for just over a year. Met him at a pub near college. He doesn't go to the LSE, by the way. Doing some arty-farty computer graphics course down the road. Talking about going to Australia, he is. Anyway, the bloke we've seen with Justin is called David Parsons. She can't stand him. She *thinks* he's got the hots for Justin but Justin's not playing.' Jimmy paused and cocked his head.

'Go on,' Gregory urged.

'Oh, you want the good news?'

'Just tell me everything.'

'She's up the spout.'

'She's —'

'Up the spout. Pregnant. With child, as they say. Justin's child.'

'Holy shit!'

'That's another way of putting it.'

'She's sure it's Justin's?'

'Dead sure. One of your faithful types. Only had it off with him. A virgin when they met. Anyway, that's what they've been rowing about.' Jimmy paused again, and then, emphasising his words with

care, he went on solemnly, 'Justin wants her to have an abortion.'
He watched his brother's reaction intently.

Gregory froze, his eyes wide, his hands clasped so tightly his
knuckles turned slowly white.

'Just like his daddy,' Jimmy added quietly.

Gregory nodded.

'But Miranda's all for keeping it. Not into abortion. Catholic. Shit
scared baby Jesus will seek revenge if she –'

'But she's still seeing Justin,' Gregory interrupted, speaking as if
to himself.

'Not any more.'

'No?'

'Dumped him tonight. In the café. Told him where to go.'

'Ah, so that's what –'

'She *says* he threatened her.'

Gregory was instantly alert again. 'What did she say exactly?'

'Told her he wasn't going to let *her* ruin *his* life.'

'That it?'

'That's all she said,' Jimmy confirmed. Then he gave a slow,
menacing grin. 'Just like his daddy didn't want *us* to ruin *his*
career.'

Gregory's head bobbed up and down: he was nodding but it looked
like an automatic gesture. 'You think she might cause him bother? I
mean . . .'

Jimmy shook his head. 'Not that sort.'

'Won't go screaming to Justin's parents?'

'No.'

'You seeing her again?'

'You want me to?' Jimmy asked with a cunning smile.

Gregory returned the smile. 'It might be useful.'

'Well, as it happens . . .'

Gregory raised his eyebrows.

'I've left it open. Said I might give her a call and take her out
Saturday.'

Suddenly Gregory interlaced his fingers and stretched his arms out in front of him. 'You've done well, Jimmy. Really well.'

'Told you I would.'

Gregory thought for a moment. 'I think we'll have to make Saturday night a bit special for Miranda. Make it a night she'll never forget.'

'I was going to do that, anyway,' Jimmy said, preening himself and grabbing his crotch.

Gregory shook his head. 'Not that way, sunshine. I mean *really* special.'

Jimmy gave him a funny, sideways look. 'Oh?'

'Really special,' Gregory confirmed.

'Like?'

Gregory started to clean his spectacles. 'Got to think that one out carefully first,' he said, and appeared to start doing so immediately. 'We need to get her to go to Justin's home. Need her to . . .' His voice trailed off. 'Can you see her again *before* Saturday?'

Jimmy shrugged. 'Don't see why not.'

'Just once.'

'No problémo. She thinks I'm an angel. Ever so sweet I am. Just the shoulder she needs to cry on. So she tells me.'

Gregory gave a cynical guffaw. 'Out of the frying pan . . .'

'You just don't appreciate what a lovely brother you have, that's you're trouble,' Jimmy answered. Gregory cackled. 'Lovely. Oh, yeah.' Then he went serious again. 'We need to get Saturday properly set up.'

'Fine.'

'We'll work out the details. Then you see her – Thursday? – and make sure you talk her into doing exactly what you want.'

'Without her knowing it, of course.'

'Exactly. Without her having a clue.'

Gary Hubbard had felt quite sad at seeing his van crushed. It had all gone smoothly enough. True, the foreman had given him a curious look when Gary had asked for the van to be crushed immediately. But after a nod and a wink, and an assurance that the van was free, he had agreed, issuing orders in the manner of a man who had been through all this sort of skulduggery before. Indeed, his line of patter appeared well rehearsed. 'Be needing a replacement, will you?'

'Could do,' Gary told him.

'Maybe I can help you there.'

Gary eyed him.

'Same thing? Van? Escort?'

'Yes, I –'

'Brother-in-law's got a place up the road. I'll give him a ring and see what he's got.'

'No. I –'

'Can't do any harm.' And then, 'Would you credit it? Got just what you want. White like your old one and all.'

'How much?'

'Have to work that out with him. Why don't you nip over there now and have a chat?'

And that was what Gary did. And now on the road outside his flat, his new, second-hand van was parked, almost identical to the old one although a year younger, taxed and with an MOT for another six months and no one any the wiser.

'You're very restless, Justin,' Helen Harvey observed, as Justin fidgeted.

'I'm bored.'

Helen sighed. 'I really don't understand you young people,' she said. 'You get bored so easily. When I was your age –'

'Ma . . .' Justin interrupted her with a sigh.

'Leave him,' Robert Harvey told his wife quietly.

'I only –' Helen started to protest, eyeing her husband.

And later, when Helen had gone upstairs, Robert asked, 'Seen Miranda?'

'Yes,' Justin told him.

'And?'

'And nothing. She won't . . . she wants to keep the baby.'

'I see. Well, there's not much you can do about that.'

'And she . . .'

'What?'

'Doesn't want to see me again.'

'Ah. I see.'

'Which doesn't mean she's not going to come after me when the kid arrives.'

'You think she will?'

Justin shrugged. 'Probably.'

Robert Harvey stared at his son for a while. Then he sighed. 'Well, we'll cross that bridge when we come to it.'

'Dad –'

'I –'

'No. Listen, Dad. You couldn't . . . I mean, if you went to her –'

'Forget it, Justin. That would be the worst possible thing to do. Believe me. I know. Any pressure from me . . . Look, I'm on your side. Just let's wait and see what happens. And remember what I said – for God's sake don't let your mother know.' He stood up, looking down at his son. 'I suppose you've tried everything to make her change her mind – Miranda, I mean?'

Justin gave a harsh snort. 'Just about everything.'

'And she won't budge?'

Justin shook his head.

'Well, we'll just have to wait and see.'

Justin nodded miserably.

'Things have a way of working themselves out.'

'Oh, sure.'

'Believe me, they do.'

And Chief Inspector Harvey certainly hoped things had a way of working themselves out, and it wasn't his son's predicament he was concerned about. It was the following morning and he had just driven to the building site where Jason Weaver had worked. DI Pope had arrived before him, and Harvey parked behind Pope's car. 'Morning. George.'

'Boss,' Pope nodded.

'I take it they *are* working?'

'They're here. Working is another matter.'

Harvey looked at him sharply. 'No joy last night, then?' he asked.

Pope gave a wry smile. 'What makes you ask that?'

'I know you, George.'

'I suppose you do. Well, Susan thinks there's one possibility. Reckon it's a bit vague myself. But . . .'

'Susan's sound,' Harvey said.

'I'm not denying that for a minute. But . . .' Pope let his voice trail off again.

'Right,' Harvey said, and straightened his shoulders. 'Better see what we can get out of this lot, then.'

'If anything.'

'Goodness!' Kate Renfrew said with exaggerated surprise. 'Don't tell me you've both got the sack?'

'No, Mum,' Gregory answered.

'It makes such a change to find you both here in the morning. I just wondered,' Kate said lightly. 'More coffee anyone?' she asked as she poured herself a cup.

'We decided to take the day off,' Jimmy told her.

'I see.'

'Well, not exactly *off*,' Gregory corrected.

Kate Renfrew raised her eyebrows slightly and came to join the twins at the kitchen table. There was no need to ask for an explanation: she knew Gregory would tell her what he meant if he felt like doing so. If he didn't feel like it, well . . .

'We thought we'd spend the day expanding our vistas,' Gregory told her.

'Expanding your vistas, eh? That sounds very grand.'

'There's money to be made out there,' Gregory went on.

'Yes, I'm aware of that.'

'We thought we'd explore other possibilities.'

'I see. Well, I'm sure that's very enterprising of you both. As long as it's legal,' Kate added with a smile. 'I wouldn't want you to end up like –'

'The Krays?' Jimmy suggested mischievously.

'Anyway, the Mini's giving trouble,' Gregory announced, hoping Kate hadn't noticed the surprise on Jimmy's face.

'Oh?'

'Nothing serious.'

'Oh, good.'

'Have to get it seen to, though.'

'Of course,' Kate agreed.

'I suppose . . . Mum, you'd let us use your car if need be?' Gregory asked.

'Well, yes, I suppose so. As long as I don't need it myself.'

Gregory gave her a big smile. 'Ta.'

'But get that Mini seen to. Today,' Kate warned.

'Yep. It's on the agenda.'

'And maybe we could meet and have lunch together?' Kate suggested.

'Hey, that would be great,' Jimmy enthused.

'That's what you do then,' Kate instructed. 'Go round this morning and get your car seen to and then come over to the studio and pick me up.'

'Sure you're not too busy?' Gregory asked.

'I'm never too busy where you two are concerned.'

Gregory smiled. 'Fine. See you for lunch. One-ish?'

'Perfect.'

'What's all this crap about the Mini giving trouble?' Jimmy wanted to know as soon as Kate had kissed them both goodbye and set off for work.

'Just preparing. Forward planning,' Gregory said mysteriously.

'Planning what?'

'Planning for Saturday.'

Jimmy looked puzzled.

'Saturday,' Gregory repeated. 'You and Miranda.'

'Oh,' Jimmy said, but still looked bewildered.

'I think we'll just have to give her a little shove in the right direction.'

Jimmy shook his head. 'You've lost me.'

Gregory stood up and ran his mug under the hot tap. 'All will be revealed,' he promised, turning his mug upside down on the draining board.

'You still want me to see her before Saturday?' Jimmy asked.

Gregory nodded. 'Oh, yes. Most definitely.'

'I'll organise that today then.'

'Good. Jimmy – she's got to really trust you. I mean, *really* trust you.'

'Hey, come on,' Jimmy said, throwing his arms wide and blinking his eyes rapidly. 'Who wouldn't trust me?'

Gregory gave a low laugh. 'Me.'

'Ah, but you don't trust anyone.'

Gary Hubbard watched the two officers chatting by their cars. He knew they were police. How he knew he couldn't tell. Perhaps, he decided, it was simply because he had been expecting them. For a moment he was not scared exactly, but anxious. And then he felt a curious exhilaration sweep over him. True, it approximated the relish he sensed when killing, but there was a new and enticing element to it. It was as though, at long last, he was about to come face to face with a formidable foe, someone who wouldn't be seduced by charm; who wouldn't, as it were, crumple in his arms. Gary smiled to himself. This, he recognised, would be a mental battle, a war of wits, and he felt cool and calm, detached almost, as he stood up and gazed unblinkingly into DCI Robert Harvey's eyes, nodding as

Harvey introduced himself, nodding again as the Chief Inspector consulted a slip of paper in his hand and asked, 'Gary Hubbard?'

And then an extraordinary thing happened. As the two men looked at each other Gary became convinced that the detective *knew* he had killed Jason Weaver. It was an impossibility, of course, but the feeling persisted. Yet, far from being frightened by this, Gary found it difficult to suppress his desire to laugh. But he did manage to suppress it, up to a point anyway, although some amusement must have shown in his eyes since the detective cocked his head and gave him a brief, baffled look. 'You've heard about Jason Weaver?' he asked, still looking mildly puzzled.

'Being killed? Someone mentioned it,' Gary heard himself say.

'You knew him, of course?'

Gary shrugged. 'He worked here.'

'So you knew him.'

'Yes.'

'Friendly with him?'

'Not particularly.'

'Go drinking with him?'

'No.'

'No?'

'No.'

'I see.' Chief Inspector Harvey looked away. 'Any idea who would want to kill the lad?'

'No. None.'

'Got on all right with . . .' Harvey waved his hand vaguely over the building site.

'Sure. I think so. Never heard of anyone not liking him.'

'You liked him?'

'Didn't know him well enough to like him or not,' Gary said, and was pleased with his answer.

'Don't know much about him, do you?'

Gary shook his head again. 'No.'

'Liked his drink, did he?'

'He drank. We all like a drink, don't we?'

Harvey smiled. 'Yes, we do, don't we? You wouldn't know *where* he drank, I suppose?'

'No idea.'

'Did he go up West often?'

Gary gave a blank stare. 'I wouldn't know,' he answered, covering his answer with a tight laugh.

'When was the last time you saw Jason?'

Gary screwed up his face. 'Dunno. Christmas, I guess. Just after. Before the frost started.'

Harvey nodded. And then, as though the thought had just occurred to him, he asked, 'You married, Mr Hubbard?'

'No.'

'Girlfriend?'

'No.'

'Live alone?'

'Yes. Why?'

Harvey gave a winning smile. 'No reason. Well, thanks for your help.' He looked down at the slip of paper. 'If we need to talk to you again you're at this address?' he asked, reading it out.

'Yes.'

'Right. Thanks again.'

Gary nodded.

Chief Inspector Harvey made as if to leave. He walked away a few paces and then stopped and turned. 'You don't seem too put out.'

Gary grimaced. 'Hardly knew him.'

'Yes. Yes, of course. So you said. Still . . . no matter.'

Gary watched Harvey walk away, keeping his eyes fixed on him even as he crouched and pretended to sort out a pile of bricks.

It was probably coincidence, but as DCI Harvey reached Gary's newly purchased van he stopped in his tracks, stared at it and then swung round, gazing back up the low scaffolding to where Gary crouched. Then he looked back at the van again, shook his head and walked over to the site office.

*   *   *

'I'm taking the twins to lunch,' Kate Renfrew announced.

'I'll put out the flags, shall I?' Hector Lord replied.

'You coming?'

'I think not.'

'Oh? I'm sure they'd love to see you.'

'We'll see.'

'What's the matter with you this morning, Hector?'

'With me? Not a thing. I don't like to intrude. That's all.'

'You wouldn't be intruding.'

'*You* might not think so.'

'Neither would the twins. They're very fond of you.'

And, generally speaking, this was true. The twins did like Hector Lord, and appreciated the help he gave their mother: the more so since he represented no threat – no fatherly instincts lurking in his breast, as Gregory put it. But when they arrived to collect Kate that afternoon they made it clear that this was one occasion when Hector Lord would not be welcome, although, as ever, they had their own way of showing it.

'You don't mind if Hector joins us, do you?' Kate asked cheerily.

'No,' Jimmy said, 'of course not,' Gregory agreed, but it was the intonation of the words that gave the lie. And the sullen unsmiling look that accompanied them.

'No,' Hector said quickly. 'I think I'll skip this one, if you don't mind.'

'Oh, Hector,' Kate exclaimed, clearly disappointed.

'We understand,' Gregory said.

'God knows, you three have little enough time as it is to chat,' Hector went on. 'We can all go out some other time.'

'If you're sure?' Kate asked.

'You *are* sure?' Gregory insisted.

'Quite sure,' Hector said. 'Quite sure.'

And so it was just the three of them who sat at the corner table

Kate preferred in Lugano Pescia – Kate in the middle, Jimmy to her left, Gregory on the right.

'This *is* nice,' Kate said. 'Now, what are we going to have?'

Harvey walked slowly back to his car. Beside him, Pope gave him a long look. 'What do you think, boss?'

Harvey didn't reply immediately. Indeed, he said nothing until they had reached their cars, then he leaned his buttocks against the front wing, almost sitting, and said, 'I'm not sure,' in a tone that was unfamiliar. 'I'm not sure, George,' he added. Then he stood upright. 'Look, I'm going to head back to the station. I'd like you to go round to –' He fumbled in his coat pocket, taking out a slip of paper. 'Go round to Gary Hubbard's address.' He passed the paper to Pope. 'See what you can find out about him. Neighbours,' he proposed quietly.

'You think –'

'Like I said, I'm not sure. Something . . .' He shook his head. 'Probably nothing. Just . . . Shit, George, I don't know. A feeling something wasn't quite right.'

'Ah.'

'Yes. Ah. That's all it is. A feeling.'

'I'll see what I can find out.'

Harvey nodded. Pope opened his car door and got in.

'I just . . . I keep coming back to what Anne Evans said. You remember. Probably just grasping at straws. But he fits, Hubbard does. Loner. And there's something about . . .' Suddenly he shook his head. 'I can't explain.'

Pope started his car. 'See you back at the station, boss.'

Harvey nodded again. 'Yes.'

Alone, driving slowly, Harvey tried to analyse what it was about Gary Hubbard that made him so uneasy. It was as though Hubbard had been just a bit too cool, too keen to be accepted as an innocent, too emotionally distant from the tragedy. The other men he had spoken to – tough, rough navvies not given to outward demonstrations of emotion – had been . . . well, gobsmacked. Some, even, close to tears. Yet Hubbard . . . Of course, it could be that he was hiding something else, some petty crime, a bit of filching from the site, for example.

Harvey turned left and increased his speed. But there was something odd and disquieting about the way Hubbard had been so determined to remove himself from even the slightest acquaintance-ship with Jason Weaver, his blunt, monosyllabic responses shutting away any possibility of a connection between him and the victim. That just wasn't right. Nor was his lack of concern. Cold, cold, cold, Harvey thought. Not a normal reaction by any stretch of the imagination. Even the omission of expletives had been strange. All the other men had effed and blinded, making it clear what *they* would do if they ever got their hands on the shitbag who killed young Jason. But not Hubbard.

'Mum, can I ask you something?' Gregory asked.

'Of course, dear.'

They had finished eating, and Kate was just enjoying the last of her wine, swilling it round and round in the glass.

'You know when Dad left you . . .'

Kate stiffened and placed her glass on the table. 'Yes?' she asked coldly.

'Did you ever think you'd like to kill him?' Gregory asked seriously, but almost instantly adopted a grin, taking the sinister edge off his question.

'Oh, many times,' Kate admitted. 'Why?'

'Just wondered.'

'But then it dawned on me,' Kate went on as though in a reverie, 'that the best revenge I could have was for you two to turn out as well as you have.' She gazed fondly from one son to the other. 'I'm so proud of you both.'

'Dad's never seen us?' Jimmy now asked.

'Good heavens, no.'

'Never?' Gregory persisted.

'No,' Kate said firmly. 'I don't think I'd have let him – even if he'd wanted to.'

'Which he didn't – right?' Gregory asked.

'No. He didn't.'

'Do you hate him?' Gregory continued.

Kate blinked. Then she shrugged. 'No. Not any more. I suppose I did at the time. But not now. He's not worth hating, really.'

'But supposing –' Jimmy began but stopped when Gregory gave him a glare.

'Supposing what, Jimmy?' Kate asked.

'Oh, nothing.'

'No – answer me. Supposing what?'

Jimmy gave Gregory a quick look of appeal. 'Supposing . . .'

Gregory said. 'Supposing something happened to him –'

'Like what?' Kate asked, surprised.

'Oh, I dunno. Lost his job. Had a car accident. You know. How would you feel?'

Kate gave an uneasy smile. 'I don't honestly know.'

'You don't still love him?' Gregory shot the question sharply at his mother.'

Kate laughed aloud. 'No, of course not. I love both of you.'

'That's all right, then,' Gregory said, and leant back in his chair.

Kate finished her wine. 'Why all these strange questions?'

'No reason,' Jimmy said.

'Just wondering about you,' Gregory explained.

Kate folded her napkin. 'Well, you don't have to wonder about me,' she said firmly. She reached out both hands and touched her sons on the cheek. 'I happen to think I came out of it rather well.' She smiled again. 'If anything happened to either of *you* . . .'

'Nothing will happen to us, Mum,' Jimmy assured her.

'That's a promise,' Gregory added.

'That's all I need to know,' Kate said lightly. And then she repeated it more seriously. 'That's all I need to know.'

*   *   *

It was still a bemused Chief Inspector Harvey who came into the incident room. He tossed his coat over the back of a chair and looked about him, his gaze coming to rest on Susan Dill. 'George says you might have found something,' he said, and then, spotting the identikits laid out on the desks, moved towards them.

In a flash Dill was at his side. 'It's just these, boss,' she said, pushing the four likenesses which had been selected across the desk. 'There's some –' she started to say, but stopped as Harvey held up one finger.

If the team had expected a reaction from Harvey it certainly wasn't the one they got. Having silenced Susan Dill, Harvey pulled up a chair and sat down. He spread out the four identikits and studied them. Then, very slowly, he began to nod. He looked up at the ceiling and closed his eyes. He looked back at the identikits again.

'Boss?' Dill ventured.

Harvey didn't hear her, it seemed. He placed his hands across one of the likenesses, leaving only the eyes visible. He did the same with the mouth. Then he took to nodding again. He slumped back in his chair. 'I think I've just been speaking to him,' he announced quietly. There was a strange, strained hiss of silence in the room. 'I think I've just been speaking to him,' Harvey said again, tapping the desk with his finger.

'Boss?' Dill tried again.

'At the building site,' he said.

'You sure, guv?' Alan Kelly asked.

'I think so. Gary Hubbard.'

'Jesus!' Jim Callaghan said.

'Something about him . . .' Harvey straightened. 'George has gone round to his home to see if there's anything.'

'Jesus!' Callaghan repeated.

But on his return, George Pope appeared to put a damper on things.

'Well?' Harvey demanded the moment Pope came into the room.

'Not a lot, boss. Nobody seems to know anything about him. Lives alone, quietly. Causes no bother. Doesn't have any visitors. Drives a white Escort van. Only person who seems ever to have spoken to him is an old dear on the same landing, a Mrs –' he gave a quick look at his notes – 'Mrs Mooney, and that was just hello and goodbye.'

'Look at this, George,' Harvey instructed, passing the top identikit to him.

Pope looked at it, pulled a face and then stared blankly at Harvey.

'Nothing?' Harvey asked as Pope shook his head. 'Reckon it could be Hubbard?' Pope shrugged. 'Wouldn't know, boss. You spoke to him. I didn't pay much attention.' He handed back the identikit. 'Sorry.'

Harvey tossed the likeness back onto the desk in disgust.

'There is one thing. Mrs Mooney says the last time she actually spoke to Hubbard was last Tuesday –'

'The day after Weaver was –' Kelly began.

'Yes. Last Tuesday morning. Hubbard was mending his flat door.'

'He was *what?*' Harvey almost shouted.

'Mending his flat door.'

'What d'you mean, mending his flat door?'

'That's what she said – mending his door.'

'For Christ's sake, George, didn't you ask if –'

'Sure I asked, boss. All she knew was that he was mending his door. She's eighty if she's a day. Lucky to get that much out of her.'

'Why would he be mending his door?' Dill asked.

Still smarting, Pope gave her a sarcastic look. 'Maybe because it was broken.'

'Why was it broken?' Dill now asked, ignoring the sarcasm.

'Because – how do I know why it was broken?'

'Because he had to break in?' Dill suggested. 'Because he hadn't got his keys?'

'Dropped them when he killed Weaver!' Alan Kelly joined in.

'Hang on,' Pope said. 'It's –'

'It's possible,' Harvey interrupted. 'It's possible.'

'Want him brought in, guv?' Kelly asked.

Harvey thought for a while. 'Not just yet. Let's see what more we can find out about Gary Hubbard before we get him in. Susan, go with Alan and see if you can't get anything more out of Mrs Mooney.' He pursed his lips and shook his head. 'No, leave it till the morning – when Hubbard's at work.' He moved his head. 'Jim, I need to know more about that white Escort. Check it out. See how long he's had it. How often he uses it. Has it been off the road recently. If –'

'Couldn't we just –'

'No,' Harvey snapped, anticipating Callaghan's question. 'I don't want to do anything to alert Hubbard. I want him to think he's in the clear for the time being.'

'*If* Hubbard is our man,' Pope said.

Harvey gave a wicked grin. 'I'll bet my life he is.'

'That's some bet, boss.'

'A certainty,' Harvey replied. 'I hope,' he added, widening his smile.

'And if he's not?'

'We lose nothing. But if he *is* . . .'

'Boss?'

'Yes, Susan?'

'Do you think we should put him under observation? I mean –'

Harvey shook his head. 'Not even that yet. I know there are risks, but I don't want to scare him off.'

'But what if he *does* decide to kill again?'

'He won't. I don't think he will, anyway. He'll be careful for a while, if I know anything about him.' Then a thought struck him. 'The MoD. George, get on to them. See if there's any record of Hubbard being in the military,' and, when Pope dithered, 'Get on to them *now*,' he added impatiently. '*Now*.'

*   *   *

'Some Romeo you are,' Gregory said disparagingly. 'I wasn't expecting you home for hours yet.'

Jimmy posed haughtily. 'I have my ways, thank you.'

'Oh, yeah?'

'Oh, yeah. I'm just being the nice, considerate, concerned type for the moment.'

'You sure you're talking about yourself?'

'Sure am. *And* she appreciated it. Told me how sweet I was – again. Anyway, Saturday's all arranged.'

'Exactly as planned?'

'Exactly as planned. I'm picking her up at seven and taking her to the Casa Fume for dinner.'

Gergory nodded. 'Good.'

'The rest is up to you.'

Gregory grinned maliciously. 'Yes, it is, isn't it?'

Jimmy flopped down on his bed, and folded his hands behind his head. 'Greg? You sure this is going to work?'

'Can't be *sure* about anything. But it will work.'

'Be some laugh.'

'Be more than a laugh, Jimmy.'

'Yeah.'

At two o'clock the next morning Frank and Eileen Delaney, returning home from their daughter's engagement party, found the naked body of Jamie Scubin in their front garden. His clothes were in a pile a yard or so from his body. He was clutching an enormous crucifix. His throat had been deeply cut.

8

'You should have listened to Susan,' George Pope remarked injudiciously.

Robert Harvey gave him a furious glare. 'I *know* what I should have done.'

Behind them, at her desk, Susan Dill shifted uncomfortably in her seat. 'There's nothing to say Hubbard had anything to do with this,' she stated loyally. 'As far as we know it's only Jason Weaver he might have –'

'We have the identikits,' Pope threw at her.

'We could be mistaken about them.'

Harvey interrupted the exchange, shaking his head. 'Thanks, Susan, but the mistake was mine,' he admitted.

'We should soon know,' Dill said, her voice consoling.

Harvey nodded wistfully.

'Where are they?' Pope asked, looking up at the clock.

And, as though to answer his question, DS Callaghan stuck his head in the door and announced, 'We're back.'

Harvey looked up. 'Got him?'

'In interview room five.'

'Right. Any trouble?'

'None at all. Quiet as a lamb – and as silent,' Callaghan said with a sardonic grin. 'If anything, he's enjoying himself.'

'Well, let's try and put a stop to that.' Harvey made for the door. 'Susan, chase up McVinnie, will you? See if there's anything we can use.' And then he was gone, tucking a blue folder securely under his arm.

'He's fucked the whole thing up,' Pope said angrily as the door closed. 'Fucked it right up,' Pope persisted, as Susan Dill ignored him.

'You'd have done better, I suppose,' Dill said, reaching for the phone.

'Any one of us would.'

'You think so – oh, Dr McVinnie, please.'

'I know so.'

'We'll see,' Susan Dill replied, and then concentrated on the phone. 'Oh. Right. Ask him to phone DC Dill in the incident room when he gets back, will you? Thanks.'

'Thank you for coming in, Mr Hubbard,' Harvey began, sitting down across the table from Gary Hubbard, and waiting for Jim Callaghan to settle into his chair beside him.

'I didn't come in. I was brought,' Gary answered, but not belligerently. His tone was calm and even; his remark sounded more like a small witticism.

'Whichever,' Harvey said.

'I'd like to know why,' Gary said.

'Just routine, I assure you. Just to follow up on our chat at the site.'

'Oh.' Gary Hubbard clearly did not believe the explanation. He tilted his head to one side and gave Harvey an almost coquettish look.

'There's nothing for you to be worried about.'

Gary smiled broadly. 'I'm not worried.'

'Good. Good. Now – about Jason Weaver. I'm trying to build up a picture of the lad –'

'I told you –' Gary interrupted, himself brought to a halt by Harvey waving his hand.

'No, Mr Hubbard,' Harvey said with an understanding smile. 'You told me all you *think* you know. And I appreciate that. But it's the small details that are so often vital. Details that are forgotten by the interviewee. You'd be surprised how many cases are solved by uncovering the tiny details.'

Gary waited.

'So, can we go back over what you told me?'

'If you want.'

'Right. I'll be frank with you, Mr Hubbard, I found it unnerving how . . . well, how uninterested you seem to be in what happened to Jason Weaver.' Harvey paused for a reaction. When Gary just blinked, he went on. 'It's almost as if you didn't care . . . or as if you already knew.' He paused again, and then, 'Did you?'

'Care or know?' Gary asked calmly.

'Know.'

Gary gave an insolent smile. 'Sure. Like I told you at the site. A mate told me.'

'Care, then?'

Gary shrugged. 'Not particularly.'

'You didn't like him?' Jim Callaghan asked.

Gary Hubbard looked at him steadily. 'Like I told *him*,' he said, nodding back towards Harvey, 'I didn't *know* him.'

'But –'

'And if I don't *know* somebody, why should I give a toss what happens to them?' Gary answered. 'I keep myself to myself. Always have done. Am I under arrest?' he demanded suddenly.

Harvey shook his head. 'No. Just helping –'

'– you with your enquiries?' Gary concluded for him.

'Yes,' Harvey confirmed.

Gary grinned. 'Not being much help, though.'

For a moment Harvey didn't reply. Then, slowly, keeping his eyes fixed on Gary's face, he pulled one of the identikits from the folder and slid it across the table. He saw the grin drop from Gary's lips, saw his eyes narrow; saw, he thought, a momentary glint of fear enter them. But then Gary was staring back at him questioningly.

'Recognise him?' Harvey asked.

Gary shook his head. 'No.'

'You're sure?'

'I'm sure. Who is he?'

Harvey didn't answer. He returned the likeness to the folder and stood up. 'Thank you, Mr Hubbard. That will be all.'

Gary placed both hands on the table as though to push himself erect.

'Oh, by the way,' Harvey said suddenly, leaning towards him. 'I hear you had a problem with the door to your flat,' he said, and felt a tingle of pleasure as Gary jumped.

But yet again Hubbard recovered quickly. 'Not a problem,' he said.

'No? Well, I heard –'

'Just changed the lock.'

'Oh? Why was that?'

Gary shrugged dismissively. 'Put a better one on, that's all.'

'I see,' Harvey said, sounding reasonable. 'Why did you suddenly do that?'

'Nothing sudden about it. Been break-ins round and about. Just put a better lock on, that's all.'

'Very sensible,' Harvey commented flatly. 'No other reason?'

'No. Like what?'

'Oh, I don't know. I thought maybe you'd lost the key to the old lock. Such things happen,' Harvey said and, without giving Gary the chance to reply, he added, 'You won't, I'm sure, have any objection to us taking a look around your flat?'

'For what?'

'Just to satisfy ourselves that –'

'You can look as much as you want,' Gary interrupted.

His willing permission came as something of a surprise. Harvey studied Gary's face for a moment before saying, 'Thank you, Mr Hubbard.' Then he turned to Callaghan: 'You and Alan go with Mr Hubbard, will you, Jim, and take a quick look round.'

Callaghan stood up.

'Oh,' Harvey went on as though it was an afterthought. 'Your van. Mind if we take a look at that too?'

'No problem,' Gary answered, something of his old bravado returning.

'That's most co-operative of you, Mr Hubbard.'

'I'll go and get Alan,' Callaghan said.

Alone with the suspect, Chief Inspector Harvey sat down again, leaning his elbow on the back of the chair, and resting his head in one hand. He had an urge to question Gary Hubbard about the killings of the rent boys, just to lob the subject into the air and see what the reaction might be. But he resisted the temptation. Let Hubbard think that Jason Weaver was the only killing they were interested in. Let him cover his tracks, let him be as smug and clever as he liked about that, and then, maybe . . . maybe he would make the one mistake that would trap him. 'It's a terrible thing – murder,' he said.

Gary nodded.

'Especially when it's someone as young as Jason.'

Gary nodded again.

'You know,' Harvey said, leaning forward now and placing both elbows on the table. 'I've seen a lot of murders but I can never understand how anyone can be so depraved as to kill a youngster.' He stared at Gary. 'Can you?'

'Can I what?'

Harvey sighed. 'Never mind.'

'Can I what?' Gary asked again, but before Harvey could reply Alan Kelly stuck his head in the room.

'We're ready, guv,' he said.

Harvey remained seated as Gary left the room. Just as Kelly was about to follow, he said, 'Alan?'

'Guv?'

'Just take a good look,' Harvey told him in a low voice. 'If you see anything, don't let Hubbard know. Don't try and take anything away. Just leave him with the impression that everything's fine.'

146

'Right, guv. That's if we *do* see anything.'

'I know, I know.'

'All ready?' Gregory asked.

'Ready as I'll ever be,' Jimmy answered, and then studied his brother. '*You* sure look the part.'

Gregory turned to the mirror and gazed long and hard at himself. And, indeed, he did look the part: with his hair flattened and wearing contact lenses instead of his spectacles, at a casual glance he could easily be mistaken for his half-brother, Justin Harvey. And not only did Gregory look like Justin, somehow the change of appearance enabled him to adopt the other's haughty façade and arrogant stance. 'All we can hope is that it works,' he said to his reflection.

Jimmy patted him on the shoulder. 'Hey, it'll work.'

'Have to be timed to perfection.'

'Don't *worry*,' Jimmy said, taking his brother by the shoulders and turning him round. 'You just have the car ready and I'll see we hit the spot on time.'

Gregory nodded.

'Just make sure you don't wreck Mum's car,' he warned. 'She'd go crazy.'

Gregory smiled. 'Yeah. She would, wouldn't she?' Then, abruptly, he swung back to the mirror. 'You're certain Miranda's arranged to meet Justin with you tonight?'

Jimmy nodded. 'Quite certain. I was right there when she called him.'

'After you've had dinner?'

Jimmy made a little noise in his throat. 'Yes. After we've had dinner.'

'Everything depends on him being away from home when –'

'I *know* that,' Jimmy answered. 'I'm not stupid.'

'No, I know you're not, Jimmy. I've just got to be sure.'

'She's supposed to meet Justin at ten o'clock in that pub near the LSE – okay?'

'Okay.' Gregory said.

Jimmy now took to looking at himself in the mirror. 'Look all right, do I?'

'Hmm?'

'Irresistible?'

'Oh, sure.'

'Jesus, I'm handsome!'

'Just let's hope Miranda agrees.'

Jimmy arched his neck. 'Miranda thinks I'm gorgeous.'

'I thought it was sweet?'

'Sweet *and* gorgeous.'

'Must be mad, the girl. Right. Let's make a move.'

'I'm ready.'

Downstairs in the kitchen Kate was poring over fabric designs spread on the table in front of her. She looked up, a ready smile on her face, as the twins came in. 'You're looking *very* smart,' she said proudly to Jimmy. 'It must be a very important date.'

'Well . . .' He gave her a coy smile.

'So it *is* . . .'

'Sort of.'

Kate Renfrew beamed. 'I *knew* it. You sly little –' And then she spotted his twin. 'Gregory?' she asked in a puzzled, amused way. 'What on earth have you done to yourself?'

'It's just a phase he's going through, Mum,' Jimmy explained.

'You look so different,' Kate said.

'My new image,' Gregory told her.

'Well, it's very nice, I'm sure, but –'

'It won't last, Mum,' Jimmy said quickly. You know our Gregory. Gets these crazy ideas. Do anything to try and look as gorgeous as me.'

'Jimmy!' Kate said with mock severity.

'It's what's inside that counts – right, Mum?' Gregory said, giving Jimmy a playful thump.

'Quite right, Gregory. Anyway, as long as –'

'Don't say it, Mum – *please*,' Gregory interrupted her.

'Say what?'

'As long as you're happy,' Gregory answered in a mincing tone.

'That's what you always say,' Jimmy pointed out.

Kate straightened her back. 'Only because I mean it.'

'We know that. But you don't have to say it *all* the time.'

Before Kate could reply, Gregory said, 'We'd better get going.'

'Ready,' Jimmy answered.

'You won't be too late?' Kate asked.

'Nope.'

'And you'll be careful with my car?'

'Mum, of *course* I'll be careful with your precious car.'

'I know you will,' Kate answered quickly. 'It's not so much the car as –'

'Mum, I'll be careful.'

Kate gave them both a grateful smile. Then she moved quickly round the table and hugged them both. 'No drinking.'

'Mum . . .'

'See you later,' Jimmy said.

Kate watched them lovingly as they moved towards the door. 'I hope she's worth it,' she called after them slyly.

The twins stopped and turned, both of them serious at first and then, in unison, breaking into a smile. 'It's nothing serious, Mum,' Jimmy said.

'Not yet, anyway,' Gregory added. 'And I'll be there to keep an eye on him.'

'I just don't want you to be hurt,' Kate explained.

'Mum, for heaven's sake. It's just a date.'

'Yes,' Kate answered, 'I know.'

After they had gone Kate Renfrew found it difficult to concentrate. The words *just a date* continued to rattle in her brain.

'Maybe the silly bitch has come to her senses at last,' David Parsons said, although there was a tinge of disappointment in his voice.

'I fucking hope so,' Justin answered.

'Why would she want to meet you otherwise?'

'You tell me. That's what worries me.'

'Want me to come along?'

Justin Harvey shook his head. 'No.'

'Well, don't you go agreeing to anything you shouldn't, you silly bugger.'

'Like what?'

'Like marrying the cow, of course.'

Justin Harvey looked up sharply at his friend. 'No chance,' he said, but not all that convincingly.

David gave a whooping laugh. 'You could always bump her off,' he suggested. 'If she gets too stroppy, of course.'

'You don't half come up with some crazy —'

'Actually,' David went on, clearly joking but nonetheless giving his preposterous suggestion a serious air, 'actually, it's not so crazy. Your dear daddy could investigate, and even if he found out you were the perpetrator, he'd never shop his darling boy.'

'Very funny.'

David stretched and yawned. 'Christ, I'm bored.'

Justin looked at his watch. 'Better make a move,' he said.

'You sure you don't want me to come along?'

'Quite sure.'

'Oh, well, an early night for me, then.'

'Do you good. I'll give you a buzz and let you know what happens.'

'Do it tonight, will you?'

'Phone you?'

'Yes.'

'Right. Might be late.'

'It'll be worth waking up for,' David said. 'I'm sure.'

Both Alan Kelly and Jim Callaghan looked dejected when they returned to the incident room and found Chief Inspector Harvey waiting for them, his eyebrows already raised hopefully. Kelly shook his head. Harvey slapped the desk with the palm of his hand, hard.

Callaghan jumped. 'Well . . .'

'Well what?' Harvey demanded.

Callaghan screwed up his face. 'Well, everything's there but nothing's –'

'For Christ's sake, Jim,' Harvey exploded.

'Okay. Okay. Sorry.'

'Tell me,' Harvey said, managing, somehow, to include a sort of apology in his words.

'Well – the door to the flat. Yes, the lock *has* been changed but –'

'But there *have* been quite a few break-ins in that area recently,' Kelly interrupted. 'I checked.'

'So, changing the lock could be legitimate,' Callaghan concluded.

'Or it could be like Susan said – he lost his keys.' Kelly added.

'Except Mrs Mooney – the old biddy who lives in the flat opposite – said, at first, that is, that she thought Hubbard's flat had been broken into.'

Harvey looked at Callaghan sternly. 'At first?'

Kelly nodded. 'When I spoke to her she said Hubbard had changed the lock because of *the* break-in.'

'Go on,' Harvey urged.

'But when I asked her specifically if Hubbard had been broken into she seemed less certain. She wasn't sure at all, in fact.'

'What exactly did you ask her?' Harvey demanded.

'Sorry?'

'The words, Alan. What exactly did you ask her?'

Kelly looked puzzled. 'Just –'

'Not just,' Harvey snapped. 'The exact question.'

'I asked –' DS Kelly paused and thought for a moment. 'I asked her if she was certain Hubbard had been broken into.'

'And she said?'

'She said, "I *think* that's what Mr Hubbard said."'

'Then?' Harvey pressured.

'Then I said, "Are you sure, Mrs Mooney, that Mr Hubbard said *he* had been broken into or was he changing the lock because of the spate of break-ins?" That's when she became uncertain. Confused, sort of.'

'Ah,' Harvey said. 'It didn't strike you that *you* had confused her?'

'Guv?'

'The old woman. Probably gets muddled up about a lot of things. She gives you a straight answer to begin with and then you suggest another possibility.'

'I just –'

'She's probably been told a thousand times by God alone knows how many people that she's mistaken, or that she's imagining things – she's bound to get confused, as you put it, if a police officer suggests there might be another explanation for Hubbard's action.'

Kelly looked suitably chastised.

'I'll get Susan to have another word with her,' Harvey decided, speaking the words quietly.

'Now, inside the flat,' Callaghan was saying.

'What's it like – the flat?' Harvey interrupted.

Callaghan stared at him.

'What's the damn flat like?' Harvey asked again.

'One bedroom, sitting-room, kitchen and bathroom,' Callaghan answered.

Harvey gave a sigh. 'That's not what I meant. Was it the sort of flat you'd expect someone like Gary Hubbard to live in?' he asked with exaggerated care.

Callaghan and Kelly exchanged glances. Then Kelly shook his head. 'Not really, I suppose.'

Harvey stared at him, waiting.

'Too tidy,' Kelly said.

'Too tidy,' Harvey repeated in an exasperated tone.

'You said that too,' Kelly told Callaghan.

Callaghan nodded. 'Not a man's flat,' he said. 'You know, guv. It was . . . well, everything was in its place. Everything neat and tidy. No clothes lying about – everything folded up. No dirty dishes. No dust.' He stared at Harvey to try to divine if that was explanation enough.

Maybe it was. Harvey nodded anyway. He leant back in his chair and thought for a while. 'Now inside the flat,' he said eventually, using Callaghan's words.

'Yes. Inside the flat. In the kitchen. He's got a right collection of knives. There must be twenty of them.'

'Eighteen,' Kelly corrected, and reddened under the withering glare Callaghan gave him.

'Not just your ordinary kitchen knives either. Proper butcher's equipment. But –'

'Here we go,' Harvey moaned. 'But –?'

'He likes cooking.'

'He said that?'

Callaghan nodded. 'And I believe him. Got all the gear. Pots, pans, woks. Spices by the bucketful. Cookbooks . . .'

'All right. All right,' Harvey said. 'What else?'

'Nothing.'

'Nothing?'

'Nothing.'

'He let you look at –'

'At everything, guv,' Kelly said. 'And there was nothing. It was funny . . . I dunno. He stood there all the time looking at us as though he knew we'd find nothing.'

'Well, he would, wouldn't he, if there was nothing to find?' Harvey pointed out.

'Yes, but – well, it was like he knew we'd find nothing because he'd made *sure* we'd find nothing. Like if he wasn't so fucking clever we *would* have found something. Oh, I dunno.'

'No, that's all right, Alan,' Harvey said gently. 'I know what you mean.' He stood up, went over to the information board and stared at the photographs of the victims. 'I know exactly what you mean,' he added quietly. Then he swung round. 'And the van?'

'Clean as a whistle,' Callaghan said. 'Got some work stuff in it, but that's all.' He looked at his notes. 'He's had the van for as long as any of the neighbours can remember.'

Harvey frowned.

'Ever since he moved into the flat,' Kelly added.

'When was that?' Harvey asked.

'Three years ago.'

'Maybe, boss,' Callaghan ventured. 'Maybe we're –'

Harvey stopped him with a violent shake of his head. He would probably have explained his reaction had not, at that moment, Susan Dill walked into the room. She looked at the three men and then made as if to retreat, as if she felt she had barged in on a private meeting.

'No, it's all right, Susan,' Harvey told her.

'I had a quick word with Doc McVinnie,' she said.

'And?'

'All he'd say to me was that he *thought* he might have something for you.'

Harvey brightened. 'Well, get him on the –'

'He's gone home, boss. Said he had a meeting this evening.'

Harvey groaned.

'Said he'd call you first thing in the morning.'

Harvey sighed. 'Not even a hint of –?'

Susan Dill shook her head.

'Oh, well. I suppose that's what we should all do. Go home.'

When Kelly and Callaghan had left, leaving Dill and Harvey alone, Susan asked, 'You all right, boss?'

Harvey nodded curtly. 'Thanks.'

'Sure?'

Harvey grunted as though he believed one could never be sure of such things.

Book Two

*   *   *

Gary Hubbard sat in the dark, the only sound his own gentle, regular breathing, and the quiet tick of a cheap carriage-clock on the mantelpiece. Yet, although he seemed unperturbed and peaceful enough, his mind was racing, thoughts clamouring for attention. From time to time he gave a little snort as though one of these thoughts struck him as ridiculous. And then, after he had been there for over an hour, he gave a long, low groan, and shook his head, almost as if this action would dislodge an idea that confused him. And Gary Hubbard was confused. He could not understand why, with the police climbing all over him, why, at a time when he should be lying low, why he should feel the strongest urge he had ever felt in his life to kill again. But it was more than that: an urge to kill again, yes, but a grand climax, a final killing, the finality of which had been taken out of his hands. So strong was this impulse that he found himself rising from his chair as if pulled from it by a force he did not recognise.

Gary stood still and silent for several minutes. Then he started to nod to himself, a strange, faraway look in his eyes, the look of someone who had solved a mystery and was pleasantly astonished at the outcome. He sat down again and crossed his legs, folding his hands across his stomach. He leant his head back and closed his eyes, a tranquil smile on his lips. He seemed to be listening, listening to music, a lullaby perhaps. And then his body began to move from side to side as though he was being cradled in someone's arms, and rocked gently in time to that music.

Robert Harvey was surprised to find his son waiting for him at the front door. And he wasn't all that pleased to see him either. He had quite enough to think about at the moment without having to deal with the lamentable result of his son's libido. Besides, it was late and he was tired. What he really wanted was a strong drink and a hot bath and a good night's sleep without interruption.

'Dad?'

'Yes, Justin?'

'Can I take the car tonight? Now, like?'

Harvey was relieved. 'Yes, I suppose so.'

'I'm going to meet Miranda,' Justin explained.

'I thought –'

'Just want to see if I can make her change her mind.'

Harvey nodded. He opened the front door. 'All right. But don't be late.'

'No.'

'And don't drink – not even half a pint.'

'No, I won't. I promise.'

Harvey grunted as though he had been given such promises before and had them broken. 'Does your mother know you're going?'

'Knows I'm going out. Not where.'

Harvey nodded, and tossed the car keys to his son, making a wry face as Justin dropped them and bent to pick them up.

Straightening, he said, 'Thanks, Dad.'

'As long as it helps.'

'I'm trying,' Justin told him.

'I know you are, Justin. I know you are,' Harvey said kindly. Then he smiled. 'And I don't mean –'

'No. I know you don't.'

Gregory Renfrew sat upright and alert behind the wheel of his mother's car, inconspicuous in the narrow street. On his left, a few hundred yards down the street was the Casa Fume, a blue neon sign over the mock-Tudor doors, and two clipped bay trees in tubs, strategically placed one on either side, trying to give the restaurant a Mediterranean look. And they would have succeeded had not the council planted a streetlamp almost opposite, its cold bright light illuminating the deception. The menu, in a glass-fronted case, was secured to the wall.

At four minutes to eleven Gregory started the engine, gunning it once then letting it idle. His palms were sweating. He rubbed his hands together roughly, then gripped the wheel tightly.

At exactly eleven o'clock Jimmy and Miranda came out of the restaurant. Gregory gritted his teeth, watching as Jimmy started to tap the pockets of his jacket. He said something to Miranda and dashed back into the restaurant. Gregory put the car in gear. Miranda moved a few paces from the entrance, then turned, walked back and studied the menu. Gregory gave a low hiss. Then Jimmy was out again, chatting, explaining, manoeuvring Miranda to the outside of the pavement. Gregory waited until they were four paces from the full glare of the streetlight. Then he released the clutch and sent the car hurtling towards them. He half mounted the pavement, his head jerking back on impact. 'Grab her, Jimmy,' he said aloud, and 'Yes!' as his brother seized Miranda, pulling her to safety but, at the same time, making certain she was facing the car. When he drew level with them, Gregory slowed fractionally and peered out of the window. Then, accelerating again, he bumped off the pavement and sped away down the narrow street.

'You okay?' gasped Jimmy, holding Miranda in his arms.

Miranda Jay didn't speak immediately. She nodded. Then, in a tiny voice, she said, 'That was Justin,' turning her head, her eyes gazing in the direction Gregory had taken.

'It was *who*?' Jimmy asked, sounding appalled.

'It was Justin,' Miranda said again.

'Nah,' Jimmy told her, starting to steer her down the street, one arm comfortingly about her shoulders. 'Can't have been.'

'It was,' Miranda insisted, pulling away suddenly and facing him. 'I saw him. I saw his face.'

'Okay, okay. Calm down,' Jimmy said gently, replacing his arm about her shoulders and continuing to walk.

'You don't believe me,' Miranda said in a whisper.

'I do. Of course I believe you,' Jimmy protested. 'It's just . . . well, you can't *really* have seen him, can you? I mean, it was all so quick.'

'I saw his face. He was looking at me.'

Jimmy stopped walking and turned Miranda so he could look directly into her eyes. 'You know what you're saying, don't you, Miranda? You're saying Justin deliberately tried to knock you down.'

Miranda didn't answer.

'That's heavy stuff,' Jimmy told her, trying hard to keep a straight face.

'I know,' Miranda said, starting to shake.

Jimmy pulled her towards him and hugged her. 'It's okay,' he whispered.

'He tried to kill me,' Miranda said in an awed voice as though the thought had just struck her.

'Shush,' Jimmy told her.

'If it hadn't been for you —'

'Shush,' Jimmy said again into her ear, allowing himself a quiet smile. 'Let's get you home.'

And, when he got Miranda back to her flat, Jimmy Renfrew was the personification of sweetness and compassion, tucking her up in bed, making her a hot drink, sitting on the edge of the bed as she drank, and then holding one of her hands and rubbing it gently.

'How *could* he?' Miranda kept asking over and over, to which Jimmy tutted and made odd little noises that suggested anything was possible as far as the despicable Justin Harvey was concerned. 'You won't leave me, Jimmy, will you?'

'Of course not,' Jimmy assured her.

He waited until she had dozed off and then went to explore her flat. He was brutal about it, reading her diary and delving into every drawer. And then he came across a wallet, an expensive wallet in pigskin with gold tips on the corners. He lifted it from the drawer and opened it. At first glance it appeared empty. There was nothing in the pockets, certainly. But, squeezing it, Jimmy felt something. He opened the back flap and pushed his fingers into the deep back recess. When he withdrew them they held a couple of cards. It was only after he placed the wallet on the dressing-table top and read the cards that he felt the hairs on the back of his neck start to tingle. A library card. A video shop membership card. A card indicating the owner wished his organs to be donated. Each card made out to Justin Harvey; each bearing his signature.

'Jimmy!'

Jimmy jumped.

'Jimmy?' Miranda called again.

'Just coming,' Jimmy heard himself say in a croaking voice. He swallowed. 'Just coming,' he said again, stuffing the cards back into the wallet. He looked up and caught sight of himself in the mirror. He gave himself a wicked smile and a reassuring nod before putting the wallet into his pocket.

'Jimmy, hold me,' Miranda said as he came into the bedroom.

Jimmy sat on the edge of the bed and reached out to hold her.

'No . . .' Miranda said.

Jimmy stood up and undressed. He slid in beside her and took her in his arms. 'That better?' he asked.

'Much.'

'You go back to sleep,' he told her.

'What are we going to do?' Miranda asked after a minute.

'About Justin?'

'Yes.'

'Easy.'

'What?'

'You know his dad's a chief inspector?'

'Yes.'

'Well, you go and see him and tell him what his precious son's been up to.'

'Oh, Jimmy, I couldn't.'

'Why not?'

'I just couldn't.'

'I'll come with you.'

'Will you?'

159

'Of course I will. Saw the whole thing, didn't I?'

Miranda kissed him on the lips. 'I don't know what I'd have done without you, Jimmy,' she said.

'Well, you don't have to do anything without me,' Jimmy told her. 'I'll look after you, Miranda,' he added, rolling her on to her back and easing himself on top of her.

'Oh, Jimmy –'

'It's okay.'

'I –'

'Shush,' Jimmy said, and started kissing her breasts.

'The bitch stood me up,' Justin told David Parsons speaking quietly into the phone.

David started to laugh.

'It's not funny.'

'I think it's hilarious.'

'Piss off, David.'

'You sure you were supposed to meet her in the pub?'

'Of course I'm sure.'

'Oh, well. Maybe she just changed her mind. You know women.'

Justin was silent for a while. 'You don't think she's gone and done something stupid, do you?' he asked eventually.

'Like?'

'Dunno. Like –'

'Topping herself?'

'That, or . . .'

'Give over, Justin. You're so dramatic.'

'It's just so unlike her not to turn up.'

'It hasn't dawned on you that maybe she simply doesn't want to see you again?'

'She said she'd be there. *She* asked *me* to meet her.'

'Like I said, she changed her mind.'

'David, I'm really worried.'

'Phone her.'

'I did. Twice. Once at half nine and again at half ten. There was no answer.'

'So, she went out.'

'Maybe I'd better go round.'

'I wouldn't. Not tonight, anyway. Leave it till the morning. Phone her again then, and if there's still no reply we'll go round together.'

'I suppose you're right. Thanks, David.'

'Anything to oblige.'

Gregory Renfrew was fit to be tied. When his brother arrived home at twenty to nine in the morning he rounded on him. 'Where the hell have you been?' he demanded.

Jimmy feigned surprise. 'Doing my job,' he retorted. Still Gregory glowered.

'Hey, come on, Greg. Everything went a treat. I just had to stay the night to calm her down.'

'Huh.'

Jimmy grinned. 'I made a *deep* impression.'

'How deep – eight inches?'

'Eight and a half, actually.'

At last Gregory smiled.

'That's better,' Jimmy said. 'Want to hear about it?'

'Course I do.'

'Mum gone?'

Gregory nodded.

'Okay,' Jimmy said, settling himself on his brother's bed. 'You were brilliant. Only fucking brilliant.'

Gregory propped himself up on one elbow. 'Naturally I was,' he said.

'No, really you were. Frightened the shit out of her. *And* she was utterly convinced you were Justin. I didn't have to say a word. Out she came with it. "That was Justin," she said.'

'And you protested?'

'Sure I protested. But she wasn't having any of that. So I took her home. Anyway, the long and the short of it is she's going to go and see our daddy and tell him what a naughty boy his son has been.'

'You serious?'

'I'm serious. Going to see him this morning. I have to pick her up at eleven and off we go to the station.' Jimmy paused and looked anxious. 'That's okay, isn't it?'

'It's only bloody marvellous.'

Jimmy beamed. 'I thought so.'

'You think you can handle it?'

'Sure I can.'

'Don't get too cocky.'

'I'm not cocky. Confident. That's the word. Confident. Can't wait to see his face. And that's not all.' I took a little nosey around her flat. Guess what I found?'

'What?'

Jimmy put his hand in his pocket and took out the wallet, tossing it casually on to the bed. 'That.'

'A wallet?'

'Look inside,' Jimmy instructed, enjoying himself enormously.

Gregory did as he was told. He took out the cards and studied them. 'Jesus holy Christ!' he said.

'Them's my sentiments exactly. We can use them, can't we?'

Gregory took his time about replying. He held the cards, fingering them as he might something fragile, something precious, thinking. Then he looked up, a huge smile spread right across his face. 'You bet we can! Jimmy, you're a genius.'

'What are we going to do with them?'

'Let me think some more about that,' Gregory told him. Then he grinned. 'I'll have it all worked out when you get back.'

'Pleased, then?'

'Oh, I'm pleased, Jimmy. Very pleased.'

'Thought you might be.' Jimmy stood up and stretched. 'Just time to have a shower and get changed.'

Gregory nodded, still gazing at the cards.

'Pity you can't come with us,' Jimmy said, making for the door.

But Gregory didn't seem to hear him. He was lying back on the pillow and staring at the ceiling, his eyes wide open and sparkling.

9

'Flour,' McVinnie said, his eyes bright behind his spectacles.

'Flour?' Harvey asked disbelievingly.

'Flour,' the doctor confirmed. 'Traces of. Only in one small area. The jeans. Lower half of the leg. None, interestingly enough, on the soles of the trainers.'

'Which means he didn't *walk* in the flour,' Harvey said vaguely.

McVinnie gave him a look that suggested he didn't believe this was the most staggering deduction ever made.

'He lay in the flour but didn't walk in it,' Harvey continued, ignoring the doctor's gaze.

'I didn't say that.'

'Hmm?'

'I didn't say he lay in the flour. I simply said there were traces of flour on the lower left leg of the victim's jeans.'

Harvey gazed at him.

McVinnie gave a little sigh. 'He *could* have been lying down with his left leg resting in an area where there was flour, but he didn't lie *in* it.'

The two men stared at each other for a short while. Harvey purposely remained silent. He knew McVinnie well enough to know that he had something up his sleeve. He liked to dole out his information piecemeal.

'I can also tell you he was dead *before* his jeans came in contact with the flour.'

Harvey didn't interrupt. He nodded until McVinnie went on.

'Although the garments from the upper half of the body are

saturated with blood, the boxer shorts, trainers and jeans are blood-free. Almost.'

'Almost,' Harvey heard himself repeat.

'Almost,' McVinnie said. 'There are two minute flecks on the lower left leg of the jeans. That blood is *under* the flour, indicating that he –'

'That he came into contact with the flour *after* he was killed.' Harvey concluded.

'Quite,' McVinnie agreed tightly.

'So, he was killed, came into contact with the flour, was stripped and transported – or visa versa – and then dumped,' Harvey said in a low voice, working out the sequence aloud. McVinnie didn't answer. 'There's no way the flour could have got on to the jeans *before* he was killed?'

'None,' McVinnie said firmly.

'You're absolutely certain, Miles?'

Miles McVinnie didn't like having his judgement questioned. He frowned briefly and gave a dismissive snort. 'Absolutely certain.'

'Thank you.'

The doctor appeared mollified. 'The flour itself is distinctive,' he said. 'It's not fresh. Been lying about for quite some time. Several months, I'd say, at a guess.'

'So if we find –'

'If you find the *right* flour I'll be able to make you a match.'

'You're a godsend, Miles.'

McVinnie blinked but looked pleased enough. His pleasure didn't last long, though. He became decidedly disgruntled when Harvey asked, 'Miles, there weren't any traces of flour on any of the others, were there?'

McVinnie bridled. 'If there had been I think I might have mentioned it,' he said waspishly.

'Yes. I'm sorry, Miles.'

Dr McVinnie accepted the apology. 'If you're trying to use the flour as a link between the killings, you can forget it. This is the only time it has been found on any of the clothes.' Harvey gave a wan smile. 'Pity. Nothing else, I suppose?'

'Nothing from a forensic standpoint. However, there is one thing that could be significant. Your killer – always assuming it *is* the same killer – is . . . Well, let me put it like this. To begin with – Peter Dunn – the depth of the incision was slight. Enough to kill, of course, but there was no great force in it. However, on James Meehan, it's considerably deeper. On Ross Douglas it's deeper still. And so on. Jamie Scubin's head was almost severed. I'd say the next time he kills, the victim could be decapitated.'

Harvey winced. 'What does that tell us, Miles?'

The doctor chortled. 'You're the detective. You need to talk to your psychiatrist friend about that.'

'Hiya,' Jimmy said.

'Hello, Jimmy,' Miranda answered.

'Feeling better?'

Miranda nodded. 'Much.'

'Good. We'll get this straightened out. Don't worry.'

But Miranda did look worried. 'I don't know if we should go to see –'

'And let Justin off scot-free? Miranda, if he tried it once he's just as likely to try again. And I might not be with you the next time.'

'I know, but –'

'Forget the buts. We're going, and that's it,' Jimmy insisted, but smiling encouragingly nonetheless.

'All right,' Miranda told him quietly. 'If you think it's –'

'I do.'

Miranda put on her coat and gave herself a last look in the mirror. 'Do I look all right?'

'You look fine. Honest,' Jimmy told her, and as they set out for the police station, he took her hand as he warned her, 'Let me do the talking, okay?'

Miranda gave him a frail, grateful smile. 'You're so good to me.'

Jimmy squeezed her hand. 'I like being good to you,' he told her convincingly.

'I wish . . . I wish I'd met you before –'

'You've met me now, haven't you?'

'Yes,' Miranda told him. 'Yes. I have.'

Chief Inspector Harvey reached for the phone. 'Yes?'

'There's a young lady down here demanding to see you, sir. A Miss Jay,' the desk sergeant said.

Harvey was puzzled. 'Who?' he demanded, trying in vain to place the name.

'A Miss Miranda Jay.'

An 'Oh' escaped Harvey before he could stop it. He closed his eyes, pressing the lids tight as if that might help him think. It had to be *the* Miranda, Justin's bloody Miranda, he thought, already steeling himself, allowing trite if brutal phrases to flick through his mind: Well, Justin didn't *force* you, did he? . . . If you'd taken even the most elementary precautions . . .

'Sir?'

'Yes. Sorry, Brian.'

'There's a young man with her.'

'Her solicitor?' Harvey asked instinctively, and immediately regretted it.

'I wouldn't say so, sir. Too young, but he's very persistent.'

Harvey sighed. 'I suppose you'd better bring them up,' he said, recovering and trying to sound casual.

The desk sergeant made a strange noise. 'Up?' he asked. 'To your office? Not an interview room?'

Harvey was flustered momentarily. 'No. I'm . . . I'm waiting for an urgent call. Up here, Brian, please.'

Harvey got up and placed two chairs, one beside the other, facing his desk. He put on his jacket and opened a file, ruffling the papers, and waited.

*   *   *

Gregory Renfrew was surprised to hear the front door slam. He went to the top of the stairs, and called down, 'Jimmy?'

'No. It's me, darling.'

'Mum? What are you doing home?' Gregory asked, coming down the stairs two at a time and following his mother into the kitchen. 'What's the matter?'

'Alice phoned. Donald's had a turn. I'll have to go up.'

'To Scotland?'

Uncharacteristically, Kate snapped. 'That's where they live, isn't it?' Immediately she was repentant. 'I'm sorry, Gregory. It sounds very serious. I mean, Alice wouldn't call me unless it was very serious.' Then she cocked her head. 'Isn't Jimmy home yet?'

'Been and gone,' Gregory told her.

'Oh, dear. I wanted . . . Never mind. Look, you'll be able to take care of yourselves for the weekend, won't you?'

'You don't want us to come with you?' Gregory asked, and if Kate had not been so distracted she might have noticed the relief in his voice.

'Oh, no. I'll fly up.'

'I'll drive you to the airport,' Gregory volunteered.

'That's kind of you, dear, but Hector's picking me up. I wasn't sure you'd be here. But thank you.'

'Okay.'

'I'll phone you tonight,' Kate said, already heading for the bedroom to pack.

'Okay,' Gregory said again, following her.

'I do hope . . . poor Alice. She'd be totally shattered if anything happened to Donald.'

'He's had turns before.'

'Yes, I know he has, dear, but Alice has never asked me to come up before,' Kate pointed out, tossing a suitcase on to her bed and grabbing clothes willy-nilly from the wardrobe.

Gregory watched her wide-eyed. 'How long are you going for, in heaven's name?'

'I don't know. Why? . . . Oh, I see,' Kate said with a swift smile, putting a couple of blouses back in the cupboard. 'You're sure you two will be able to manage?'

'Mum . . .'

'I know *you* will, dear. But Jimmy . . .'

'I'll look after Jimmy,' Gregory promised.

'Thank you,' Kate said, touching his cheek with her fingertips as she passed, walking quickly into her bathroom, collecting toiletries and hurrying back to the bedroom again.

'*You'll* have a turn if you don't slow down,' Gregory told her.

'Hector will be here in a minute.'

'He'll wait.'

'Yes, dear, but the plane won't.'

Packed, Kate looked about the room, sucking the tip of one finger. Then she went to pick up the suitcase.

'I'll take that,' Gregory volunteered.

'Thank you, Gregory. Now, you're quite sure you'll –'

'Mum . . . yes. I'm quite sure.'

They were halfway down the stairs when the front doorbell shrilled. 'That'll be Hector. I just made it,' she said, as though this was a major achievement.

Robert Harvey eyed the two people sitting opposite him. He had started by saying, 'I don't have a lot of time,' but had become unnerved by the cold, unwavering stare the young man bestowed on him when he replied, 'I'm afraid you'll have to make time, Chief Inspector.'

Jimmy, for his part, was enjoying every minute of it. Well, maybe not enjoying it: fascinated by the situation was more like it. He found it hard to believe he was sitting opposite his father. He had a desperate urge to sneer, but he restrained himself. With Gregory's warnings ringing in his ear, he adopted instead an attitude of objective seriousness, consoling himself with the thought that this puffed-up, arrogant son of a bitch hadn't a clue who he was – no clue, either, of what was in store for him.

'I'm listening,' Harvey said coldly.

Jimmy took his time about replying. He was on his own now, with no Gregory by his side to prompt him, to step in and take over if he made a mess of things. But it was Gregory's tone that coloured his words when he finally asked, 'You are the father of Justin Harvey?'

Harvey nodded.

'This is Miranda Jay.'

Harvey nodded again.

'You know the name?'

'I've heard it.'

'I'm sure you have, Chief Inspector. Miss Jay is an *ex*-girlfriend of your son.'

Harvey nodded for the third time. 'Justin has told me.'

'And did he tell you Miranda is pregnant?' Jimmy asked with a thin smile.

'Yes,' Harvey admitted, and was pleased to see, for the first time, a flicker of surprise creep into the young man's eyes; less pleased when Jimmy recovered in a flash.

'And that he, Justin, your son, is the father?'

'That, as I understand it, is what Miss Jay maintains.'

'It's true,' Miranda put in suddenly.

Harvey pursed his lips.

'I assure you it *is* true, Chief Inspector,' Jimmy said. 'As you're no doubt aware, such things can be proved.'

Harvey rose from behind the desk and walked to the window. Staring out, his back to Jimmy and Miranda, he asked, 'Let us suppose it *is* true – what do you expect me to do about it?'

There was silence. Harvey swung round. Jimmy smiled up at him. 'Oh, nothing,' he told the chief inspector brightly.

Astonished, Harvey blinked. 'I'm sorry?'

Jimmy kept smiling. 'Nothing. We don't expect you to anything about it.'

'Then why are you here?'

'Because of something we think your son might have neglected to tell you.'

Harvey came back to his desk. He stood behind it, his hands deep in his trouser pockets. 'And what would that be?'

Jimmy gazed up at him innocently. 'That last night he – your son, Justin, tried to kill Miranda,' he announced.

For a moment Harvey looked as if he had been struck. His whole body stiffened. He swayed. And then, as if his emotions had taken on a life of their own, he heard himself start to laugh. 'He *what?*'

'He tried to kill Miranda,' Jimmy repeated.

Harvey sat down. 'Now, look –'

'You have a dark-blue Audi, don't you? Well, last night your son, driving a dark-blue Audi, tried to kill Miranda,' Jimmy said.

'Don't be –' Harvey began, about to tell the young man not to be absurd, but thought better of it. 'You . . . you recognised Justin?' he asked.

'I didn't, but Miranda did. And I think you'll agree she knows him well enough to know when she sees him or not.'

'It's true, Mr Harvey,' Miranda said. 'I wouldn't lie about something like this. I wouldn't try –'

Harvey stopped her by lowering himself into his chair. 'Tell me,' he said. 'Tell me exactly what happened.'

It sounded very much like Gregory speaking when Jimmy answered: 'It's very simple. Miranda and I were out for a meal. When we left the restaurant at about eleven your son drove your car at Miranda. He mounted the pavement at high speed and tried to knock her down. If I hadn't been there to pull her out of the way he'd probably have succeeded. He didn't stop. He drove off. That's it.'

Harvey stared at Miranda. 'Are you . . . are you absolutely certain it was Justin?' he asked intently.

171

'She's absolutely certain,' Jimmy told him.

'I was asking Miranda.'

'Absolutely certain,' Miranda confirmed.

Jimmy wasn't happy with the snub. 'He's been trying to make Miranda have an abortion,' he said.

Harvey nodded. Or rather, his headed nodded as though his mind was on other things.

'She wouldn't agree, of course. Vile things, abortions,' Jimmy went on. 'So . . .' He left the conclusion hanging in space.

It seemed a very long time before Harvey said, 'I'll talk to Justin.'

Jimmy gave a scoffing laugh. 'You'll have to do a lot more than just talk to him.'

Harvey stared at Jimmy in silence as though the full ramifications of what he had been told were finally penetrating his consciousness. 'The matter will be investigated,' he said finally.

'By you, I suppose,' Jimmy said scornfully.

'Initially.'

'And then?'

'Depending on what Justin says –'

'Not good enough, Chief Inspector,' Jimmy told him, and took great pleasure in seeing Harvey wince.

'Mr Harvey, I don't . . .' Miranda started, and then glanced at Jimmy. Harvey regarded her hopefully. Jimmy nodded. 'Chief Inspector, I don't want to cause . . . I mean . . .'

'What Miranda means, Chief Inspector, is that she doesn't want to do anything that would damage *your* career. I mean, we both recognise how *very* important your career is to you.'

'So what is it you *do* want?' Harvey demanded, a note of exasperation in his voice.

Jimmy decided to let him stew for a while, and during the silence he recalled the speech he and Gregory had rehearsed so gleefully. 'The reason we came to you directly, Chief Inspector, is because Miranda, and I, well, we both understand it was probably a moment of madness on Justin's part. But it's worrying that first your son wants to have the baby killed –'

Harvey flinched.

'– aborted,' Jimmy corrected. 'But it's the same thing, isn't it, really? And when that fails, he attempts to kill both mother and child. Miranda simply wants you to warn your son that we know it was him, and if he should ever try –'

'You're saying?' Harvey interrupted.

'Miranda's saying that this isn't – what do you call it? – isn't an official complaint. You can investigate it as much as you like. You can talk to Justin for as long as you want. All Miranda wants is for you to be aware what your son is up to . . . what he is capable of, and to make sure he doesn't try anything like this again.'

Harvey suddenly felt suspicion creep into his mind. It was ridiculous to suppose that that these two had come to see him just to have him slap Justin's wrists. But, 'I see,' he said.

In his mind's eye Jimmy saw Gregory beaming at him. 'After all,' he now told Harvey, 'it wouldn't be doing the baby any favours if it started life knowing its father had tried to kill it, would it, now?' He raised his eyebrows. Harvey didn't reply. 'And it *is* Miranda's intention to have the baby,' Jimmy continued, leaving the matter in no doubt whatever.

Harvey nodded, but said nothing.

'I'm sure *you* wouldn't encourage Justin to keep pressing for an abortion.' Jimmy let his voice rise towards the end of the statement, turning it into a question.

Harvey shook his head, his eyebrows twitching as if something still puzzled him, or as if he had solved the conundrum and found the answer even more disconcerting.

'I knew you wouldn't.' Jimmy stood up and offered Miranda his hand. Together, hand in hand, they walked to the door. Then Jimmy turned and looked directly back at Harvey. 'It's an abomination, isn't it?'

Whether it was something about the icy way the young man asked the question, or whether the chief inspector genuinely just realised it, he said suddenly, 'I didn't get *your* name.'

'James,' Jimmy told him. 'My friends call me Jimmy.'

And, before Harvey could pursue it further, they had left the office.

That day Gary Hubbard worked as hard as he'd ever done. It was as though he was filled with a monstrous energy that somehow had to be expended. It was also a cleansing. As he worked, feeling the perspiration trickle down his back despite the cold wind that blew steadily in from the river, Gary convinced himself that his labour, and the exhausting nature of it, was preparing him for the biggest challange of his life, greater even than killing – and getting away with it, of course. Yet it wasn't, as far as he could tell, a mission precisely. It was something more momentous than that. And whatever it was would come to *him*. All he had to do was wait, and during the waiting prepare himself.

'Gary!' one of his workmates called. 'Hey, Gary!'

But Gary pretended not to hear. He continued working, heaving breeze-blocks into place, their rough edges cutting into the flesh of his hands. But even this discomfort seemed to have a significance. Through pain to purity, he remembered reading somewhere, and remembered, too, that he had scoffed at the idea. It was different now, though.

'Sod you, then,' his workmate shouted.

From his vantage-point high up in the scaffolding Gary saw the building crew knock off for their lunch break, saw them enter the small hut, some of them opening packets of sandwiches as they went. Meat paste came to Gary's mind. That's what most of them ate, meat paste. Too lazy, too ignorant to make anything better, they settled for meat paste, scraping the last remnant from the jar. Waste not, want not, someone had said to him once. He paused and tried to recall who it was. He couldn't remember.

That was the trouble: so many people had said so many things to him throughout his life. Stupid things. What were they called? Platitudes, that was it. He smiled to himself, pleased that he had recalled the word, but suddenly also remembering: 'Do you recognise him?', remembering himself staring at a likeness that could have been him, almost certainly was him, yet denying it was him. Gary frowned. That, he thought, was wicked. People making him deny . . . He went back to work.

The instant Robert Harvey came into the incident room, before he had uttered a word, George Pope and Alan Kelly, the only two members of the team there, realised that he was in a foul mood. He didn't acknowledge either of them, walking instead directly to the information board and staring at it.

It was both foolish and ill-timed but Pope chose that moment to say: 'The Super's been looking for you, boss.'

'Let him look,' Harvey growled.

He leant closer to the board, fixing his gaze on the photograph of Jamie Scubin which had recently been added. 'McVinnie says there were traces of flour on Scubin's jeans,' he said.

'Flour? You mean –?' Pope started to ask.

'Flour. You know – the stuff you make bread with,' Harvey told him huffily, ignoring the fact that he had reacted in much the same way when the doctor mentioned the flour to him.

'That's new,' Kelly observed. 'There's nothing connecting Hubbard to a bakery, though, is there?'

'He doesn't *have* to be connected to a bakery. The flour was on the lad's jeans. Only on his jeans. Nothing on his trainers. At some point the left leg of his jeans lay in some flour.'

'Could have picked it up anywhere, boss. Could have been on his jeans for ages. Not the cleanest little sod, was he?' Kelly said. 'Maybe the flour . . .'

'McVinnie is positive the boy was killed *before* he came in contact with the flour. The flour is on top of the blood.'

'Oh.'

'It's only in the one small area,' Harvey continued. 'Just on the lower half of the left leg of the jeans.' He peered closer at the photograph as though attempting to see the flour stain.

'What if he was killed, stripped, and only the *jeans* thrown on to the flour?' Pope suggested.

Harvey nodded. 'I'd thought of that.'

'The van,' Kelly said suddenly. Harvey and Pope looked at him. 'If Hubbard killed Scubin and used the van to transport the body to where we found it –'

But already George Pope was objecting. 'There'd have been traces of flour on the other bodies.'

'Not necessarily,' Kelly insisted, none too happy at having his idea shot down without a proper hearing. 'It only means that the others didn't happen to touch the flour. The boss said there was probably only a small area of it.' He paused. 'Or maybe Hubbard only bought the flour *after* he'd killed the others.'

'Jim said the van was clean as a whistle,' Pope said.

'He wasn't looking for a bit of flour, was he?' Kelly asked dismissively.

'Well, my bet is if Hubbard's our man and if he's been using his van to transport the bodies, there'd have been *some* forensic evidence common to them all.'

'Did anyone check to see how long he'd owned the van?' Harvey asked suddenly.

'Yep. Jim did. Had it for years.'

'Shit!' Harvey swore. 'I thought maybe . . . I'm inclined to agree with you, George. If the van has been used, there should be something in forensics to link the victims.'

Pope looked pleased. He gave Alan Kelly a wink. But his smugness evaporated when Harvey went on, 'So, maybe he hasn't been using the van at all. Christ! Maybe Hubbard isn't our man.' He sounded thoroughly frustrated. 'Anyway, I'd better go and see what the Super wants, I suppose.'

'Take the wind out of his sails, boss,' Kelly said encouragingly.

'Using what?' Harvey demanded, slamming the door behind him.

'If only you could have seen his face!' Jimmy Renfrew waltzed about the bedroom.

'Sit down, will you, Jimmy?' Gregory said.

'Jesus, Greg, I wouldn't want to be pretty-boy Justin when his daddy gets his hands on him.'

'Are you going to tell me about it or not?' Gregory demanded.

'Tell you . . . ? Oh, yeah. Sure.' Jimmy sat down at the desk beside his brother, pulling up his knees and hugging them. 'You'd have been really proud of me, Greg,' he said.

'Just tell me what happened and then I'll tell you whether I'm proud of you or not.'

'Well, in we went. When I introduced Miranda he knew exactly who she was. He –'

'You didn't give him *your* name?' Gregory interrupted anxiously.

'Of course not. What d' you take me for?'

'Okay. Sorry. Go on.'

'Well, he knew who she was but decided to play it cool. By the way, Justin's already told him he's the father of Miranda's brat.'

Gregory made a pouting face that indicated he had expected as much.

'Anyway, I let him think we were there about the baby, and he asked what we expected *him* to do about it.' Jimmy broke into a manic cackle. 'He was totally gobsmacked when I said we didn't expect him to do a damn thing.'

Gregory nodded his approval.

'But when I told him Justin had tried to knock Miranda down . . . well, he was only fucking shattered.'

Gregory frowned. 'He believed you?' he asked as if he found this disturbing.

'Not at first. But we convinced him. Yeah, we convinced the bastard, all right.'

'What did he say to that?'

'Didn't give him a chance to say much. Tell you what, though, he got very suspicious when I said we weren't making a formal complaint. I could see it in his beady eyes. Couldn't understand why Justin was being let off so lightly.'

'But he accepted your –'

Jimmy nodded. He cackled again. 'Even got him to say he didn't approve of abortion. I called it an abomination, I did, and he agreed. Jesus, Greg, it was just perfect.'

'How did you leave it?'

'Just that he was going to *talk* to Justin. Made no secret of the fact that if anything untoward happened to Miranda again we'd know where to look for the culprit.'

Gregory nodded. 'You did well, Jimmy.' Then he grinned. 'I *am* proud of you.' He reached out both arms and gave his brother a hug.

'Knew you would be.'

Gregory leant back in his chair, swinging on the back legs. He folded his hands behind his head and gazed at Jimmy. Finally he brought the chair back on all fours with a thump. 'I think we can move on to the next phase.'

'Yes!' Jimmy said, and punched the air.

'Miranda,' Gregory said.

'What about her?'

'We don't need her any more. She could become a liability. Dump her.'

'Aw, Greg. I was just getting to –'

'Dump her.'

'I'm supposed to phone her later,' Jimmy protested.

'Then phone her and dump her.'

'I have to?'

Gregory nodded.

'Whatever you say,' Jimmy agreed reluctantly. 'What the hell am I going to say to her?'

'You'll think of something. Just get rid of her,' Gregory told him sternly.

'Sorry, Miranda, you're dumped,' Jimmy practised.

Gregory gave a thin smile. 'That'll do.'

'Oh, sure. I couldn't just leave it for a day or two?' Jimmy asked hopefully.

Gregory shook his head slowly.

'No. I suppose not.'

'I suppose not,' Chief Inspector Robert Harvey replied to Superintendent Peter Donnelly's observation that things didn't appear to be moving too swiftly. 'But we have a suspect,' he added.

The Superintendent nodded. 'So I'm told,' he said, turning over a couple of pages that lay on the desk before him. 'Gary Hubbard?' He looked up questioningly.

It was Harvey's turn to nod.

'Is he a *prime* suspect?'

Harvey blew air from his mouth. 'He's our *only* suspect.'

'But you don't have enough to charge him?'

'Not yet, no.'

Superintendent Donnelly took to shaking his head sadly. 'Robert, Robert,' he sighed. 'I have purposely kept out of your way. I've given you a free rein, have I not? You have had my complete confidence. And yet . . .' The superintendent stopped and eyed Harvey, seeming to expect an answer.

But Robert Harvey was reluctant to give him one. He stared back, not directly at his superior but at some point an inch or so above his head. He didn't trust himself to look the man directly in the eye. Certainly Donnelly had kept out of the way. Certainly he had given him a free rein. And Harvey knew precisely why: let him, Harvey, arrest the killer, charge him, and in would step Donnelly to claim all the credit. As to having Donnelly's complete confidence – that was a laugh, a sardonic laugh, but a laugh nonetheless. 'We're getting there,' he said finally.

Donnelly waited.

'Getting there slowly,' Harvey repeated, almost as if he was trying to convince himself.

'Too slowly, I'm afraid, Robert,' Donnelly said.

It was Harvey who now waited.

'How many bodies do we have?' Donnelly asked. Without waiting for an answer he consulted the papers on his desk again. 'Dunn, Meehan, Douglas, Salmon, Weaver and now Scubin. Six bodies, Robert. Six bodies. How many more do you need, for heaven's sake?'

'We're not sure about –'

'Not sure? Not sure?' Donnelly interposed.

'We're almost certain Hubbard killed Weaver. We're not sure he's responsible for the others. It's likely, but not certain.'

'Almost certain, not sure, likely, not certain?' Donnelly repeated with distaste. 'A litany of incompetence if ever I heard one.'

Robert Harvey was finding it difficult to control himself. His body tensed and his face reddened. And perhaps the superintendent realised he had overstepped the mark. In a less sarcastic tone he asked, 'You've questioned this man Hubbard?'

'Yes.'

'And?'

'There are inconsistencies.'

'And you've checked these inconsistencies?'

'We're in the process of checking them.'

Superintendent Donnelly pushed back his chair and stood up. 'Robert . . . I regard you as more than just a colleague,' he said, turning away as he spoke, giving Harvey the chance to give a wry smile unobserved. 'We've had our differences, certainly, but . . .' Maybe even the superintendent appreciated the hypocrisy in what he was saying. Anyway, he stopped, swung back and asked: 'Can I expect a result in the *near* future?'

Harvey committed himself. 'Yes.'

Donnelly's attitude changed yet again. He became expansive. He threw out his arms. 'That's all I wanted to hear.'

Robert Harvey was smarting as he made his way down the corridor to his own office. And his humour wasn't about to be improved.

'Sir?'

He swung round and saw Susan Dill and Jim Callaghan chasing after him. He stopped, allowing them to catch up. 'What is it, Susan?'

Dill looked at Callaghan and back to Harvey.

'What is it?' Harvey demanded again.

'It's about the van, guv. Hubbard's van,' Callaghan said in a timid way.

'What about it?'

'George and Alan were just saying –'

'What about the van?' Harvey asked, setting out for his office again.

'About having it checked.'

Harvey kept moving. 'You *did* check it?' he asked on the trot. But when Callaghan didn't answer, he stopped and rounded on him. 'You *did* check it?' he asked again, coldly.

Callaghan took a deep breath. 'Well, no. I –' He stopped when he saw the fury on Harvey's face.

'My office. Both of you,' Harvey shouted, leaving them to follow.

He was behind his desk, seated, livid, by the time Callaghan and Dill came into the office and shut the door. 'I – told – you – to – check – that – van,' he said, using a finger to jab home each word.

Callaghan hung his head.

'Didn't I?'

'Yes, boss.'

'And you didn't?'

'The neighbours said he'd had it for –'

181

'Neighbours? Oh, I see. So that's what you base your investigation on, is it? What the neighbours tell you?'

'No, boss, but –'

'Shut up, Callaghan,' Harvey said, turning away in disgust and allowing himself an enormous sigh. Still not looking back, he said,

'Susan, would you *kindly* check out that van for me?'

'Yes, boss.'

'You want me to –' Callaghan began.

Harvey turned and glared at him. 'You know what I want you to do, Callaghan. I want you to get out of my sight,' he bellowed, and waited, staring at them, as they retreated.

10

It was as though Gary Hubbard knew he would soon be arrested. He got home at just after four in the afternoon: heavy rain had forced the site manager to call it a day early.

Gary parked his new van in its usual space, and walked quickly to his building, turning up his collar and hunching his shoulders as he went. Inside his flat, he shut the door and cocked his head, listening.

On tiptoe, he walked down the narrow hallway and stopped outside the sitting-room door. It was ajar. As he had seen the police do so often on television, American cops mostly, guns at the ready, he silently pushed the door wide open. Then, swiftly, he entered the room, flicking his eyes about, a look of genuine disappointment descending on his face when he found it was empty.

Gary Hubbard was play-acting. He enjoyed play-acting. He knew full well the sitting-room would be empty, but the pretence that the enemy, whoever that might be, would be lurking there was all part of the fun. So much fun that, on this particular afternoon, he carried out the same charade in each of the rooms in the flat, moving, silent as sin, from sitting-room to bedroom, from bedroom to bathroom, from bathroom to kitchen. And only when he had inspected the entire flat did he relax and, with a shake of his head, cease his dramatics. There were things to be done, he told himself. And he had little time in which to do them.

Gray began to prepare himself. He wanted everything in order. He wanted to be sitting in his armchair, a beer in his hand, perhaps browsing through a newspaper. He wanted to be able to look up and smile without fear when the police arrived. But that would be later, much later.

Gary Hubbard had something else he wanted to do first.

'Who was that on the phone?' Jimmy asked, coming into the bedroom from the bathroom, drying his hands before tossing the towel on the bed.

'Mum,' Gregory told him, eyeing the towel. 'Hang that up.'

Jimmy pulled a face behind Gregory's back, but he picked the towel from the bed and slung it over the back of a chair.

'In the bathroom where it belongs,' Gregory said.

'In a sec,' Jimmy replied, combing his hair. 'What did Mum want? How's Uncle Donald?'

'Distraught. Bad.'

'What?'

'Mum's distraught. Uncle Donald's bad.'

'How bad?'

'Probably won't make it.'

'Oh.'

'Comes to us all,' Gregory said philosophically.

'Wow, I never knew that,' Jimmy said, and put down the comb.

Gregory gave him a look.

Jimmy returned a forced and phony grin. 'I take it Mum's staying up there a bit longer?'

Gregory shrugged. 'Depends. She'll let us know.'

Jimmy concentrated deeply for a moment. 'You don't think . . . if Uncle Donald *does* snuff it – you don't think Mum would be daft enough to ask fat Alice to come and live down here – with us?'

'Of course she won't,' Gregory said. 'You don't think Mum's going to let anyone intrude into our cosy little set-up, do you? Shit, she'd end up strangling Alice within a week.'

'I hope you're right.'

'Course I'm right. Anyway, Donald Duck hasn't gone up the yellow brick road yet.'

'True.'

'We'll worry about Alice if he does.'

Jimmy brightened. 'Right,' he replied, and immediately dismissed his concerns from his mind. He gathered up the towel from the back of the chair and headed for the bathroom.

'You phoned that Miranda yet?' Gregory called after him.

'I told you, I'm calling her this evening.'

'We've got work to do this evening,' Gregory said.

Instantly Jimmy was back at the bedroom door. His eyes shone as he slapped aftershave on to his cheeks, wincing and hissing as the alcohol stung. 'What work?'

'Phone Miranda,' Gregory told him.

'What's the time?'

'Half four.'

'No point. She won't be there.'

Gregory gave Jimmy a disbelieving look.

'Honest,' Jimmy protested. 'Told me she wouldn't be home till round about seven.'

'You lying to me?'

'Would I?'

'You –'

'I'll call her at seven-thirty. Promise. What work?'

'I'll tell you *after* you've given Miranda the good news,' Gregory bartered with a wicked grin.

'Bastard!'

'You and me both.'

At the moment Gregory was confirming their illegitimacy Robert Harvey arrived home, slamming the front door behind him and storming into the living-room. Helen Harvey looked up from her magazine in surprise. 'You're home early, Robert,' she commented, although without too much interest.

'Where's Justin?' Harvey demanded.

'Upstairs in his room. Why?'

'I want to talk to him,' he said, making for the door.

Immediately Helen was on the alert. 'What's happened, Robert? He's not in any trouble, is he?'

'I hope not. I need to talk to him.'

Robert Harvey made it as far as the foot of the stairs before he realised his wife was following. 'No, Helen. You stay here. I need to talk to him alone.'

Helen shot both hands to her face. 'He *is* in trouble,' she said in a sort of wail.

'I'll tell you all about it when I come down.'

'Robert –'

'When I come down,' he told her adamantly, and went up the stairs two at a time.

Justin Harvey didn't hear his father come into his room. He was lying on his bed, his face to the wall, enormous earphones clamped over his ears. He stared in astonishment as his father wrenched them off. 'What –'

'Sit up,' Harvey ordered.

Justin did as he was told, swinging his legs off the bed, sticking fingers in both ears and jiggling them as though the music still thundered there.

'I had Miranda Jay in my office this morning.'

'Oh, shit. I'm sorry, Dad. I never thought she'd –'

'She claims you tried to kill her last night,' Harvey said bluntly.

Justin sat bolt upright. He made a funny little gurgling noise that seemed to come from somewhere in his chest: a wheezy sort of laugh. He started to shake his head in bewilderment. He kept shaking it for a long time, for as long as his father stared at him and was silent.

'Say something,' Harvey eventually demanded.

'Say what? She's lying. I never tried to kill her. I never even saw her last night.'

'You told me you were going to see her,' his father pointed out.

'I was *supposed* to see her. She rang me and asked me to meet her. I went but she never showed up.'

'Huh,' Harvey grunted.

'It's true, Dad. She never showed. I didn't see her last night.'

'How come, then, that she and another witness saw you, in my car, drive up on to the pavement and deliberately try to knock her down?'

'They couldn't have! Dad . . . look, ask David. I phoned him late last night, after I got home, and told him Miranda had stood me up.'

'Covering your back?'

'I wasn't covering my back,' Justin insisted, just about screaming.

'Both Miranda and her companion saw you,' his father insisted.

Justin took to shaking his head again, helplessly now. 'They can't have. They can't have. Must have seen someone else and *thought* it was me.'

Harvey shook his head too. 'They both saw my car with you driving it.'

'Dad!' Justin wailed.

'You had my car last night, didn't you?'

'Yes, but –'

'Justin –'

'Dad –'

Robert Harvey sat on the bed beside his son. He didn't look at him. He folded his hands, letting them hang between his legs, and studied them. 'Why would Miranda concoct such a story?' he asked in a reasonable voice. 'And don't say she wants revenge on you because of the baby. Please.'

'It's the only reason I can think of,' Justin said miserably.

'That simply doesn't make sense, Justin. All right, she wants to have the baby, you want the pregnancy terminated. You've had words. You've split up. Why would she –'

'I don't *know!*' Justin was close to tears.

'She seemed a perfectly sane girl to me,' his father observed.

'She *is*, Dad, but –'

'But you're asking me to believe that this sane girl can somehow

187

manipulate people to such an extent that she can get someone else – a young chap, about your age, who seemed every bit as sane to me – to conspire with her in some outrageous figment of her imagination?' He started to shake his head again. 'I'm sorry, Justin, I just cannot –'

'Dad, I've told you the truth.'

'You haven't threatened her?'

'Threatened her?' Justin was shocked.

'You haven't given her any ultimatum about the baby?'

'No. No, I haven't. I told her I didn't want the baby. I tried to make her understand the best thing – for both of us – would be for her to have an abortion. That's all. There were no threats. I swear, Dad.'

'Just have an abortion. That's all,' Harvey repeated, but in a softer tone than he'd been using.

'That's all,' Justin assured him.

Harvey sighed, and stood up.

Justin looked at him. 'Dad, what's going to happen?'

His father gazed at him. 'Nothing. She doesn't want anything to happen.' He gave a quick, nervous little smile. 'That's the one thing that makes me think you *might* be telling the truth. To go to all that trouble, confronting me . . .' He stopped talking and thought for a moment. 'It doesn't make any sense at all,' he concluded finally, mostly to himself, walking heavily towards the door. Then he swung round, his anger returning. 'If I ever, ever find out that you lied to me –'

'Dad, I swear on my life I've told you the truth.'

'I certainly hope you have – for your sake,' Harvey told him. He put his hand on the door as if to open it and leave. Then he turned and stared at his son. 'You're not to go out of this house until we've had a chance to talk again – understood?'

Justin nodded.

'I mean it, Justin,' Harvey warned.

'I won't leave the house,' Justin said.

Harvey straightened his back. 'I've got to get back to the station. We'll —' he began, and then another thought struck him. 'Your mother,' he went on. 'She'll want to know what's going on.' He fell silent, frowning. 'Tell her . . . tell her you were done for speeding,' he instructed, and left the room without another word.

In his haste to get out of the house, Robert Harvey almost tripped over his wife. She was sitting on the stairs, camped there, it seemed, until she discovered what all the fuss was about. She stood up and faced her husband. 'Now, Robert —'

'*Not* now, Helen,' he told her. 'I have to get back to the station. I'll explain everything tonight.' He squeezed past her and made for the front door.

'Robert!'

'Later. It's nothing serious.' He opened the door. 'I might be late,' he said, and was gone.

There is sometimes, in madness, another person who thinks for you, unpegs your mental washing and carries it in as clouds presage rain, shuts and bolts the mind's window against what it cannot encompass: but there is always a door left open in the mind for the entrance and reception of the unprecedented, the tumultuous confusion that disorientates, that makes it impossible to distinguish right from wrong, that makes wrong take on the guise of right. And it was through this mental door that Gary Hubbard, still in his flat, now perceived that something approaching menace was wrapping itself around him. And perhaps it was to rid himself of this threat that Gary started to clean his flat, the word *purification* rising into his mind. He scrubbed, he dusted, he polished, inspecting each area and item, standing back and surveying his efforts in the manner of an ageing woman expecting a last-chance lover to call, or a priest, or death perhaps.

His task completed, Gary took a bath. He added a little Radox to the water, watching it bubble and foam. Then he added more, emptying the container as though he would not have any use for it in the future.

Bathed, and with the bath scrupulously cleaned, he began to dress. He was punctilious about this also, taking his time about choosing what to wear, changing his mind even when he appeared to have made his final decision. He was curiously serene, however, as though changing his mind was part of the ritual also. It was twenty past five by the time he was satisfied with his appearance.

It was twenty past five, also, when Chief Inspector Harvey got back to the station and made his way directly to the incident room.

'Boss,' Susan Dill greeted him.

'Where is everybody?'

'Alan and George have nipped down to the canteen,' Dill explained.

'And Callaghan?'

Dill looked uneasy. 'Obeying orders,' she said finally.

'What?'

'Keeping out of your way, boss.'

Harvey ignored that, leaving Susan Dill even more uneasy. And it was probably to leapfrog this disquiet that she said, 'I've checked the van, boss. It's not registered to Gary Hubbard.'

It took a moment or two for the information to sink in. 'Not registered to Gary Hubbard?' Harvey asked.

'Not yet. He only bought it a few days ago. From a garage.'

'Wait a minute, wait a minute. What was Callaghan on about, then? The neighbours –'

'Prior to buying *this* van he owned another. Another Ford Escort. Same colour. A bit older.'

'Jesus!' Harvey exclaimed. 'Susan, you're a gem.'

'His new van – his new, second-hand van – was previously owned by a Matthew Ball,' Dill told him. 'I managed to get hold of Ball. He's unemployed. Lives in Clapham. His last job was in an abattoir. When that closed he had to sell the van. Couldn't afford to run it, he says.' Dill paused, her mouth slightly open, her tongue flicking in and out twice. Harvey eyed her. 'I asked him if he ever carried flour

190

in the van,' Susan went on. 'He laughed at that. He said I'd make commissioner. It appears one of the last things he did before he sold the van was to go shopping. He bought a bag of flour among other things. The bag burst inside the van,' Susan Dill concluded, a little smugly.

'Christ, Susan, I wish I had more like you. That's brilliant work. Well done.'

'Thanks, boss.'

Harvey placed his buttocks on the edge of Dill's desk. 'This garage – Ball sold it directly to them?'

'Yes.'

'How long ago?'

'Three . . . four months.'

'And nobody else used the van between the time he sold it and the time Hubbard bought it?'

Susan Dill shook her head. 'No.'

'It fits, Susan. McVinnie said the flour on Scubin's jeans was several months old. The van was sold by Ball several months ago. It fits. It bloody fits. We've got him.' Harvey rubbed his hands together. 'Susan, get George and Alan back up here immediately.'

'Yes, boss,' Dill said, rising.

'And find Callaghan too.'

'I don't know where he –'

'He's got a mobile, hasn't he?'

'Yes.'

'Try that. I want everyone in on this.'

When Susan Dill had left the room, Harvey made his way slowly towards the information board. In a strangely tender gesture he reached out and touched each of the photographs with the tips of his fingers, almost caressing them.

Gregory and Jimmy Renfrew sat in front of the computer. There was one name on the screen:

DAVID PARSONS

'Right,' Gregory said. 'What do we know about him?'

'Why him?' Jimmy wanted to know.

'Because, James dear, he is going to be our secondary victim.'

Jimmy stared at his brother uncomprehendingly.

'It's going to be through Parsons that we get at Justin,' Gregory explained.

'And through Justin we get at –'

'Precisely,' Gregory said. 'Now, what do we know about him?'

'We know where he lives,' Jimmy said, and watched as Gregory put that into the computer.

'What else?'

'We know he's loaded,' Jimmy said.

'How loaded?'

'*Seriously* loaded, according to Miranda. Parents divorced. Mummy gives him anything he wants, when she's around. Not around much, though. Travels. Enjoying her alimony, I suppose.'

Gregory added all this into the computer, numbering each salient point in the margin. 'Next?'

'At the LSE.'

'Right. Next.'

'Sausage jockey.'

'*What?*'

Jimmy laughed. 'Bent. Queer. Ho-mo-sex-ual.'

'Thought you'd have put that in at number one, the fright it gave you,' his brother smirked.

'Huh.'

'Bent,' Gregory repeated as he tapped it in.

'Fancies Justin,' Jimmy said.

'Do we *know* that?'

Jimmy shrugged. 'Miranda says he kept trying to steal Justin away from her.'

'Not just being bitchy, was she?'

192

Jimmy gave this consideration. Then he shook his head. 'Not the bitchy sort,' he said. 'Anyway, we've seen the two of them together – Justin and David. Pretty obvious they're a bit more than chummy. Or Parsons would like them to be.'

'Good.' Gregory watched the information come up on the screen. 'Anything else?' he asked. 'What was the name of that gay bar he went into?'

'Forget it,' Jimmy said with a look of distaste. 'We know where it is, though.'

Gregory nodded, and tapped some more. 'You said he gave you the once over in the pub, didn't you?'

'Bloody stripped me,' Jimmy said.

FANCIES OUR JIMMY, Gregory added to the information.

'Fuck that,' Jimmy told him.

'It's just for the record,' Gregory answered. 'Just for the record.' He leant back. 'That's about it.'

'Not much there, is there?'

'Oh, enough to be getting on with, I think.'

'If you say so.'

Justin Harvey held the phone close to his mouth, and spoke in a low tone. 'David, can you come over this evening?'

'I *could*, but I was going to –'

'It's important, David. Really important.'

Justin's tone and insistence alerted David Parsons. 'You all right?'

'Yes, I'm okay. It's just . . . something's happened.'

'What?'

'I'll tell you when I see you.'

'Miranda?'

'Yes. But –'

'Well, you can't say I didn't warn you.'

'It's not just – look, come over, will you?'

'I said I would.'

'Thanks.'

193

'Be after nine.'

'Any time.'

DCI Harvey faced the team. They were all there, Callaghan included. Without prelude, Harvey told them what Susan Dill had uncovered.

'So we can arrest him, then – Hubbard?' Kelly asked.

'Yes,' Harvey confirmed. 'We arrest him. We tear his flat apart. We get that van into forensics.'

'Yes!' George Pope hissed.

'All right, all right. Calm down,' Harvey said, 'and listen to what I have to say. Jim,' he was gratified to see Callaghan jump. 'I want you and George to effect the arrest.'

Callaghan and Pope leapt to their feet.

'Listen to me,' Harvey warned. 'When you arrest him, make it clear the arrest is in connection with the death of Jason Weaver. Got that? Jason Weaver. Not Jamie Scubin. Jason Weaver.'

It was Alan Kelly who stated what was clearly going through all their minds. 'We've nothing that connects him with Weaver's killing, guv.'

'You think I don't know that?'

'So –'

'Just do what I say. I know what I'm doing.'

Kelly shrugged. 'You're the boss.'

'I sometimes wonder,' Harvey replied. He turned to Dill. 'Susan, you and Alan search the flat. Be thorough, please.'

'Right, boss.'

'I'll get on to McVinnie and have the van brought in.' He turned back to Callaghan. 'Jim, I don't want either you or George to so much as touch the van.'

Callaghan nodded.

'And above all don't let Hubbard go near it. I want that van to reach McVinnie exactly as it is. Understood?'

'Understood,' said Pope.

Callaghan nodded again.

'Well, get going.'

Harvey watched the team leave. Only when they had gone and shut the door behind them did he permit himself a huge grin and the luxurious stretch of a confident man.

11

'I thought you said we were working tonight,' Jimmy Renfrew remarked.

'Changed my mind,' Gregory told him. 'We need to think this thing out thoroughly.'

'*What* thing?' Jimmy asked anxiously. 'You don't tell me anything.'

'I tell you everything,' Gregory said. He looked at his brother archly. 'On a need-to-know basis,' he added. 'Anyway, by thing I mean our plan of action.'

'Oh.'

'I . . . *we* want everything to tie in neatly,' Gregory went on. 'Somehow we have to get –' He stopped abruptly, switched on the computer and started tapping in words.

Jimmy looked over his shoulder, mouthing the words as they appeared.

1. Chief Inspector Robert Harvey investigates serial killings.

Gregory looked at Jimmy. 'Right?'

'Right,' Jimmy agreed.

Gregory peered intently into his eyes. 'What I'd *like* to do is somehow have Justin arrested for those killings,' he said very quietly.

Jimmy gasped. 'That's crazy!'

'You think?'

'Course it's crazy. Maddest thing you've ever come up with,'

Jimmy replied, but then he grinned. 'Be brilliant if we could, though.'

'I think maybe we can,' Gregory said. 'Just maybe.'

2. According to papers all victims have their throats cut.

'True?'
'True.'

3. David Parsons is found dead – with his throat cut.

'Jesus!' Jimmy exclaimed.

4. Beside his body there's a wallet containing a library card, a video card, a donor card. Owner: Justin Harvey.

'You're out of your tiny mind,' Jimmy said gleefully.

Gregory didn't appear to hear him. He chewed on his bottom lip for a while, and then asked, 'Harvey wouldn't be allowed to investigate if his son was thought to be involved, would he?'

'Shouldn't think so.'

'I'm sure he wouldn't. Conflict of interest or something, isn't it?' Gregory asked, but didn't wait for a reply.

5. Chief Inspector Harvey removed from case. New investigators find out Justin has allegedly attempted to kill his ex-girlfriend, Miranda Jay. Find out his father knew and did nothing.

Gregory leant back. 'How's that for starters?'

'We'd have to kill Parsons?' Jimmy asked.

'Oh, yes,' Gregory told him in a matter-of-fact voice.

Jimmy wasn't fazed. 'How do we do that?'

Gregory smiled beatifically. '*You* use your charm, sunshine.'

'I don't get you.'

'You will. I'll explain in a minute,' Gregory told him. 'Right now you go and phone Miranda and get her off our backs.'

Jimmy was hesitant.

'Go and phone her,' Gregory insisted.

'Greg –'

'What's the matter with you? Don't tell me you've fallen for her or something?'

'Shit, no,' Jimmy replied quickly. 'Don't give a toss about her.' Then he grinned. 'Wouldn't mind getting my leg over again, though.'

'You're a pervert,' Gregory told him.

'Okay, I'm a pervert. But a fuck's a fuck, and she wasn't that bad.'

Gregory was getting impatient. 'Just go and phone her, will you? If this –' he tapped the computer screen '– is to have any chance of working, we can't have bloody Miranda Jay moping about, making lovey-dovey eyes at you.'

Jimmy sighed.

'Besides, if you and she are an item the police would want to question you and –'

'They'll want to question me if it comes out Justin tried to run her down. I was there, remember?'

'They'll be looking for a Jimmy.' Gregory paused. 'A James,' he corrected himself. 'We should have Justin well stitched up before they get round to you – if they ever do.' He gave Jimmy a piercing stare. 'She doesn't know your last name, does she?'

'Never told her.'

'You're sure?'

'Yeah, I'm sure.'

Gregory looked suspicious. 'She never asked?'

198

'Sure she asked.' Jimmy stretched. 'Told her it was —' Then he burst out laughing. 'Can't remember what I told her. It sure wasn't Renfrew, though.' He stood up and walked to the phone on the table between the beds. He slumped down on his bed, and looked at his brother. 'What do I tell her?'

'Goodbye,' Gregory said curtly.

'Yeah, I know, but she's going to want to know why.'

'Oh, tell her anything you want. Tell her she was a lousy shag,' Gregory suggested cruelly.

'I can't tell her *that*,' Jimmy protested.

'Sure you can.' Gregory laughed. 'Just tell her whatever you want, but dump her.'

Jimmy picked up the phone and dialled Miranda's number. As he waited for her to answer, he asked hopefully, 'Couldn't I simply not see her again?'

Gregory gave him a look that said no, he couldn't simply not see her again.

'Hello? Miranda?'

'Hi, Jimmy. How are you?'

'Me? Oh, I'm fine,' Jimmy said, giving Gregory a grimace as his brother silently mimicked him. 'Miranda, I'm not going to be able to make it this evening.'

'That's too bad. I —'

'I've been thinking,' Jimmy said.

'He's been thinking,' Gregory whispered in quiet despair.

'I've decided it would be better for both of us if —'

'Oh, Jimmy,' Miranda cut in, anticipating the news.

'I'm not going to see you again,' Jimmy told her.

Gregory nodded his approval.

'Why, Jimmy? What have I done?'

'You haven't done anything. It's just —' Jimmy paused.

'Just that you're a lousy shag,' Gregory said in a stage whisper and rocked with silent laughter.

Despite himself, Jimmy let out a guffaw, looking about as though to find something to throw at his brother: Gregory moved his body from side to side, preparing to evade the missile, covering his mouth to suppress his merriment.

'Jimmy?' Miranda called plaintively.

'It's just that you're a lousy shag,' Jimmy told her, and heard her start to sob before he slammed down the phone.

For a moment there was dead silence, and then the twins began to roar with laughter – Jimmy rolling on the bed and kicking his legs in the air; Gregory, fists clenched, thumping his chest, tears streaming down his face. 'Poor cow,' he said between spasms of laughter. 'Poor fucking cow.' Then, 'You're an evil uncaring bastard, James Renfrew.'

'You told me to say it,' Jimmy protested, spluttering the words.

'I never thought you *would*, though.'

'Always do what I'm told, I do.'

That simple statement seemed to bring Gregory back down to earth. He clicked off his laughter as though by some switch in his brain. 'I'm counting on that, Jimmy,' he said seriously. '*Absolutely* counting on it.'

'You've done everything by the book?' Harvey demanded.

Jim Callaghan nodded.

'Read him his rights?'

'Yes.'

'How was he?'

Callaghan glanced at Pope.

'If it wasn't mad I'd say he was expecting us,' George Pope said.

Harvey didn't find it mad. 'Maybe he was,' he said. 'Right, let's go.'

At the door he paused. 'And don't forget, either of you, that as far as Hubbard is concerned, we're only questioning him about Jason Weaver.'

Callaghan and Pope nodded.

'I don't want him to get any inkling we suspect him of the other killings. Not till I'm ready. Clear?'

'Yes, guv.'

'I'm not expecting any joy from him this evening, if the previous interview was anything to go by. But that suits me. He can stew in the cells overnight. Might even give him something to think about. If *I* can think of something, that is,' he added with a tight smile.

'Yes, guv,' Callaghan said a bit too quickly.

'Ready?'

'Ready.'

Gary Hubbard had not, as he had dreamed, been sitting quietly, sipping a beer and browsing through a newspaper when the police came for him. He had been in his kitchen, his hand outstretched to take a knife from the rack, when the pounding started on his front door. Very slowly Gary withdrew his hand. A smile rippled on the corners of his lips; a minute, two minutes at most, later, and he would have been leaving the flat, the knife in his pocket.

And now, sitting once again in the interview room, avoiding the gaze of the young uniformed officer who stood, still as a statue, by the door, he wondered if that tiny trick of time was to prove an omen. In his mind he gave a shrug.

And he shrugged his shoulders when Chief Inspector Harvey enquired: 'You understand why you have been arrested?'

Gary hadn't, in fact, spoken a word for several minutes, remaining sullenly silent as the tapes were placed in the machine and DS Callaghan gave out the time and date and year, and the names of those present.

'Is that a yes?' Harvey asked.

Gary smiled. 'It was a shrug,' he said.

Harvey smiled back. 'Does it mean yes?'

Gary nodded. 'It means yes.'

'Fine. Now, do you want legal representation?'

Gary Hubbard just stared blankly, and Harvey wondered if he had been understood. 'Do you want a solicitor?'

'No.'

'You're sure?'

'Quite sure.'

'Right, well, if as we proceed you feel it would be advisable to have a solicitor, you *can* have one.'

'I know.'

'Right, Gary – you don't mind if I call you Gary?' Harvey asked affably, and when Hubbard failed to reply, he continued. 'Good. Now, Gary, I'll be frank with you. We are not at all satisfied that you have told us all you know about the death of your workmate Jason Weaver.'

Gary raised his eyebrows.

'So, it's back to the beginning, I'm afraid. You told us you worked with Jason but didn't know him. Right?'

Gary nodded.

'I'll accept that. You also said that you never saw him apart from the hours when you were working together. Right?'

Again Gary nodded.

'My problem with that is that we have two witnesses who tell us they saw you standing over Jason Weaver's body.'

Gary frowned. 'Is that what they said? They saw *me*?' he asked quietly, reasonably.

'You or someone very like you,' Harvey allowed, controlling his breathing.

Gary nodded. 'Someone very like me,' he repeated. He nodded again. 'Maybe they did see someone very like me,' he admitted, 'but they didn't see me, did they? Not for definite.'

Harvey let Gary bask in his smugness for a while, and then, out of the blue, he asked, 'How long have you owned your van, Gary?' and felt his heart thump as Gary froze, his eyes taking on a steely, hunted aspect.

'My van?' Gary asked finally, recovering, his voice casual.

'Your van,' Harvey repeated.

'Not long.'

'How long? A year? A month? A week? How long, Gary?'

Gary's reply was barely audible.

'I didn't catch that,' Harvey told him. 'A little louder, please – for the tape.'

'A few days.'

'A few days?' Harvey asked, loading his question with exaggerated surprise. When Gary didn't answer, he asked, 'Where did you buy it?'

'Dagenham.'

'Dagenham? That's a long way to go to –'

'Garage there had the one I wanted.'

'And before that what did you drive, Gary?'

'Another van.'

'Another van. Same make? Same colour? Almost identical apart from the year?'

Gary Hubbard stared straight into Harvey's eyes, but stayed silent.

'You said that the garage in Dagenham had the one you wanted – am I right? I'd also be right in suggesting that you therefore specifically wanted a van that was all but identical to your old van, would I?'

'They're good vans.'

'I'm sure they are. Just a bit odd you went for the same colour too, though, isn't it? Like you were trying to fool people into thinking they were one and the same van, or am I being a bit too suspicious?' Harvey asked with what he hoped was a disarming smile.

'Most Ford Escort vans are white,' said Gary sullenly.

'You sold your original van, I take it. To whom?' Harvey asked, ignoring him.

Gary shook his head. 'Dunno.'

Harvey leant back in his chair and folded his hands behind his head. 'You don't know to whom you sold your original van?'

Gary looked away.

'Someone walked up to you on the street and said, "Hey, there, Gary, I want to buy your van" – is that how it was?'

Without wanting to, Hubbard gave a tiny sneer.

'Or maybe it was that famous man in the pub? Some guy you've never seen before met you in a pub – you won't remember the name of the pub, of course – and did a deal to buy your van?' Harvey asked and waited.

Gary frowned as though he was thinking – about that, or something quite different.

'No?' Harvey asked.

'No,' Gary confirmed quietly.

'You advertised it?'

'No.'

'You have me really baffled now, Gary. I mean, it's such a simple question: what did you do with your original van?'

Gary took a deep breath. 'Had it scrapped.'

'You had it scrapped,' Harvey said as if that was the answer he had been waiting for. 'Fine. You had it scrapped. Where?'

'Dagenham.'

'Dagenham again!'

'The engine seized.'

'I see. The engine seized, so how did you get it to Dagenham?'

'It seized *in* Dagenham.'

'Ah, that explains that,' Harvey said, and then gave a hearty, good-natured laugh. 'Don't tell me it seized right outside the scrapyard gates?'

'It did, as a matter of fact.'

'Well I never. Some people have all the luck, eh?'

Still jovial, Harvey got up from the table and wandered, almost casually, over to George Pope who was seated in the corner of the room. He bent down. 'Get on to Dagenham. Ask them to check any scrapyards. Fax them a copy of the identikit. See if any scrapyard manager can put Hubbard's face to it.' Then he wandered back to the table, waiting for Pope to leave before sitting down. Seated, he waited for Callaghan to feed the information of Pope's departure into the tape.

'Before it seized, Gary, was the van going all right?'

'So-so.'

'No major problems? You could drive to work?'

'When there was work.'

'Ah, yes. The weather. Tell me something, I have one hell of a job getting my car to start these winter mornings. The van started up okay, did it?'

'Yes,' Gary answered, but there was a tiny hesitation in his reply.

'Oh, by the way, I've just sent that detective to see if we can't locate the van. Be a great help if we could find it. Great help to you too, incidently.'

Gary couldn't restrain himself. 'To me? How?'

Harvey glanced at Jim Callaghan like someone unsure of what he was about to do. 'Can't make any difference, I suppose. Telling you. You see, we're certain whoever killed Jason took him there in some sort of vehicle,' Harvey lied, gambling that Hubbard wouldn't remember that vehicles couldn't be taken into the underpass. 'That being said, there would definitely be forensic evidence in the vehicle. No question whatever about that. Now, if we had your van and could find *no* forensic evidence, you'd be in the clear.'

Gary's mind raced. Everything Harvey said was reasonable enough. And yet, and yet . . .

'Tell you what,' Harvey was saying. 'Let's take a break. See if the detective comes up with anything. If he does – finds your old van, I mean – we'll have it checked, and if it's clean . . .' Harvey waved his arms to indicate freedom. 'Bet you could use a cup of tea, anyway. I know I could,' he said, and nodded to Callaghan, smiling pleasantly at Gary while the tape was shut down.

In the corridor outside, Harvey and Callaghan watched Gary being taken back to the cells.

'Guv?'

'Yes, Jim – oh, by the way, I owe you an apology –'

'My fault, guv.'

'I'm sorry,' Harvey said anyway.

'Can I ask what you're up to?'

'You make me sound devious, Jim. What am I up to? Well, I'm trying, to put it crudely, to fuck the bastard's head up. I know we can't pin Weaver's death on him, but I really need him to think that's all we're interested in him for. We'll let him go in the morning. By that time we'll have McVinnie's report on the flour. *He* assured me that if we gave him the *right* flour he could match it to the flour on Scubin's jeans. If McVinnie gives us the match we rearrest Hubbard, this time for Scubin, and we're in business.'

Callaghan shook his head. 'Yeah,' he said. 'That's devious.'

Harvey laughed. 'Now, we all go home and try and get some sleep.' He started off down the corridor, and there was a new spring to his step. 'Do me a favour, Jim. Nip down to the incident room and tell George I'll need him here first thing in the morning.'

'Sure, guv.'

'Leave a message for Dill and Kelly, too. Same thing. First thing in the morning.'

'Right.'

'Thanks, Jim.'

'Thanks, guv.'

Chief Inspector Harvey gripped Callaghan's arm, and squeezed it.

'Sounds pretty grim,' Jimmy Renfrew said, putting the phone back in its cradle thoughtfully.

'What did Mum say?' Gregory asked.

'Same as she did to you, I guess.'

'That old Donald's just about snuffed it?'

'Yeah. Pity. I like Uncle Donald.'

'Hope he hangs on for a while,' Gregory said. 'Don't want to have to traipse all the way up to Scotland for a funeral just at the moment.'

'You're all heart, Greg.'

'You know what I mean.'

'Oh, I know what you mean all right,' Jimmy said. And then, 'Greg, I've been thinking –'

'Oh, God.'

'No. Seriously. There's no way we'll be able to pin all those murders on Justin.'

To Jimmy's surprise his brother nodded in agreement. 'I've been thinking that too. Too much to hope for, I suppose. Just have to get him done for being a nutter. A copycat killer. They're just as bad, really.' He smirked. 'Got carried away, I did. Tell you what's going to be our main problem: making sure Justin's out of his home at the time we kill Parsons. Not too clever having him in the middle of a *tête-à-tête* with his mummy when he's supposed to be hacking off the head of his best mate.'

Jimmy pulled a face. 'Hacking off his head? That's what you're going to do?'

'That's what *we're* going to do,' Gregory corrected.

'You couldn't think of something a bit more –'

'Got to be the old head chop if he's a copycat killer, stupid.'

'Oh yeah. I suppose so.'

'No supposing about it.'

'I'll probably throw up.'

'You won't dare.'

'Okay, so I'll choke on my own vomit just to make you happy.'

'That's a good boy.'

'And, see? If you hadn't made me dump Miranda we could have got her to get Justin out of the house when we wanted him out.'

Gregory gave a laugh. 'I was wondering when you'd come up with that.'

'It's true, though, isn't it?'

Gregory nodded, and gave Jimmy an odd, conspiratorial look.

'Oh, no,' Jimmy responded immediately. 'You can forget that. There's no way I'm calling Miranda again after what you made me say to her.'

'Just a thought.'

'You can think it as much as you like, Greg. I ain't doing it, and that's final.'

'Okay, okay,' Gregory said in a pacifying tone. 'Have to think of something else, that's all. Or call the whole thing off,' he added dolefully.

'Don't try and guilt trip me,' Jimmy told him. 'You're the one doing all the planning, so you're the one who can come up with the solution.'

'And I will.'

'That's fine, then.'

'Be a laugh, though, wouldn't it – if you called her back again and –'

'A laugh for you, maybe. Not for me.'

'Might get your leg over again.'

'Greg, will you shut it?'

'Oh, dear,' Gregory sighed. 'It's hell living with someone who's got no sense of humour.'

'Speeding?' Helen Harvey said. 'I thought he'd murdered someone the way you went on.'

'He was in *my* car,' her husband pointed out without flinching.

'All the same, speeding. Really, Robert. You do overreact when it comes to Justin.'

Harvey grunted.

'Anyway, I'm off for my bath. There's pheasant casserole in the oven.'

'Thanks. Justin – upstairs?'

'Yes,' Helen said in a tight voice. 'You going up to see him?'

'I was going to, yes.'

Helen nodded. 'Good.'

'Why good?'

'Because he has that Parsons boy up there with him. In his bedroom.'

Harvey gave a lewd guffaw. 'Better knock before I go in then,' he said.

'Robert!'

But Robert Harvey did knock. He always knocked before going into his son's bedroom, allowing Justin, he believed, that sense of privacy to which all teenagers were entitled to.

'Oh, Dad. You're home,' Justin said.

Harvey nodded. He nodded to David Parsons. A curt nod. 'David.'

'I've been waiting for you,' Justin said.

'Oh?'

'I asked David to come over so he can confirm what I told you. About Miranda. About phoning him up to say she'd stood me up.'

'Justin, we've been through all that.' His father sounded weary.

'It's perfectly true,' Parsons said.

For some odd reason, at that moment, Robert Harvey found himself sharing his wife's dislike for David Parsons. He felt affronted that this arrogant, spoilt teenager should presume . . . he wasn't quite sure what David Parsons was presuming. He heard himself say, 'I never doubted my son's word,' in a ridiculously pompous tone. He transferred his gaze to Justin. 'I only came up to see if you were all right.'

'I'm fine, Dad. Thanks.'

Harvey nodded. 'Good. Right. Goodnight.' He turned to leave. 'Dad?'

Harvey swung round and raised his eyebrows.

'There's nothing . . . I mean, you meant it when you said it wasn't being taken any further? Nothing's going to happen?'

Harvey pursed his lips. He couldn't understand why his son's questions disturbed him so. But there was something about them, something . . . He shook his head. 'No. Nothing's going to happen.

The matter is closed. Unless . . . unless Miranda decides – look, to the best of my knowledge the girl is not going to pursue this further. I suggest you put it out of your mind. Forget it.' He gave Justin a short, paternal smile. 'Think you can do that?'

'I'll try.'

'And I'll help,' David chipped in.

'Justin will get all the support he needs from his mother and me.'

'I was only offering to help.'

'Thank you,' Harvey said coldly. He looked back at his son. 'And keep away from Miranda Jay,' he warned.

'Don't worry. I will.'

'Even if *she* phones *you* and asks for a meeting, keep away from her.'

'I will, Dad. I promise.'

'And if she *does* phone, tell me. I'll deal with it.'

'Thanks, Dad.'

'Right. Goodnight again.'

''Night, Dad.'

David Parsons waited until Robert Harvey had just about shut the door before calling, 'Good night, *Chief* Inspector,' after him in an impertinent, singsong, mocking way.

Robert Harvey shut the door tight.

Alone in his cell, Gary Hubbard sat crosslegged on his bunk. He held a mug of tea in both hands. From time to time he rocked back and forth, humming. He looked happy enough.

Indeed, one could be forgiven for thinking Gary found himself in familiar surroundings; either that or he had developed an aptitude for survival in confined spaces.

. . . Away, away, away, Gary thought, away back to a rarely recalled children's home, a brutal unloving place where the moustachioed tyrant, Mother Margaret of the Sisters of Charity, rejoiced in making the children suffer just as the Lamb of God had suffered, she said, whatever she meant by that. 'Cupboard, and no supper,' she would cry at the least misdemeanour, her voice, even now, whistling through Gary's mind like an ill wind. And Gary had been prone to misdemeanours, spending many long nights, supperless, locked in the cupboard on the third landing. But it was in there, sitting crosslegged on the floor just as now that his fantasies took shape, floating into his mind on the wings of memory.

Gary sipped his tea. It had gone cold and tasted strongly of tannin, making him suck in his cheeks, just as he had sucked in his cheeks when Mother Margaret made him chew soap when he lied, telling him that it was akin to the taste of sin.

But Mother Margaret forgot or maybe never knew that even the most bitter of forfeits can become familiar and unthreatening when paid often enough. And Gary found himself longing for that acid taste and the seclusion and privacy of the dark, cramped space of the cupboard. It was there he created his mothers: the wicked, uncaring one who had abandoned him to this dreadful place; the loving, beautiful one who waited, arms outstretched, for the time to come when he would leave.

He gave a low moan as he reached down awkwardly and placed the mug on the floor of his cell. As he straightened, in his mind's eye he saw himself, naked, his arms trying to shield his thin little body from the calloused hand of the sadistic nun as she beat him and screamed, 'You don't have a mother! You don't have a mother!' becoming incensed at the gaze the child bestowed on her, a gaze that insisted he knew better.

Gary Hubbard allowed himself to topple over on his cot, unravelling his legs only when he was on his back. Someone, in a cell further down the corridor, roared drunken obscenities, changed to pleading, back to cursing again, then sobbing. Gary had heard this devilish sequence before, but for the moment he couldn't quite remember where. He closed his eyes. Perhaps he had cursed and pleaded and sobbed himself, he thought, and he fell into a fitful sleep.

12

It all depended on what McVinnie came up with: a match between the flour on the floor of Gary Hubbard's new van and the residue found on the leg of Jamie Scubin's jeans, and they were in business. No match – Harvey didn't dare allow himself to think about such a possibility. So it was with some trepidation that he took the phone call from the doctor.

'Miles?'

'Ah, Robert. Yes. Well, I've done the tests,' McVinnie said, and to Harvey's alarm didn't sound all that pleased.

'And?'

Miles McVinnie gave a wicked chuckle. 'We have a match,' he said.

'You bugger,' Harvey told him.

'Not often,' McVinnie replied.

'That's great news, Miles. I owe you.'

'You most certainly do.'

'There's no doubt?'

'No doubt whatever. The sample of the flour we took from the van is identical to that we got from the lad's jeans. That helps you, I take it?'

'Does more than that, Miles.'

'You want the rest of the news, then?'

'Miles –' Harvey said threateningly.

'The other items which that rather pretty WPC brought me –'

'Yes?'

'Well, the knives are clean.'

'Damn.'

'But any one of the three larger ones could have been the weapon.'

'Not good enough, Miles,' Harvey said, disappointed.

'I know, I know. Now, the items of clothing belonging to your suspect . . .' McVinnie paused. Harvey held his breath.

'The clothes worried me . . . well, maybe worried isn't the word. They raised my curiosity, more like. None of them had been recently washed or dry-cleaned, that's the first point. The second point is a puzzle. Despite the fact that none of them had been cleaned recently, and taking into account the match we have between the two samples of flour, there was no trace whatever of blood or any fibres we could match up with the victims on any of your suspect's clothes. Yet from the *way* the victims were killed, there really *should* have been blood spatters on the clothes. The conclusion being that he didn't wear any of the clothes found in his flat when he committed the murders.'

'So you're saying he had other clothes elsewhere?'

'I'm saying that, in my opinion, if this *is* the man you're looking for, he wore other clothes when he committed the murders. Whether he still has them or not is another matter. He could have destroyed them, I suppose.'

Harvey sighed. 'Okay, Miles. Thanks.'

'I'm not finished,' McVinnie said quickly.

'Oh. Sorry.'

'On the assumption that he was unlikely to change his clothes anywhere other than his flat, I asked a couple of likely lads from the department to go back to his place and take another look.' McVinnie paused for breath; Harvey didn't dare interrupt. 'In the kitchen there are some wooden chairs. On one of the stretchers between the legs we found a minute smear. Easily overlooked. The sort of smear that would be caused by a trouserleg brushing against it if one was sitting down with one's legs tucked under the chair.'

'Smear of what?'

'Oh, blood,' McVinnie said casually.

213

Harvey heard himself gasp.

'It matched the blood of the second victim, James Meehan,' McVinnie paused again, this time for effect. 'Good, eh?'

Harvey was smiling broadly to himself. 'What would I do without you, Miles?'

'Be back on the beat, probably.'

Harvey laughed. 'Probably,' he agreed. 'That everything?'

'That's your lot for now.'

'Thanks, Miles.'

'You're welcome.'

Harvey put down the phone and sat motionless for several seconds. He gave no sign of the good news he had just received. Then, as though the devil was on his tail, he hurried from his office and down to the incident room.

The team looked up anxiously as he entered. And perhaps it was their anxiety, an anxiety with which he was only too familiar, that made the chief inspector uncharacteristically attempt the same impish jest that McVinnie had played on him. 'I've just had a call from McVinnie,' he announced glumly.

The team waited. Harvey shook his head. The team wilted.

Suddenly Harvey laughed. 'We've got a match,' he shouted. 'We've got a bloody match!'

The atmosphere in the incident room instantly became electric. 'Yes!' Kelly and Callaghan hissed in unison.

'Brilliant!' was how Pope expressed his feeling.

Susan Dill smiled and nodded as though she had expected nothing less.

Chief Inspector Harvey bounced as he walked about the room. 'Not only that but forensics have found a trace of blood on one of the kitchen chairs in Hubbard's flat. It matches –' Harvey marched to the information board and tapped the second photograph in the line-up of victims '– James Meehan.' Before the team had the chance to assimilate the news fully, he went on. 'Right. Here's what we do.' He looked at his watch, and then nodded several times as though

214

counting. He cleared his throat. 'First thing tomorrow morning we release Gary Hubbard –'

'Boss –'

'We *have* to. We arrested him in connection with the death of Jason Weaver, don't forget. We've nothing to charge him with on that.' Then Harvey smiled. 'George, and you, Jim, both of you outside the station when he's released. The minute he sets foot outside, rearrest him – for Meehan and Scubin.'

The whole team grinned.

'The instant you arrest him it's into the interview room for questioning. I don't want his feet to touch the ground between the time he's arrested and the time we start on him – clear?'

'Clear, guv,' Callaghan said, speaking for them all.

'And no cock-ups.'

Jimmy Renfrew fidgeted nervously. 'You sure it will work?' he asked.

'Has to,' Gregory told him.

'I know it *has* to, but will it?'

'Yeah,' Gregory said. 'If you're at your seductive best,' he added with a sly grin.

Jimmy wasn't amused. 'Why is it always me who has to do the –'

'Because you're so good at it,' Gregory interrupted. 'Besides, I have to drive the car, don't I?'

'I know, but . . .'

'Look, Jimmy, if you don't want to go through with it –'

'I do,' Jimmy answered quickly. 'Course I do. It's just –'

'It'll work, I tell you. Hey, it worked fine with little Miranda, didn't it?'

'That was different.'

Gregory shrugged. 'Not that much different.'

'We didn't –' Jimmy began.

'Kill her?' Gregory asked.

Jimmy nodded.

'No. But we *could* have,' Gregory pointed out.

'I suppose,' Jimmy agreed, unsure of the logic.

'You know we could. And Parsons – it'll be just as easy.'

Jimmy wasn't so sure. Gregory watched anxiously as he thought for a while. 'Okay, how do we get Justin out of his house when we deal with Parsons?' Jimmy asked.

'We phone him,' Gregory answered blandly.

Jimmy snorted. 'Oh, sure. Just like that? "Hey, Justin, would you mind stepping out of your house for a couple of hours so we can bump off your pal and get you blamed for it?" Just great, that is.'

Gregory beamed. 'Something like that,' he said.

'You're out of your mind, Greg.'

'Listen,' Gregory said, and waited for Jimmy's full attention. 'You phone him –'

'*Me?*'

'Okay. *I'll* phone him and say that I know what Miranda's game is, telling people he tried to kill her. I'll tell him I want to meet him. Shit, I'll tell him to bring some cash to pay me. Make it sound good and realistic.'

'He won't fall for that,' Jimmy said.

'Oh, yes, he will. I'll convince him,' Gregory insisted. 'I know I can do it.

'And if he *doesn't* fall for it?'

'We think of something else,' Gregory replied, seeming not in the least worried.

'And how do we get Parsons into that gay bar at the same time?'

'That's the first thing,' Gregory explained. 'We wait till Parsons goes to the bar and *then* I call Justin.'

'And if Parsons doesn't play ball?'

Gregory shrugged. 'No harm done. Dear Justin will just put the call down as a hoax.'

'But you won't be able to call him again.'

'So, I'll think of something else, won't I?'

Jimmy said nothing.

'Anyway, it's up to you to see that Parsons *does* play ball, as you put it.'

Jimmy wasn't convinced. He still wavered. But Gregory had expected that. 'Is it a yes or a no?' he asked after a minute, peering at his brother through his spectacles.

Jimmy Renfrew took a deep breath. Then he grinned. 'What the hell. Yes.'

Gary Hubbard woke in the very early hours of the morning. For a moment he couldn't remember where he was: it was very quiet, except for a sort of whimpering that came sporadically from another cell. Slowly his brain began to function. He rolled on to his back and put his hands behind his head, staring into the darkness. That, he thought, was what they had been like, those years of childhood and adolescence that returned to haunt him from time to time: staring into darkness. But, as everyone knew, there was light at the end of every tunnel, and Gary felt a warm glow as he realised he would soon emerge into that light. Why he would shuffle off the gloom, or how, he had no idea, but he was certain he would, and soon.

It was one of the curiosities of Gary's mind that it didn't play tricks on him. Although quirky, never allowing him to recognise that his killings were damnable, it permitted him to admit, if only to himself, that he was a victim of madness, but a madness that he donned willingly, a madness that clothed him in comfortable delusions. Saints, he reasoned, were consumed by a sort of insanity too, were they not? And Gary certainly believed himself to be good, even though, as far back as he could remember, he had been told he was wicked.

'You're a wicked boy, Gary Hubbard,' Mother Margaret told him, slapping him and taking him by the ear, twisting it cruelly, and marching him off to the cupboard.

'You're wicked,' his evil mother told him from time to time, pushing him away from her.

But there was another voice too, a kind and tender voice that consoled him. And, although a figment, it was this voice Gary yearned to hear now. He raised his head and listened hopefully. Only the whimpering, more fretful now, could be heard, and Gary Hubbard found he was crying quietly to himself.

'That's good news,' Jimmy said.

'. . . Yes,' Gregory agreed hesitantly.

'You didn't *really* want Uncle Donald to snuff it, did you?'

Gregory looked shocked. 'No, of course I didn't.'

'Well, then?'

'It's just with him getting better it means Mum will be home. And that means we'll have to get a move on. Won't be at all easy to do what we want to do if Mum's here.'

Jimmy didn't look too displeased.

'She tell you when she's coming back?' Gregory asked.

'Two or three days, she said.'

'Two or three days. Not much time.' Then Gregory smiled. 'Should be enough, though, with a bit of luck.'

'Can't,' Justin Harvey said.

'Why not?' David Parsons demanded.

'Got things to do,' Justin lied. 'Besides . . .'

'Besides?' David urged.

'I don't want to go out.'

'Oh.'

'Dad said –'

'Oh, I get it.'

'I just want to . . . Look, David, I simply want to stay at home for a bit.'

'Jesus, you're miserable.'

'Okay, I'm miserable,' Justin agreed. 'And I'm fucking scared,' he admitted after a pause.

'Of what, for Christ's sake? Not bloody Miranda?'

218

'Yes, if you must know.'

'What's she going to do?'

'That's just it, David. I don't know. Anything. She seems to be capable of anything. I just don't want to give her the chance to do –'

'So you're becoming a recluse, then?' David asked with a mocking laugh.

'If you like. Just for a bit. Until things cool down.'

'There's nothing *to* cool down,' David insisted.

'Whatever.'

'So you won't come out this evening?' David tried again.

'No. But there's nothing stopping *you* going out.'

'Too right there's not.'

Justin gave a small laugh. 'I'm sure you'll enjoy yourself.'

'I intend to.'

'Cheers, David.'

If Gary Hubbard was confused or distraught, he didn't show it. Indeed, he had shown considerably more bewilderment when he was released than when he was rearrested. And now, sitting in the interview room again, there was an air of calm about him. And the smugness, so apparent in the first interview, had gone. It seemed almost as though he was relieved: he had about him something of an old lag's furtive gratitude: pleased to be released but petrified at having to face a world he could no longer cope with.

At the moment it was quiet in the interview room. The tape, running, gave a tiny hum. Chief Inspector Harvey had a new seriousness about him, Gary observed, but it was a severity tempered with concern.

'I still think you should have your solicitor here, Gary,' he said now.

Gary gave him a long, steady stare. Then he shook his head.

'Very well,' Harvey said, leaning forward. 'You understand why you have been rearrested?'

Gary nodded. He had his head bowed, staring at his hands. It was six o'clock in the evening, and between the time he had been rearrested and now, Gary had been kept in a cell (to sweat, Harvey had said, changing his mind about immediate questioning) and for all those hours he had sat on his bunk, head bowed, staring at his hands. Sometimes he would hold out one hand in front of him and wiggle the fingers, scrutinising them: not pretty fingers, short and thick and stumpy, but scrupulously clean. 'Hands,' Mother Margaret demanded, and they would all line up and hold their little hands out for inspection. And down the line she would march, a birch cane waving, and being brought down with horrendous force on any hand that failed.

'It would save so much time and trouble if you would admit to these killings,' Harvey said reasonably. 'We might even be able to help you if you told us why you killed Meehan and Scubin.' He let his statement sink in for a moment before asking, 'Why *did* you kill them, Gary?'

Gary Hubbard looked up, and for a split second Harvey thought he was about to reply, to say something like, 'You wouldn't understand.' But Gary didn't answer. He hung his head again, shaking it slowly.

'Very well,' Harvey said, sounding disappointed. 'If that's the way you want it.' The statement was almost interrogative, as if giving Hubbard one final chance to change his mind.

Gary gave a small smile of what could have been appreciation, but remained silent.

Harvey sighed. He glanced over his shoulder. 'Susan,' he said, 'could you organise some coffee? It seems we're in for a long night.'

Susan Dill left the room, and Jim Callaghan recorded her departure on the tape.

'A long night,' Harvey repeated.

It certainly seemed as if Gregory Renfrew, judging by the choices he made, had luck on his side. In the first place he chose the evening of Gary Hubbard's rearrest to put into action his plan to eliminate the unfortunate David Parsons. Yet it wasn't as though he and his brother had set out on spec, hoping that everything would fall into place. From the outset there was an extraordinary conviction in Gregory's actions. And, in the second place, he chose to wait for David, not outside his home which would have been the logical place to linger, but outside the bar he and Jimmy had seen him frequent. Of course, he had explanations for both when Jimmy questioned him: 'Got to do it some time – may as well be this evening' and 'More going on in Green Park – stop you getting bored' were the words he used to pacify his brother.

And so, sitting in the Mini, the twins waited. They waited in silence. They had nothing much to discuss now, having been over and over the plan, honing the details.

'Right,' Gregory had said. 'Let's go over it one more time. We wait outside the bar until David goes in.'

'*If* he goes in. *If* he even turns up,' Jimmy said.

Gregory was having none of that. 'We wait outside the bar until David goes in,' he repeated. 'Then you go in after him. You make it clear you're interested and let him chat you up.'

'*If* he chats me up –'

'While you're in the bar, I'll phone Justin and get him to come and meet me.'

'*If* he'll come and meet you.'

'Then you come out with him –'

'*If* he'll come with me.'

'Just shut up, Jimmy,' Gregory ordered.

'I'm being reasonable,' Jimmy protested.

'If it doesn't work, it doesn't work. We'll find another way. But it will work,' Gregory said adamantly. Then he relented. 'The power of positive thinking,' he told Jimmy. 'That's all it takes.'

'Takes a lot more than that, mate. For me, anyway. *I'm* the one who has to let that creep drool all over me.'

221

Gregory grinned. 'You'll be terrific. Who could resist you?'

'Piss off.'

'Now, where was I?'

'You had me and that queer coming out.'

'Oh, yes. Right. You get a taxi and go straight to Mum's shop. But don't forget, you've got to stop the taxi away from the place a bit. Don't want the taxi driver seeing you go in, do you?' Gregory gave Jimmy a winning smile. 'Then, you take him round the back, down the alley, and in the back door, into her storage room. Okay with that so far?'

Jimmy nodded.

'Meantime, as soon as I see you get into the taxi I'll shoot off and go to the shop. I'll be waiting in the storeroom when you arrive. I'll have everything ready. And then –' Gregory shrugged. 'Bingo!'

'Jesus, Greg, I worry about you – you're so . . . so –' Jimmy couldn't find the word he wanted.

'Charming?' Gregory suggested.

'Oh, sure.'

'Anyway, don't worry about me. Everything's going to go like clockwork.'

'I wish I was that sure.'

'*Be* sure, Jimmy. Be positive. Be . . . be *optimistic*,' Gregory said. 'Be confident,' he added as though his brother had unexpectedly landed the leading role in some much vaunted play and was about to make his entrance on opening night.

'You got the keys to Mum's?' Jimmy now asked as they waited outside the bar.

'Yes,' Gregory said, and tapped his pocket, making the keys jangle for good measure. He tapped his inside pocket also. 'And Justin's wallet.' Jimmy looked across at his brother as though to ask another question but he didn't get the chance. 'See?' Gregory asked. 'What did I tell you?'

'Huh?'

'Coming up the street . . . lover boy,' Gregory pointed out.

And sure enough, up the street came David Parsons, strolling in his languid gait, a cigarette dangling from his fingers.

'Shit,' Jimmy said.

Gregory grinned mischievously. 'Pretty, ain't he?'

They watched David reach the bar. He hesitated for a moment at the door, looking about him. For a second it looked like he might change his mind about going in. 'Go on!' Gregory hissed to himself. And David flicked his cigarette away and obediently went into the bar. 'Time to go, Jimmy.'

Jimmy gave a sigh. 'Guess so.'

'Good luck. And don't worry,' Gregory told him, giving his brother's hand a squeeze.

'Easy for you to say.'

'It's not as if you have to *do* anything with him.'

'Oh, no. Just help you cut his fucking head off, that's all.'

Gregory gave a cackle. 'Could be worse,' he said. He waited until Jimmy was halfway out of the car before adding, 'Be nice to him.'

'I swear, Greg, if he touches me I'll kill –'

'There you go,' Gregory smirked.

'You make sure you're at Mum's when we get there,' Jimmy warned.

'I'll be there.'

'Just make sure you are.'

'Smile,' Gregory said.

Jimmy glowered.

'Aw, come on. Give Gregory a great big smile.'

And despite himself, Jimmy Renfrew grinned.

Kate Renfrew suddenly shuddered, and her sister asked, 'Cold, dear?'

Kate shook her head. 'Someone just walked over my grave.'

Now it was Alice Johnson's turn to shudder. 'I hate that saying. It's so silly. So *morbid*.'

They were sitting in the bay window of the living-room, staring out at the lights of the town blinking below them. Donald was home: weak and frail, but home, safely tucked up in bed.

'You've been so very kind, Kate,' Alice said.

Kate gave her a smile.

'No, really. I don't know what I'd have done without you,' Alice insisted.

'You'd have coped. You always were able to cope, Alice.'

'You're the one who's coped.'

'That's different. I have the twins,' Kate replied, the thought of her sons bringing a tender smile to her eyes. 'I can tell you one thing, Alice – without them . . .' She fell silent. And then, 'I can't wait to see them.'

'They *are* good boys,' Alice agreed.

Kate gave a sad smile. 'Not boys any more, Alice. Young men.' She sighed. 'I expect, any day, they'll be leaving me.'

Alive gave a sympathetic little chuckle. 'Not for a while, I'd say. Far too comfy at home. They know which side their bread is buttered on.'

'Jimmy's got a girlfriend,' Kate said as though she had not heard her sister's observation, as though having a girlfriend was the beginning of the end.

'And about time,' Alice said.

'I suppose.'

'Of course it is. You can't mother them for ever, you know.'

'Oh, I know, I know.' Kate laughed. 'But I *want* to.'

'You have to let them spread their wings,' Alice told her.

'I do. Honestly, I do. It's just – they're so *special*.'

13

Chief Inspector Harvey was in no hurry. Certainly it would have suited him better if he could have got the matter dealt with quickly, but he had no intention of trying to hasten a conclusion at the risk of having Gary Hubbard clam up altogether. He realised that the small, burly man sitting opposite him sipping the coffee that Susan Dill had brought to the interview room, the man who killed without remorse, it seemed, and without reason, was one of those suspects who had to be allowed breathing space. If he was to confess, it would be on his own terms and in his own time. Harvey recognised also that Hubbard was not the sort of person who would suddenly hold his hands up and admit to his crimes: he would want to do more than that. He would want to explain everything in detail, not, Harvey suspected, by way of making excuses, not even to try to justify his terrible actions, but in an attempt to find that curious peace so many murderers inexplicably seek. And Harvey wanted to hear it all. He cleared his throat. 'James Meehan and Jamie Scubin,' he said clearly.

Gary looked up at him. Harvey raised his eyebrows questioningly. Gary stared at him.

'The names mean anything to you?'

Gary thought for a moment and then shook his head before looking back at his coffee.

'They should,' Harvey told him quietly.

'They don't,' Gary answered.

'I'll try and refresh your memory, Gary,' Harvey said. He opened the file that lay on the table between them and took out two photographs. Then he pushed one towards Hubbard. 'That's James Meehan.' He pushed the second one across the table. 'That's Jamie Scubin.'

Gary didn't move.

'Look at them,' Harvey ordered.

Obligingly, Gary Hubbard raised his eyes and stared at the two photographs. He gave a small frown as though puzzled.

'Recognise them?' Harvey asked.

Very slowly Gary shook his head. And then, taking Harvey by surprise, and still shaking his head in denial, he said, 'I've seen them.'

Chief Inspector Harvey felt something inside his head thud, and it took a serious effort not to let any reaction show on his face, but he managed. 'Where did you see them, Gary?' he asked, surprising himself with the calmness of his voice.

'Can't remember.'

'Think.'

Gary appeared to think. He made as if to reach out and pick up the photograph of Jamie Scubin, but stopped as his hand hovered over the dreadful image. He withdrew his hand slowly. But it was a strange action. It was as though some unseen force had grabbed Gary's elbow and was deliberately restraining him, so that his hand recoiled in spasms.

'You can pick it up,' Harvey told him.

Gary looked up at him. Harvey indicated the two photographs as if to emphasise his invitation. Gary continued to stare into Harvey's face. Then, expressionless, he shook his head.

'Afraid to pick them up, are you, Gary?' Harvey asked.

'Oh, no,' Gary answered quickly.

'Then . . . ?'

'They're dead,' he said quietly.

Mistaking the statement for a question, Harvey answered, 'Yes, they're dead, Gary.'

Gary nodded. 'They're dead,' he said again.

'And you killed them,' Jim Callaghan cut in, making Harvey jump at the ferocity of his tone and give Callaghan an equally ferocious glare.

And then: 'Did I?' Gary asked.

Instantly the interview room was becalmed by an eerie, prickling silence.

There was nothing insolent about Gary Hubbard's question. There was no hint of a taunt in it. It was a question asked pathetically and in all seriousness.

'We think you did, Gary,' Harvey heard himself say.

Hubbard took to nodding again.

'Did you?'

'I'd have to think,' Gary said in a distant tone.

Jim Callaghan was in again like a shot. 'There's nothing to think about. Either you –'

Chief Inspector Harvey silenced him by catching his arm and squeezing it, without taking his eyes off Gary Hubbard. 'Of course,' he told him. 'I can understand that.'

Gary gave him a tired smile.

'We'll take a break. You think about it, Gary. Take all the time you want. When you're ready we'll –'

'Thank you,' Gary interrupted.

'You don't think you should have pressed on?' Callaghan asked when Hubbard had been taken back to the cells.

Harvey shook his head. 'Not with him, Jim. Not with him.'

Clockwork was a word Gregory Renfrew liked to use. Everything would go like clockwork. And for a while it seemed a most appropriate word.

The bar was about half full and could have been mistaken for a gentlemen's club, with most of the clientele dressed in business suits, some with briefcases by their feet, some with furled unbrellas; a gentlemen's club, except for the gloom and the posing and the occasional high-pitched nervous laughter.

But on the whole they were a sober lot, having an after-work drink before going home. Indeed, dressed casually as he was, Jimmy Renfrew felt even more out of place, and chose to sit at the far end of the bar. As his eyes became accustomed to the dim light he noticed he wasn't the only teenager there: at a table in one corner a gaggle of young men held cigarettes by the tips of their fingers and talked earnestly, punctuating their conversation with glances towards the door whenever it opened to allow someone new to enter, giving him a critical gaze and then putting their heads together again. And there was David Parsons, of course, although he, standing aloof with what looked like a glass of white wine, managed to look older than his years and, for a moment, gave the impression of a serious and sober young man, or rather, of a man who had found the secret of youth and appeared younger than he actually was. And attractive, it seemed, since Jimmy noticed a number of the customers eyeing him. David, if aware of the attention, pretended not to notice, and if anyone showed any sign of approaching he would adopt a haughty air and turn his head away to discourage any unwelcome advance.

And it was on just such an occasion, turning his head as someone in a pinstriped suit was so bold as actually to murmur a tentative word or two, that David noticed Jimmy, noticed Jimmy before Jimmy was aware of it, and started to weave his way towards the far end of the bar.

Gregory Renfrew, also, was on the move. He gave Jimmy a couple of minutes inside the bar before leaving the Mini and making for a phone box. Anyone taking a close look might have been surprised at the way he muttered to himself as he walked, and even more surprised at the curious accent he was rehearsing.

In the phone box he took a deep breath, staring at the telephone number Miranda Jay had given Jimmy. Then he dialled.

'Well, hello,' said David Parsons.

'Hello,' said Jimmy.

'Hello?' said Justin Harvey. There was silence. 'Who is this?'

'Haven't I seen you here before?' David asked.

228

Jimmy gave him a smile. 'Doubt it.'

'I'm sure –'

'Haven't been here before,' Jimmy interrupted quickly.

'Just shut up and listen,' Gregory told him.

'Who are you?'

'Maybe just wishful thinking on my part,' David said.

'Probably,' Jimmy agreed.

'Want to know what's going on?' Gregory asked.

'Who is this?' Justin Harvey demanded.

'You haven't got a drink,' David observed.

'Service stinks,' Jimmy answered.

'Yes,' David drawled. He held up a finger and immediately the barman came to him. 'What will you have?' David asked Jimmy.

'Just listen,' Gregory ordered. And then, as though suspecting Justin was about to hang up on him, he added, 'Want to know what Miranda's up to?' he asked.

There was a pause. 'I'm listening,' Justin said.

'A beer,' Jimmy told the barman.

'I'm David.' Parsons held out his hand.

'Christopher,' Jimmy told him, taking David's hand and shaking it.

'How do you do, Christopher,' David said in a curiously old-fashioned way.

Jimmy nodded. 'Hiya.'

'It'll cost you,' Gregory said.

'I'm listening,' Justin Harvey said again.

'Bring fifty quid and meet me.'

'I can't –'

'Then fuck you.'

'Wait. Wait. I –'

'You goin' to do what I say?'

'Yes.'

'Okay, then.'

'God, it's so *dreary*,' David observed. 'Dreary place. Dreary people.'

'Thanks,' Jimmy said.

'Oh, I didn't mean *you*, Christopher.'

But Jimmy decided to play hurt. Deliberately he bent his head and looked past David. He let his eyes linger on the men at the corner table, and although none of them looked at him, he smiled and nodded as though one of them had.

David took a step closer. 'You have to be careful, you know,' he warned.

Jimmy looked up at him. 'I'm always careful.'

'There are some very odd types floating around.'

'Think I don't know that?'

'Bring the money and meet me in half an hour outside the Body Shop in Piccadilly,' Gregory ordered.

'I'll never make it in half an hour —'

'You'll make it. Then I'll tell you everything.'

'Who are you?' Justin asked.

David finished his drink, and stretched. He looked intently at Jimmy and made a decision. 'Want to go somewhere else?'

'Like where?'

'Like another bar.'

Jimmy shook his head. 'Not into drinking much.'

'What are you into, Christopher?' David Parsons asked.

'Action,' Jimmy answered, and could hardly believe he'd done it.

'Never mind who I am. I know what Miranda has in store for you and it ain't pretty, I can tell you. See you in half an hour. If you're not there, well, tough shit.'

'I'll be . . . how will I know you?' Justin asked.

'I'll know you. That's all that matters. You're wasting time.'

'Is anyone allowed to join in the action?' David asked, clearly interested.

'Not just anyone.'

'Me?' David asked pointedly.

Jimmy shrugged. Then he grinned wickedly. 'Yeah, why not?

Gagging for it, are you?' David looked affronted for a moment, but relaxed and smiled when Jimmy added, 'I am.'

'We could go to my place,' David said.

Jimmy Renfrew decided to take a leaf from David's book, and put on a mildly insulted expression. 'Got my own place,' he snapped.

'Oh, I didn't mean to imply . . . Your place would be fine.'

Jimmy finished his drink in one gulp and placed the glass on the bar, twisting it a couple of times. He glanced at the clock. He'd been in there twenty minutes. 'Okay,' he said. 'What are we waiting for?'

'He wants to see you, boss,' Susan Dill announced.

Harvey nodded and rubbed his hands. 'Right. Let's go,' he said. He stopped by the door of the incident room and tapped the inside pocket of his jacket, then nodded again, this time to himself.

'Got everything, guv?' Jim Callaghan asked.

'Oh, yes.'

Their footsteps echoed as they hurried down the corridor to the interview room, Harvey in the middle, flanked by Callaghan and Dill. They had almost reached the door when Alan Kelly came quickly after them. 'Guv. Guv,' he called.

Harvey stopped and swung round, almost colliding with Dill. 'What is it?' he demanded testily.

'Your son's on the phone, guv.'

'Justin?'

'Says it's urgent.'

Harvey hesitated. He took one stride towards Kelly as if about to go and take the call. Then he changed his mind. 'Tell him I'll call him back,' he said. 'Tell him I'm busy. Say I'll call him right back when I'm free.'

'Right, guv.'

'Take a message,' Harvey called after him.

'Right, guv,' Alan Kelly said.

But Harvey didn't hear him. He was already entering the interview room, nodding to Gary Hubbard who sat there waiting.

Gregory Renfrew had just closed the door of the Mini and settled back in his seat when Jimmy and David Parsons came out of the bar. Gregory slid lower in his seat, peering out. For a moment he panicked as Jimmy deliberately led David across the street towards the Mini. He allowed David to squeeze through the space between the Mini and an Astra before following him, giving himself time to wink at Gregory and flick an absurdly limp wrist.

As soon as they were out of sight Gregory hastily got out of the car: there was something he wanted to do, something he hadn't mentioned to Jimmy, a little touch that pleased him.

'No need for all that, is there?' Jimmy had asked, eyeing his brother who had flattened his hair and put in his contact lenses just as he had done when he had driven the car at Miranda.

'Might as well,' Gregory had answered, making it sound like a whim.

But it had been no whim. And now, as he crossed the street and made for the bar, he straightened his shoulders and drew himself up, adopting the swaggering walk he had seen Justin effect. He went straight in and up to the bar, leaning across to the barman and asking, 'You know David Parsons?'

'David? Yes. You just missed him.'

'Shit,' Gregory said, making as if to hurry out again.

'Any message?' the barman asked obligingly. 'He might be back.'

Gregory hesitated. He shook his head. Then he said,' Yeah, tell him Justin's looking for him urgently.'

'Justin?'

'Yeah. Justin.'

'If he comes back I'll tell him. Want a drink?'

But Gregory was already at the door, hauling it open and letting it slam behind him. Once inside the Mini he had a fit of the giggles, and he was still chuckling away to himself as he drove up the King's

Road towards his mother's shop. He was about a hundred yards from the turn-off when he spotted Jimmy and David Parsons getting out of the taxi. He drove carefully past them, not daring to look too closely. He parked the Mini and dashed up the alley, fumbling for the keys as he went. He was panting quietly. He eased open the door and went inside. He didn't put on the lights but stood stock still to let his eyes get accustomed to the gloom. Then he walked deliberately towards a small pile of packing cases. Beside them, on a shelf, was a small iron crowbar used for opening the wooden cases. He grabbed it, then he went back to the door, stood behind it, and waited.

'I'll go first,' he heard Jimmy say. 'And get the lights.'

Gregory tensed and took a firmer grip on the crowbar, raising it over his shoulder. Jimmy pushed open the door and came in. Gregory took a deep breath, holding it as Jimmy strode across the small storeroom. Then, suddenly, David Parsons was standing there, his back to him. Gregory brought the crowbar down on his head as hard as he could. With a tiny grunt David buckled at the knees. He fell forward and hit the concrete with a dreadful, dull thud.

'Quick,' Gregory said. 'Bring some of that plastic wrapping and shove it under his head.'

And when that was done the twins stood staring at the body. Then they looked at each other. They were both smiling.

'Well?' asked Chief Inspector Harvey abruptly once the tape was running and they were all seated.

'I've been thinking about it,' Gary Hubbard said seriously.

'And?'

'I don't think I'm the one you're looking for,' Gary stated, still serious and reasonable, giving the impression he was willing to help.

'You don't, eh?' Callaghan asked.

Gary shook his head.

'What would you say if we could *prove* it was you, Gary?' Harvey asked.

Gary wouldn't say anything, it seemed. He looked puzzled for a moment, cocking his head and staring at Harvey, but made no reply.

'All right. Let's start with James Meehan. You say the name means nothing to you?' Harvey asked.

Gary shook his head.

'And you say you don't recognise him from the photograph I showed you earlier.'

Gary shook his head again.

'Suppose I told you that we found blood that matched James Meehan's in your flat, Gary?'

What Gary Hubbard thought of that was anyone's guess. He certainly didn't appear alarmed by Harvey's words. It was almost as if the significance of the find didn't register with him, or as though it reminded him of something else, something amusing. He gave a tiny smile.

'It's not funny, Gary,' Harvey told him sharply.

Hubbard looked up quickly. 'Oh . . . no. I was thinking . . . no. Not funny.'

'The chairs in your kitchen. How long have you had them?'

'The kitchen chairs?'

'That's right. How long have you had them?'

'A while. A couple of years, maybe.'

'That's where we found Meehan's blood,' Callaghan revealed. 'On one of your kitchen chairs.'

It wasn't that Gary Hubbard was inspired or cunning. He looked directly at Jim Callaghan and asked in a concerned way, 'You sure it was Meehan's?' And when Callaghan didn't answer, he went on. 'It's just so odd . . . how his blood could have got into my flat.' He shook his head as though genuinely bewildered. 'Maybe it's just the same type but not his?' he asked politely. Then, 'It might be mine,' he suggested.

'What blood type are you, Gary?' Harvey asked, an edge to his voice as if he was being forced down a path he had no desire to take.

Gary beamed at him. 'No idea. I'm sorry. No idea.'

'You won't mind if we take a sample?'

'Oh, no. I'm trying to help.'

Callaghan gave a sneer.

'Let's move on to Jamie Scubin,' Harvey said. 'Again, the name means nothing to you and you didn't recognise him from the photo?'

Gary nodded his agreement.

'And you never met him?'

Hubbard gave that deliberate consideration. 'No,' he said finally.

'Then how do you explain our forensic evidence which proves he was in your van?'

Hubbard looked astonished. Then he narrowed his eyes as if he suspected some trick was being played on him. 'You can't have,' he said flatly.

'Oh, but we do, Gary.'

'*Can't* have,' Hubbard insisted, and there was something about his tone that made Harvey lean forward and study his face closely, before saying in a compassionate and understanding way, 'You know, Gary, I think you've forgotten you killed Meehan and Scubin.'

'I wouldn't forget –'

'You might. If you wanted to.'

'I *couldn't* forget something like that,' Gary insisted. And then he looked appealingly at Harvey. 'Could I?'

Harvey nodded slowly. And then, still nodding, he put his hand into the inside pocket of his jacket and took out Jamie Scubin's large crucifix. He placed it carefully, reverently almost, on the table between himself and Gary Hubbard.

For a second Gary was transfixed, and then, in a series of little jerks, he recoiled, pushing himself as far back in his chair and as far from the crucifix as he could.

'You remember that, don't you, Gary?' Harvey asked and, when Gary nodded, Harvey gave Callaghan a swift glance of satisfaction.

'She always wore it,' Gary said.

Instantly the smile of triumph vanished from Callaghan's face, and Harvey snapped his head round to face Gary Hubbard again. 'What was that, Gary?'

'She always wore it,' Gary repeated.

'*She?*'

Gary nodded.

'Who?'

Hubbard was breathing in a sharp, panting way. He looked up at the ceiling, blinking as though to prevent tears. He shook his head, moaning quietly.

Chief Inspector Harvey looked at Callaghan for assistance, but Callaghan wasn't much help: he grimaced and spread his hands as though flummoxed. 'We'll take another break,' Harvey said, drawing a finger across his neck to indicate he wanted the tape stopped. But as Callaghan started making the appropriate entry, Harvey restrained him, placing a hand on his arm, and eyeing Hubbard with concern. 'We'll take another break now, Gary,' he said, and when Hubbard didn't react: 'Gary?'

Gary Hubbard opened his eyes and stared about him in a dazed way. Slowly, very slowly, it seemed to dawn on him where he was.

'We're taking another break, Gary,' Harvey said again.

Hubbard nodded.

And Chief Inspector Harvey nodded also, to Callaghan, permitting him now to stop the tape.

... A man has been arrested in connection with the so-called Rent Boy Murders. Although it has been stressed that the man is only helping police with their enquiries, sources close to the investigation say he is expected to be charged shortly.

The announcement came over the car radio shortly after ten o'clock. 'What a clever chappie Daddy is,' Gregory said, thumping the steering wheel gleefully with one fist. 'Well, we'll see just *how* fucking clever he is, won't we?' he asked Jimmy. But when his brother didn't answer, Gregory glanced at him. 'What's up with you?'

Jimmy shook his head. 'Nothing.'

'Oh, no?'

'You didn't have to . . .' Jimmy began, but stopped abruptly.

'Didn't have to what?'

'You know,' Jimmy told him, jerking his head in the direction of the boot.

'Oh, *that.*'

'Yes. That.'

'Not getting squeamish, are we?'

'No. It's just . . . well, killing him and dumping him out there was enough.'

Gregory shook his head. 'No. I need it,' he said. 'The final touch. Anyway, can't do much about it now, can I?' he asked with a grin. 'Can't go and stitch the bloody thing back on.'

'You're sick.'

'Terminally,' Gregory agreed, bringing the car to a stop outside their home. They sat there in silence for a while. Then Gregory said brightly, 'Right. Out you get.'

Jimmy looked at him. 'You're not –?'

'Got something to do,' Gregory told him mysteriously.

'Oh.'

'You go get the kettle on. Make us both a nice cup of tea. Be dying for it when I get back, if you'll pardon the pun.'

And he certainly seemed to enjoy his tea when he did get back to the house three quarters of an hour later, adding a tot of whisky to it, and savouring it as though it were some sublime vintage. Then he started to laugh, putting the mug on the table as his body shook. 'Christ, I wish I could be there when they find it,' he announced.

'Where did you –'

'Ah-ha, that'd be telling.'

Oddly, Jimmy didn't press him. He sat down beside his brother and stared at him. 'Greg, what happens if we get caught?' he asked quietly.

'We *won't* get caught. No way will we get caught,' he replied confidently.

'But suppose we do?' Jimmy insisted.

Gregory shrugged. 'Won't have to go near the Job Centre for a while then, will we?' he asked with a laugh. 'We won't get caught,' he said again. 'It's over. It's done. All we have to do now is sit back and watch that bastard suffer.' Then he reached out and took Jimmy's hand. 'Just think of it as claiming legitimate compensation.'

'Greg – we just killed someone,' Jimmy said as though the true horror of what they had done had just struck him.

'You don't say.'

'You think I should have pressed on?' Harvey asked.

Jim Callaghan shrugged, but made the shrug say that, yes, that's what he thought.

Harvey sighed. He shook his head wearily, fixing his eyes on the chair where Gary Hubbard had been sitting. 'All we're left with is the flour. You fancy trying to get a conviction on that, eh?'

Jim Callaghan shrugged again.

'We don't even have enough to charge him. I've got to get a confession. Without that . . .' Harvey let the thought hang in the air.

'And if he doesn't confess?' Callaghan asked.

Harvey drummed his fingers on the table. 'He'll confess,' he replied. 'He *wants* to confess.'

Callaghan wasn't convinced. 'And what was all that about him *forgetting* he'd killed Meehan and Scubin – and the others?' he asked, his tone as derisory as he dared make it.

Harvey caught Callaghan's tone and gave a little snort, making it clear he was laughing at himself alone. 'Something that psychologist Anne Evans said. I think it was her who said it. Maybe I read it.' He stood up. 'It's not forgetting exactly. Blocking out, more like.' He gave another little mocking laugh. 'Crap, eh?'

Callaghan inclined his head.

'Maybe it is. I hope not, though.' He gathered up the file from the table and tucked it under his arm. Then he turned to Susan Dill. 'You're very quiet,' he observed.

But before Dill could reply, Alan Kelly was at the door, saying, 'Guv –'

Harvey turned to him and frowned. Then he nodded quickly. 'I'll call him straight away. Thanks, Alan,' he added, and made as if to walk to the door.

'No, sir. It's not about Justin. It's – can I have a word?'

Perhaps it was the fact that Kelly had addressed him as sir or perhaps it was the almost furtive glances he gave to both Callaghan and Dill that made Harvey hesitate.

'In private, sir?'

'Oh?'

Kelly looked deliberately at Callaghan and Dill. It was Dill who took the hint. 'I could use a coffee anyway. Jim – you coming too?'

Kelly stood aside to let them leave the room, and then shut the door. He waited until Harvey had rested his buttocks on the edge of the table. 'Sir, there's been another. Another killing.'

Harvey felt himself go cold. He gaped at Kelly. And then it dawned on him that there was something more Kelly wanted to say, or rather, something he didn't want to say but was obliged to. 'Go on,' he said.

'George Pope is at the scene. He wants you down there urgently, guv.'

Harvey made a small gesture of irritation. 'I can't –'

'Sir. He said that no matter what you were doing you *had* to get over there.'

'Did he say –'

'I've got my car ready, sir,' Kelly interrupted.

Irked for some reason, 'I've got my own car,' Harvey snapped.

'I'll drive you, guv.'

'Alan –' Harvey began threateningly.

'I'm only doing what George told me to.'

Harvey looked thoroughly bemused. 'He asked you to drive me there, did he?'

Kelly nodded. 'Immediately.'

Harvey sighed and heaved himself upright. 'Well, we 'd better do what our DI says then, hadn't we?' he said as Kelly opened the door. 'Perhaps you'd nip down to the canteen and tell Susan and –'

'George said immediately, sir.'

Chief Inspector Harvey looked as if he was about to protest, but something in Kelly's expression stopped him. He gave a curt nod. 'Immediately it is, then.'

Book Three

14

'Wonder if they've found him yet,' Jimmy Renfrew asked, wandering back into the bedroom in his dressing-gown. Any despondency or anxiety he had shown had long since dissipated. 'Bit of a let-down, really, not being there to see everything.'

Gregory Renfrew, also in his dressing-gown, his hair damp and tousled from the shower, and wearing his spectacles, nodded his head in agreement. 'Adds to the tension a bit, though, doesn't it – not knowing exactly what's going on?'

'Sure does,' Jimmy said. 'Sure does.'

'Could be they won't find him until the morning,' Gregory said.

'Poor sod, lying out there in the cold all night,' Jimmy remarked.

'Terrible, isn't it?' Gregory asked. 'Like Aunt Alice says, I don't know what the world is coming to.'

Jimmy started to brush his hair. He looked at the reflection of his brother in the mirror. 'We thought of everything, didn't we?' he asked, and saw Gregory nod emphatically. 'You sure, Greg?'

Gregory was very sure. He was certain he had thought of everything. Every detail of the plan had been followed to the letter, and the entire evening had gone without a hitch. Nevertheless he closed his eyes and swung backwards on his chair, nodding from time to time as though checking a list and giving each item on that list a little mental tick as he ran it through his mind.

Once David Parsons had been poleaxed with the crowbar and the plastic wrapping placed under his head to collect any seeping blood, they had acted swiftly. Still in the vague hope that Justin might be linked to the spate of killings already under investigation, they set about putting the information they had gleaned from the tabloids into action. Gregory produced two pairs of surgical gloves from his pocket and, without a word, tossed one pair to Jimmy. They put them on carefully. They stripped Parsons, crudely giggling when Gregory nudged his penis with his foot and remarked, 'No wonder he's bent.' They folded the clothes and placed them in a pile. Then they wrapped the body in more plastic and carried it out to the Mini, grunting with exertion as they jammed it onto the back seat. They put his clothes on top of it. Then they drove to a car park at the back of a building society in Battersea. Gregory had selected this car park: it wasn't overlooked by any flats, and it appealed to him that all the spaces had RESERVED painted on them in white. They caught one end of the plastic wrapping and rolled the body out onto the concrete. Then they laid David Parsons out ceremoniously, straightening his legs and folding his arms across his chest. Jimmy put the clothes next to the body. Gregory wasn't happy with the way they looked. With his foot he scattered them, looking at Jimmy for approval. Jimmy nodded.

Then, like a conjuror pulling a rabbit from his pocket, Gregory took out Justin's wallet. Holding it, he looked carefully about the scene. He walked to the body, turned, and carefully measured out six strides. Then he dropped the wallet on the ground, once again glancing at Jimmy for approval, and again Jimmy nodded.

For several minutes they stood there, Jimmy watching Gregory intently as he surveyed the scene, then started hopping from foot to foot and saying, 'Come on, Greg. Let's get out of here.'

But Gregory wasn't quite finished. He collected the plastic sheet in which David had been wrapped and crumpled it into a monstrous ball. He handed it to Jimmy. 'You go to the car, Jimmy,' he instructed quietly.

'Huh?'

'Go and wait in the car. Put the wrapping and your gloves in the boot. And wait.'

'What are you –'

'Just go and wait in the car.'

Jimmy Renfrew waited in the car, frowning when he saw Gregory coming out of the car park carrying what looked like a bulging shopping bag. He swung the bag nonchalantly in one hand. When he reached the car he dumped the bag in the boot. He took off his gloves and threw them in after the bag. He closed the boot, not slamming it, just pushing down on it until the lock clicked. Then he got into the car beside his brother. He gave a sharp little blow like a silent whistle.

'What was that?' Jimmy asked.

Gregory started the car. 'You don't want to know.' He swung the car out of the car park, turned left, and picked up speed.

'What was it, Greg?' Jimmy insisted.

Gregory leaned forward a little, peering through the windscreen. 'His head,' he said casually, not taking his eyes off the road.

And then it was back to the storeroom behind their mother's shop, Gregory taking a black plastic rubbish bag and the crumpled shroud from the boot of the Mini with him. Jimmy carried a holdall.

Inside the storeroom Gregory opened the bag and dropped the crowbar in. Then he stuffed the plastic wrapping in on top of it, and on top of that the square of wrapping on which David's head had rested. 'Okay?'

Jimmy nodded.

'Right,' Gregory said, and started undressing, putting each item of clothing into the rubbish bag as he removed it. 'Hurry up!' he snapped at Jimmy.

When they were naked Gregory opened the holdall and took out two pairs of jeans, two jumpers and two pairs of trainers, tossing one of each to Jimmy, and saying, 'Catch.'

Dressed, Gregory tied the rubbish bag with a piece of cord and carried it to the door. He left it there and returned to stand beside his brother, his eyes bright, flicking about the scene. 'Clean as a whistle,' he said under his breath.

Jimmy nodded towards the rubbish bag. 'Gloves in there?'

'Yep. Let's get out of here.'

For what was undoubtedly the longest time ever when in each other's company the twins remained silent, as Gregory drove the car to Docklands. On the journey they were silent. When Gregory took the rubbish bag from the boot they were silent. When he returned to the Mini having dumped the bag in the river, watching it sink under the weight of the crowbar, they were silent. Indeed, it was only as Gregory braked and turned the car into their own street that Jimmy made his remark about it having been unnecessary for Gregory to decapitate Parsons.

Gregory shrugged. He stopped the car, and pursed his lips, frowning.

Jimmy was already getting out. He gave Gregory a look. 'What's up?'

'Nothing.'

'Well, come on, then.'

Gregory shook his head. 'You go on. There's something –'

'What?' Jimmy demanded.

'Just something I have to do. You go on in. I'll be back in a little while.'

Jimmy hesitated.

'It's just something I want to check,' Gregory said nonchalantly. 'You go put the kettle on,' he added with a grin and drove away.

And an hour later, in the bedroom, Gregory stopped swinging on his chair and let the front legs hit the ground with a thump. 'Yep,' he announced. 'We've thought of everything.'

Jimmy finished brushing his hair. He got into his bed and lay back. 'Greg?'

'Yeah?'

'Where did you go?'

Gregory ignored the question.

'It had something to do with the head, didn't it?'

Gregory smiled. 'Maybe.'

'What did you do with it?'

'You'll find out soon enough.'

Jimmy accepted this. He yawned. 'What time's Mum getting home tomorrow?'

'Some time before lunch, she said.'

'We meeting her?'

'I offered but she said she wasn't sure exactly *what* time she'd be in. Getting a taxi.'

'Oh.'

'Oh, what?'

'Oh, nothing . . . Going to be hard . . . you know, keeping . . . with Mum here and all.'

'Keeping what – quiet?'

'Yes. Sort of.'

'Just act natural. Easy.'

'Mum's not stupid, you know. She'll know if –'

'She won't *know* anything. She can *think* what she likes.' Gregory suddenly burst out laughing. 'Anyway, she's never going to think for a minute that her two little jewels *killed* someone, is she?'

Jimmy joined in the laughter. 'No.'

'There you go, then.'

And an uncharacteristic silence, also, had fallen between DCI Harvey and DS Alan Kelly. True, as they sped away from the station, Harvey had demanded, 'What's all this about, Alan?'

Kelly had replied curtly. 'I don't know, sir,' he claimed. 'Just what I told you. George asked me to get you down there as soon as possible. If not sooner.'

'Down where?'

'Battersea, sir.'

'You know a lot more than you're saying, Alan,' Harvey observed, but not in an accusatory way, and let the matter drop, settling back as Kelly drove at speed towards Battersea.

And there was another subterfuge in store as Kelly stopped the car in front of a building society, and said quickly, as Harvey made to open his door, 'Would you wait here, sir? Please?' although there was nothing interrogatory about his words.

'Alan –'

'Please, sir,' Kelly insisted, scrambling out of the car and running round the side of the building.

And moments later it wasn't Alan Kelly who returned to the car, but George Pope. He got in quickly and shut the door. He looked grim. 'Boss,' he said.

'Are *you* going to tell me what all this cloak-and-dagger stuff is about, George?'

'I wanted a quick word with you alone, boss,' Pope told him.

'I'm listening.'

'The Super's here.'

'Donnelly?'

'Yes. I wanted to talk to you before he . . . Boss, there's another body round the back.'

'I know that. Alan told me there's been another.'

'This is different, boss.'

'Oh?'

'We can definitely identify this victim. Student card in the back pocket of his trousers,'

Harvey waited.

'It's a David Parsons, boss.'

It took a moment or two for the name to register. Then Harvey stiffened.

'Beside the body, boss, we found a wallet.'

Chief Inspector Harvey slowly turned his head to look Pope full in the face.

Pope looked away. 'From certain documents inside the wallet we can identify the owner.'

Harvey felt his jaw drop involuntarily. It was as though he knew what was coming.

'It belongs to your son, boss. Justin.'

For an unbelievably long time Harvey didn't react. Then, very slowly, he said, 'Oh, my God,' and gave a low moan. 'I must—' He opened his door and started to get out, but Pope grabbed his arm.

'Sir, the Super's instructions are that if you turn up you're not to be allowed near the scene.'

Harvey fell back into his seat, shaking his head in a bewildered way. 'Not allowed –'

'That's why I wanted a word with you first. Out here. I didn't want the Super to have the chance to –'

'No. No.' Harvey said although he didn't appear like someone who knew quite what he was agreeing with. 'Thank you, George.'

'I'm going to get Alan to take you home, sir.'

Harvey nodded.

'As soon as I get the chance I'll call round and fill you in.' Again Harvey nodded.

'I'm sorry, boss.'

And Harvey continued to nod. 'There must be some explanation,' he muttered to himself.

'If there is, we'll find it.'

'Yes,' Harvey said vaguely.

'I'll just get Alan.'

'Yes,' Harvey agreed, and then asked, 'George? . . . Justin?'

'The Super's already sent –'

'To arrest him?'

'Yes, boss. I'm sorry.' Pope got quickly out of the car as Kelly came furtively round the building.

'I'll have to see him,' Harvey said in a distant voice.

Pope leant down. 'Just stay at home, boss. Please. I promise I'll be round to see you as soon as possible.'

'Won't Donnelly *let* me see him?' Harvey suddenly asked.

'I don't know, boss. I don't know what he's going to do. I'll tell you as soon as I do.' And then Pope was signalling Kelly with a jerk of his head to take his place in the car. But just before Alan Kelly got behind the wheel, George Pope put his lips close to his ear. 'The boss home, and then you straight back here.'

'Right.'

'And when you get back –'

'I know. I haven't seen the boss.'

'Good man.'

Gary Hubbard, sitting in his cell, wondered what was going on, why nobody had recalled him to the interview room. He wasn't bothered, though. Someone was comforting him. 'It's going to be all right,' the voice told him. 'Come and give me a cuddle. Everything's going to be just fine.'

Gary cuddled himself.

Helen Harvey was close to hysteria. She threw her arms about her husband's neck, sobbing wildly. 'Robert, they've arrested Justin. They just came in and –'

'Shh. I know. I know.'

'They wouldn't tell me anything.'

'No.'

'What's happened, Robert?'

'I don't know, Helen. I just don't know.' He took hold of her hands. 'Helen, did Justin go out this evening?'

'What?'

'Did Justin go out this evening?'

'Yes. Yes, he did. For a couple of hours.'

'You don't know where he went?'

'No. He didn't say. He just asked if he could borrow my car, and went,' Helen explained. 'Why?'

'He didn't mention going to see David Parsons?'

'No. He wouldn't. Not to me. Is that it, Robert?'

Harvey looked at her curiously.

'Has that David Parsons got Justin into trouble?' And then without waiting for an answer, 'I knew it. I just *knew* it. I asked you to speak to him about that boy. But would you? Oh, no. What did you do? You laughed at me, Robert. Made a joke about them being upstairs alone together. And now –'

'David didn't get Justin into any trouble, Helen.'

'That's what you say –'

'David's dead, Helen.'

Helen snatched away her hands, recoiling as though her husband had slapped her hard across the face. Indeed, she touched her cheek with one hand as though feeling the pain. 'Dead?' she asked finally, her voice a tiny squeak.

Harvey nodded.

'An accident?' Helen asked. She frowned. 'But he doesn't drive.'

'Not an accident, Helen.'

'I don't understand.'

Harvey took a deep sigh. 'He was, it seems, murdered.'

Helen Harvey raised both hands to her face now, palms outwards as though protecting herself from some invisible evil. And then slowly she lowered them. 'Robert, they don't think Justin –' she began to ask.

Harvey looked away.

'Oh my God!' Helen screamed. Suddenly she was running away from her husband, racing up the stairs.

'Helen –' he called after her helplessly.

'I've got to get to him,' Helen called back.

'You can't. They won't let anyone –'

'He'll need things,' Helen was saying. 'Soap. And shaving things. And clean clothes.'

'Helen!' Harvey shouted. But it was to no avail. Helen Harvey had made up her mind.

He was still standing in the hall when she came down again, carrying her own overnight bag. 'Helen, listen to me, will you? They won't let anyone see him yet.'

'I'm going, and that's that,' she insisted, pushing past her husband and opening the door.

251

'They won't let you see him.' Harvey tried again.

'Well, I'll wait until they do,' Helen shouted. 'No one is going to prevent me seeing my own son.' Then she rounded on her husband. 'You coming?'

'I *can't*, Helen.'

She was already leaving the house, snapping on the outside light and slamming the door behind her.

Making one last effort to stop her, Robert Harvey opened the door and called, 'Helen –'

But Helen Harvey was busy trying to fit her keys into the boot of her little Fiat. Annoyance flicked across her face when she saw it was broken and incongruously the thought occurred that she must scold Justin. She opened the boot and swung the overnight bag towards it. Then she stopped, all movement frozen. Then she started to scream, a wild, daemonic wail, her gaze fixed on the dull and sightless eyes protruding from David Parsons' head.

15

It was a night when nobody slept; nobody except Helen Harvey, that is, who had been given a sedative. Yet even she was fitful and restless in her induced slumber.

The twins couldn't sleep. Or perhaps they could but didn't want to. At three o'clock in the morning Jimmy lifted his head from the pillow and looked across to his brother's bed. 'Greg?'

'Hmm?'

'Don't suppose we could drive back over to Battersea and take a look? See if anything's happening?'

Gregory gave a laugh. 'I was just thinking that,' he admitted.

'Well, could we?'

'Later.'

'Why not now?'

'Not enough traffic about. We'd be spotted too easy.'

'Oh. You're right.'

'Later, though.'

Jimmy lay back.

'Good, wasn't it?' Gregory asked suddenly, the dark adding to the sinister edge in his voice.

'Yeah,' Jimmy agreed. 'Some buzz.'

'I can see why they do it.'

'See why who does what?' Jimmy asked, propping himself up on one elbow.

'Why killers kill,' Gregory explained. 'Serial killers, I mean. The buzz. Hard to stop once you've started.'

Jimmy sat bolt upright. 'You're not planning to –'

'No. Of *course* not.'

Jimmy relaxed.

'Mind you . . .' Gregory said in his teasing way.

'Mind you nothing,' Jimmy replied quickly, and, after a moment's silence, they both laughed.

And Gary Hubbard didn't sleep. He didn't even lie down on his cot and make himself comfortable. He had assumed his favourite position, crosslegged, on his bunk, and sat quite still most of the time. Occasionally he gazed up at the small window set high in the wall as though to stare out at the night beyond, but the thick glass prevented that, so he took to imagining what it was like outside, just as he had spent dark hours in the cupboard wondering what the other children in the home were doing. It had never been a depressing experience. He liked imagining things. Making them better. Making them pleasant. Making them pain-free and comforting. Peopling his world with nice people, people who were nice to him, that is. Thinking about how *he* would be nice when he grew up. How he would help people. How he would ease their suffering. How he would take them with him to his happy world.

And Chief Inspector Robert Harvey didn't sleep. He sat hunched in an armchair in his bedroom, watching his wife in her uneasy sleep, grateful that she was unable, for the time being, anyway, to demand of him answers he was unable to give.

Only when the doctor had been and administered the sedative, and Helen had been put to bed, had he reported the horrific discovery she had made. And as he reported it, he had felt a consuming sense of betrayal, aware that he was making matters worse than ever for his son. For one wild moment he had even considered taking Parsons' head from the Fiat and dumping it somewhere far away from the house, and he was surprised how difficult he found it to reject this option. So he had phoned the incident room. 'Susan?' he asked automatically when Susan Dill answered, and could not suppress a wry smile at the tiny gasp she gave.

'Boss?'

'Yes.'

'I'm so –'

'It gets worse, Susan.'

'I'm so sorry,' Susan Dill told him. And then, as if her superior's statement had just registered, 'How do you mean – worse?'

'Parsons' head. Helen just found it in the boot of her car. The lock had been forced and –'

Susan Dill gave a strangled cry of astonishment.

'You'd better get on to George and tell him.'

'Boss, the Super's taken over.'

Harvey ignored that. There was real anger in his voice when he continued. 'Get in touch with George and tell him,' he said coldly.

'Right.'

Harvey's voice softened. 'Have you seen Justin?'

'Only when he was brought in, boss.'

'I see.'

'He'll be all right. I promise.'

'Don't make any rash promises, Susan.'

And so they had arrived and taken Helen's Fiat away, tactfully making as little fuss as possible, discreetly avoiding looking up at the window from where Harvey watched.

Later, true to his word, George Pope had visited, starting by saying, 'I don't know what to say.'

'George, I don't want you to say anything that might –'

'I know. I know.'

'Just tell me what the situation is.'

'Donnelly's taken over.'

'And I'm to –'

'In the morning – this morning – you'll be officially removed from the case,' Pope told him.

Harvey began to nod, accepting the inevitable. And then he looked at Pope sharply. 'Wait a minute. What do you mean, George?'

'Boss –'

'I know I can't investigate anything that involves Justin, but Hubbard – that's *my* case. They can't –'

George Pope shifted uneasily. 'Boss,' he tried again.

'They're two separate cases, George. They can't just –'

'Donnelly doesn't think so,' Pope blurted.

'Donnelly doesn't –'

'He says he believes Parsons' death is linked to the others.'

'You mean he thinks Justin killed . . .' Harvey began, astounded. 'The man's mad,' he concluded.

Pope shrugged. 'Anyway, the word is he wants to see you first thing in the morning.'

'Oh, he'll see me all right.'

'I'd better get back.'

'Yes, George, of course. Thank you for – you know.'

George Pope hesitated. 'Boss, look, don't go crazy or anything, but . . . but there is a chance Justin *did* –'

'He *didn't*,' Harvey hissed.

'You don't know that yet.'

'I know my son.'

Pope sighed. 'You sure?'

'Robert, Robert, Robert,' Superintendent Peter Donnelly said, taking Harvey by the arm and leading him to a chair in a friendly, sympathetic way. And when Harvey was seated Donnelly walked ponderously round behind his desk and seated himself before shaking his head and saying, 'This is the most appalling situation.'

He sounded sincere enough, but Harvey gave him a suspicious look.

'I won't even pretend to understand what you must be going through,' Donnelly went on. 'However, there are certain things that have to be done, and there's no easy way to do them. You are, as of this moment, Robert, removed from the case, and I suggest that our official announcement is that you are taking leave.'

'My son didn't—' Harvey tried to reason quietly.

Donnelly held up one hand. 'I really cannot discuss this with you, Robert. It's a question not only of public confidence but . . . well, you know quite well you cannot be allowed to investigate any charges against your son.'

'*Has* he been charged?' Harvey demanded.

'Not yet. But it's only a matter of time.'

'And what about Hubbard?'

'Hubbard is to be released. There simply isn't enough to charge him. Besides –'

'You've made up your mind that Justin –'

'I've made up my mind about nothing yet, Robert. Your son has been questioned. Briefly. Further questioning will take place shortly.'

'He hasn't admitted   '

'No.'

'What *did* he say?'

Donnelly twisted in his chair. 'Nothing.'

Harvey allowed himself a tight smile.

'Which is why the interview was brief,' Donnelly explained, sounding peeved. 'He has requested, quite rightly, that his solicitor be present.' He looked down at some notes on his desk. 'Mr Poyser?'

Harvey nodded.

Donnelly peered at his watch. 'He's due here at nine thirty.'

'Can I see him?'

'Of course.'

'I meant Justin. Can I see my son?'

'Ah. Well . . . No, I'm afraid that would be inappropriate at the moment, Robert. Later, of course. By all means.'

'Will you keep me informed as to what happens?'

'Insofar as I can,' Donnelly agreed.

Harvey stood up. He shoved his hands into his coat pockets and stared down at Donnelly. 'You're wrong about Hubbard, you know.'

'I'll be the judge of that,' Donnelly answered.

'And about Justin.'

'I have made no decision one way or the other about your son, Robert. As I said, we have only had a brief, preliminary interview. When I've talked to him at length and made the necessary enquiries, then I'll decide whether he is to be charged or not.'

Harvey nodded and turned towards the door.

'Robert, there's nothing *you* want to tell me, is there?'

Harvey swung round. 'About what?'

'About anything I should know.'

'Like?'

Donnelly shrugged. 'Anything.'

Harvey studied the Superintendent's face. There was a hint in his voice that suggested he knew something, and was giving Harvey the chance to explain it. 'No. Nothing.'

'Very well.'

Harvey opened the door. 'Peter – unofficially – would you mind if I –'

Donnelly knew what was coming. He shifted in his chair again and his eyes narrowed.

'Anything I find will be passed on to you,' Harvey told him. '*Anything.*'

'And *everything*?' Donnelly asked, relaxing a little.

'Everything,' Harvey assured him.

'Even if –'

'Yes. Even if.'

Superintendent Donnelly picked up a pencil and tapped it on his desk. 'What you do when you're on leave, Robert, is your own affair.'

'Thank you, Peter.' Harvey gave him a curt nod and left the office.

It made the lunchtime news. *Police revealed this morning that what appears to be another victim of the so-called Rent Boy Murders was discovered late last night in Battersea. This brings the total to seven. A police spokesman also announced that Chief Inspector Robert Harvey, the officer heading the enquiry, has been removed from the case and is taking extended leave. John Farrar reports.*

Gregory and Jimmy Renfrew were glued to the television, Gregory transfixed and motionless, Jimmy nibbling his nails. Without looking at each other they both smiled at the news of Robert Harvey's dismissal from the case.

Yes, John Farrar was saying. *There appear to have been a number of developments overnight. I understand that the man arrested yesterday in connection with these killings is to be released, but that another man has been arrested and is currently helping the police with their enquiries. No reason has been given for the removal of Chief Inspector Robert Harvey from the case, although it is being stressed that it is not the result of any incompetence on his part. The most police will say is that Superintendent Peter Donnelly has taken over and that a new approach is deemed necessary.*

'You think it's little Justin they've arrested?' Jimmy asked gleefully.

'Bet my life on it,' Gregory wagered.

'So we've done it!'

Gregory reached out and threw an arm about his brother, hugging him. 'Yep. We've done it!' he confirmed. 'Now all we have to do is sit back and watch the shit hit the fan.'

Jimmy pulled back and looked at him.

'What?' Gregory asked.

'I thought this was it. That it was over. What more –'

'Lots,' Gregory interrupted. 'I want the bastard thrown out of his job, not just sent off on paid leave. I want him out, and that's exactly what's going to happen.'

Jimmy didn't understand.

'Just wait and see,' Gregory told him. 'I have it all worked out.'

'So what do we have to do now?' Jimmy wanted to know. Gregory smiled. 'Nothing. That's the beauty of it. It's all been done.'

Gary Hubbard stood outside the police station. He was confused. He was confused because he felt he had been denied the chance to explain himself, to explain his actions, to make the sympathetic Chief Inspector Harvey understand. He turned and stared back at the building, just as he had turned and stared back at the home when he was dismissed from care. It was sleeting now just as it had been then. Gary turned up the collar of his jacket. It was dull and cold, and the lights from the police station sent withering reflections out onto the road. But there were no faces at the window, no small, pinched faces gaping down at him, no faces terrified by the punishment for sin.

He started to walk away from the station, his shoulders hunched. That was it, of course. Sin. Sin and the expiation thereof. He stopped walking suddenly and cocked his head. *We must be prepared to die rather than commit sin.* Gary shuddered. And indeed, he thought, something of him had died in penance for his sins.

'I'm home!' Kate Renfrew called from the foot of the stairs, putting her suitcase on the floor and listening. Then she threw out her arms as the twins came hurtling down, ready to embrace them.

'Hiya, Mum,' Jimmy said.

'Hello, Mum,' Gregory said.

'Let me look at you,' Kate said, standing back as though expecting a massive change to have taken place during her brief absence. If she spotted any she didn't admit to it. She gave Jimmy an extra squeeze, and said, 'It's so good to be home.'

'Yeah,' Jimmy told her. 'We missed you.'

Kate beamed. That was just what she wanted to hear, allowing her to reply, 'And I missed you too.'

'How's Uncle Donald?' Gregory asked.

'Uncle Donald is fine. As well as can be expected, anyway,' Kate said, taking off her coat. 'Now tell me: what's been happening here?'

The twins looked at each other. Jimmy nodded. 'Quite a lot, actually,' Gregory announced.

Kate gave a tiny concerned frown.

'Oh, nothing *here*,' Jimmy said quickly.

The frown cleared. 'Ah.'

'You haven't seen the news?' Gregory asked. 'On the telly?'

'No. What news?'

'You won't believe it, Mum,' Jimmy said.

'Won't believe what?'

'What's happened,' Gregory said enigmatically, turning and walking towards the kitchen.

'Well, tell me, for heaven's sake,' Kate said, following.

'We're going to,' Jimmy said, bringing up the rear.

In the kitchen Gregory pulled out a chair and waited for his mother to sit. 'Something *very* funny going on,' he announced, walking to the fridge and taking out a bottle of tonic and the tray of ice.

'Goodness,' Kate said, not sure whether to be concerned or just intrigued. She watched Gregory pop some ice cubes into a glass, and add gin and tonic.

'We've no lemon,' he said in an aggrieved tone, looking at Jimmy as though blaming him for the shortage.

'Never mind the lemon, Gregory,' Kate said. 'Tell me. What's all this funny business you're being so mysterious about?'

Gregory handed his mother the drink and sat down. He looked up at Jimmy and nodded, waiting for him to sit down too. Then he said, 'Well, to begin with, you know *he* was heading the investigation into all those killings –'

'You mean Robert?' Kate interrupted, starting to frown once more.

'Yes. Him. Well, he's been taken off the case.'

'Oh?' Kate didn't sound all that interested. 'I don't see –'

'*And* his *son* has been arrested,' Jimmy announced dramatically.

Kate had just taken her first sip. She swallowed and then coughed. 'Robert's son? He has a son? Arrested?' she asked incredulously, and then in an appalled way, 'Not for those terrible murders?'

'Seems like it.'

'His *seventeen*-year-old son,' Gregory stressed.

'Good, eh?' Jimmy added, starting to smile but quickly feigning seriousness again as Gregory gave him a warning scowl.

'Good?' Kate asked, puzzled.

'What Jimmy means is,' Gregory interrupted, 'it's ironic, isn't it?'

Kate was now totally baffled. 'I'm sorry. I don't –' She shook her head. 'Ironic?'

'Yes, well, you know, Mum,' Gregory was trying to explain. 'After what he did to you . . . to us . . . to us all . . .'

But still Kate couldn't fathom what they were getting at. Indeed, to the twins' dismay she looked both horrified and sad. 'Are you sure?' she asked quietly.

'Seems so,' Jimmy said.

Kate sat very still for several seconds, eyeing her drink as though pondering whether to drink more of it or not. Then she shook her head. 'Poor Robert,' she said. She jumped when Gregory repeated her words, shouting them and making them into a question.

'Poor Robert?' he exploded.

'Gregory!' Kate said, shocked.

'What d'you mean, Mum? "Poor Robert"?'

Kate shook her head. 'It's just so . . . I was thinking if it had been one of you who had been –'

'Jesus, Mum. You're something else,' Gregory said mockingly.

Kate looked at him. 'Well, you didn't think I'd be pleased, did you? It's terrible.'

'It's what he deserves,' Gregory insisted. He stared at his mother. 'You *still* don't get it, do you? He was shagging *her* at the same time as he was –'

'Stop it!' Kate said.

'And he kept bloody Justin,' Jimmy said.

'Justin?'

'Yes, Mum. Justin. His son. Didn't want him aborted, did he? Oh, no. Just us.'

Kate Renfrew stood up suddenly. 'I'm sorry,' she said, shaking her head as if the action would sort out the turmoil in her mind. 'I just want to go upstairs for a bit.' She walked swiftly from the kitchen, still shaking her head.

'Didn't count on *that*, did we?' Jimmy asked.

Gregory was furious. 'She's feeling *sorry* for the bastard,' he said in a disbelieving way.

'Tell me about it,' Jimmy said, equally bewildered.

'I thought she'd be really –' Gregory began.

'Pleased?' Jimmy asked, and shook his head. 'Mum wouldn't be pleased about something like this. We should have guessed, really. She feels sorry for everyone.'

'But Robert fucking Harvey!'

'Well, they were – you know – they had a thing going once. Hey, you think she still loves him?'

'Don't be so effing stupid, Jimmy,' Gregory snapped.

'Just wondering,' Jimmy answered lamely. Then he brightened. 'Doesn't really matter, does it?'

Gregory leapt to his feet, sending his chair scudding back across the polished kitchen floor. 'Of course it matters, you prat. Why do you think we arranged it all?'

'For us. You and me,' Jimmy said.

'Yeah, for us, sure. But for Mum too,' Gregory said.

'But mostly for us,' Jimmy suggested, trying to calm his brother down.

And it seemed to work. Gregory collected his chair and brought it back to the table. He sat down again. He put his head in his hands and ruffled his hair with his fingers. When he finally looked up at Jimmy he seemed better. 'You're right, Jimmy,' he conceded. 'It was mostly for us.'

'Doesn't really matter if Mum can't see it our way, does it?'

Gregory shook his head. 'Not really, I suppose.'

'We know he's paying for what he tried to do to *us*,' Jimmy pointed out.

'Yeah.'

'You and me – that's all that matters.'

Gregory Renfrew stared hard at his brother. Then he nodded. 'Yep, I guess so,' he said seriously.

'That's *all* that counts, isn't it?'

Gregory nodded again. 'Yes,' he agreed firmly as though he had made up his mind about something. 'That *is* all that counts. You and me. *That's* what counts.'

16

'I have no option,' Superintendent Donnelly said severely. 'You have left me no option, Robert. You are suspended until this enquiry is completed, and then it will be up to others to decide your future.' He held up his hand as Harvey looked as if he was about to say something. 'I gave you every opportunity,' Donnelly went on. 'I specifically asked you if there was anything you wanted to tell me, and you refused categorically to confide in me. What the hell did you think you were playing at, Robert?'

Harvey said nothing.

'Did you really think it wouldn't come to light?'

Harvey made no reply.

'Good God, man, you of all people should have known the correct procedure.' Donnelly started shifting files about his desk as if in the midst of some exotic board game; as if, maybe, this was the requisite preliminary to what was now definitely about to take place.

Still Harvey remained silent.

'I can tell you this much, Robert. You haven't done your son a damn bit of good. How could you try and conceal –'

'I wasn't trying to conceal anything.'

'You didn't tell anyone, did you?'

'No.'

'Well, if that's not concealing, what is?'

'I didn't think it would –'

'Precisely. You didn't think. Well, you're supposed to think. That's the one thing you are most definitely meant to do.'

'I didn't believe it,' Harvey tried lamely.

'What you believed or didn't believe doesn't enter into the question. It was reported to you that your son attempted to at the very least cause grievous bodily harm to that girl and you kept that information to yourself. You didn't, correct me if I'm wrong, so much as look into the matter in even the most peripheral way.' Donnelly shook his head. 'I'm sorry, Robert, but you have left me no alternative. You are suspended and will remain so pending a full enquiry. And I'm bound to say that I see your dismissal from the force as a very real possibility.' Donnelly now had the files neatly piled on his desk and seemed momentarily at a loss as to what to do with his hands. He folded them eventually, and leant back in his chair.

If this was a sign that the conversation was over, Harvey didn't interpret it as such. He stayed in his chair, staring wearily at his superior. Although he had been prepared for a reprimand, now that it had come and in such severe terms, he was shattered. Indeed, just as he had been plunged into turmoil when George Pope had called to see him the previous evening, and said, 'Bad, boss, I'm afraid.'

'How bad?'

'Very bad,' Pope informed him, and then, in a disappointed voice, added, 'You could have told me, boss.'

Harvey looked surprised. 'Told you what?'

'About Justin and the girl,' Pope told him. 'She's told us every-thing.'

Harvey dismissed that with a scowl. 'That was domestic, George.'

'Oh? Since when did attempted murder become domestic?'

Harvey felt himself start to shake. 'Oh, God,' he sighed. 'I thought you meant –'

'The baby?'

Harvey nodded.

'That's the motive,' Pope said. 'That's what Donnelly calls the motive, anyway. Apparently quite a few people, students mostly, at the college – people Parsons and your son knocked about with

– knew that Miranda and Justin were having problems.' Pope blew out air. 'Being students they put two and two together.'

Harvey buried his face in his hands.

'Why in Christ's name didn't you tell someone, boss? To cover your own back if nothing else.'

Harvey shook his head, keeping it hidden in his hands. 'They told me they didn't want to press charges,' he answered through his fingers but in a tone that admitted this was hardly an excuse.

'And that's another thing,' Pope went on. 'Donnelly wants to know the identity of the bloke who accompanied Miss Jay to your office.'

Harvey looked up.

'She says she can't remember. Just Jimmy. That's all she could tell us.'

Harvey nodded again. 'That's what he told me. James. Jimmy to his friends.'

Pope looked astonished. 'And you let it go at that? You didn't even bother to –'

'No, I didn't,' Harvey said angrily, getting up and walking to the fireplace.

And that was exactly what Superintendent Donnelly now asked. 'And you let it go at that? Miranda Jay and some stranger walk into your office and accuse your son of trying to run her down and you don't even bother to find out who this person is?' Clearly he couldn't believe it. He gave a scoffing laugh. 'If it had been my son they'd accused, you can be damn sure I'd want to know who the hell was accusing him.'

'I know, I know,' Harvey interrupted. 'I know I should have reported it. I know I should have pursued it. I know, I know, I know.' He stared long and hard at Donnelly. 'But I didn't.'

'No; you didn't. You swept the whole incident under the carpet,' Donnelly told him. 'You covered it up,' he added.

'It wasn't like that,' Harvey protested.

'Really? What was it like, then?'

Harvey gazed at Donnelly as though in a dream. And he had gazed at George Pope in the same way when he asked, 'You think Justin is guilty, don't you, George?'

'I don't know what to think,' Pope had answered, sounding miserable. 'But what's the alternative? That he's been set up?'

It could have been that Harvey was willing to clutch at any straw, or it could have been something in Pope's tone that made him grasp at the possibility. 'What makes you say that, George?'

'Well . . .' Pope hesitated.

'Is there something?'

'Boss, I shouldn't tell . . . I shouldn't even *be* here. If Donnelly ever found out . . .'

Harvey nodded. 'I'm sorry, George. You're quite right. You'd better not –'

Pope suddenly laughed. 'Oh, fuck Donnelly. Look, boss, there are a couple of things. The wallet. Justin claims he lost it months ago. And as Donnelly says – he would, wouldn't he? But Miranda Jay does say she thinks – only thinks, mind – she remembers seeing the wallet in her flat recently.'

'Only thinks, though.'

'Only thinks. However, there's something not right about the wallet. There's not a single fingerprint on it. Wiped clean. If Justin *had* dropped it at the scene, why weren't his fingerprints on it? And if someone *else* left it there, why weren't their prints on it? Unless . . . ?'

'Nothing on the cards either? The cards in the wallet?' Harvey asked.

Pope flinched. 'How did you know about them?'

'The cards? You told me. The other night.' Harvey gave Pope a shrewd look. 'Don't you remember?' He didn't wait for an answer. 'Any prints on *them*?'

Pope shook his head. 'Nothing.'

A glimmer of hope came into Harvey's eyes. But in the manner of a man used to disappointments, used to discovering that things are never quite what they seem, he just nodded and said, 'You said there were a couple of things.'

Now Pope nodded. 'His clothes. Justin's. As far as we can tell they're all accounted for and there's not a trace of Parsons' blood on any of them.'

Harvey didn't look so happy with that. 'Who says they're all accounted for?'

'Justin himself, and his mother. Perhaps you could –'

'George, I haven't a clue what clothes Justin has.' Harvey rocked on the balls of his feet. 'Donnelly had tests done on Justin himself, I suppose?'

'Oh, yes,' Pope said emphatically. 'They were negative too.'

'So –'

'So apart from the wallet and the fact that Parsons' head was found in your wife's car –'

'There's nothing to connect Justin –'

'Except for the fact that he's shown himself *capable* of . . . Boss, if only you had reported . . .'

To deflect yet another reminder of his stupidity, Harvey asked, 'So what is Donnelly doing now?'

'Trying to trace Parsons' movements on the night he was killed,' Pope told him.

And that was what Donnelly admitted to now, watching as Harvey stood up. 'Parsons was seen leaving his home at twenty past seven. We know that Justin left your house about thirty minutes later. Driving his mother's car.' He made the timing of the two departures sound significant.

'That doesn't mean –' Harvey began.

'Of course it doesn't,' Donnelly agreed with considerable largesse.

Harvey nodded.

'I *am* sorry, Robert,' Donnelly said.

'Yes. Thank you.' Harvey walked to the door. 'Can I see Justin now?' he asked.

Superintendent Donnelly sucked in his breath. 'I would prefer you to leave it for another twenty-four hours, Robert,' he said.

'You've asked for an extension then?'

Donnelly nodded. 'Yes,' he said crisply.

'Very well.'

'Just go home, Robert. Take my advice. Just go home. As soon as there are any developments I will personally see to it that you are informed.'

'Yes. Thank you. Thank you, Peter.'

'And Robert –'

Harvey swung round and raised his eyebrows.

'If it does come to an official enquiry into your behaviour, I will be on your side. You know that.'

Harvey knew no such thing, but said, 'Yes, I know that, Peter. Thank you.'

'And if you have anything else you think we should know . . .'

Harvey shook his head.

'Very well,' Donnelly said, and made a great show of just what a busy man he was, putting on his spectacles, and opening one of the files on his desk.

Gary Hubbard decided to walk home. It was a long walk but that didn't bother him. In a sense he felt it was to be a definitive walk, away from something, or towards something, towards some conclusion maybe and away from all that remained unresolved. And as he walked he talked to himself in his mind, telling himself that life would be different now, that he would no longer have to skulk in shadows, seeking something other people could not fathom, continually, relentlessly searching as ghosts are said to do.

And as he moved away from the police station, moved through the hubbub of people going about their business, he suddenly felt overwhelmed by loneliness. What had struck him as that elusive chance to explain himself had somehow escaped him, had slipped through his fingers, had been whipped away from him, and Gary Hubbard realised it was unlikely ever to return.

'Don't look at me like that, Gregory,' Kate Renfrew said, pleading rather than scolding.

'Like what?'

'Like –' Kate gave a nervous laugh. 'Like I'd done something awful.'

Gregory grimaced and shrugged.

'Like I'd let you down or something,' Kate added.

'Are you working today?' Gregory asked.

'Of course. Well, I'm going in, if that's what you mean. I'm not sure if I'll be there all day. I need to talk over a few things with Hector, that's all. Why?'

'Just wondered.'

'My, you're in a grumpy mood.'

'No, I'm not.'

Kate walked to the sink and rinsed her mug under the tap. She placed it upside down on the draining board, turned and stared at her son. 'Gregory, just because things didn't work out between me and your father doesn't mean I have to hate him, you know.'

Gregory stared back.

'After all, if it hadn't been for ... well, for Robert, I wouldn't have you and Jimmy, would I?'

Gregory shook his head in amazement. 'You really don't get it, do you, Mum?' he asked.

'Get what?'

Gregory continued to shake his head but the look of amazement had vanished. 'Oh, forget it,' he said coldly.

'No. You tell me. What don't I get?' Kate demanded.

'I said forget it, Mum,' Gregory answered and made as if to leave the kitchen.

Suddenly Kate was angry. 'Don't you dare walk away from me

271

like that,' she snapped. 'Come back here this instant and tell me what's on your mind.'

Gregory stopped walking and turned slowly. 'All right,' he said, and the word *venomous* came to Kate's mind when she heard his tone.

'I'm listening,' she said despite herself.

'A question first. You still love him?'

'Robert?' Kate asked fatuously, and gave a nervous little laugh, tossing her head. 'No, of course I don't still love him,' she said, and then, before Gregory could reply, she continued, 'but that doesn't mean I hate him either. I *did* love him. I loved him very much, and you can't help . . . *I* can't help but feel sorry for him if his son –'

'*I'm* his son,' Gregory said in an icy voice. 'Jimmy's his son,' he added.

'Yes, I know, but –'

'And he wanted you to have us killed off.'

Kate gave a tiny cry. Then instinctively she crossed the kitchen, holding out her arms to embrace her son, but Gregory moved himself out of her reach. 'It wasn't like that,' Kate heard herself say lamely.

Gregory gave a derisive laugh.

'You don't understand,' Kate tried.

'I'm not fucking stupid, Mum,' Gregory shouted back. 'Don't understand?' He laughed again. 'Oh, don't you have any doubts about that, Mum. Jimmy and I, we understand all right.'

'Gregory, Gregory,' Kate pleaded, reaching out again, and then withdrawing her arms almost guiltily as Jimmy came bouncing into the room. He stopped dead in his tracks and stared.

'Interrupting something, am I?' he asked.

'Gregory and I were just –'

'Mum thinks we don't understand,' Gregory said immediately.

'That's not fair, Gregory,' Kate countered.

'Understand what?' Jimmy asked, and when neither his mother nor his brother answered, he asked again, 'Understand what?'

'Tell him, Mum,' Gregory said.

As always, when backed into a corner by one of her sons, Kate Renfrew became flustered. 'How can I?' she asked. '*You* haven't explained to me what it is *I* don't appreciate,' she said. 'All I know is that it's something to do with your father,' she went on, instantly regretting the remark as now Jimmy, too, gave her a long cold stare. 'Something to do with Robert,' she corrected. 'And the way I reacted last evening,' she went on, wanting to stop but feeling compelled to continue. 'Apparently your brother thinks I should be pleased that his son –' Again she faltered. 'That Justin has been arrested.'

'You're not?' Jimmy asked.

'No,' Kate replied quickly. 'Of course I'm not *pleased.*'

To her complete surprise, and Gregory's if the look on his face was anything to go by, Jimmy just shrugged, said, 'No big deal,' and went to get himself a mug of coffee. When neither of them answered, he turned and saw both Gregory and his mother staring at him. 'What?' he asked.

'Why – nothing,' Kate told him, while Gregory continued to stare.

'That takes care of that, then,' Jimmy said. He held up the coffee pot. 'No?'

'No,' Kate said. 'Thank you, Jimmy. I must –' She flicked her wrist and glanced at her watch. 'I must make a move.' Then she turned back to Gregory. 'Maybe this evening, when I get home, we can discuss . . . ?'

Gregory gave a long slow blink.

'Right,' Kate said. 'I'll see you both this evening,' and walked swiftly from the kitchen.

The twins waited until the front door closed behind her. Indeed, they waited until they heard their mother start her car and drive off, before relaxing. At least Jimmy relaxed. 'What was all that about, Greg?'

'She still loves that bastard,' Gregory told him.

'That what she said?'

273

'No. She said she didn't love him.'

'But you know better, that it?'

'I can tell.'

'Clever you. How?'

'You saw her. Running upstairs last night and crying her eyes out.'

'Means nothing. Well, just means she was thinking about when she did love him, probably. Women is funny things, you know, Greg.'

Gregory gave a wisp of a smile.

Jimmy grinned. 'That's better. She's never going to see things the way we do. You know that. I mean, she wasn't the one heading for the chop, was she?'

Suddenly Gregory was laughing. 'Jesus, Jimmy, you're the greatest!'

'I've been telling you that for years. Good job I came in when I did, eh? Smooth things down. No point in getting Mum all knotted up, is there?'

Gregory shook his head. 'No, you're right. Doesn't matter *what* Mum thinks, does it?'

'Like you keep telling me – it's us who count. You and me. Just us.'

For the best part of a minute, separated by the width of the table, the twins looked at each other. And it was as if they were continuing their conversation secretly, not needing words, their thoughts passing between them with curious, unfettered ease.

Then the postman rattled the front door as he pushed letters through the box.

'Anything new on the news?' Jimmy asked, going to collect the post, returning with two bills, and asking again, 'Anything new on the news?'

'Haven't heard. Probably not.'

Jimmy agreed. 'Take their time, don't they?'

Gregory leered. 'Got to be sure, they have.'

'Oh, indeed. Got to be certain positive,' Jimmy added. 'Never do if they made a nasty mistake.'

But there was news, although it wouldn't be broadcast until that evening.

17

DI Pope got away from the station as soon as he could and drove directly to Chief Inspector Harvey's home. It was a meeting he had been dreading ever since Justin Harvey had been arrested; ever since Superintendent Donnelly had convinced himself that Justin was guilty. So Pope was pleased when Susan Dill chased after him, reaching him as he opened his car door. 'George – are you going where I think you're going?'

'No,' Pope lied.

'Liar.'

Pope gave a sheepish grin.

'I'm coming with you – if you don't mind?' Dill said.

Pope wasn't so sure. 'He won't like it.'

'The boss?'

'He'll say you're compromising yourself.'

'Okay, so I'm compromising myself.'

Pope smiled. 'Just as long as you make it clear you twisted my arm.'

'Twisted anything you like, George,' she said with a grin.

'Best offer I've had in months.'

But as they drove to Harvey's house, Pope's attitude changed. His face was grim when he asked, 'What do you think, Susan?'

'About Justin?'

'Yes.'

Susan Dill thought for a moment. 'Tell you the truth, George, I'm not doing that much thinking about him. It's the boss I'm worried about.'

'But do you think he killed Parsons?'

Susan Dill turned her head and looked at Pope. 'You don't?' she asked.

'I'm asking you.'

'Well, if he didn't someone's done a pretty good job of making us think he did.'

'So you *do* –'

'I didn't say that.'

She didn't say anything else either until they reached Harvey's home. Neither of them did. But on the doorstep, listening to the bell echo inside the house, Pope finally said, 'I'm dreading this.'

'Justin's been charged, hasn't he?' Chief Inspector Harvey said moments later as he stood with his back to the unlit fire, staring morosely at Pope.

'I'm afraid so, boss,' Pope told him. 'It was the barman who clinched it as far as Donnelly was concerned.'

'I'm sorry?' Harvey ran his fingers across his brow.

'We've traced Parsons' movements on the night he was killed,' Pope went on, and then, as though in an effort to delay the news, he asked, 'Did you know he was gay – Parsons?'

Harvey clearly couldn't follow where Pope was leading. He frowned. 'I didn't *know*, no. Helen always thought he was, but neither of us *knew*. Why?'

'Well, he went to a gay bar that night,' Pope said, and stopped to bite on his lower lip.

'So?'

'Justin has claimed all along that he never saw Parsons that night,' Pope continued reluctantly.

'Go on.'

'He claimed he never set foot in that particular bar,' Pope said, and glanced at Susan for support.

'George, would you just tell me –'

'The barman says that shortly after Parsons left the bar someone came in looking for him,' Susan Dill volunteered.

Harvey stared at her as though registering her presence for the first time.

'This person left a message that if Parsons came back he was to contact –' Now Susan Dill broke off, and looked down at her hands. Then she looked up again, and almost defiantly continued, 'He was to contact Justin urgently.'

In a ludicrous, absent-minded gesture Harvey turned his back on them, facing the fireplace, even holding out his hands as though to gain heat from the unlit fire.

Perhaps Pope thought it best to get the whole thing over while Harvey's back was towards him. 'The barman has identified Justin as the person who came in looking for Parsons and left the message.'

Harvey's outstretched hands folded themselves into tight fists. Yet his voice was remarkably calm when he asked, 'Is he positive, George?'

'Picked Justin out without a problem from –'

'All right. All right,' Harvey interrupted. He left the fireplace and slumped into an armchair. Then, with a horrible grin, a grin that was probably meant to be one of resignation, he said quietly, 'Well, that would appear to be that, wouldn't it?'

'Boss,' Susan Dill said quickly. 'It only means he lied about *looking* for Parsons.'

Harvey gave a forlorn snort. 'Just like he appears to have lied to me about trying to run down that girl – Miranda Jay,' he said wearily.

'There's still one glimmer of hope,' Pope now said, and Harvey looked up slowly, disbelievingly. 'Parsons did leave the bar before Justin came in,' he said.

'The person who *said* he was Justin,' Susan Dill corrected, and gave an encouraging smile in return for the look of gratitude Harvey threw her.

'Yes,' George agreed. 'And Parsons left with someone. Another man,' he said. Then he gave an exasperated sigh. 'Unfortunately the barman can't give us a proper description of this person –

apart from the fact that he was young, casually dressed and not a regular.' He fell silent again for a moment. 'We've managed to contact several people who were in the bar that evening but – well, they weren't much help with the description either. A few said he was good-looking, and one said he thought he heard him tell Parsons his name was Christopher, but –'

'But is there a chance *he* could –'

'There's always a chance, boss,' Susan Dill interrupted.

'However,' Pope jumped in, not wanting his superior to raise his hopes only to have them dashed again, 'it's Donnelly's contention that, because of the time element – Parsons had only left the bar a minute or two . . . before the man saying he was Justin came in – he could easily have caught up with him.'

'Justin, you mean?'

Pope nodded.

'We *are* still doing everything we can to trace this Christopher character,' Susan Dill said encouragingly.

'I'm sure, I'm sure,' Harvey said, sounding as if he meant it.

George Pope and Susan Dill stood up. There seemed to be nothing more to say.

Buttoning his overcoat, Pope said, 'By the way, boss, I did hear Donnelly say you would be wanting to see Justin.'

Harvey looked up quickly, expectantly.

'He instructed that you were to be given every facility to do just that.'

'Thank you, George.'

Harvey walked them to the front door. 'And thank you too, Susan.' He gave a wan little smile. 'You shouldn't have brought Susan, you know, George,' he admonished.

'I wanted to come, boss,' Dill said.

'You twisted his arm, I suppose?'

She gave a smile. 'You could say that.'

'Thank you both.'

'We just wanted you to know before it was made public, boss,' Pope said.

'I appreciate that. Thank you.'

It was made public at five o'clock in a brief news summary on BBC2 but the twins didn't see it then: as usual they waited for their mother to come home, have her drink, and watch the news at six o'clock.

Kate Renfrew was still fretting about all that had been said that morning although she tried hard to hide it, being overly bright and talkative and making no reference to what had taken place. But it was certainly in a strained silence that they all watched the news, especially when the newsreader announced: *Chief Inspector Robert Harvey, who until recently has headed the investigation into the so-called Rent Boy Murders, has been suspended from duty. For news on that and other developments here's our Crime Correspondent, John Farrar.*

John Farrar battled with the wind for a moment, settling stray strands of hair back into place. *We reported last week that Chief Inspector Robert Harvey had taken extended leave. A police spokesman now confirms that he has, in fact, been suspended, although it is stressed again that this is not for any mishandling of the so-called Rent Boy Murders. And in another development, the man originally arrested and questioned in connection with the serial killings of rent boys has been released. A few hours ago Superintendent Peter Donnelly stated that another man had been arrested, and has now been charged with the murder of David Parsons, the young man found dead in Battersea, although his death has not yet been officially confirmed as having any connection with the previous killings. And while the new suspect has not been named, sources close to the investigation have suggested he may be the son of Chief Inspector Harvey, although I must stress that this has not been stated officially. I understand that Superintendent Donnelly is to give a press conference later this evening and we'll have the details of that in our next bulletin.*

Gregory took the remote control and switched off the sound, plunging the room into a tingling silence. Blatantly, the twins turned and stared at their mother. Kate pretended not to notice. She kept

280

her eyes on the silent screen, concentrating as though lip-reading what the newscaster was now mouthing.

'Wonder why they *suspended* him?' she heard Gregory ask.

'Have to, wouldn't they, if his *son* is the killer,' she heard Jimmy reply.

'Nah, not *suspend* him. Take him off the case, sure, but not *suspend* him,' she heard Gregory say.

'Maybe he knew all along that his *son* was the killer,' she heard Jimmy suggest.

'And covered it up?' she heard Gregory ask.

'Could be,' she heard Jimmy surmise.

Kate's head snapped round. 'Will you two just stop it?' she demanded angrily, slopping her drink in the process. 'Now look what you've made me do.' She pulled a hankie from her pocket and wiped the drops from her skirt.

'Didn't *make* you do anything, Mum,' Jimmy protested.

'Stop what?' Gregory asked with enormous innocence.

'You know perfectly well what I'm talking about.'

'Oh, you mean about *him*?' Gregory said, nodding towards the screen.

'Gregory, I'm going to get really angry in a minute,' Kate said tightly.

'We were only talking, Mum,' Jimmy chimed in. 'It's interesting. I mean, he *is* our father, isn't he?'

The question made Kate even more upset. 'Yes, Jimmy. Precisely. He is your father,' she said.

'That don't make him no saint, though, do it?' Gregory asked, deliberately fouling up his grammar.

'No. No, it doesn't,' Kate agreed. 'But there is such a thing as loyalty,' she announced, and instantly wished she could have bitten back the words. She looked away and winced as the twins hooted with derision.

'Jesus, Mum, you don't half come out with some good ones,' Gregory told her. 'Loyalty! To *him*?'

281

'To *me*,' Kate said quietly, and then she repeated it, shouting as though a loud voice would make her point more valid. 'To *me!*'

'Oh, I get it,' Gregory mocked, 'be loyal to you and nice to him, is that it?'

'No, that's *not* it. I –'

'And we . . . Jimmy and I . . . we don't come into it at all. We're just two little *bastards* who –'

'Gregory!' Kate almost screamed.

'Well, that's what it seems like to us – right, Jimmy?'

'Seems like it,' Jimmy agreed.

Kate Renfrew was close to tears. She stared at her sons and shook her head. 'You're so mistaken if –'

'Mistaken?' Gregory interrupted. '*We're* mistaken? I like that one. Come on, Jimmy. Let's get out of here,' he said, standing and marching to the door.

'Don't either of you dare walk out on me like that,' Kate shouted, rising also.

The door already open, standing there with his brother behind him, Gregory turned and faced his mother. 'You know something, Mum? The only mistake was made by you. You didn't fall in with the bastard's plan to have us killed off. You had us – that's the mistake,' he said in cold, unblinking fury.

Very slowly, as though her body was gently collapsing of its own volition, Kate Renfrew sat back down in her seat. Away in the distance, or what appeared to be the distance, she heard the front door slam. She heard the Mini start. She heard it drive away. Suddenly she hurled her glass against the wall, smashing it to smithereens. Then she folded her arms across her breasts, and took to moaning, rocking herself. 'Damn you, Robert Harvey,' she whispered. 'Damn you. Damn you. Damn you.'

And perhaps Robert Harvey felt damned. He certainly looked it as he went to confront his son: his face was drawn and grey, his shoulders drooped like an old man's, his step was heavy. And when he spoke his voice rasped. 'How are you, Justin?' he asked, aware that the words were absurdly banal in the circumstances. 'Stupid question,' he added.

Justin gave a wan smile.

Harvey sat beside his son and placed a comforting arm about his shoulders. For quite some time they sat like that, neither of them speaking. In truth, there seemed nothing to say, nothing that would alleviate the desperate sadness. But, finally, Harvey said quietly, 'Justin, Justin,' sounding bewildered.

'Dad, what's happening?' Justin asked in a tiny voice, a voice that reminded Harvey of his son as he had been years ago, a child filled with curiosity, a child forever wanting to know the answers.

'You've been charged, Justin,' Harvey said, thinking that was what his son wanted to know.

'That's not what I meant, Dad. It's this whole thing – Dad, I didn't kill David. You've got to believe me. I never touched him,' Justin said in a lost voice. 'I never even *saw* him that night.'

'Justin . . .'

Abruptly Justin pulled himself away. 'You don't believe me either,' he said in a frightened voice. 'You think I *did* kill –'

'Justin, I don't know what to believe – your wallet, Miranda, the barman, I mean . . .' Harvey stopped talking, and then in a desperate tone, he pleaded, 'Explain it to me, Justin.'

'I *can't*,' Justin answered, sounding desolate. 'I didn't try and run Miranda down. I didn't kill David. I don't know what's going on . . . Dad – help me, please.'

For the first time in his life Robert Harvey felt utterly powerless. He gave his son a long, pained stare. 'I can't, Justin,' he admitted.

'Dad –'

'It's all been taken out of my hands. I'm suspended. I can't do anything to help.' He gave something approximating a wail. 'I wish I could, but I can't.'

And it was as though Justin had somehow convinced himself that his father, the all-powerful, would be able to rescue him; and now, bereft of this hope, he crumpled. He buried his face in his hands and burst into uncontrollable sobs.

And the most terrible thing was that Robert Harvey could do nothing about it. He could not console his son. Worse, he suddenly realised he could do nothing to console himself. He knew it was the wrong thing to do, knew it was unforgivable, but he got to his feet and walked quickly out of the room.

'You were a bit hard on her,' Jimmy said, but didn't sound all that reproachful.

Gregory glowered. 'It had to be said.'

'Yeah, but there's a way of saying things, Greg.'

'And mine wasn't the way?'

Jimmy grinned. 'Let's just say you sure ain't no fucking diplomat.'

They had parked the Mini about fifty yards from the house, and now Gregory thumped the steering wheel with his fist. 'How *could* she –' he began.

'She didn't,' Jimmy interrupted.

'Oh, no?'

'No. You know Mum – she starts to whimper if she sees a dead cat on the side of the road.'

'Okay, a cat. I can understand a cat. But *him!* Feeling sorry for *him!*'

'That's Mum for you.'

'She's ruined everything,' Gregory complained bitterly.

It seemed that for a while Jimmy agreed. But then he shook his head. 'It'd have been better if she'd been pleased, but she hasn't really ruined everything. I mean, it's not exactly as if she's in on it.'

'So?'

'So, *we're* the ones who have to be chuffed.'

Gregory looked mildly appeased. 'I suppose.'

'Sure we are. And I am, for one,' Jimmy told him.

Then Gregory broke into a smile. 'And me!'

'There you go!'

They were silent again for a while before Gregory said, 'Suppose we should go back.'

'Yep.'

'And I'll have to apologise.'

'Yep.'

'Oh, Christ.'

'Yep.'

And Gregory did apologise. 'Mum, look, I'm really sorry for what I said,' and was nonplussed for a minute when Kate Renfrew seemed about to be unforgiving, glaring at him as though doubting his sincerity. 'Really, Mum. I was well out of order.'

'He means it, Mum,' Jimmy chipped in.

And, of course, Kate's defences, if that's what they were, collapsed. She opened her arms wide and welcomed Gregory into her forgiving embrace, hugging him, whispering into his ear. 'I know, darling. I know you're sorry. I'm sorry too. Honestly I am. I should have tried harder to see things from your point of view. To understand more.'

'I'm forgiven then?'

'Of course you are, darling. And is Mummy forgiven?'

'Can we call a halt to this now?' Jimmy asked with a grin. 'It's getting really maudlin.'

And suddenly they were all laughing, albeit nervously, Kate wiping a tear from her eye with a delicate flick of her finger.

The bedroom was dark and still: not even his breathing made a sound.

Gary Hubbard lay naked on his bed, his arms folded neatly over his chest. He was convinced they would stay that way even when he slept, and he smiled to himself at the thought of escaping a beating. Or maybe he smiled to himself just as he had done the night before he was due to leave the children's home, because Gary Hubbard had decided to make another move, a move, to his mind, every bit as momentous. He was going to leave his flat, to move on rather than out, as he thought of it. Indeed, this was an even more special move: it was a move of his own choosing, off and away to a new beginning. He was going to walk out, taking only his clothes and a couple of precious possessions, leaving behind all the things that might remind him of where he'd been and what had happened. Already his van was packed, the clothes he would wear carefully laid out on a chair at the foot of his bed. Even his shoes were specially polished, bright and shiny, and not just for Jesus this time.

'How *could* I?' Helen Harvey asked when her husband remonstrated against her return. 'How *could* I stay away and let you go through all this alone?'

'Oh, Helen –' was all that Robert Harvey could manage.

They sat far apart, one on each side of the fireplace. But the fire was lit now, cheery and bright and warm, very much at odds with the anguish that had etched itself on their faces.

'I feel so useless,' Harvey confessed after a while.

'Is there nothing we can do?' Helen asked, shaking her head at the same time as though already admitting to herself the futility of the question.

'Nothing.'

And again the terrible silence fell between them, both staring into space, both wrapped in their private hopelessness. Then, out of the blue, and in a tone that smacked of despair, Helen asked, 'Robert, *could* Justin really have done it, do you think?'

Robert Harvey could not bring himself to look at his wife: he fixed his eyes on the flames, and nodded. 'He could have, Helen,' he replied, and he flinched as though feeling the betrayal again.

'But . . .' Helen began, and then shook her head. 'Justin? *Our* Justin? We'd have known,' she said, and then, pleading, 'wouldn't we?'

'I don't know, Helen. I just don't know.'

Helen made up her mind. 'Of course we would, Robert. He just *can't* be guilty.'

Her husband retreated into the security of professional jargon. 'All the evidence points to his guilt, dear.'

'The evidence must be wrong then,' Helen said.

'And the witnesses?' Harvey asked. 'They are wrong too?'

'Mistaken,' Helen said.

Harvey shook his head.

'People do make mistakes, don't they?'

'Helen – don't. Please.'

'We can't just sit here and do nothing,' she insisted but in a lost, forlorn way.

'There's nothing we *can* do, Helen.'

'I just cannot believe that Justin –'

'Helen . . . Helen. It doesn't *matter* what you can or cannot believe. It doesn't matter what *I* can or cannot believe. On the evidence available, Justin has been charged with murdering David Parsons and we're going to have to wait and see what happens at his trial.'

It was as though Helen Harvey had forgotten about the trial. She repeated the word in a whisper, putting her hands to her mouth as if in an effort to stifle the word. Then she allowed her hands to flutter from her face. 'Maybe something will turn up between now and then?' she asked with desperate hope.

'Maybe,' her husband told her. 'Maybe.'

A log on the fire spat like gunfire, making them both jump.

At ten o'clock Trevor McDonald donned his most serious face, sounding like an undertaker as he told his viewers the astonishing news. It had been confirmed, he said, that the man charged with the murder of David Parsons was the son of Chief Inspector Robert Harvey.

'That's it then,' Jimmy said firmly.

'That's it,' Gregory agreed. There was a wistful note in his voice.

'Mission accomplished.'

'Mission accomplished,' Gregory repeated. 'Almost.'

'Almost?'

'Got to get the conviction.'

'Oh. Yeah.'

'Need him to get life.'

'Yeah.'

Gregory pawed the air in a complicated stretch. 'Then it'll be mission accomplished.'

'Right. When will that be? The trial?'

Gregory shrugged. 'God alone knows. Could be months yet.'

'So what do we do now?'

Gregory shrugged again. 'Wait. That's all we *can* do. Wait.'

And that was all Justin Harvey could do: wait. And the waiting was interminable. On remand, he was a far cry from the handsome, cocky young man he had once been. His eyes, black-rimmed, seemed to have sunk into his face, and he had the gaunt look of someone who had been witness to unspeakable horror.

Alone at night Justin would curl up and wonder how all this had befallen him; wonder, too, how easy and practical it might be to end the entire episode, to hang himself as some had done, or slice through his wrists. There were times when he seriously considered this as an option. He was not, he learned, somewhat to his astonishment, afraid of dying, but dying in prison was another matter. To die alone, caged, as though admitting guilt, struck him as particularly awful. And so he continued to wait, allowing the melancholy to settle about him like a shadow, following him wherever he went.

And Kate Renfrew waited. Although she gave no indication of it to her sons, she was appalled by what had happened. Justin Harvey, conceived of the same seed as her own children, came constantly into her mind, and although she had never met the boy, never even seen him, she felt that he was in some mysterious way a part of

288

her, and it troubled her that the twins could be so callous, even gleeful, about his terrible predicament. Alone, sometimes when she was driving but more often at night, she argued with herself. Yes, she could understand why Gregory and Jimmy might hate their father, although hate was an emotion she found difficult to comprehend. And, yes, she could with effort understand why they took pleasure in the fact that Robert had been suspended and, if the reports were to be believed, was facing diciplinary action and possible dismissal. Yes, she could understand all that. But the lack of concern they had shown towards the boy, guilty or not, alarmed her, if only because it seemed to prove that she barely knew the children she had always thought she was so close to.

But then she would scold herself. Tell herself that, really, the whole fiasco was no concern of hers. It was nothing to do with her if Robert's son had turned out to be a monster. And night after night she would end up saying a quick but heartfelt prayer to a God admitted to only in times of crisis, thanking Him that *her* sons were good boys, boys she could be proud of, boys who loved her and whom she loved.

And away to the north, sitting quietly in his new bedsit in Doncaster, Gary Hubbard waited, although, had he been asked, he would not have been able to explain what exactly he was waiting for.

18

T hen the waiting was over, eleven months of it, and the trial began. Jimmy Renfrew was furious he couldn't attend, but reluctantly agreed to stay away, swayed by his brother's relentless logic. 'What you going to do?' Gregory demanded sarcastically. 'Put on a wig and a false beard?'

'No, but –'

'You can't run the risk, Jimmy. *We* can't. All it takes is for that bastard to recognise you – or Miranda, for that matter – and the whole thing goes up the spout. Can't you see that?'

'I suppose. But I can go for the verdict?'

'Oh, yes. Most def-in-ite-ly yes. We'll all be there that day. Mum too.'

'And you promise to tell me everything that happens?' Jimmy asked.

'Every single word. And all the stuff that doesn't get on the news.'

'Okay then.'

Gregory might not have reported every single word but he certainly gave his brother an accurate commentary, relishing his role. Every morning he trotted along to the Old Bailey in good time, making sure of getting a decent seat in the gallery. And when the day's session was completed he would hurry home and lock himself away with Jimmy in the bedroom, and relate everything that had taken place.

'I tell you, Jimmy, it's creepy, that Old Bailey. I mean, *really* creepy. Like it's filled with ghosts or something. So fucking creepy it kind of makes you want to giggle.'

'Yeah?' Jimmy asked, wide-eyed.

'Really pompous too.'

'I bet.'

'The place was packed, but ever so quiet. Bit like a funeral, really. You know. Everyone dying to have a right good natter but nobody daring 'cause of the place they were in.'

Jimmy nodded, intrigued.

'Well, *he* was there, of course. Right in the front row. With his tart. Trying to put on their concerned parents' faces.' Gregory gave a snigger. 'Tell you something else. He's had the stuffing well and truly knocked out of him. Remember how he was on the telly when we first saw him? All supercilious and condescending, trying to convince the plebs what a clever bunny he was? Well, he ain't like that now, I can tell you. Talk about having your world collapse about you! Shit, Jimmy, he's *fucked*!'

For a while Jimmy shared Gregory's delight, but then he looked puzzled, and asked, 'What about Justin?'

It was Gregory's turn to look baffled. He frowned and thought for a moment. Then he grinned. 'You know, I didn't pay much attention to him. Doesn't really matter a lot, does he? Not in the greater scheme of things, anyway.'

'I'd say it matters to him, though,' Jimmy said.

'Oh, I'm sure it does, but that's his problem. Doesn't matter to us.'

'Okay. Go on. Tell me all that happened,' and was angry when Gregory answered. 'Not a lot, really.'

'You promised to tell –' Jimmy began hotly.

'No, truly. Very little happened. Just a lot of palaver about what the case was all about so the jury wouldn't – hey, you should see *them*! Right lot of dumbclucks, if you ask me – so they wouldn't have to tax their little brains too much. Nothing ever happens for the first few days, Jimmy. It won't hot up for a while. Really, I'm not holding anything back.'

'You'd better not be,' Jimmy warned.

'If you don't believe me – read the rags tomorrow. Bound to be in them. Maybe on the box too. You'll see I'm not telling lies.'

'Better not be,' Jimmy said again.

And Gregory wasn't lying: it took several days before the barristers got down to the nitty-gritty and started calling witnesses.

'Oh, it's not looking at all good for poor old Justin,' Gregory reported. 'Ta,' he added, accepting a can of lager from Jimmy and settling back to give his daily rundown of events. 'The thing about Miranda was that she acted so *dumb* she was convincing. Like the jury were thinking no one that stupid could make up a story like that.'

'About me and her and the car?' Jimmy asked.

Gregory nodded and sipped his beer. 'Tell you another thing – motherhood hasn't done her a lot of good. You should see what a year has done to her. She looks *old*.' He gave a shudder. 'Like a hag. Tits all saggy. And *fat*.' He added a grimace to his shudder. 'Never get a father for the little bastard at the rate she's going.' He placed the lager on the desk and adopted a pompous, judicial pose: 'Tell me, Miss Jay, isn't it extraordinary that you don't even know the *name* of this young man whom you claim took you out for what I can only imagine was a romantic evening?'

'That's me,' Jimmy said.

'Oh, that's you,' Gregory confirmed. 'Rather convenient, is it not? Almost as convenient as the fact that the police, despite strenuous efforts, have not been able to locate this young man.'

'What did she say to that?' Jimmy asked.

'Not a lot. "It's true," she said. "True that it's remarkably convenient?" the barrister asked. "No," she said, "my story." "Ah, your *story*. Thank you, Miss Jay."' Gregory dropped his pose and took another drink. 'Still, the jury believed Miranda, I'm sure of it.'

'Who else did they call?'

'The barman from the gay bar,' Gregory said. 'He called you insignificant,' he smirked.

'How d'you mean?' Jimmy asked, bridling.

'That's what he said. When he was asked how come he recognised

Justin so easily as the person who came in looking for Parsons, why he couldn't give even a vague description of you, he said it was because you were insignificant.'

'Fuck him,' Jimmy swore.

'So now you know,' Gregory teased.

Jimmy hurled a pillow at him.

'Why?' Helen Harvey demanded.

'I'd just prefer it if you weren't there,' her husband told her.

'You mean I might hear something else you didn't tell me?' Helen asked.

'No. I –'

'How *could* you, Robert. Good God, I should have been the first person you told. I'm his mother, aren't I?'

'Helen . . . Oh, God. Look. I didn't want you upset. I . . .'

'Upset?' Helen demanded. 'Of course I'd have been upset. Some little trollop accuses my son of making her pregnant and then trying to kill her – of course I'd have been upset. But I should have been told. How do you think I felt having to learn about it in open court?'

'I'm sorry, I'm sorry. I thought it was sorted. I mean –'

'You mean –' Helen began and then reached for a newspaper and threw it across the room towards her husband. 'You mean that all these stories are true, is that what you mean? That you tried to cover up the fact that –'

'No, Helen, no. The girl . . . Miranda Jay . . . and the lad she came with told me they didn't want to take it any further. They just wanted me to warn Justin to stay away from her. From Miranda. I didn't see any point in . . . Oh, forget it, Helen.'

'Oh, that's lovely. Forget it. Well, the prosecution aren't going to forget it, are they?' Helen screamed. And then her voice took on an icy edge. 'You're going to help convict our son,' she said accusingly. 'And if that happens –' She stared at him for a moment, then swung round and stormed out of the room.

'Helen!'

His wife ignored him. The bedroom door slammed. Robert Harvey felt totally alone.

John Farrar was standing outside the Old Bailey in the blustery December evening. He cleared his throat. *Geoffrey Cavendish QC for the prosecution has indeed hinted at what he called 'murky goings-on'. However, we understand that the accused's father, Chief Inspector Robert Harvey, who was suspended without any clear reason being given, is to be put on the stand tomorrow. So we should learn a lot more at that point.*

'Big day tomorrow, then,' Jimmy said, switching off the television and looking enviously across at Gregory. 'I don't suppose –'

Gregory immediately shook his head. 'No chance. Sorry, Jimmy. Just too risky.' Then he gave a little laugh. 'Can't you just see him up there in the witness box and suddenly he spots you and shouts, "There he is!" Be bloody bedlam!'

Jimmy laughed too. 'Liven things up.'

'Oh, I think things are going to get quite lively enough without that,' Gregory told him. 'It's perfect. Just perfect. When that QC is finished with him I bet it's going to sound like he thinks his precious son *is* guilty, and if *he* thinks that, what are the jury going to think, eh?'

Jimmy didn't know what the jury were going to think. He knew, though, what he was now thinking. 'Mum's gone very quiet since it started, hasn't she?' he observed.

Gregory shrugged. 'Just doesn't want to talk about it in case we have another row.'

'You don't think she suspects we had anything to do with it?'

'Hell, no,' Gregory shot back quickly. 'What makes you ask that, Jimmy?'

'Dunno. Kind of giving us looks, isn't she?'

'Is she? I hadn't noticed.'

'Yeah, sort of watching. And listening. Like she was waiting for us to say something she could jump on.'

Gregory shook his head. 'You're imagining it.'

'Maybe. Yeah. Maybe I am.'

And if Kate Renfrew had been privy to the conversation she would have agreed that, yes, Jimmy was certainly imagining it, although she would have conceded that she had been watching her sons more closely than usual, and listening carefully to everything they said. But it wasn't because she believed they had anything to do with the dreadful events: such a thought would never have entered her head. She watched and listened because she was worried what effect the grim drama was having on her beloved sons. Nothing could erase the fact that there was a link between the Harveys and the Renfrews. And it was as though she felt that any stigma attached to the Harveys would inevitably leave a mark on her sons, a thumbprint of guilt.

She made an excuse, recognising it as feeble: a chill coming on, she said, and went to her room immediately she came home. And from her room she watched John Farrar's report. Now, almost before she realised what she was doing, she was hurrying downstairs in her dressing-gown and slippers.

'Mum!' Jimmy exclaimed in surprise. 'Can't you sleep?'

Kate stood in the doorway looking embarrassed. 'No, I –' she began wondering why, indeed, she had come downstairs. 'I was worried, I think,' she heard herself explain.

'About what, Mum?' Gregory asked, loading his question with filial concern.

Kate shook her head.

'Come on, Mum,' Jimmy insisted. 'Tell us what you're worried about.' He got up and took his mother by the arm, leading her to his chair.

Kate sat down. 'I'm not sure.'

Jimmy and Gregory waited.

'This whole business –'

Still the twins waited.

'I'm worried you'll be startled by it,' she said, and instantly knew that 'startled' was not the word she had wanted to use. 'Be hurt by it,' she amended. 'Be scarred by it,' she tried as if 'hurt' wasn't the right word either.

The twins looked at each other. Then Jimmy encouraged his brother with a surreptitious nod.

'Hey, Mum,' Gregory said seriously but kindly. 'You don't have to worry about us. Really you don't.'

Kate gave a wan smile. 'It's just that you both seem so . . . so . . .' she broke off, floundering.

Jimmy perched on the arm of the chair and put his arm around her shoulders. 'So *what*, Mum?' he asked gently.

Kate shook her head again. 'I don't know how to put it. So *cold*, maybe,' she concluded but making it a question as though she was open to other suggestions.

'Well, you don't really expect us to weep, do you?' Gregory asked.

'That's not what Mum means,' Jimmy told him.

'No, it's not,' Kate agreed.

'What then?' Gregory urged.

'I just wish –'

'What Mum means is that she wishes we'd be a bit more compassionate,' Jimmy said. 'Isn't that it, Mum?'

Kate beamed up at him. 'Yes, darling. That's exactly what I mean.' She reached awkwardly over her shoulder, took his hand and squeezed it. And before Gregory could reply she went on, 'I *do* understand that you both feel bitter about the way . . . you know . . . about –'

'The abortion,' Gregory interposed harshly, cruelly.

'Yes. Yes. But –'

'Mum, you've got it all wrong,' Jimmy interrupted, giving Gregory an admonishing look. 'Okay. Sure, we're not too happy about him wanting you to have us aborted –'

'Not too happy,' Gregory mimicked.

'But, I mean, we're civilised, aren't we? We . . . well, you want to know the truth? We're really feeling sorry for them all. Him. And his wife. And Justin. We were just talking about it before you came down, weren't we, Gregory? Saying how really awful it must be to have your whole world come down about your head like a ton of bricks. Weren't we, Gregory?' Jimmy demanded with a warning glare.

Gregory nodded.

'Were you really, darling?'

'You don't think we're enjoying it all, do you?' Jimmy asked. 'We can see just how upset *you* are, and that's enough in itself for us to feel really upset by everything.'

'Oh, Jimmy,' Kate said.

'Actually, what we were saying was wouldn't it be great if we could find out that Justin was innocent, could find out who the real killer was, and bring everything to a happy conclusion.'

Kate Renfrew reacted as she did to all fairytales. She gave a longing smile and her eyes filled with tears. 'I just *knew* I was being silly,' she confessed. 'How could I ever have thought – come here, both of you, and give me a great big hug.'

Jimmy was already there with her so he gave her the first hug. And Gregory got up from his chair and gave her another one. When he straightened up, he advised, 'Now you go back to bed and have a good sleep, Mum.'

'Yes,' Kate agreed, and stood up.

'And don't be so silly in future,' Jimmy said.

'No. No, I won't. Oh, I love you two so much I could eat you both,' she added with a gay little laugh.

'Oh no,' Jimmy said. 'Be like cheese. Eat cheese before you go to bed and you have nightmares.'

'Oh, I don't think I'll be having those tonight,' Kate said.

'Not if you don't eat us,' Gregory said, and his mother laughed happily as she made her way back upstairs.

'What in the name of Jesus was all that crap you came out with?' Gregory demanded, leering.

'Had to say *something*,' Jimmy told him.

'"Find out that Justin was innocent, find the real killer, bring everything to a happy conclusion"?' Gregory mocked.

'That's what she wanted to hear,' Jimmy said.

Gregory suddenly went serious and his eyes clouded. He nodded. 'You're quite right, Jimmy. That's just what she wanted to hear,' he said in a distant voice.

'And that's what counts.'

Gregory nodded again. 'That's what counts.'

'Helen,' Robert Harvey called quietly from the bedroom door.

'Go away, Robert.'

'Helen —'

'Go away!' she said harshly.

'I want to explain —'

'There's nothing *to* explain, Robert. I've told you. If your stupidity does anything to make people believe my son is guilty I'll never forgive you.'

'That's —'

'It's a fact, Robert.'

Robert Harvey went slowly back downstairs, making tiny pauses on the stairs, swinging each foot forward in an exaggerated way. It seemed there was to be no end to his misery. He looked back up towards the bedroom door. His job, his marriage, his son, most of all his son, slithering away from him. He jumped when the doorbell rang shrilly.

'George!' Harvey said, surprised.

George Pope held a bottle of whisky aloft. 'I thought, maybe . . .'

'Come in. Come in.'

Pope followed Harvey into the sitting-room. 'I thought maybe you could use a drink,' he said.

'Need more than a drink, George.'

Pope nodded understandingly.

'Need a miracle. Let me get glasses.' Harvey looked about him in an addled way and made for the kitchen. 'I appreciate this, George,' he said when he returned.

'Well, you know . . .'

Harvey nodded as though he did, indeed, know.

'Susan says to say hello,' Pope said. 'And the others.'

Again Harvey nodded.

'Boss, if there's anything any of us can do –'

'I know you would, George,' Harvey said, passing Pope a tumbler. 'I know you would.' He looked hard at Pope. 'The terrible thing is, George, sitting there in court, hearing the evidence, I'm beginning to believe the boy might be guilty.' He gave a huge sigh and swallowed a mouthful of whisky. He waited for Pope to pooh-pooh any such idea, and looked surprised when no such contradiction came. 'You think so too?' he asked wearily.

'Boss, it's something we've got to face. He *might* have done it. I'm sorry, but . . . you know . . . Jesus, how many times have we charged someone with murder and found it impossible to believe he could be guilty?'

It was a while before Harvey took his eyes from Pope's face and walked across the room to sit down. He held his tumbler in both hands, swilling the liquid round and round. 'I've been thinking that myself. It's just . . . my own *son* . . .'

George Pope looked uncomfortably about him before sitting down also.

'You think you know them, don't you?' Harvey asked. 'Your children. You really think you know them. And then something like this happens and . . . oh, I don't know, George. I honestly don't know what to think.'

'How's Mrs Harvey? Is she coping?'

Harvey shrugged. 'She's coping as best she can,' he said. 'As best she can under the circumstances.' He gave a tight little laugh. 'I was thinking, just before you arrived, that – you believe in fate, George?'

'I haven't given it much thought, boss.'

'No,' Harvey said wistfully, 'I don't suppose you have. Maybe we have to pay for mistakes we've made. What d'you think? Have to make reparation.' He was rambling, he knew. Talking nonsense. 'I'm sorry.'

'That's okay.'

'Anyway, not long now. I'm being called tomorrow, I understand.'

Pope didn't reply.

'And no matter what I say I'm going to make matters worse.'

'You don't know that, boss.'

Harvey gave a huge, bitter laugh. 'Oh, I know it, George. Believe me, I know it. And when I do –'

'Boss –'

'When I do, George, I'm finished,' Harvey said, mostly to himself. Then he looked up. 'Helen will leave me, you know. Oh, yes,' he insisted as Pope began to protest. 'She's as good as told me. How's that for an outcome, eh? No job. No son. No wife. Nothing.' He gulped down the remainder of his whisky. 'Some prospect, isn't it?'

'Maybe this wasn't such a good idea,' Pope said. He stood up.

'Maybe not good,' Harvey agreed. 'But kind, George. Very kind.' He rose and followed Pope to the front door, opening it.

'We'll be thinking of you, boss. Tomorrow.'

'Thank you.'

'Yes. Well.' George Pope turned abruptly and walked down the short driveway to his car without looking back.

Harvey shut the door and leaned his back against it. He let his head droop. Then, with what could have been a sob or a growl, he heaved himself upright and walked deliberately to a small room at the back of the house. He switched on the light and gazed at the chaos that confronted him. Everything unwanted or unused, it seemed, had been dumped in there. He spotted what he wanted. Stepping carefully, he reached up to the top shelf and lifted down a large black box. He placed it on the floor outside the room. Then he went back in and took another box from the same shelf, a smaller, oblong one.

Back in the sitting-room, the slide projector on a card table beside him, he eased himself back into his chair and started to flick slowly through the slides. All of them were of Justin: from the day he was born to the age of about thirteen: learning to walk, his first day at school, playing football, running, acting the fool, laughing. The boy's laughter rattled in Harvey's head. He started to shake, and for a moment he thought he was laughing also. But then the pictures projected onto the wall started to blur, and Robert Harvey knew he was crying. Instantly he switched off the machine. And in the darkness, he sobbed quietly to himself.

19

*Y*ou're absolutely right, John Farrar confirmed. *Quite extraordinary scenes. The entire day was given over to the questioning of Chief Inspector Robert Harvey, the father of the accused, Justin Harvey, and again Geoffrey Cavendish QC for the prosecution made reference to what he described yesterday as 'murky goings-on'. Although admonished by the judge, Justice Raphael Havelock, Mr Cavendish referred again to the fact that an earlier witness, Miss Miranda Jay, claimed that she had approached the chief inspector and informed him that the accused had attempted to run her down – in a car of the same make and colour as the chief inspector's – but that the chief inspector had suppressed this information. Mr Cavendish countered the judge's warning with the assertion that he was seeking to prove that the chief inspector was a hostile and unreliable witness, a man, he said, who would go to the ultimate limits to protect his son even if this meant using his position to conceal evidence. Mr Cavendish then enumerated the police findings to the chief inspector and asked, 'As a police officer, would it not be fair to say that with all the evidence before you, and based on your own experience and shedding any feelings of paternal obligation, you would, like the police, like myself, like most sane and intelligent people, come to the conclusion that the accused, Justin Harvey, was guilty of this brutal murder?' The chief inspector agreed it was a reasonable conclusion. At that point his wife, Mrs Helen Harvey, screamed and ran from the gallery. Immediately the judge called a brief recess. There is no doubt that the chief inspector's admission has had a devastating effect on the case. Most people I spoke to are now of a mind that Justin Harvey is guilty, and although, of course, he has not been charged with any other offence, the general feeling seems to be that he could well be responsible for the so-called Rent Boy Murders as well. This feeling has been compounded by the defence's announcement that the accused will not now take the stand* *as was expected, so the trial could be over in a few days.*

'How awful,' Kate Renfrew said with a shudder.

'Terrible,' Gregory said, straight-faced.

'Poor Justin,' Jimmy said, and gave his mother a morose and compassionate look.

'That's not what I mean,' Gregory said. 'I meant it must be terrible for *him*. It was *him* who put the final nail in his own son's coffin. How's he going to live with that?'

'Don't, Gregory,' Kate said. 'It doesn't bear thinking about.'

But Gregory was relentless. 'He'll get life now. Might as well be dead, really. Locked up for the rest of his natural life. Best part of it, anyway. And it'll be *him* who killed him,' he persisted. 'Just like he nearly killed us,' he concluded, but keeping malice from his voice, making it sound as though sadness and disbelief were in his mind. And then, as if he realised what he was saying only when the words had been uttered, he turned to his mother. 'Oh, Mum. I'm so sorry. I didn't mean to . . . I shouldn't have said that.'

'No, you shouldn't,' Jimmy told him, his voice severe but his eyes sparkling. 'Don't pay any heed to him, Mum. It's just that we're all upset.'

Kate nodded, but in a vague way, as if she was agreeing with something else entirely, some thought that had occurred to her on the spur of the moment.

'Mum?'

She swung her head sharply to face Jimmy. 'Yes. Oh. Yes, of course I know Gregory didn't mean it. We *are* all desperately upset, aren't we?'

'Won't be for much longer,' Jimmy said consolingly. 'Be over soon.'

'Yes, dear. It'll be over soon,' Kate agreed.

'And then we can put it all behind us,' Gregory decided.

Kate gave him a thin smile. 'Yes.'

Gregory left his chair and walked to his mother. He knelt on the floor in front of her, leant forward and buried his head in her lap. Kate stroked her son's head, gentle, even strokes as though smoothing silk. 'Mum?'

'Yes, Gregory?'

'Would you mind if we went to court to hear the verdict?'

Kate stopped her stroking for a second, her hand suspended over Gregory's head. She looked across at Jimmy in a puzzled way. And then, as if her puzzlement was something never to be solved, she said. 'No, I don't mind.'

'It's not that we're being morbid or anything,' Gregory said, peering up into her face. 'Is it, Jimmy?'

Jimmy shook his head.

'It's just that we think that we *should* be there, isn't that right, Jimmy?'

Jimmy nodded.

'Kind of support,' Gregory added.

The puzzlement flickered back across his mother's face. 'I understand,' she said quietly.

'We think you should come too, Mum,' Gregory told her.

Kate stiffened. 'No,' she said quickly. 'I couldn't. I couldn't possibly. I –'

'Okay . . . okay,' Gregory reassured her.

'It would be just too dreadful –'

'I said it was okay, Mum,' Gregory told her, taking hold of one of her hands and kissing it.

'We just thought it would be . . . well, a *kind* thing to do,' Jimmy said quietly.

'Kind?'

'Yes. You know. I mean, can you imagine how *he* must be feeling right now? We thought it would be really nice for him to know that someone was . . . No. You're right. Forget it, Mum. It would be dreadful for you.'

'We didn't think it out properly, Mum,' Gregory said remorsefully.

'Why should you bother to support him after what he did to you?

We must have been crazy even to think you'd go.'

'That's not the reason,' Kate said sharply.

'Sorry?' Gregory said.

'It's not because of what happened between us that I don't want to go.'

'Why, then, Mum?' Jimmy asked.

Kate looked down at Gregory's head and started stroking it again. 'You'll only be angry if I tell you,' she answered.

'*I* won't,' Jimmy said.

'*I* won't either,' Gregory affirmed, but he got up from his knees and went to join Jimmy on the settee.

Kate took a deep breath. 'Well, it's because . . . because I still have . . . have . . . feelings for Robert that I don't want to go there and see him humiliated.'

Gregory nodded. 'Yeah, okay, I can understand that, Mum,' he said reasonably.

'Still,' Jimmy said, 'I'd have thought you'd want to be there *because* you still had feelings for him. Sort of back him up. You know, show support.'

Gregory nodded soberly. 'He has a point, Mum.'

Kate stood up and crossed the room to stare at herself in the mirror over the fireplace. 'I'll think about it,' she said finally. She swung from the mirror. 'Now, if you'll excuse me, I'm going to have a bath.'

'Let's put it this way, Mum,' Gregory said. 'If you decide to go we'll look after you.'

'Thank you, dear.'

'And if all gets too much for you and you want to leave, we'll leave with you,' Jimmy assured her.

Kate smiled at Jimmy. 'I'll think about it,' she said again.

The twins stared at each other after their mother left the room. 'What d'you think?' Gregory asked.

Jimmy gave him a glare. 'I think you should have told me his wife screamed and ran out of court,' he said.

'I did.'

'No, you didn't. All you said was she gave a yelp and walked out.'

'A yelp. A scream. What's the difference?'

'Big difference. You promised to tell me *everything*.'

'I have told you everything.'

'Not exactly as it happened, though.'

'Near enough.'

'Okay. Tell me now. What really happened?'

Gregory gave a sigh. 'She gave a yelp –'

'A scream.'

'A scream, then, and ran from her seat in the gallery.' Gregory laughed. 'Nearly knocked some old bloke over as she scuttled out.'

'And what did *he* do?'

'Daddy?'

'Yes.'

Gregory gave another laugh. 'I thought he was going to jump out of the witness box and go chasing after her. Kind of opened his mouth to yell at her, and took a bit of a step. Then just seemed to freeze. Looked really shattered, he did. Really devastated.'

And if he looked really devastated in court, Robert Harvey was even more so when he got home.

At first he presumed Helen had taken to her bed – her usual reaction when angry or under stress. He went into the kitchen and brewed a pot of tea. He filled one cup, added a splash of milk but no sugar, and carried it up to the bedroom. He hesitated on the landing, surprised but not alarmed to find the bedroom door open. He walked in. Before he could do anything about it the cup of tea slipped from his fingers and thudded onto the floor, spraying tea onto the carpet and the pale-green floral wallpaper.

Rigid, Robert Harvey gazed about the bedroom. The doors of the built-in wardrobe were wide open, many of Helen's clothes missing, their hangers scattered about the floor. The drawers of her dressing table were open also, all of them empty, although much of their contents, underclothes mostly, was strewn on the bed. 'Helen?' he called in a futile way. 'Helen?' There was no reply.

Very carefully, methodically, he moved about the room, shutting the wardrobe, closing the drawers, picking up Helen's garments from the bed, folding them and placing them in a pile on the chair. Then he lay down on the bed and stared at the ceiling. He seemed to shrivel, looking like an old man, an old man who guessed he had taken to his bed for the final time. And with each small movement he grimaced, as though his body was racked with pain.

Gary Hubbard drove at a steady pace. It was still early afternoon but the streetlights had already been switched on by some ill-informed computer. They shone uselessly, determined to hasten the dark.

He had settled in nicely. Finding a job had not been a problem: he was a good and willing worker, happy to do part-time, and builders were glad to take him on.

He drove slowly past the railway station. He spotted the young men lingering there, and his eyes brightened as they turned their heads and appeared to follow his progress; he smiled to himself as he imagined they were calling to him. And then, struggling down the pavement came an ageing man, a sandwich board hanging like a yoke about his neck. DELIVER US FROM EVIL it proclaimed. Deliver us from evil, Gary thought. Deliver us from evil, he heard, and wondered if that was what the young men had been calling to him. Deliver us from evil.

Gary Hubbard swung his van to the side of the road and stopped. He bowed his head. 'Amen,' he said quietly to himself.

20

The public gallery was packed. Even though they got there in good time, there were no spaces for the twins and their mother to sit together. But Gregory and Jimmy were in fine fettle, had been since they got up, particularly since Kate had announced, 'I've decided you're both right. I *should* be there.'

'So you're coming with us?' Gregory asked.

'Yes.'

'Okay,' Jimmy said. 'I'll make extra sandwiches.'

Kate looked astonished. 'Sandwiches? I didn't think you could eat in –'

'Only joking, Mum.'

'Oh,' Kate said, and smiled. 'I see. You made it sound like a picnic,' she added as a mild reprimand. 'Which it's not.'

'Indeed not,' Jimmy agreed.

Gregory studied his mother's clothes. She looked very smart: every inch the successful businesswoman, her neat, tailored suit clearly expensive. It was black and Gregory was about to comment that it wasn't a funeral they were going to either, but decided against it. It was, after all, he thought, a funeral in a sense – terminal, anyway, which was all that counted. 'You look terrific, Mum,' he said.

And so they took their places, Kate in the back row, the twins one row below and directly in front of her, together, on the aisle.

There was certainly an air of sombre expectancy. Nobody spoke much, not even the journalists, and when they did it was in whispers.

Jimmy turned in his seat to look up at his mother, just to make sure she was all right, and was enjoying herself. She didn't notice him. She was staring down towards the front row of the gallery, unblinking, a look Jimmy had never seen before in her eyes, a look of great sadness and longing. He swung back round and followed her gaze, his eyes settling on Robert Harvey, who sat with his head bowed, his hands between his knees. Jimmy nudged Gregory, and nodded towards Harvey.

'I know,' Gregory whispered to him. 'Been in the same place all through the trial.'

'Don't look round, but Mum's spotted him.'

Gregory gave Jimmy a shrewd look. 'That's the reason she came, isn't it? To have a look at him. See what he's like in the flesh now.'

'Where's the wife?' Jimmy asked. 'Bet Mum'd like to see her too.'

Gregory looked about the gallery, scanning the faces. 'Not here. Funny. Always sat beside him.'

'Maybe after she ran off –'

Gregory nodded. 'Maybe.'

They looked at each other and giggled, lowering their heads and covering their mouths with their hands so no one would notice.

'Wish they'd hurry up,' Gregory said through his fingers.

'Yeah,' Jimmy agreed. 'Shame to keep poor Daddy in suspense.'

They started giggling again, and Kate leant forward, touching both of them lightly on the shoulder. The twins looked up, Jimmy raising his eyebrows questioningly. 'I thought you two were laughing,' Kate said.

The twins looked at her as though appalled. 'Mum!' Jimmy admonished.

'I'm sorry,' Kate apologised.

'Not much to laugh at, is there?' Gregory asked.

'No, dear, there isn't,' Kate answered and sat back.

'Not much,' Gregory said quietly to a grinning Jimmy. He strained his neck and peered down into the court. 'Something's happening,' he said.

''Bout time.'

There was an inevitability about the verdict when it was delivered: guilty. But there were no shouts from the gallery, no curses hurled at the accused, no harridans screeching that revenge had successfully been wreaked. David Parsons' mother was there, looking strained but suntanned. She was very dignified about the whole thing, although later Jimmy was to swear he had seen the mink collar on her cashmere coat bristle; for a moment it did look as if she was about to applaud the sentence of life imprisonment. Indeed, she parted her hands as though to bring them together in a clap but it was a gesture she could equally well have used for drying her nails.

As the judge rose, everyone stood, including the twins and nobody noticed they were holding hands.

When the judge had gone to his chambers people started to leave, chattering animatedly now, discussing the events they had witnessed, critics all of them.

Chief Inspector Robert Harvey had raised his head to watch his son being led away. But he had given no signal to Justin: he had not smiled or nodded or raised a hand. He had simply stared at the boy, and Justin had stared back disbelievingly.

And then Robert Harvey started to make his way from the gallery, taking the steps slowly as though suddenly finding them too steep. He paused after every second step, apparently thinking, his face ashen, his head lolling from side to side. His hands, too, appeared out of control, the fingers curling and straightening rapidly like talons seeking a firmer grip on their chosen roost. He seemed unaware that people were jostling him, pushing past him in their hurry to leave and tell their friends what an exciting time they'd had.

The twins watched as Robert Harvey climbed closer to them, their faces expressionless, but their eyes glistening, their lips parted. Kate

Renfrew watched also, one hand over her mouth as if suppressing cries trying to escape her.

Suddenly Robert Harvey looked up. For a while there was nothing but dullness and pain in his eyes. Then he focused on Gregory's face and a small frown skittered across his brow. Although he didn't move he appeared to look closer, giving the impression he had come across someone he should know, did know, but to whom he could not give a name.

Gregory, his eyes half closed, turned his head deliberately as though orchestrating Harvey's gaze towards Jimmy. And Harvey took the cue. He looked directly at Jimmy. For a second his face relaxed. He even gave a tiny nod as though relieved Jimmy was someone he *did* recognise. Then, as if this recognition had only plodded through his mind, it dawned on him that Jimmy was the young man who had accompanied Miranda Jay to his office. He visibly recoiled. He gave a tiny gasp. His lips curled and froze in a horrible twist of incredulity or hatred.

And it was as hatred that Kate Refrew interpreted it. Instinctively, she reached forward and placed her hands on the twins' shoulders, claiming them, protecting them, her head thrown back, all compassion gone from her face.

Harvey saw the hands appear on the shoulders of the boys, and allowed his eyes to follow the arms upwards. He saw Kate Renfrew staring down at him defiantly. And it was as though he had been struck. He staggered back, losing his footing. He grabbed hold of one of the benches to prevent himself falling, his body sprawled across the back of the bench, his head twisted back, staring in bafflement at Kate and the twins. As the realisation of who they were and the implication of the smile on the boys' faces sank into his consciousness he made an effort to stand upright. But it was an effort which for the moment was too much for him.

Gregory looked up at his mother. 'Ready to go, Mum?' he asked.

Kate nodded curtly. 'Yes, dear.'

The twins let Kate leave the court first. Just before they followed her through the door they turned and stared back at Robert Harvey. They smiled and nodded to him. Then they shook hands, turned away from him, and hurried after their mother.